HEART OF DARKNESS

HEART OF DARKNESS

Joseph Conrad

edited by D. C. R. A. Goonetilleke
second edition

broadview literary texts

National Library of Canada Cataloguing in Publication

Conrad, Joseph 1857-1924.
    Heart of darkness.
(Broadview literary texts)
2nd ed.
Includes bibliographical references.
ISBN 1-55111-307-4

I. Goonetilleke, D.C.R.A.   II. Title.   III. Series.

PR6005.04H42   1999   823'.912   C99-931796-2

Broadview Press Ltd. is an independent, international publishing house, incorporated in 1985. Broadview believes in shared ownership, both with its employees and with the general public; since the year 2000 Broadview shares have traded publicly on the Toronto Venture Exchange under the symbol BDP.

We welcome comments and suggestions regarding any aspect of our publications — please feel free to contact us at the addresses below or at broadview@broadviewpress.com.

North America
PO Box 1243, Peterborough, Ontario, Canada K9J 7H5
3576 California Road, Orchard Park, NY, USA 14127
Tel: (705) 743-8990; Fax: (705) 743-8353
email: customerservice@broadviewpress.com

UK, Ireland, and continental Europe
Plymbridge Distributors Ltd.,
Estover Road, Plymouth PL6 7PY
Tel: (01752) 202301; Fax: (01752) 202333
email: orders@plymbridge.com

Australia and New Zealand
UNIREPS, University of New South Wales
Sydney, NSW, 2052
Tel: 61 2 9664 0999; Fax: 61 2 9664 5420
email: info.press@unsw.edu.au

www.broadviewpress.com

This book is printed on acid-free paper containing 100% post-consumer fibre.

Text design and composition by George Kirkpatrick

PRINTED IN CANADA

Contents

Preface

It was a great pleasure to have been invited to edit Conrad's *Heart of Darkness*. It is to me the most absorbing of Conrad's works — and I am clearly not alone in that judgement. Professor David Leon Higdon, the editor of Conradiana, stated in 1990 that twenty-five percent of the submissions for his journal focus on this novella. It has captivated the general reader, too; it is perhaps the twentieth-century literature classic most commonly read — and enjoyed. Chinua Achebe is probably right that it is "the most commonly prescribed novel in twentieth-century literature classes" and, in my experience, students are fascinated by it. To cap it all, the tale was a favourite of Conrad; he called it "my pet *Heart of Darkness*," in his letter of 3 December 1902 to Elsie Hueffer. It seems to me that it expresses the essence of Conrad.

I wish to thank Dr. Marcus Milton, Deputy Director of the British Council, Colombo, Sri Lanka, and the University of Kelaniya, Sri Lanka, for grants which enabled me to research this edition in The British Library, London, and the Library of the Joseph Conrad Society (UK); Professor David Leon Higdon for advice regarding the choice of text; and my wife, Chinchi, whose cooperation is indispensable in all my academic endeavours — and is always readily given.

D.C.R.A.G.

Introduction

What most differentiates this edition of *Heart of Darkness* from the many others available is the extent to which it is devoted to placing the text in context. To this end the reader will find a chronology of Conrad's life, a chronology of the Congo, a select bibliography, and—perhaps most importantly—a very substantial selection of contemporary documents, including comments by Conrad on the text, contemporary reviews, and a variety of historical documents that may help to give a sense of the time out of which *Heart of Darkness* emerged.

The Place and its History

The Congo refers both to Africa's second-largest river and to its watershed—then, as now, a landscape dominated by tropical forest. The earliest inhabitants of the area were Pygmies, who were largely displaced between 500 and 1000 AD by Bantu invaders from the northwest. We know that Bantu peoples were mining the copper in the south of the region (what is now Katanga province) as early as 700 AD, and that they formed a variety of independent states, many of them of considerable complexity.

The first contact with Europeans came in 1482 with the visit of Diogo Cam of Portugal. The slave trade began to affect the coastal regions shortly thereafter, and it continued here longer than elsewhere; though slavery was eliminated in most areas of Africa by the late 1860s, some slave trading (primarily by Arabs) continued in the Congo, Nigeria and Nyasaland (now Malawi) until about 1903.

The central event in the colonization of Africa was the Berlin Conference of 1884-85, at which the colonial powers carved up the continent among themselves. Whereas other colonies were set up as subject to European nation-states, the area that is now Congo became the Congo Free State in 1885, with King Leopold II of Belgium as its independent owner. The system proved to be even more brutal than those imposed elsewhere in Africa, but it was not until 1908 that under international pressure (following criticism of exploitation of native labourers, particularly on Congolese rubber plantations), the Congo was granted a conventional colonial charter.

After the establishment of the Congo Free State the process of exploitation became fairly rapid, and the Congo at the time of Conrad's 1890 journey was less undeveloped than he portrays it. This predating facilitates, among other things, the introduction of a dimension to the jungle as symbolic of dark urges and enables Conrad to incorporate Marlow's sensation that "going up that river was like travelling back to the earliest beginnings of the world." (We should remember in reading this that Conrad was writing well before any theory of Africa being humanity's ancestral home had become widespread.)

It is also important to remember both that *Heart of Darkness* was in no way intended to provide an accurate description of Africa, and that the Africa that does appear in the novella is a version of the continent as seen through late nineteenth-century European eyes. The "mysterious Africa" of that time has been laid bare by "development" and modernization. That said, however, the Congo has probably altered less in the past century than have most other areas of the world. As late as the 1970s V. S. Naipaul observed: "The airplane that goes from Kinshasa to Kisangani flies over eight hundred miles of what still looks like virgin forest."[1] And even today the Congo remains perhaps the least developed of all African countries. The country did not emerge from the coarse colonial rule of Belgium until 1960; after five years of turmoil the situation was stabilized under the rule of Mobutu Sese Seko, whose path to power had been smoothed by Belgian forces and by the operations of the American Central Intelligence Agency. Mobutu ran one of the world's most corrupt governments and he became one of the world's richest men as he solidified his position as dictator, but the people of Zaire (as the country was called under Mobutu) have remained among the world's poorest. If anything, their plight may have worsened

---

[1] V.S. Naipaul, "A New King for the Congo: Mobutu and the Nihilism of Africa" (1975), in *The Return of Eva Peron with the Killings in Trinidad* (New York: Knopf, 1980) 179.

under Mobutu; in one memorable description of the country in the 1980s a visitor from Zimbabwe described the state of development at Kisangani (the former Stanleyville and Stanley Falls) as being "at about 1910—and heading rapidly for the turn of the century."[1] And turmoil has continued since Mobutu's overthrow in 1997.

The possibility of Conrad working in Africa happened accidentally, when he was in search of employment, and he may well have accepted the position offered in the absence of anything better: it was more remunerative than a command at sea. But the idea is also likely to have touched him; his boyhood enthusiasm for Africa[2] would in all probability have been already re-awakened by the current excitement about the continent. As Conrad's early biographer, G. Jean-Aubry, observed in *The Sea Dreamer*:

> In 1889 the Congo was very much in the foreground. Since September 1875, when King Leopold had founded the International Association for the Civilization of Central Africa, and since Stanley's expedition from Zanzibar to the lower Congo in 1876 and 1877, Africa had aroused at once the most ardent interest and the most violent greed. A few months earlier, on February 17, 1889, Stanley, repeating the exploits of his search for Livingstone, had discovered and joined Emin Pasha in Kavali's camp. Scientific, journalistic, and political circles in Europe had followed these excursions with attentive and breathless interest.[3]

It was Henry Morton Stanley's phrases, "the Dark Continent" and "the immense heart of Africa," that passed into general parlance and that figure in Conrad, and the adventurer appears to have indeed been very much a presence behind *Heart of Darkness*; he may well be one of the models for Conrad's portrayal of Kurtz. The brash young American reporter had made his reputation by

---

1 Reported by Michael Valpy, Harare-based reporter for *The Globe and Mail* (Toronto) 1984.
2 See Appendix A, Document 1.
3 G. Jean-Aubry, *The Sea Dreamer* (London: William Heinemann, 1927) 122.

"finding" Livingstone in 1871; his many subsequent African involvements were considerably less savoury. His first Congo journey, made at the urging of Leopold II, was an exploration in 1875-77, westwards from Lake Victoria in search of a way to the Atlantic via the Lualaba. At terrible cost to both himself and his party he discovered that the Lualaba became the Congo, and he followed it to the sea; he also established relations with Tippu Tip, a trader in ivory and slaves from Zanzibar who was soon to become the most powerful figure in Central Africa. This was a key voyage in opening up Central Africa to the Europeans, but Stanley's triumph was tainted (as much of his future behaviour would be) by accusations that he was prone to mistreat the native population. At various times he was accused of shooting natives and even of kicking them to death, of attacking defenceless villages, of countenancing looting, of collusion with the slave trade, and of a range of other crimes. Dr. John Kirk, the British Consul at Zanzibar, reported that the 1877 expedition had been "a disgrace to humanity," and Stanley's own words do little to reassure doubters. His many accounts of his expeditions are filled with discussions of appropriate punishments to be inflicted on natives, and he writes in his *Autobiography* of how when his blood was up he would pursue Africans

> up to their villages; I skirmish in their streets, drive them pell-mell into the woods beyond, and level their ivory temples; with frantic haste I fire the huts, and end the scene by towing the canoes to mid-stream and setting them adrift.[1]

By 1878 he had been taken on in Leopold's employ, having helped to convince the Belgian king of what he had been unable to convince his fellow Britons: the Congo could be an enormous source of profit for the European. Between 1879 and 1885 Stanley was the chief figure behind the "development" of the Congo for the Belgians. In 1887-89 he was again in the Congo, this time on

---

1 Henry Morton Stanley, *The Autobiography of Sir Henry Morton Stanley*, ed. Dorothy Stanley (Boston, 1909) 327. See also, for example, Thomas Pakenham, *The Scramble for Africa* (New York: Random House, 1991) 62.

a mission to Emin Pasha on Lake Albert, who had been reported to be in dire need of assistance. Before the journey Stanley persuaded Leopold to appoint Tippu Tip Governor of Stanley Falls, and when he arrived he obtained the (sometimes unreliable) support of the trader. Nevertheless he encountered appalling obstacles in the overland trek from Basoko to Lake Albert; when Stanley found Emin Pasha the Arab ruler was clearly much less in need of assistance than was Stanley himself. All in all, the journey was far from an unqualified success, but by the time Stanley had returned to Brussels in 1890 he was greeted as a hero. Leopold gave him the lion's share of the credit not only for his successful expeditions but also for helping to swing the climate of public opinion behind Congo development and for helping to establish the Belgian company that had built a railway to Stanley Pool. Now, in April 1890, Stanley was awarded the Order of Leopold and a new honour, the Grand Cross of the Congo. One month later Conrad was given his Congo posting and set sail for Central Africa.

Heart of Darkness was written in late 1898 and early 1899 (within a two-month period, while Conrad was in the middle of *Lord Jim*), but it was based on a trip Conrad had taken eight years earlier, when he was thirty-three. As Conrad puts it in the Author's Note, "*Heart of Darkness* is experience ... pushed a little (and only very little) beyond the actual facts of the case." He had signed a contract with the Société Anonyme Belge pour le Commerce du Haut-Congo, a commercial company Stanley had been associated with, now headed by the unsavoury M.A. Thys. The understanding was that Conrad was to command a river steamer for the duration of the three-year contract, but things went badly wrong. Conrad arrived in Kinshasha on 2 August, but discovered that the ship he was to command was disabled. He was then assigned as second-in-command to a Captain L.R. Koch leading a relief expedition in the steamer *Roi des Belges* to Stanley Falls; the agent at the Stanley Falls station, Georges Antoine Klein (a Frenchman who had been in the Congo for a year and a half), had become very ill. The ship arrived 1 September, by which time Koch had also been taken ill. On the instructions of Camille Delcommune, Acting Manager for the Company, who was also among the party, Conrad was put in command of the ship for the return journey. As well as carrying the invalided Klein and Koch the steamer pulled two barges, probably filled with ivory. Klein died on board on 21 September, shortly before the ship reached Kinshasha. Conrad was then to have accompanied Alexandre Delcommune (brother of Camille) on "a new expedition on the Kasaii River"[1] to the Katanga region, which was to have lasted several months.

We know that Conrad was on bad terms with Camille Delcommune[2] and that his own health had suffered badly, but we do not know the exact circumstances under which he parted company from the Société. All we can say for certain on this score is that he sailed for Europe from Matadi on 4 December. His Congo experience had lasted only eight months, but it is clear that the journey had an enormous impact on him. As Edward Garnett reports of Conrad,

> in his early years at sea he had "not a thought in his head." "I was a perfect animal," he reiterated, meaning of course that he had reasoned and reflected hardly at all over all the varieties of life he had encountered.[3]

Heart of Darkness, Imperialism, and Race

Conrad's Congo journey took place at the high tide of imperialism and racism in European history. It was a period of high-flown ideals as to the supposed "civilizing" influence of European civilization—and a period in which it would not have occurred to many Europeans to think of non-whites in terms of words other than "savage" and "nigger."[4] Even those who were among the

---

1 Conrad, letter to his cousin Mariette, 24 September 1890, in *The Collected Letters of Joseph Conrad* vol. 1 1861–1897, ed. Frederik R. Karl and Laurence Davies (Cambridge: CUP, 1983).

2 See Conrad's letter to Marguerite Poradowska, 26 September 1890. (See Appendix A for full text.)

3 Edward Garnett, "Introduction" to *Letters from Conrad: 1895–1924* (London: The Nonesuch Press, 1928) xii.

4 Interestingly, the word "nigger" seems to have taken on a cast that was recognized by its

most enlightened on such issues held some views that are likely to strike modern readers as condescending; indeed, they may sometimes seem to resemble the outright racists of their day in finding the native peoples of Africa or of Asia "backward" or "childlike." Perhaps the central difference is that for the one group the differences were thought to be built in; Africans were inherently backward, were in their very *essence* "no better than animals." The more enlightened, by contrast, felt that the perceived backwardness was merely a product of circumstance—that in other circumstances, with education and so on, native peoples of the world could become just as "enlightened" as themselves. The essentialist view was the foundation for racist brutality, whereas the anti-essentialist view (ethnocentric though it unquestionably was) laid the path for progress away from imperialist oppression, and indeed away from racism of any sort.

We may add that imperialist and racist sentiments are typically founded on simplistic dichotomies. As Abdul R. JanMohamed points out:

> the colonial mentality is dominated by a manichean allegory of white and black, good and evil, salvation and damnation, civilization and savagery, superiority and inferiority, intelligence and emotion, self and the other, subject and object.[1]

As we shall see, Conrad subverts this manichean allegory in his novella, from the very beginning blurring or inverting the conventional dualities. But let us begin by posing the questions: to what extent is the text imperialist? to what extent (if at all) is it racist?

It has become a commonplace of Commonwealth literary criticism to condemn works such as *Heart of Darkness* and Joyce Cary's *Mister Johnson* because they are alleged to distort cultural or political reality and hence are wanting in "truth" which is considered a necessary quality of good literature; such critics perceive

---

users to be pejorative rather earlier in the United States than in Britain and the British Empire.

1   Abdul R. JanMohamed, *Manichean Aesthetics: The Politics of Literature in Colonial Africa* (Amherst: U of Massachusetts P, 1983) 4.

a discrepancy between the real world and the world created by a writer in his work. Chinua Achebe is impassioned on this point:

> Conrad was a bloody racist.... And the question is whether a novel which celebrates this dehumanization, which depersonalizes a portion of the human race, can be called a great work of art. My answer is: No, it cannot.[1]

Edward Said, for his part, argues: "Chinua Achebe's well-known criticism of Conrad ... does not go far enough."[2]

Even those critics who disagree with Achebe and Said (and it may be noted that among their number are many African writers[3]) must recognize the value of the perspective in which they have placed the text; the book *is* in important ways about imperialism and racism, and these issues must not be brushed aside. This may seem an obvious truth, but it has not always been recognized. While most of the early reviews treated the text at least in part as a commentary on imperialism, and Belgian imperialism in particular (most, though not all, feeling that it presented an attitude highly critical of European behaviour), several laid these themes entirely to one side; it was this second critical tendency that took hold in Conrad criticism as the century moved forward. For generations an exclusively white community of literary critics treated a variety of thematic and stylistic issues (often with great subtlety and insight) while largely ignoring *Heart of Darkness* as a commentary on imperialism or racism. As recently as the 1970s the most influential North American textbook anthology, *The Norton Anthology of English Literature*, summarized *Heart of Darkness* in this fashion:

---

1   Chinua Achebe, "An Image of Africa," in *The Massachusetts Review* (Vol. 18, 1977) 788.
2   Edward Said, *Culture and Imperialism* (London: Chatto & Windus, 1993) 200.
3   "In conversations with me Lewis Nkosi ... and Matthew Buyu, the Kenyan poet and scholar, have both defended *Heart of Darkness*, emphasising that by the standards of its times it offers a valuably sceptical account of imperialism." Cedric Watts, "Introduction" to *Heart of Darkness* (Oxford: OUP, 1990). Nkosi also makes his case in *Tasks and Masks* (Harlow: Longman, 1981) 80. Watts offers further instances of Third World scholars who have defended *Heart of Darkness*; see also *Conradiana*, xiv (1982) 163-87.

In *Heart of Darkness* he draws on his Congo River experience to create an atmosphere of darkness and horror in the midst of which the hero recognises a deep inner kinship with the corrupt villain, the Belgian trader who has lost all his earlier ideals to succumb to the worst elements in the native life he had hoped to improve.[1]

Not only does this summary skim over the appalling oppression of the native population by Kurtz and the imperialist system, but it even appears to blame the natives (in very much the same way as some of the less attractive early reviews did) for the evil that Kurtz perpetrates. Notice in this connection the word "succumb"; it is hard to avoid the connotation that somehow the natives are partly to blame, as if they were somehow holding out temptations to Kurtz. One might almost imagine from this summary that Kurtz is as much victim as villain.

In fact—as we shall see in considerably more detail shortly—the weight of Conrad's text cannot fairly be taken to support any such reading. Much as it may indeed suggest complexities in the nature of evil, on certain things the text is absolutely clear—among them, that the appalling atrocities that the book catalogues are hugely disproportionately the work of whites rather than blacks, and that, rather than succumbing to any native temptation in carrying out his demonic acts, what Kurtz succumbed to were the worst impulses in his own nature: "things about himself that he did not know, things of which he had no conception till he took counsel with this great solitude...."

In large part, as a result of the insistence of such critics as Achebe and Said, it is not now possible to gloss over the issues of imperialism and race. Today even those critics who feel that the most important meanings of the text may concern the souls of individuals, or may concern the heart of humanity as a whole rather than anything connected with Africa or with race, must nevertheless recognize that the text emerges out of the very

---

1   M.H. Abrams et al., *The Norton Anthology of English Literature* (New York: W.W. Norton & Co., third edition, 1974) Vol. 2, 1829. [David Daiches is credited as the editor of the twentieth-century material.]

centre of racism and imperialism, and that no matter how much it may say on one level about humanity as a whole, at another level it has much to say about the treatment of black Africans by white Europeans. As much as it may say something about individuals it also says something about groups; as much as it says something symbolic it also says something about the palpably real. Let us turn, then, to the text itself.

It is significant that the darkness we are first introduced to is not in Africa, but in England. That in Britain's past and present history and in all imperial ventures there is an exploration of darkness is the suggestion in Marlow's opening words: "And this also has been one of the dark places of the earth." The suggestion is elaborated in Marlow's comparison of the Roman Empire and contemporary empires—a comparison which recalls one made by Stanley (see Appendix C), but which introduces an irony absent in Stanley in Conrad's treatment of "light" and "darkness." Conrad goes on to suggest that white men have turned the map of Africa into a Dark Continent—thus inverting the conventional view of the Europeans as the harbingers of light. (Later in the tale, Kurtz's painting may be taken to intimate the same inversion of roles.)

It is only when we have before us an image of Britons at the receiving end of colonialism that we are offered Marlow's harsh truths and brutal ironies about the present imperialist venture. The structure of the narrative has already reinforced the anti-essentialist sentiment: there is no essential difference between Britons and Congolese other than that the latter have "a different complexion and slightly flatter noses":

> But these chaps were not much account, really. They were no colonists; their administration was merely a squeeze, and nothing more, I suspect. They were conquerors, and for that you want only brute force—nothing to boast of, when you have it, since your strength is just an accident arising from the weakness of others. They grabbed what they could get for the sake of what was to be got. It was just robbery with violence, aggravated murder on a great scale, and men going at it blind—as is very proper for those who tackle a

darkness. The conquest of the earth, which mostly means the taking it away from those who have a different complexion or slightly flatter noses than ourselves, is not a pretty thing when you look into it too much. What redeems it is the idea only. An idea at the back of it; not a sentimental pretence but an idea; and an unselfish belief in the idea— something you can set up, and bow down before, and offer a sacrifice to....

It is difficult for the modern reader here to be sure of the degree to which Marlow's view "as is very proper for those who tackle a darkness" is to be taken "straight" or as brutal sarcasm. Is the irony here Marlow's, or Conrad's? And to the modern reader it seems incomprehensible that any idea could redeem such barbarity; but, as the documents in the appendices illustrate, imperialism *was* was of course "justified" time and again not as murder and theft but as "something higher." What *Heart of Darkness* shows with subtlety but with devastating clarity is just how vague and how empty the idea was. Its central expression is in Kurtz's report for the International Society for the Suppression of Savage Customs: seventeen pages of high-flown phrases, of "burning noble words" that "appeal to every altruistic sentiment"... "though difficult to remember you know." There was no practical advice whatsoever to interrupt the "magic current of phrases"— or almost none: the sole "practical hint," as Marlow sarcastically terms it, is the "valuable postscriptum" scrawled in an unsteady hand at the foot of the final page, the appalling revelation of the naked racist brutality at the heart of Kurtz and the heart of imperialism: "Exterminate all the brutes!" That is perhaps the ultimate expression of the essentialist extreme in imperialism: "they" are "brutes," different from "the civilized" in every essential quality, irredeemable and expendable.

The narrative gathers momentum as the centre shifts to Brussels, the headquarters of the Belgian empire. The scene when Marlow bids farewell to his aunt, who had exercised her influence to obtain for him an appointment as the captain of a river-steamboat, is by no means irrelevant. Conrad introduces conventional Western notions of imperialism (these were naturally more prominent in the metropolitan countries than in the colonies) through the aunt, and exposes their falsity through Marlow. Marlow can see the difference between her conception of his role as "an emissary of light" and the real pettiness of his job, between the sentimental idealism centring around imperialism and its economic basis. Conrad dramatizes the actual working of the head office of an imperial company. There are the memorable figures of the two unconcerned women at the door knitting black wool, who go with such an office. They recall the classical Fates. Moreover, the slim knitter is "herself a fate—a dehumanised death in life to herself and to others, and thus a prefiguring symbol of what the trading company does to its creatures"[1] and what Western industrial civilization does to its members.[2] There is Conrad's presentation of the medical examination with its suggestions of callousness in the operation of the company, and of the likelihood of derangement and the death of its employees. The whole city, in fact, seems to Marlow "a whited sepulchre." Its deathlike attributes, along with the implications of hypocrisy, link up with the inhumanity of the empire, and Conrad suggests how the "achievement" of the metropolitan country is founded on imperialism.

Despite Marlow's common sense and these disquieting experiences, his vigour and keenness for the Congo journey remain. After all, he has as yet hardly experienced imperialism. The realities en route are as much an integral part of the portrayal of imperialism as are realities in Belgium and in the Congo itself.

Marlow's first contact with black Africans is crucial in establishing the novella's underlying attitude: these "black fellows" in boats give Marlow "a momentary contact with reality":

The voice of the surf heard now and then was a positive pleasure, like the speech of a brother. It was something

---

1   Ian Watt, *Conrad in the Nineteenth Century* (London: Chatto & Windus, 1980) 192.
2   Cf.   When lovely woman stoops to folly and
          Paces about her room again, alone,
          She smoothes her hair with automatic hand,
          And puts a record on the gramophone.
                                    (T.S. Eliot, *The Waste Land*)

natural, that had its reason, that had a meaning. Now and then a boat from the shore gave one a momentary contact with reality. It was paddled by black fellows. You could see from afar the white of their eyeballs glistening. They shouted, sang; their bodies streamed with perspiration; they had faces like grotesque masks — these chaps; but they had bone, muscle, a wild vitality, an intense energy of movement, that was as natural and true as the surf along *their coast. They wanted no excuse for being there.* They were a great comfort to look at. [Editor's italics]

Though there may be more than a hint here of an adaptation of the "Noble Savage" myth (as there is later in the description of Kurtz's native mistress), the attitudes expressed are hardly racist. Even the phrase "like grotesque masks" merely serves to intensify the sense of their alienness, their otherness, to Marlow. It thus gives additional grip and emphasis to the response drawn from him, the instinctive approving recognition: "natural and true as the surf along *their coast. They wanted no excuse for being there."* The natives are like the surf, and the voice of the surf is to Marlow "like the speech of a brother." If these natives are alien to him, he is clearly entirely at peace with them — and perhaps closer to them than he is to "all these [white] men with whom he had no point of contact" or to those on the French man-of-war "incomprehensible, firing into a continent … a touch of insanity in the proceeding…."

This passage sets the tone for the attitude taken throughout towards native Africans. Conrad breaks with nineteenth-century stereotypes of unrestrained savagery. The Africans at first are seen only as strange, inexplicable, and then as akin. Conrad not only deploys and deconstructs the binary opposition between the self and the Other, but brings them together.

The contrast between this image of natives still free from oppression and the next image of black men that we are given could hardly be more marked: this is the chain gang, enslaved labourers building a railway. Here for the first time Marlow's tale brings the reality of imperialism home to the reader. In this context of radical oppression Western terms and concepts such as

"criminals," "rebels," "labourers" do not fit and law itself is outraged by the oppression of the colonizers:

> Another report from the cliff made me think suddenly of
> that ship of war I had seen firing into a continent. It was the
> same kind of ominous voice; but these men could by no
> stretch of the imagination be called enemies. They were
> called criminals, and the outraged law, like the bursting
> shells, had come to them, an insoluble mystery from the sea.

Marlow allows to his audience that "you know I am not particularly tender," but clearly even he is shocked by the brutality of the
"devils that drive the men who are responsible."

From here on we are given a continuing litany of appalling
human acts. In vivid detail Conrad brings out the suffering
caused by imperialism to Africans. They are tortured, killed,
exploited, dehumanized in almost every conceivable respect. In
the grove of death black men have been reduced by the ravages of
disease and starvation to "black shapes," "bundles of acute angles."
The manner in which the text presents these images suggests
vividly the extent to which the natives have been dehumanized
by the brutal treatment they have received—but the distancing
mechanisms make the horror that the images call up more vivid
rather than less so. Far from the portrayal "glorifying" this dehu-
manization, both pity and horror are palpably present; Marlow
describes his own reaction as being "horror-struck," and it would
be an extraordinary reader who did not share the feeling.

The horrors continue. A middle-aged man with a bullet hole
in his forehead has been abandoned in the road. A man blamed
for starting a fire is beaten horribly, and his cries provide a recur-
ring reminder of the savagery of the "pilgrims." Again and again
the whites are shown to be crude, sordid and violent. Perhaps the
most extreme example of their casual brutality is presented with a
devastating understatement that only adds to its power:

> I pulled the string of the whistle, and I did this because I saw
> the pilgrims on deck getting out their rifles with an air of
> anticipating a jolly lark. At the sudden screech there was a

movement of abject terror through that wedged mass of bodies. "Don't! don't you frighten them away," cried someone on deck disconsolately. I pulled the string time after time. They broke and ran, they leaped, they crouched, they swerved, they dodged the flying terror of the sound. The three red chaps had fallen flat, face down on the shore, as though they had been shot dead. Only the barbarous and superb woman did not so much as flinch, and stretched tragically her bare arms after us over the sombre and glittering river.

And then that imbecile crowd down on the deck started their little fun, and I could see nothing more for smoke.

It would be hard to imagine a more damning indictment of imperialism than the litany of horrors that are perpetrated here by the Europeans. The effect is to undermine for the reader the sort of imperialistic discourse — "civilizing influence," "blood-thirsty natives," "light-bringers" and so on — that today has long ceased to be taken seriously but that in Conrad's time was almost universally accepted at face value. Indeed, it is a remarkable indicator of the power of ingrained prejudice that although most contemporary reviewers read *Heart of Darkness* as "a criticism of Belgian colonialism,"[1] a minority were able to convince themselves that it should not "be supposed that Mr. Conrad makes attack upon colonisation, expansion, even upon Imperialism."[2]

The figure of Kurtz, however, may be an even more extreme example of the savagery of the white man. It is Kurtz who hides beneath his veneer of "enlightened imperialism" the brutal sentiment, "Exterminate all the brutes!" Kurtz who has been the most ruthless of the ivory-traders, Kurtz who arranges for the heads of the dead to be displayed on poles, Kurtz who had ordered the attack against the steamer on the river. Here again we may see how the text subverts traditional stereotypes. The attack by spear-throwing natives is almost a cliché, a page from what Said has

---

1   Robert F. Haugh, *Joseph Conrad: Discovery in Design* (Norman, Oklahoma: U of Oklahoma Press, 1957) 35.
2   See Appendix B, Document 3.

termed the "library of Africanisms." But as we learn after the fact, the chief responsibility for the savagery does not lie with the "savages":

> He informed me, lowering his voice, that it was Kurtz who had ordered the attack to be made on the steamer. "He hated sometimes the idea of being taken away — and then again…. But I don't understand these matters. I am a simple man. He thought it would scare you away — that you would give it up, thinking him dead. I could not stop him.

By comparison with the brutality of the imperialists the savagery of the blacks is a paltry thing indeed. They never initiate violence, and even the discussion of cannibalism inverts conventional notions of savagery. Eating other human beings is to the Western imagination perhaps the ultimate in savagery, but Conrad does not make an undue moralistic fuss over cannibalism. Indeed, he seems to accept it as a part of the African way of life. In contrast to the pointless cruelty of the Europeans, the savagery of the natives is regarded as understandable, excusable:

> I would no doubt have been properly horrified, had it not occurred to me that he and his chaps must be very hungry: that they must have been growing increasingly hungry for at least this month past.

Marlow actually attempts a phatic, a gratuitous, communication with the headman of his African crew, not a command or request. Marlow is aware of him as a person, a human being, not just a tool of convenience. Nor is the African subservient: he is curt, dignified — and businesslike. Marlow is so far from attributing any positive qualities to the whites that he coolly considers the possibility that it is disgust which keeps the cannibals from eating their employers and rejects it only because he realizes that disgust is not a sufficient barrier for starving men. The blacks, then, do not in this text fit the racist stereotypes of the time any more than the Europeans who do not fall into the mould of Empire builders.

It would be foolish to deny, on the other hand, that traces of condescension may be discernable from time to time in the text, as it would be foolish to suggest that the text at any time takes on the viewpoint of the native blacks. We have already seen that the view of native peoples presented in the text occasionally partakes of the idealized "Noble Savage." And unquestionably Marlow shares the tendency common even among the most "enlightened" Europeans to assume that the operation of the mind of the semi-educated African was always influenced by superstition:

> He was useful because he had been instructed; and what he knew was this—that should the water in that transparent thing disappear, the evil spirit inside the boiler would get angry through the greatness of his thirst, and take a terrible vengeance.

Marlow—and perhaps Conrad—sees the native Africans as at a stage of culture through which his own race had passed. At a time when the view of history was melioristic, inevitably he saw Africa as the childhood of human history—childhood being given to whirling, howling, strong griefs and rages, but neither condemned nor condoned.

But if there is occasional condescension or even disdain in Marlow's (if not Conrad's) view of native blacks half-trained in the white man's ways, it is hard to find support for Said's assertion regarding Conrad's standpoint: "the lesser or subject peoples were to be ruled."[1] Contrast the way in which the fireman and the helmsman are presented with the glow that is cast over the original image we are shown of Africans free from European influence and control. A key phrase employed to describe imperialism in the tale is "fantastic invasion"—"invasion," with its connotations of forcible, wrongful intrusion, and displacement. When the text does portray the Africans as primitive, it also suggests that they are best left to themselves—that the white man should not be in Africa. Perhaps the worst fate for the black African, the text seems to suggest, is to obtain only a little of the "white man's

---

1   Said, *Culture and Imperialism*, 26.

learning"—to become like Marlow's fireman, "a dog in a parody of breeches," ironically called "an improved specimen," a hybrid product of two cultures.

It should not be forgotten, though, that Marlow assigns even to the disparaged helmsman a higher moral value than he does to Kurtz: "I can't forget him [Kurtz], though I am not prepared to affirm the fellow was exactly worth the life we lost [the helmsman's] in getting to him." If such attitudes as these amount to a damning racism, then even the most enlightened nineteenth-century European was irredeemably racist.

Eloise Knapp Hay thinks that the chief among the drawbacks of *Heart of Darkness* as a teaching text is "Conrad's deliberate obscurantism, hiding the part that England played in opening the Congo for free trade in the 1880s."[1] But Conrad does take this into account imaginatively: the young African in the grove of death has "a bit of white worsted round his neck"; Kurtz's disciple is equipped with a Martini-Henry and Towson's *An Inquiry into some Points of Seamanship*; one of his pockets is bright red, and the other dark blue and white, a veritable Union Jack!

It should be admitted that Conrad downplays the active opposition of blacks to the imperialists in the Congo. In Conrad's presentation of the death of Fresleven the reader sees the white Fresleven beating a passive chief, whereas in the original, actual incident a ruffled, offended chief repudiated a gift of two brass rods to his child and threatened to attack a steamer captain called Freiesleben; the dispute was not about a trivial matter of hens as in *Heart of Darkness* but one of pride, followed by the threat of a native rising.[2] Similarly, although Arthur Eugene Constant Hodister was one of the models for Kurtz, the novella includes nothing suggestive of the fate of the 1892 Hodister expedition, as it was reported in *The Times*: "The reception at Riba Riba was distinctly unpleasant. Arabs and natives refused absolutely to recognize the Government of the Congo State and insisted that the flag should be hauled down."[3]

---

1   Eloise Knapp Hay, Abstract for "Rattling Talkers and Silent Soothsayers: The Race for *Heart of Darkness*" (1990 MLA Convention), in *Joseph Conrad Today* (Vol. 16, Nos. 1 & 2, 1991) 3.
2   Norman Sherry, *Conrad's Western World* (Cambridge: CUP, 1971) 17-20.
3   Ibid., 110.

Readers today should be careful to see such narrative details in the context of the time, however. Whereas to us it seems inappropriate to downplay resistance to oppression on the part of black Africans, at the time Conrad was writing any suggestions of "aggression" by blacks could be—and were—taken as justification for further oppression.

It should also be admitted that there is no sustained attempt in the text to represent African culture. But given the role of Marlow, neither is this possible. Marlow sees no more than a man on a river trip can see and understand of the natives. Marlow's ignorance is explicable and defensible; but he does not condemn what he does not understand. He commits himself only regarding the culture he knows—European culture—and, as we have seen, in almost everything said about the Europeans the text subverts the melioristic view of history with a damning critique of "progress" and civilization. Moreover—and quite extraordinarily for the time—Marlow is able to imagine the tables turned, the roles of blacks and whites reversed:

> The population had cleared out a long time ago. Well, if a lot of mysterious niggers armed with all kinds of fearful weapons suddenly took to travelling on the road between Deal and Gravesend, catching the yokels right and left to carry heavy loads for them, I fancy every farm and cottage thereabouts would get empty very soon. Only here the dwellings were gone, too.

It is almost impossible for the modern reader not to be brought up short by the word "nigger" in this passage. We almost have to force ourselves to go beyond the understanding we now have of the racist connotations of the word to understand what the sentence as a whole is saying: "no wonder these people are making themselves scarce; we would too if they had invaded our country in the way we have invaded theirs and were treating us in the fashion we are treating them." Once again the anti-essentialist attitude is plain; the difference between "them" and "us" is purely one of circumstance.

Conrad and the Text

For the most part we have spoken of the attitude of the text to these questions. But it is notoriously difficult to separate an attitude that the text inherently expresses from the attitudes of the narrator, the expected attitudes of the reader, and the intentions of the author. It may be impossible to settle such questions conclusively, but they should at least be posed. What are the attitudes here of Marlow and of Conrad? Is the reader led towards any position? On this point Edward Said argues:

> Conrad's readers of the time were not expected to ask about or concern themselves with what became of the natives. What mattered to them was how Marlow makes sense of everything, for without his deliberately fashioned narrative there is no history worth telling, no fiction worth entertaining, no authority worth consulting. This is a short step away from King Leopold's account of his International Congo Association, "rendering lasting and disinterested services to the cause of progress," activities described by one admirer in 1885 as the "noblest and most self-sacrificing scheme for African development that has ever been or ever will be attempted."[1]

But can we find any basis for these assertions in the text? Surely Said in fact takes Marlow as totally other than he is as a character. Far from being represented as infallible or as a moral guru, Marlow is often a voice of shifting uncertainties. He sits Buddha-wise, but the "enlightenment" he has received is the awareness of an ineluctable darkness; the only positives he clings to—work, duty and restraint—are constructs, deliberately set up and used to save a mind from disintegration.

From the beginning we are told that Marlow is distinguished from the other seamen by stories that lack the neat and satisfying conclusions of the sort that listeners normally expect. And while Marlow's comments make it clear that his audience does indeed

---

1 Said, *Culture and Imperialism*, 200.

hold attitudes that place little value on "what became of the natives," Marlow repeatedly asks them to rethink their position:

> I missed my late helmsman awfully — I missed him even while his body was still lying in the pilot-house. Perhaps you will think it passing strange this regret for a savage who was no more account than a grain of sand in a black Sahara. Well, don't you see, he had done something.

It is Marlow's audience, and by extension Conrad's original readers, who could be expected to think of a native as of "no more account than a grain of sand"; the text, through Marlow, consistently works against that view.

To any reader Marlow's tale must act to some extent to subvert the imperialistic reality it describes. But to the modern reader the evidence Marlow presents also sometimes acts to subvert his own assessment of it. We see some of his attitudes towards the natives — enlightened though they may have been at the time — as patronizing or condescending. Even more centrally, "the idea" of a higher purpose behind the exploitation of the natives, which Marlow at least intermittently seems to want to believe in, is for the modern reader entirely discredited. But is that the way Conrad intended the text to work? Did he in fact share Marlow's views pretty much in their entirety? What if anything do we know of the author's own beliefs and intentions?

Conrad was a Pole, but he was genuinely attached to the country of his adoption, England, and undoubtedly had a soft corner for some aspects of its ideals. During the Boer War, and two days after he began writing *Heart of Darkness*, he wrote to a cousin, Aniela Zagorska, who was living in Brussels where Belgian and British sentiments were in conflict: "that they (the Boers) are struggling in good faith for their independence cannot be doubted; but it is also a fact that they have no idea of liberty, which can be only found under the English flag all over the world."[1] In the

---

1   Conrad, letter to Aniela Zagorska, 25 December 1899, in *The Collected Letters of Joseph Conrad*, Vol. II, 1898-1902, eds. Frederick R. Karl and Laurence Davies (Cambridge: CUP, 1986) 230.

light of this, Marlow may be seen as an alter ego. But to what extent was Conrad aware of the ironies inherent in the British struggling to suppress the Boers in the name of liberty — or of the liberty of Zulu and Xhosa being valued so differently? We may never be entirely sure. On the one hand it should be admitted that Conrad's other writings are not entirely free of the sort of racism that was conventional in his age. In his earlier tale *The Nigger of the "Narcissus"* (1897), for example, he describes James Wait as having "a face pathetic and brutal: the tragic, the mysterious, the repulsive mask of a nigger's soul."[1]

But if he was occasionally prey to the prejudices of his time, in his best writing at any rate Conrad seems to have had the integrity and courage to follow through to the full the implications of his vision even when they may have challenged aspects of his own prejudices. (It may well have been the case that in *Heart of Darkness* he was even able to transcend, in a sense, his own persona.) There is also ample evidence that his lapses into prejudice were precisely that — lapses — and that Conrad for the most part genuinely believed that imperialistic oppression was a moral outrage. As to the behaviour of the white man in the Congo his statements could hardly be plainer:

> ... curious men [go] prying into all sorts of places (where they have no business) and come out of them with all sorts of spoil. This story, and one other, not in this volume, are all the spoil I brought out from the centre of Africa, where, really, I had no sort of business.[2]

In "Geography and Some Explorers" he is even more blunt, describing the white man's enterprise in the Congo as "the vilest scramble for loot that ever disfigured the history of human conscience and geographical exploration."[3]

There is ample evidence as well that Conrad genuinely regarded human beings as human beings, whatever their race (not a

---

1   Joseph Conrad, *The Nigger of the "Narcissus," Typhoon and Other Stories* (London: Penguin, 1963) 27.
2   From the Author's Note.
3   See Appendix A, Document 1.

common attitude in turn of the century Europe). In his 1895 *Author's Note* to *Almayer's Folly*, for example (the manuscript he was working on during his Congo journey), he responds to the complaint that his tales are "decivilized" by dint of depicting "strange people" and "far-off countries." Making no apology for portraying "honest cannibals," Conrad concludes:

> I am content to sympathize with common mortals, no matter where they live; in houses or in tents, in the streets under a fog, or in the forests behind the dark line of dismal mangroves that fringe the vast solitude of the sea.

Perhaps more poignantly telling is Conrad's recounting of one of the incidents from his Congo experience that was not included in the fictionalized version—his recovery from illness:

> lying sick to death in a native hut, tended by an old negress who brought him water from day to day, when he had been abandoned by all the Belgians. "She saved my life," Conrad said, "the white men never came near me."[1]

Moreover, Conrad unequivocally supported the efforts of those (such as Roger Casement) who were campaigning against the savage oppression he depicted.[2] It is true, of course, that Conrad was himself a writer rather than a political activist, and a writer, moreover, who saw truth as complex and elusive, and who had an aversion to polemic even when he did wish to make a clear point. Said argues that Conrad "does not give us a fully realized alternative to imperialism."[3] Well, no. Neither does Shakespeare give us a fully-realized alternative to Christianity—nor does he attempt to

---

1 Edward Garnett, "Introduction" to *Letters from Conrad: 1895-1924;* see Appendix A.

2 On 21 December 1903, for example, Conrad wrote to Roger Casement: "There exists in Africa a Congo State, created by the act of European powers where ruthless systematic cruelty towards the blacks is the basis of administration.... I do hope we shall meet before you leave. Once more my best wishes go with you on your crusade. Of course you may make any use you like of what I write to you." From *The Collected Letters of Joseph Conrad*, Vol. III, 1903-1907, eds. F.R. Karl and Laurence Davies (Cambridge, CUP, 1988) 95-96, as quoted by Watts, "Introduction," *Heart of Darkness* (Oxford: OUP, 1990).

3 Said, *Culture and Imperialism,* 28.

do so. Nor does Kate Chopin give us a fully-realized alternative to patriarchy — or in any way attempt to do so. Within the mainstream of literature, on the other hand, extraordinary texts are able to transcend the limitations of the ideological principles of their times by revealing ironies, showing contradictions, and by depicting in memorable fashion the tragic consequences of the applications of those principles. In such ways does Shakespeare subvert Christian prejudice, Chopin subvert patriarchal values — and Conrad subvert the racist and imperialist impulse.

In large part it may have been Conrad's multinational experience and his Polish origins that enabled him to transcend conventional thinking and gave him a unique perspective on the limitations of Englishness and, indeed, of Western civilization in his time. Poland had no Empire and was, in fact, subject to Russian imperialism; as a Pole, Conrad had thus been at the receiving end of imperialism and had seen it kill his parents. His family tradition, on both his father's and mother's side, had a nationalist aspect. He was a member of a ruling class (the gentry) which itself was a suppressed class in Poland.

When Conrad settled in England, writing in Polish for publication seemed unrealistic. He did entertain the possibility of writing in French, but that too seemed not practical. From boyhood he had taken to literature in English (which he read in Polish or French translation), and especially to Shakespeare, whom his father translated into Polish. The influence and pressure of his immediate environment would tend to make Conrad write in the sole language of that society, English. He felt that he was competent in the language, though he always found writing in English difficult. He learnt it only when an adult and, at the beginning, mainly from such seemingly unpromising sources as navigation manuals and seamen's talk.

Narrative Strategies

The form of the novella and its thematics are so closely intertwined as to be virtually inseparable. Ambiguities, uncertainties and ironies are echoed in the layered narrative structure of *Heart of Darkness*, through which it is often impossible to be sure of one's bearings—and indeed, often difficult to be sure on first reading of what is happening or who is speaking. In its density the style has tellingly been likened to a tropical forest. This is most obviously the case with Conrad's strategy of including narratives within Marlow's narrative, and enclosing Marlow's narrative itself within that of an anonymous narrator.

The anonymous frame narrator is a beneficiary of imperialism, yet, like Marlow before his river journey, he is ignorant of imperial realities. He undergoes a process of education as he listens to Marlow's tale, yet at the very beginning he possesses the intelligence to characterize it accurately—

> The yarns of seamen have a direct simplicity, the whole meaning of which lies within the shell of a cracked nut. But Marlow was not typical (if his propensity to spin yarns be excepted), and to him the meaning of an episode was not inside like a kernel but outside, enveloping the tale which brought it out only as a glow brings out a haze, in the likeness of one of these misty halos that sometimes are made visible by the spectral illumination of moonshine.

The narrator establishes himself as a reliable agent to relay Marlow's narrative. From one perspective, the narrative structure subverts the seaman's yarn. From another, Conrad employs the narrative mode of the sahib recounting his colonial experiences, a mode established in *Blackwood's Edinburgh Magazine* to which Conrad contributed *Karain, Youth, Lord Jim* and *Heart of Darkness* itself, to subvert the sahib view of imperialism. Marlow's suitability as a first-person narrator is crucial to the success of the novella. As he ruminates on his experiences at the Central Station in Congo, he confesses that his temperament is such that he hates lies. He may compromise with truth and utter white lies on occasion—to cope with the exigencies, limitations and imperfections of our world. But his dissimulation is not of the sort to impair integrity and he is candid about it. His kind of honesty is one reason why the reader accepts his tale.

That Marlow is a certain type of Englishman is also important. When Marlow is in the waiting-room of the Belgian imperial company, he observes a map of the world with all the colonies marked: "There was a vast amount of red—good to see at any time, because one knows some real work is done in there." Though Conrad and Marlow overlap, Marlow is essentially a projection of the middle-class Englishman, still rather extrovert and enthusiastic about British imperialism—*before* his experience of imperial realities. Through Marlow Conrad can examine British attitudes to imperialism; Marlow also remains a perfect narrative vehicle because his nationality does not inhibit his clear-sightedness and frankness in confronting the colonialism represented by a foreign nation, Belgium.

Conrad's presentation of the imperial theme begins, not in the Congo or even in Brussels, but in London. Marlow talks of his connection with the Belgian Congo because of his "propensity to spin yarns." The "propensity" is released in a situation conducive to it—Marlow on board a yawl in the Thames at dusk with three cronies who are joined by "the bond of the sea." The atmosphere and setting are interwoven with meaning: the dominant metaphorical motif of darkness and light arises naturally, given the time and place; the Thames is like "an interminable waterway," suggesting no limits of place or time on the tale's significance; Marlow's cronies are a Director of Companies, a Lawyer and an Accountant, pillars of capitalism and thereby implicated in the thematics.

The Buddha tableaux enclose the tale, the comparison to the Buddha suggesting Marlow's role as a seeker after truth. Yet the tale is really open-ended and "inconclusive," thereby involving the reader in active exploration and assessment and ensuring "a continued vibration" that, as Conrad hoped in his Author's Note, "hangs in the air and dwells on the ear." Moreover, Conrad, by emphasizing the Buddha tableaux and lingering over Marlow's technique of story-telling, warns the reader that s/he must be prepared to hunt for meaning.

Conrad is a studied writer and, like any great artist, he possessed a semi-independent interest in form. As his letters show, he was conscious of having done something new, profound and wonderful in writing *Heart of Darkness*.[1]

---

1   See Conrad's letters in Appendices.

Kurtz, Conrad, and Nietzsche

The Kurtz phase is the climax of Conrad's story — Kurtz being the chief character of the tale, not Marlow as the generality of critics have argued. Here the imperial theme expands to include an account of moral isolation — Kurtz's story in the heart of Africa — from one perspective. The direct presentation of Kurtz occupies only a few pages and he speaks very little, but he is extensively discussed both before and afterwards. He is presented mainly through the eyes of others, both as a great man and as the most absolute of sinners. His "greatness" is, ironically, linked to completely ordinary facts. He wishes to "make his pile," the common motivation of colonial employees, and is both more successful and even less scrupulous than most in doing so. He thinks that each station should be a centre for trade, but he is also a painter, a poet, a musician, a journalist, an orator — a man of varied talents. Above all, he comes to the Congo "equipped with moral ideas." It is for this reason, not so much for his outstanding success in gathering ivory (which is what matters to the other colonial employees), that Marlow's attitude of indifference to him changes. One of Kurtz's stated ideals is: "Each station should be like a beacon on the road towards better things, a centre for ... humanizing, improving, instructing."

Critics have argued for a number of models for Kurtz — Georges Antoine Klein,[1] Hodister,[2] King Leopold II of Belgium, and Stanley.[3] From an aesthetic point of view it may be argued that the dynamics of Conrad's tale demand a figure such as Kurtz. But it also seems very likely that the ideas of Friedrich Nietzsche (1844-1900) had something to do with the creation of Kurtz. Nietzsche attacked Christianity, liberalism, democracy and socialism alike as embodying a "slave morality." Christianity's antithesis was "beyond good and evil" — a morality appropriate to superior individuals who were capable of rising to greater heights; these "overmen" or "supermen" — Nietzsche's ideal world was if anything more sexist than mainstream nineteenth-century European

---

1 Jocelyn Baines, *Joseph Conrad* (London: Weidenfeld & Nicolson, 1993) 117.
2 Sherry, *Conrad's Western World*, 95.
3 Watt, *Conrad in the Nineteenth Century*, 142-6.

society—would embody the "will to power," the height of self-assertion and self-mastery. In what most scholars see as a perversion of his doctrines, Nietzsche's writings were later drawn on by Nazi theorists claiming racial and national superiority for the German people. Nietzsche enjoyed the shock that his writings engendered, and by the time Conrad was writing, his ideas had become widely disseminated in Europe.

The key to the transformation of Kurtz is found in Marlow's realization that "he had kicked the very earth to pieces." Kurtz is perhaps a specimen of the "free spirit" who has gone "Beyond Good and Evil" and answered in the affirmative Zarathustra's question, "can'st thou give thyself thine own evil and thy good, hanging thy will above thee as a law?" The strong drives in human nature are allowed to emerge in all their force. Lust for women results in "gratified and monstrous passions." The lure of the alien is permitted to affect Kurtz. He is both drawn and repelled by a culture he despises; it is he who orders the Africans to attack Marlow's steamer which was intended to rescue him. Their arrows "might have been poisoned but they looked as though they wouldn't kill a cat"—an effective trick: it does not avoid the realistic possibilities of the arrows being lethal, yet leaves a flavour of harmlessness, very much in tune with the fact that it is an attempt to repel, not kill, the whites. Kurtz's avarice and lust for power, whose seeds precede his life in Africa, and of which the human skulls around his dwelling are a symbol, are unrestrained. He betrays the native people, corrupting and ruthlessly exploiting them. He employs African villagers to fight their fellow men exclusively for his benefit, so that he can amass the maximum possible quantity of ivory. He perverts "pure, uncomplicated savagery" into "some lightless region of subtle horrors," including "unspeakable rites offered up to him."

Conrad is implicitly critical of Nietzschean thought. Kurtz's kind of progress is a circular regression: to rely totally on intellect and will, to reject all religious and social taboos, is to be beyond man—but also to be less than man. At the end, Kurtz, stripped of his daemonic vitality, is quite simply undignified.

Kurtz's role suggests meanings on political, economic, social, religious, moral, psychological and philosophical levels. It also intimates meaning on the archetypal level. Cedric Watts seems to me right in asserting that behind Kurtz "stands the Christian legend of Lucifer."[1] Kurtz is guilty of pride, pride of self, in keeping with the Luciferian legend which has something in common with the classical concept of *hubris*. Marlow remarks that "his [Kurtz's] stare ... was piercing enough to penetrate all the hearts that beat in the darkness." Perhaps Kurtz also sees a vision of Hell and the damnation awaiting him.

Kurtz is remarkable in that he can win loyalties and appeal to fellow human beings even during moments of darkest savagery. He is admired by the Russian disciple, by the Africans, indeed by all those who come to know him, even by Marlow himself in an ambivalent way. At the beginning of his journey into the interior, Marlow makes an important distinction between the "strong, lusty, red-eyed devils, that swayed and drove men," on the one hand, and "a flabby, pretending, weak-eyed devil of a rapacious and pitiless folly," on the other. He prefers the former category, which Kurtz falls into, while the "pilgrims," the Manager and brickmaker belong to the despicable second category. In Marlow's view, Kurtz is a genuine devil who can inspire horror, whereas the Manager "was obeyed, yet he inspired neither love nor fear, nor even respect. He inspired uneasiness." He keeps up appearances and pretences continuously, whereas Kurtz commits himself totally to the free expression of the self and believes in action. The *postscriptum*, "Exterminate all the brutes!," to his report for the International Society for the Suppression of Savage Customs has to be taken seriously because it figures as a principle of action. (In Nietzsche's view, pitilessness was a virtue.) While the Manager plots against Kurtz and plans to prevent help from reaching the sick man until he perishes, he is very cautious; even his evil is negative, weak and mean. Marlow calls "the first-class agent," also known as "the brick-maker," a "papier-mâché Mephistopheles." The ordinary unidentified pilgrims are the worst. All of them are essentially alike in that they suffer from moral impotence and vacancy. They cannot do evil for they are never involved in making a moral choice for good or evil, and, certainly, cannot go

---

1   Cedric Watts, *The Deceptive Text* (Sussex: Harvester Press, 1984) 77-8.

beyond morality as Marlow suggests Kurtz does. Kurtz is, in Marlow's view, man enough to make a decision and peculiarly honest in acting by it. It is to this honesty in Kurtz that Marlow turns "for relief"; this is why he prefers the "nightmare" of Kurtz to that of the other colonial employees, though it is far more unsettling. Conrad's view here is an extension of T.S. Eliot's:

> So far as we are human, what we do must be either evil or good; so far as we do evil or good, we are human; and it is better, in a paradoxical way, to do evil than to do nothing: at least, we exist. It is true to say that the glory of man is his capacity for salvation; it is also true to say that his glory is his capacity for damnation.[1]

From this vantage point, Kurtz is "man enough" (or *human* enough) to be damned. The other colonial employees are not; they can be neither saved nor damned. It is Kurtz's soul that goes mad (Nietzsche literally lost his sanity), whereas the other employees do not possess souls and so cannot go mad. In Marlow's words, "You may be too much of a fool to go wrong—too dull even to know you are being assaulted by the powers of darkness. I take it, no fool ever made a bargain for his soul with the devil."

Marlow's encounter with Kurtz is the climax of Conrad's tale. The episode itself reaches its climax with Kurtz's death. His final cry, "The horror! The horror!," is rich in meaning. It is interpreted by Marlow as "complete knowledge" and a "moral victory"; some critics (for instance, J.I.M. Stewart and Ian Watt) have seen it as on one level a rejection, a rejection of "going native."[2] To Lionel Trilling, Kurtz's cry "refers to the approach of death or to his experience of savage life."[3] But it seems to me that it can no less validly be seen to include more meanings. The "horror" represents the gap between the ideals of civilization—the ideals

---

1 T.S. Eliot, "Baudelaire," in *Selected Essays* (London: Faber, 1951) 429.
2 J.I.M. Stewart, *Joseph Conrad* (London: Longman, 1968) 79; Watt, *Conrad in the Nineteenth Century*, 236.
3 Lionel Trilling, *Beyond Culture*, quoted from *Conrad: Heart of Darkness, Nostromo and Under Western Eyes: A Casebook*, ed. C.B. Cox (London: Macmillan, 1981) 64.

which Kurtz has mouthed—and the realities (torture, domination, exploitation) as well as a recognition of their common source. It is also the response elicited from Kurtz as he faces the emptiness of a world without moral criteria, a nihilistic view of life and death.

(We may note here in passing connections to somewhat later classics of modern nihilism. Both the African wilderness and the Marabar Caves in Forster's *A Passage to India* engender "ouboum"—the ultimate nullity. "Mistah Kurtz—he dead" was used by Eliot as an epigraph for *The Hollow Men* (1925). Kurtz's cry, "The horror! The horror!" could well have been an appropriate epigraph to *The Waste Land* (1922), given Eliot's view of the depravity of man and the deadness of Western civilization as well as the darkness beyond good and evil, though he was dissuaded from using it by the less perceptive Ezra Pound.[1])

Kurtz is a representative or symbol of European civilization and of imperialism ("His mother was half-English, his father was half-French. All Europe contributed to the making of Kurtz."). But he also acquires a wider significance as a human being. The heart of darkness is in one sense the centre of Africa, but more important is the suggestion that it is the unknown, the evil in humanity, the hidden self and the negation at the back of all things.

Style, Image, and Symbol

Two statements by Conrad help explain the style that he employs:

... explicitness ... is fatal to the glamour of all artistic work, robbing it of all suggestiveness, destroying all illusion.[2]

I wish at first to put before you a general proposition: that a work of art is very seldom limited to one exclusive meaning and not necessarily tending to a definite conclusion. And

---

1   Valerie Eliot (ed.), *T.S. Eliot, The Waste Land: A Facsimile and Transcript of the Original Drafts* (London: Faber, 1971) 125.

2   Conrad, letter to Richard Curle, 24 April 1922, in *Conrad to a Friend*, ed. Richard Curle (New York: Doubleday 1928) 113.

this for the reason that the nearer it approaches art, the more it acquires a symbolic character.[1]

These principles are at work behind his methods of description and suggestion as much as they are behind his narrative structures. Ian Watt, Cedric Watts and other critics have remarked on Conrad's technique of delayed decoding, by which events are described in such a way that it only gradually becomes clear to the reader what is happening.[2]

More obvious, perhaps, is Conrad's penchant for adjectives that attempt to describe the indescribable: "ineffable," "incomprehensible" and so on. This tendency has often been criticised, beginning with F. R. Leavis's strictures on the "overworked vocabulary," "the adjectival insistence upon inexpressible and incomprehensible mystery" as applied to the Congo and to "the evocation of human profundities and spiritual horrors."[3] More recent critics (for instance, C.B. Cox and James Guetti)[4] argue that Conrad's kind of language represents not a failed attempt to capture experience but rather an effort to suggest an experience for which normal language is inadequate. It may be, however, that Conrad's narrative indirections, and the fact that he unquestionably overworks such adjectives in certain of his other works (in *Arrow of Gold* the habit verges on self-parody), may lead some to believe that he employs them in *Heart of Darkness* more frequently than is in fact the case. "Incomprehensible" is used four times and "inscrutable" five, but "ineffable," "inexpressible" and "indescribable" are in fact never resorted to.

Heart of Darkness quite quickly came to be regarded as an important text in the development of modern symbolism. One critic, Marvin Mudrick, has gone so far as to suggest that "after

---

1   Conrad, letter to Barrett H. Clark, 14 May 1918, in G. Jean-Aubry, *Life and Letters* (London: Heinemann 1927) 204-205.
2   See Watt, *Conrad in the Nineteenth Century*; Watts, *The Deceptive Text*; and Bruce Johnston, "Conrad's Impressionism" and Watt's "Delayed Decoding," in *Conrad Revisited*, ed. Ross C. Murfin (Tuscaloosa: U of Alabama Press, 1985).
3   F.R. Leavis, *The Great Tradition* (London: Penguin, 1962) 196-7.
4   C.B. Cox, "Introduction," in *Conrad: Heart of Darkness, Nostromo and Under Western Eyes: A Casebook*, 16-7.

Heart of Darkness, the recorded moment—the word—was irrecoverably symbol."[1] The ways in which the symbolism of light and darkness are employed, of course, have an extraordinary complexity to them. As well, ivory forms an important real and symbolic leitmotif in the tale. Ivory is to the Congo what silver is to Costaguana in *Nostromo*. It is the actual raw wealth which private individuals, colonial companies and imperial powers covet, as well as a symbolic centre for their self-aggrandizing motives. Amidst pretences, the white man's desire for ivory is unmistakably real and prominent. The search for it is the expression of Kurtz's baser motives—of his brutality towards the natives as well as of his greed.

> Hadn't I been told in all the tones of jealousy and admiration that he had collected, bartered, swindled, or stolen more ivory than all the other agents together?

> He had been absent for several months ... with the intention to all appearance of making a raid either across the river or down stream. Evidently the appetite for more ivory had got the better of his—what shall I say?—less material aspirations.

Ivory has a wider symbolic application too. It is white and shiny on the outside but it is really dead matter, and thereby points to a paradox at the heart of Western civilization. (It is significant that the Accountant keeps up appearances, but his accounts are false and he is insensitive and dried-up within.) Conrad chooses to focus on ivory rather than rubber, though in the Congo rubber was no less important, because it suits his purposes better. Ivory is thematically and metaphorically richer.

In discussing the symbolic structure of the tale many commentators have remarked that Marlow's journey into the interior becomes, at the same time, an interior journey: at a symbolic level

---

1 Marvin Mudrick, "The Originality of Conrad," in *Conrad: A Collection of Critical Essays*, ed. M. Mudrick (New Jersey: Prentice-Hall, 1966) 44.

the journey into the Congo becomes also a journey into the depths of man's unconscious, revealed in all its darkness.

It is quite clear that Conrad intended the reader to draw such symbolic inferences — though almost certainly he would not have been comfortable with a thoroughly Freudian or Jungian approach of the sort that some critics have attempted,[1] analyzing the perceived connections between the tale and Conrad's own psyche. The connections between the Congo journey and Conrad's boyhood dreams (reported in "Geography and Some Explorers") have been made much of by some, for example, and others have not implausibly suggested that Conrad may have in part been motivated by a desire to expiate guilt at the part he had himself played in the imperialistic adventure. Conrad would no doubt have had none of it; in 1921, three years before Conrad's death, H.R. Lenormand, a young French playwright and admirer of Dostoevsky and of psychoanalysis, met Conrad at Ajaccio and was shocked by his refusal to read Freud, whose books he had lent him, or to discuss the subconscious motives influencing the behaviour of his characters.[2]

Heart of Darkness and Gender

An aspect of *Heart of Darkness* that many modern readers find problematic is the attitudes towards women that are displayed in it — from the frank lusts of Kurtz to the patronizing tone that Marlow adopts:

> Then — would you believe it? — I tried the women. I, Charlie Marlow, set the women to work — to get a job.

> I ventured to hint that the Company was run for profit.
> "You forget, dear Charlie, that the labourer is worthy of his hire," she said, brightly. It's queer how out of touch with

---

1 See, for example, A.J. Guerard in *Conrad the Novelist* (Cambridge, Mass.: Harvard UP, 1958); Frederick R. Karl, "Introduction to the *Danse Macabre*: Conrad's *Heart of Darkness*," in *Heart of Darkness: A Case Study in Contemporary Criticism*, ed. Ross C. Murfin (New York: St. Martin's Press, 1989).

2 Zdzislaw Najder, *Joseph Conrad: A Chronicle* (Cambridge: CUP, 1983) 460.

truth women are. They live in a world of their own, and there has never been anything like it, and never can be. It is too beautiful altogether, and if they were to set it up it would go to pieces before the first sunset. Some confounded fact we men have been living contentedly with ever since the day of creation would start up and knock the whole thing over.

As at so many other places, though, at this point the text as a whole acts to subvert the sentiments being expressed. Marlow good-humoredly belittles the idealistic sentiment of the woman who suggests that the value of the labourer should be placed above the profit motive. Yet the text as a whole shows with appalling clarity the effects of the profit motive being let loose without restraint—and the effect in particular of unrestrained *male* capitalism.

The contrast between Kurtz's black mistress—whose portrayal may remind us of the "Noble Savage" motif but is yet more than that—and his Intended has often been commented on as a fairly conventional dichotomy of Virgin/Whore. But it is misleading to apply this dichotomy. The real antithesis in the text is between the Intended as virginal, cerebral, idealistic (her forehead is highlighted) and the African as passional, yet with dignity as her distinguishing trait: she is theatrical, statuesque, yes, but not a whore, not cheap or mercenary in sex. The two women, finally, appear as different sides of a single archetypal woman. Kurtz's disciple presents Kurtz's African woman, from *his* perspective, as a shrew, a virago, but, from the reader's perspective, she appears jealous and possessive, not sexually but in regard to sharing Kurtz's attention.

What of the final scene? Does it imply that women as a group are naïve and must be protected from horror, sheltered from the truth? Johanna M. Smith has plausibly argued that the scene embodies "the ideology of separate spheres" for men and women,[1] and there can be no question that gender roles have an

---

1   Johanna M. Smith, "'Too Beautiful Altogether': Patriarchal Ideology in *Heart of Darkness*," in *Heart of Darkness: A Case Study in Contemporary Criticism*, ed. Ross C. Murfin (New York: St. Martin's, 1989).

important part to play in the final scene. It would be difficult to suggest that the final scene holds *only* a gender-related message, however. Indeed, insofar as a message concerning the necessity of protecting ourselves from "the appalling face of glimpsed truth" is concerned, it is surely at least as plausible to see such a theme running throughout the book: to see it surface as much in the illusions that Marlow constructs for himself as in those he allows to remain undisturbed in the heart of Kurtz's Intended. It is Marlow, after all, who in the face of the purest horror strives desperately to find his "Idea," to find somehow in this evil

> an affirmation, a moral victory paid for by innumerable defeats, by abominable terrors, by abominable satisfactions. But it was a victory! That is why I have remained loyal to Kurtz to the last, and even beyond, when a long time after I heard once more, not his own voice, but the echo of his magnificent eloquence thrown to me from a soul as translucently pure as a cliff of crystal.

If the Intended is deemed unable to truly face the horror, may we not say the same of Marlow himself ? Finally, it is not women who must be protected somehow from too much reality, but all humanity.

★ ★ ★

Marlow's African journey ends at the key places from where he set out — Brussels, the headquarters of the Congo Empire, and London, the headquarters of the British Empire. The final phase in Europe is pitched on a lower key than those in Africa. This is appropriate, perhaps necessary, not merely to a tale drawing to a close, but to convey and underline its final wisdom. Conrad directs his irony at conventional, ordinary living and the values of work, duty and restraint found in it, and suggests a preference for the kind of exploration of the self that has occupied Kurtz in Africa. Through Marlow's account of his return to "the sepulchral city" (reiterated), during which he refers to physical details in the Intended's house such as the fireplace with "a cold and monumental whiteness," a piano like a "sarcophagus," even the woman's perfect yet pallid skin, Conrad is able to confirm, without any forcing of the symbolism, that the secure opulence of Europe is able to maintain itself intact only by a radical ignorance of the raw savageries which ultimately pay for it.

The Intended is a rich pun. It refers to Kurtz's fiancée, to his intentions regarding her, to Africa and to himself, and to his will, which he wanted to use to better Africa and which he used to break free of Western morality. Marlow thought that "the culminating point" of his experience was the Kurtz episode. This was so in regard to Africa as well as to wider life. The final scene with the Intended is a necessary extension of his experience. In his conversation with her, he suppresses the dark truth of Kurtz and concludes by uttering the biggest of his white lies, that Kurtz's last words were not "The horror! The horror!", but her name. Marlow has become more aware of deeper and darker things, but now he sees that illusions, ethics, ideals are necessary for the survival of the individual and of civilization itself, however debatable its value.

> The lights must never go out,
> The music must always play,[1]

even if on the keys of dead and deathly ivory that grin like a death's head in the Intended's drawing-room. A sustaining illusion is necessary to all but the strongest minds—like Marlow who has found a Buddha-like "enlightenment," the knowledge of the dark. At the very end, the Thames merges with the Congo (one is reminded of Marlow's opening words, "This also has been one of the dark places of the earth"), and the reader is left gazing at the heart of darkness, still in the grip of the world of the novella:

This world: a monster of energy without beginning, without end; a firm, iron magnitude of force that does not grow

---

1   W.H.Auden, "September 1, 1939," in *Poetry of the Thirties*, ed. Robin Skelton (Harmondsworth: Penguin, 1964) 282.

bigger or smaller, that does not expend itself but only trans-
forms itself; ... enclosed by "nothingness" boundary.[1]

There is a — let us say — a machine. It evolved itself (I am
severely scientific) out of a chaos of scraps of iron and
behold! it knits.... And the most withering thing is that the
infamous thing has made itself; made itself without thought,
without conscience, without foresight, without eyes, without heart.... It knits us in and it knits us out, it has knitted
time, space, pain, death, corruption, despair and all the illusions — and nothing matters. I'll admit however that to look
at the remorseless process is sometimes amusing.[2]

In an edition that is intended for a wide variety of readers (all
of whom may interpret the text in rather different ways), it may be
best in closing to turn the direction from the author's viewpoint
to that of the reader. Conrad himself was acutely aware of the
essential and rich obscurity of his tale and, anticipating postmod-
ernism, looked upon the reader as an imaginative collaborator.
"For one writes only half the book," he insisted to Cunninghame
Graham in 1897, "the other half is with the reader."[3]

★ ★ ★

In addition to a variety of relevant writings by Conrad and a
selection of contemporary reviews, I have included in the
Appendices a selective presentation of contemporary documents
to give a vivid picture of the historical context out of which *Heart
of Darkness* emerged, sometimes illustrating the novella and also
giving substance to all those hints as to the "unspeakable" of
Marlow. As postcolonialism occupies the centre of the stage

---

1 Friedrich Nietzsche, *The Will to Power*, quoted from Edward Said, "Conrad and
   Nietzsche," in *Joseph Conrad: A Commemoration*, ed. Norman Sherry (London:
   Macmillan, 1979) 73.
2 Conrad, letter to Cunninghame Graham, 20 December 1897, in *Joseph Conrad's Letters
   to R.B. Cunninghame Graham*, ed. C.T. Watts (Cambridge: CUP, 1969) 56-7.
3 Conrad, letter to Cunninghame Graham, 5 August 1897, in *Joseph Conrad's Letters to
   R.B. Cunninghame Graham*, 46.

today, it is necessary to provide a re-entry into the earlier, very different, heady age of the high tide of imperialism, 1880-1920, when *Heart of Darkness* was written, an age now long past, remote and alien. I begin with documents of exploration to serve as a kind of prelude—exploration preceding exploitation, and conveying the sheer excitement of Africa and the white man's perception of himself and the Other. Stanley's responses are unreflective and unsophisticated when compared to Conrad's, but they are the stuff of the age. So too is the excerpt from the diary of William G. Stairs, who accompanied Stanley up the Congo on the ill-fated Emin Pasha expedition only three years before Conrad's own journey, for much of the time travelling on the steamer *Florida* that Conrad was hired to captain. Both the advocates and the critics (a minority) of imperialism are represented. The documents of exploitation such as Roger Casement's "The Congo Report" (11 December 1903)[1] contain instances of colonial discourse (such as the specious justification of "impositions" on the Africans by the Companies) which Conrad subverts in his novella. I close with accounts of the Benin massacre (1897). Coming between Conrad's Congo journey (1890) and the writing of *Heart of Darkness* (1898-99), the massacre, which kept the savagery of the Dark Continent before the public eye for several weeks, would have enkindled Conrad's own memories of Africa and acted as a catalyst. In any case, Conrad did not tie his narrative specifically to the Congo, and the realities of Benin are relevant: in R.H. Bacon's *Benin: The City of Blood*, the accounts of human sacrifice and the absolute power of the ruler over religion relate to Kurtz; in the emphasis on Benin as bloody and bigoted, the alert reader sees the colonizer justifying his presence. The Benin documents are useful as illustrating the general European/English perception of Africa as a whole.

The Benin group of documents is prefaced by a selection describing civilization in Benin in a somewhat earlier period—an excerpt from *Equiano's Travels*. The Equiano text may set the later

---

1   Roger Casement, "The Congo Report," in *The Black Diaries: An Account of Roger Casement's Life and Times, With a Collection of His Diaries and Public Writings*, ed. P. Singleton-Gates (Paris: Olympia Press, 1957).

accounts of "savagery in Benin" in useful relief. But more than that, as one of the very few narratives—by far the best-written and most reliable—by Africans that give a real sense of the pre-Colonial period in any Bantu society, the Equiano text offers us as close as we are ever likely to get to a shadowy glimpse of what life may have been like in the neighbouring Bantu societies of the Congo in the pre-Colonial period.

For the second edition two appendices of visual material have been added. The first of these consists of various images of people and scenes relevant to the novel. The Harris photographs were thought to warrant a separate appendix; these extraordinary images of Belgian Congo atrocities were very influential in swaying public opinion in Britain against Belgian colonialism in the region. (In the context of the recent violence in the region, these images stand as well as a horrific historical reference point.)

Altogether, the documents provide a cross-section of attitudes in regard to the political, economic and social facts relating to imperialism in Africa; they may serve to provide a series of perspectives on the reality out of which this particular fiction emerged, and simultaneously serve to highlight the perceptiveness, complexity and profundity of Conrad's fictional approach.

Select Bibliography

Biographical studies

Jocelyn Baines, *Joseph Conrad: A Critical Biography* (London: Weidenfeld & Nicolson, 1993 edn.).

Frederick R. Karl, *Joseph Conrad: The Three Lives, A Biography* (New York: Farrar, Straus & Giroux; London: Faber and Faber, 1979).

Zdzislaw Najder, *Joseph Conrad: A Chronicle* (New Brunswick, NJ: Rutgers UP; Cambridge: CUP, 1983).

Cedric Watts, *Joseph Conrad: A Literary Life* (London: Macmillan, 1989).

Bibliographies

Jetty de Vries, *Conrad Criticism 1965-1985: Heart of Darkness* (The Netherlands: Phoenix Press, 1988).

David Leon Higdon, et al., *Conrad Bibliography: A Continuing Checklist, Conradiana* (Lubbock, Texas: Texas Tech. UP, 1968).

Bruce E. Teets and Helmut E. Gerber (eds.), *Joseph Conrad: An Annotated Bibliography of Writings About Him* (De Kalb, IL: Northern Illinois UP, 1971).

Bruce E. Teets, *Joseph Conrad: An Annotated Bibliography* (New York: Garland, 1990).

Studies

Patrick Brantlinger, *Rule of Darkness: British Literature and Imperialism, 1830-1914* (Cornell: Cornell UP, 1988).

Jacques Darras, *Joseph Conrad and the West: Signs of Empire* (London: Macmillan; New York: Barnes & Noble, 1982).

D.C.R.A. Goonetilleke, *Joseph Conrad: Beyond Culture and Background* (London: Macmillan; New York: St Martin's Press 1990).

John W. Griffith, *Joseph Conrad and the Anthropological Dilemma* (Oxford: Clarendon Press, 1995.)

Albert J. Guerard, *Conrad the Novelist* (Cambridge, MA: Harvard UP, 1958).

James Guetti, *The Limits of Metaphor* (Ithaca, NY: Cornell UP, 1967).

Jakob Lothe, *Conrad's Narrative Method* (Oxford: Clarendon Press, 1989).

Gene Moore (ed.), *Conrad on Film* (Cambridge: Cambridge UP, 1997).

Benita Parry, *Conrad and Imperialism: Ideological Boundaries and Visionary Frontiers* (London: Macmillan, 1983).

Edward W. Said, *Culture and Imperialism* (London: Chatto & Windus, 1993).

Norman Sherry, *Conrad's Western World* (Cambridge: CUP, 1971).

Brian Spittles, *Joseph Conrad: Text and Context* (London: Macmillan, 1992).

Ian Watt, *Conrad in the Nineteenth Century* (London: Chatto & Windus, 1980).

Cedric Watts, *Conrad's Heart of Darkness: A Critical and Contextual Discussion* (Milan: Mursia International, 1977).

Joseph Conrad: A Brief Chronology

1857   3 December: Jòzef Teodor Konrad Korzenioswki born, in the Ukraine, of Polish parents.

1861   His father, Apollo Korzeniowzski, poet and translator, arrested for anti-Russian (patriotic) conspiracy.

1862   The Korzeniowskis exiled to Vologda, Russia; Conrad accompanies them.

1865   Death of his mother Eva (née Bobrowska).

1869   Death of Apollo Korzeniowski in Krakow; Conrad adopted by his uncle, Tadeusz Bobrowski.

1874   Leaves Poland for Marseilles to become a trainee seaman in the French merchant navy. Voyage on *Mount-Blanc* to Martinique.

1875   Voyage on *Mount-Blanc* to West Indies as an apprentice.

1876   Steward on the *Sainte-Antoine*; goes to Caribbean.

1877   Possibly involved in smuggling arms to the "Carlists" (Spanish royalists) from Marseilles.

1878   *March:* shoots himself in chest in Marseilles but is not seriously injured; his uncle, Bobrowski, clears his debts. *April:* joins his first British ship, the *Mavis*, probably as apprentice. Later, *The Skimmer of the Sea* as able-bodied seaman.

1884   *17 November:* fails his first mate's examination. *3 December* (his twenty-seventh birthday): repeats and passes the examination.

1886   *28 July:* fails master's examination; *18 August:* becomes a nationalized British subject; *10 November:* successfully passes master's examination.

1887   Sails to Java on the *Highland Forest* as first mate, sustains a back injury, hospitalized in Singapore. Later, joins the *Vidar* as first mate, trading between Singapore and the Dutch East Indies, Borneo and Celebes.

1888   Conrad accepts his only permanent command, the barque *Otago*, joining it in Bangkok.

1889   Resigns his command and returns to London. Begins *Almayer's Folly*.

1890   *February:* visits his cousin, the writer Marguerite
        Poradowska in Brussels and is interviewed by Albert
        Thys of the *Société Anonyme Belge pour le Commerce du
        Haut-Congo.*
        February-April: first vist to Poland in 16 years.
        29 April: returns to Brussels to learn his "Aunt"
        Poradowska has secured him a three-year appointment
        with the *Société* as the master of one of its ships.
        June-December: in the Belgian Congo; disenchanted and
        malarial, Conrad returns to Brussels in late January
        1891.

1891-3 First-mate on the *Torrens,* his pleasantest berth; meets
        E.L. Sanderson and John Galsworthy, who became life-
        long friends.

1894   End of Conrad's sea career. Bobrowski dies, leaving
        Conrad about £1,600. *Almayer's Folly* accepted for pub-
        lication by T. Fisher Unwin. Conrad meets Edward
        Garnett, who is his early mentor and lifelong friend.

1895   *Almayer's Folly* published and Joseph Conrad adopted as
        his pen name. Finishes *Outcast;* late 1895 begins *The
        Sisters* (a fragment) and *The Rescuer,* completed in 1919
        as *The Rescue.*

1896   *An Outcast of the Islands* published. Marries Jessie
        George.

1897   Conrad meets Henry James and Stephen Crane. Begins
        lifelong friendship with R.B. Cunninghame Graham.
        The Nigger of the "Narcissus" published.

1898   Borys Conrad born. *Tales of Unrest* ("Karain," "The
        Idiots," "An Outpost of Progress," "The Return," "The
        Lagoon") published. Finishes "Youth." Collaborates
        with Ford Madox Ford [Hueffer] on "Seraphina"
        (*Romance*). Throughout the year fitful progress on *The
        Rescue.*
        December: begins "Heart of Darkness."

1899   *6 February:* finishes "Heart of Darkness" (*Blackwood's,*
        February-April). Collaborates with Ford on *The
        Inheritors.* Works on *Lord Jim* (*Blackwood's* October
        1899-November 1900).

1900   Collaboration with Ford on *Romance* continues. Conrad begins a twenty-year association with J.B. Pinker the literary agent, who "stakes" his feckless client generously. Stephen Crane dies.

1901   *The Inheritors* published; works with Ford on *Romance*.

1902   *Youth and Two Other Stories* published ("Youth," "Heart of Darkness," "The End of the Tether").

1903   *Typhoon and Other Stories* ("Typhoon," "Amy Foster," "Falk," "To-morrow") and *Romance* (with Ford) published.

1904   Roger Casement visits Conrad to solicit support for his movement to expose the atrocities of King Leopold of the Belgian Congo. Jessie injures both legs in a bad fall, the beginning of a permanent disability. *Nostromo* published.

1906   John Conrad born. *The Mirror of the Sea* published.

1907   *The Secret Agent* published. The Conrads move to "Someries," Luton.

1908   *A Set of Six* published.

1909   Moves to Aldington, Kent.

1910   Finishes *Under Western Eyes*. Suffers a severe breakdown. Rents Capel House, Orlestone. Awarded a Civil List Pension of £100 per annum.

1911   *Under Western Eyes* published.

1912   *A Personal Record* and *'Twixt Land and Sea* ("A Smile of Fortune," "The Secret Sharer," "Freya of the Seven Isles") published.

1913   *Chance* published.

1914   *Chance* his first popular succes; the earlier work now attracts a larger public. The Conrads visit Poland. War breaks out.

1915   *Within the Tides* ("The Planter of Malata," "The Partner," "The Inn of Two Witches," "Because of the Dollars") and *Victory* published.

1917   *The Shadow-Line* published; Conrad begins to write "Authors' Notes" for the collected edition of his works.

1918   Conrad takes up cause of Polish freedom and finishes "The Crime of Partition."

1919 *The Arrow of Gold* published. Moves to "Oswalds," a spacious house, in Bishopsbourne, near Canterbury.

1920 *The Rescue* (begun in 1896) published.

1921 Visits Corsica for research on *Suspense*. Conrad in poor health. *Notes on Life and Letters* published. The Heinemann *Collected Edition* begins to appear.

1923 Visits America and is lionized.

1924 *May:* Declines offer of a Knighthood.
   3 August: dies of a heart attack at "Oswalds."

1924 *The Nature of a Crime* (collaboration with Ford) published.

1923–7 Collected ("Uniform") edition by Dent.

1925 *Tales of Hearsay* ("The Warrior's Soul," "Prince Roman," "The Tale," "The Black-Mate") and *Suspense* published.

1926 *Last Essays* published.

1928 *The Sisters* (fragment) published.

A Congo Chronology

1482   Diogo Cam, Portuguese navigator, discovers the mouth of the Congo. He made two other voyages there, in 1485 and 1487.

1491   Arrival of the first missionaries in the Congo.

1813   Birth of Livingstone.

1816   British scientific expedition to the mouth of the Congo; death of its leader, Captain J.K. Tuckey, R.N., who had penetrated beyond the first cataracts.

1840   Livingstone lands at the Cape.

1841   Birth of Stanley (born John Rowlands).

1851-52   Livingstone explores the Upper Zambezi and the Upper Kasai.

1858   *February:* The Englishmen, R. Burton and J.H. Speke, discover Lake Tanganyika.

1859   Burton goes up the Congo as far as the Falls of Yellala.

1865   Leopold II, King of the Belgians, ascends the throne.

1871   Livingstone reaches the River Lualaba (Upper Congo) and stays at Nyangwe.
         November: Stanley "finds" Livingstone at Ujiji, on the shores of Lake Tanganyika.

1873-75   V.L. Cameron, British naval lieutenant, crosses Africa from east to west and discovers the course of the Congo.

1873   Death of Livingstone at Chitambo, on Lake Bangweulu. His tomb is in Westminister Abbey.
         Failure of expedition of British naval lieutenant W. Grandy (assault of the cataracts and ascent of the Congo towards Nyangwe).

1874-77   Stanley's crossing of Africa, from Bagamoyo to Boma.

1875   First voyage of Savorgnan de Brazza to Libreville.

1876   *September:* First meeting of the International Geographical Conference at Brussels. Founding of the Association Internationale Africaine (A.I.A.).

1877   *October:* First Belgian expedition of the A.I.A. along the east coast of Africa.

1878   De Brazza returns to Europe; audience with King
Leopold at Brussels.
Stanley lands at Marseilles.
June: Leopold-Stanley talks.
November: Comité d'Études du Haut-Congo
(C.E.H.C.) founded.

1879   *January:* Stanley is appointed leader of the expedition of
the C.E.H.C.
May: The second expedition of the A.I.A. lands on the
east coast of Africa.
July: C.E.H.C. expedition arrives at Banana.
August: Stanley, coming from Zanzibar, lands at Banana.
September: C.E.H.C.'s first station founded at Vivi.
November: C.E.H.C. dissolved. Birth of the Association
Internationale du Congo (A.I.C.).
December: S. de Brazza embarks on behalf of the A.I.A.

1880   *January:* The third and fourth Belgian expeditions of
the A.I.A. leave the east coast of Africa for Karema.
September: S. de Brazza establishes a French post at
Stanley Pool (left bank of Congo).
October: De Brazza treaty with Makoko of Mbe (right
bank of Congo).
November: Stanley–de Brazza meeting near Vivi (right
bank of Congo).

1881   *February:* Second station of C.E.H.C. founded at
Isangila.
April: Third station of C.E.H.C. founded at Manyanga.
May-June: Stanley, prostrate with fever, prepares for
death.
August: Ngalyema authorizes Stanley to settle in his
country.
October: Stanley crosses the River Congo and installs
himself on the left bank, not far from Ntamo
(Leopoldville).
December: Foundation of fourth C.E.H.C. station at
Stanley Pool.

1882   *March:* Colonel Strauch becomes President of the
Association Internationale du Congo (A.I.C.).

April: Stanley and Ngalyema become "blood brothers." Stanley Pool station named Leopoldville.

May: Stanley discovers Lake Leopold II. Foundation of the C.E.H.C.'s fifth station at Mswata.

June: de Brazza returns to Europe.

July: Stanley, having completed the first part of his mission in the service of King Leopold II, sails for Europe.

November: The stations set up by de Brazza are formally ceded to France.

December: Foundation of the sixth C.E.H.C. station at Kwa. Return of Stanley to Vivi.

1883   Stanley reaches Stanley Falls (Stanleyville).

1884   *February:* Anglo-Portuguese Treaty.

April: America recognises the A.I.C. as a State. The A.I.C. grants priority rights to France (confirmed at Paris in December 1908, following the annexation of the Congo by Belgium).

June: Stanley, his mission in Leopold II's service fulfilled, finally returns to Europe.

November: Germany recognizes the A.I.C. as a State. Opening of the Berlin Conference.

December: Great Britain recognises the A.I.C. as a State.

1885   February: France, Russia, Portugal and Belgium recognize the A.I.C. as a State. End of the Berlin Conference and adoption of the General Act.

July: Formal Proclamation of the Congo Free State.

1887   Stanley's expedition for the relief of Emin Pasha.

1889   August: Will of King Leopold II bequeathing the Congo to Belgium.

November: Opening of Anti-Slavery Conference at Brussels.

1898   Inauguration of the Matadi-Leopoldville railway, the achievement of General Albert Thys.

1904   *10 May:* Death of Sir Henry Morton Stanley (buried at Surrey).

1905   *14 September:* Death of Count Savorgnan de Brazza at Dakar.

1908   *August:* The Belgian Parliament votes the Annexation
        of the Congo.
        October: Belgian Colonial Charter.
1909   *17 December:* Death of King Leopold II.

A Note on the Text

After completing *Youth* (1898), Conrad returned to his struggle with *The Rescue* and at the same time was expected to finish "Jim" (envisaged as a short story) for serialization in *Blackwood's Edinburgh Magazine*. But *The Rescue* was still recalcitrant and Conrad left it, this time to write *Heart of Darkness*. Richard Curle in his "Introduction" to Conrad's *The Congo Diary* states: "I remember Conrad telling me that its 40,000 words occupied only about a month in the writing. When we consider the painful, slow labour with which he usually composed, we can perceive how intensely vivid his memories of this [African] experience must have been, and, to judge from the parallel passages, how intensely actual." Though written with extraordinary rapidity, a comparison of the manuscript with the final version shows careful revision. For instance, in the manuscript Conrad gives a detailed account of Boma, the seat of government at the mouth of the Congo which he evidently disliked, but the novella only refers briefly to "the miserable little wharf" and "these government chaps." It looks as though Conrad eliminated personal impressions to sharpen focus. This also illustrates how the story, characteristically for Conrad, had "grown upon him." It seems to have been originally envisioned as (like "An Outpost of Progress") socially-centred—colonialism, its ill effects on Black and White—but developed into a driving obsessive exploration of man and the validity of his ideals. It is significant that it was initially planned for two serial instalments of *Blackwood's* but, finally, covered three, appearing in the February, March and April issues of 1899.

"Jim" grew into a full-length novel, *Lord Jim*, published in 1900 as a book after serialization in *Blackwood's* (1899-1900). Conrad then published *The Inheritors* (collaboration with Ford Madox Ford) in 1901. He completed "The End of the Tether" in July 1902, and "Youth," "Heart of Darkness" and "The End of the Tether" were issued as a single volume, long overdue, in November 1902.

In trying to decide upon an authoritative text for my edition, I first considered the 1921 Heinemann *Youth* volume, but found the text most unsatisfactory because so much of the repunctuation, the capital letters and so on were handled by the printers rather than the author. I opted for the 1923 Dent Collected text— directly set from slightly revised plates of the first edition, the Sun-Dial Collected, as far more satisfactory for my purposes, especially as I wish the reader to acquire an accurate impression of the style of *Heart of Darkness*. The style is a marked idiolect, influenced by Conrad's foreignness as well as by the rhythm and emphases of the narrators' voices, altogether generating a unique power.

HEART OF DARKNESS

Joseph Conrad

AUTHOR'S NOTE

[Preface to the 1923 edition of *Youth: A Narative and Two Other Stories*]

THE three stories in this volume lay no claim to unity of artistic purpose. The only bond between them is that of the time in which they were written. They belong to the period immediately following the publication of the "Nigger of the Narcissus," and preceding the first conception of "Nostromo," two books which, it seems to me, stand apart and by themselves in the body of my work. It is also the period during which I contributed to *Maga*; a period dominated by "Lord Jim" and associated in my grateful memory with the late Mr. William Blackwood's encouraging and helpful kindness.

"Youth" was not my first contribution to *Maga*. It was the second. But that story marks the first appearance in the world of the man Marlow, with whom my relations have grown very intimate in the course of years. The origins of that gentleman (nobody as far as I know had ever hinted that he was anything but that)—his origins have been the subject of some literary speculation of, I am glad to say, a friendly nature.

One would think that I am the proper person to throw a light on the matter; but in truth I find that it isn't so easy. It is pleasant to remember that nobody had charged him with fraudulent purposes or looked down on him as a charlatan; but apart from that he was supposed to be all sorts of things: a clever screen, a mere device, a "personator," a familiar spirit, a whispering "dæmon." I myself have been suspected of a meditated plan for his capture.

That is not so. I made no plans. The man Marlow and I came together in the casual manner of those health-resort acquaintances which sometimes ripen into friendships. This one has ripened. For all his assertiveness in matters of opinion he is not an intrusive person. He haunts my hours of solitude, when, in silence, we lay our heads together in great comfort and harmony; but as we part at the end of a tale I am never sure that it may not be for the last time. Yet I don't think that either of us would care much to survive the other. In his case, at any rate, his occupation would be gone and he would suffer from that extinction, because I suspect him of some vanity. I don't mean vanity in the Solomonian sense. Of all my people he's the one that has never been a vexation to my spirit. A most discreet, understanding man....

Even before appearing in book-form "Youth" was very well received. It lies on me to confess at last, and this is as good a place for it as another, that I have been all my life — all my two lives — the spoiled adopted child of Great Britain and even of the Empire; for it was Australia that gave me my first command. I break out into this declaration not because of a lurking tendency to megalomania, but, on the contrary, as a man who has no very notable illusions about himself. I follow the instincts of vain-glory and humility natural to all mankind. For it can hardly be denied that it is not their own deserts that men are most proud of, but rather of their prodigious luck, of their marvellous fortune: of that in their lives for which thanks and sacrifices must be offered on the altars of the inscrutable gods.

"Heart of Darkness" also received a certain amount of notice from the first; and of its origins this much may be said: it is well known that curious men go prying into all sorts of places (where they have no business) and come out of them with all kinds of spoil. This story, and one other, not in this volume, are all the spoil I brought out from the centre of Africa, where, really, I had no sort of business. More ambitious in its scope and longer in the telling "Heart of Darkness" is quite as authentic in fundamentals as "Youth." It is, obviously, written in another mood. I won't characterize the mood precisely, but anybody can see that it is anything but the mood of wistful regret, of reminiscent tenderness.

One more remark may be added. "Youth" is a feat of memory. It is a record of experience; but that experience, in its facts, in its inwardness and in its outward colouring, begins and ends in myself. "Heart of Darkness" is experience, too; but it is experience pushed a little (and only very little) beyond the actual facts of the case for the perfectly legitimate, I believe, purpose of bringing it home to the minds and bosoms of the readers. There it was no longer a matter of sincere colouring. It was like another art altogether. That sombre theme had to be given a sinister resonance, a tonality of its own, a continued vibration that, I hoped, would hang in the air and dwell on the ear after the last note had been struck.

After saying so much there remains the last tale of the book, still untouched. "The End of the Tether" is a story of sea-life in a rather special way; and the most intimate thing I can say of it is this; that having lived that life fully, amongst its men, its thoughts and sensations, I have found it possible, without the slightest misgiving, in all sincerity of heart and peace of conscience, to conceive the existence of Captain Whalley's personality and to relate the manner of his end. This statement acquires some force from the circumstance that the pages of that story — a fair half of the book — are also the product of experience. That experience belongs (like "Youth's") to the time before I ever thought of putting pen to paper. As to its "reality," that is for the readers to determine. One had to pick up one's facts here and there. More skill would have made them more real and the whole composition more interesting. But here we are approaching the veiled region of artistic values which it would be improper and indeed dangerous for me to enter. I have looked over the proofs, have corrected a misprint or two, have changed a word or two — and that's all. It is not very likely that I shall ever read "The End of the Tether" again. No more need be said. It accords best with my feelings to part from Captain Whalley in affectionate silence.

1917   J.C.

I

THE *Nellie*, a cruising yawl, swung to her anchor without a flutter of the sails, and was at rest. The flood had made, the wind was nearly calm, and being bound down the river, the only thing for it was to come to and wait for the turn of the tide.

The sea-reach of the Thames stretched before us like the beginning of an interminable waterway. In the offing the sea and the sky were welded together without a joint, and in the luminous space the tanned sails of the barges drifting up with the tide seemed to stand still in red clusters of canvas sharply peaked, with gleams of varnished spirits. A haze rested on the low shores that ran out to sea in vanishing flatness. The air was dark above Gravesend,[1] and farther back still seemed condensed into a mournful gloom, brooding motionless over the biggest, and the greatest, town on earth.

The Director of Companies was our captain and our host. We four affectionately watched his back as he stood in the bows looking to seaward. On the whole river there was nothing that looked half so nautical. He resembled a pilot, which to a seaman is trustworthiness personified. It was difficult to realize his work was not out there in the luminous estuary, but behind him, within the brooding gloom.

Between us there was, as I have already said somewhere, the bond of the sea. Besides holding our hearts together through long periods of separation, it had the effect of making us tolerant of each other's yarns — and even convictions. The Lawyer — the best of old fellows — had, because of his many years and many virtues, the only cushion on deck, and was lying on the only rug. The Accountant had brought out already a box of dominoes, and was toying architecturally with the bones.[2] Marlow sat cross-legged right aft, leaning against the mizzen-mast.[3] He had sunken

---

1   Gravesend] the eastern-most town in the Thames estuary, twenty-six miles east of London, opposite Tilbury (until recently an important port).
2   bones] a slang term for dominoes; until well into the twentieth century these were typically made out of ivory, indented with black dots.
3   mizzen-mast] the rear mast of a three-masted ship.

cheeks, a yellow complexion, a straight back, an ascetic aspect, and, with his arms dropped, the palms of hands outwards, resembled an idol. The director, satisfied the anchor had good hold, made his way aft and sat down amongst us. We exchanged a few words lazily. Afterwards there was silence on board the yacht. For some reason or other we did not begin that game of dominoes. We felt meditative, and fit for nothing but placid staring. The day was ending in a serenity of still and exquisite brilliance. The water shone pacifically; the sky, without a speck, was a benign immensity of unstained light; the very mist on the Essex marshes was like a gauzy and radiant fabric, hung from the wooded rises inland, and draping the low shores in diaphanous folds. Only the gloom to the west, brooding over the upper reaches, became more sombre every minute, as if angered by the approach of the sun.

And at last, in its curved and imperceptible fall, the sun sank low, and from glowing white changed to a dull red without rays and without heat, as if about to go out suddenly, stricken to death by the touch of that gloom brooding over a crowd of men.

Forthwith a change came over the waters, and the serenity became less brilliant but more profound. The old river in its broad reach rested unruffled at the decline of day, after ages of good service done to the race that peopled its banks, spread out in the tranquil dignity of a waterway leading to the uttermost ends of the earth. We looked at the venerable stream not in the vivid flush of a short day that comes and departs for ever, but in the august light of abiding memories. And indeed nothing is easier for a man who has, as the phrase goes, "followed the sea" with reverence and affection, than to evoke the great spirit of the past upon the lower reaches of the Thames. The tidal current runs to and fro in its unceasing service, crowded with memories of men and ships it had borne to the rest of home or to the battles of the sea. It had known and served all the men of whom the nation is proud, from Sir Francis Drake to Sir John Franklin, knights all, titled and untitled—the great knights-errant of the sea. It had borne all the ships whose names are like jewels flashing in the night of time, from the *Golden Hind* returning with her round flanks full of treasure, to be visited by the Queen's Highness and thus pass out of the gigantic tale, to the *Erebus* and *Terror*, bound on other conquests — and that never returned.[1] It had known the ships and the men. They had sailed from Deptford, from Greenwich, from Erith[2] — the adventurers and the settlers; kings' ships and the ships of men on 'Change;[3] captains, admirals, the dark "interlopers"[4] of the Eastern trade, and the commissioned "generals" of East India fleets. Hunters for gold or pursuers of fame, they all had gone out on that stream, bearing the sword, and often the torch, messengers of the might within the land, bearers of a spark from the sacred fire. What greatness had not floated on the ebb of that river into the mystery of an unknown earth!... The dreams of men, the seed of commonwealths, the germs of empires.

The sun set; the dusk fell on the stream, and lights began to appear along the shore. The Chapman lighthouse, a three-legged thing erect on a mud-flat, shone strongly. Lights of ships moved in the fairway — a great stir of lights going up and going down. And farther west on the upper reaches the place of the monstrous town was still marked ominously on the sky, a brooding gloom in sunshine, a lurid glare under the stars.

"And this also," said Marlow suddenly, "has been one of the dark places of the earth."

He was the only man of us who still "followed the sea." The worst that could be said of him was that he did not represent his class. He was a seaman, but he was a wanderer, too, while most seamen lead, if one may so express it, a sedentary life. Their minds are of the stay-at-home order, and their home is always with them — the ship; and so is their country — the sea. One ship is

---

1 Sir Francis Drake (*c.* 1540-96) was the captain of the *Golden Hind* under Queen Elizabeth I. His adventurous voyages were motivated partly by the urge to make discoveries and partly by the urge for plunder. The *Erebus* and the *Terror* were the ships taking part in the last expedition of Sir John Franklin, Rear-Admiral, F.R.S. (1786-1847), the famous Arctic explorer; Franklin was searching for the North-West Passage, but did not return.

2 Deptford ... Greenwich ... Erith] three ports between London and Gravesend.

3 'Change] loosely, any place of business and financial activity (such as, the Royal Exchange in London); hence "men on 'Change," businessmen, merchants.

4 interlopers] vessels trespassing on the rights of monopolies held by such trading companies as the East India Company.

very much like another, and the sea is always the same. In the immutability of their surroundings the foreign shores, the foreign faces, the changing immensity of life, glide past, veiled not by a sense of mystery but by a slightly disdainful ignorance; for there is nothing mysterious to a seaman unless it be the sea itself, which is the mistress of his existence and as inscrutable as Destiny. For the rest, after his hours of work, a casual stroll or a casual spree on shore suffices to unfold for him the secret of a whole continent, and generally he finds the secret not worth knowing. The yarns of seamen have a direct simplicity, the whole meaning of which lies within the shell of a cracked nut. But Marlow was not typical (if his propensity to spin yarns be excepted), and to him the meaning of an episode was not inside like a kernel but outside, enveloping the tale which brought it out only as a glow brings out a haze, in the likeness of one of these misty halos that sometimes are made visible by the spectral illumination of moonshine.

His remark did not seem at all surprising. It was just like Marlow. It was accepted in silence. No one took the trouble to grunt even; and presently he said, very slow —

"I was thinking of very old times, when the Romans first came here, nineteen hundred years ago — the other day.... Light came out of this river since — you say Knights? Yes; but it is like a running blaze on a plain, like a flash of lightning in the clouds. We live in the flicker — may it last as long as the old earth keeps rolling! But darkness was here yesterday. Imagine the feelings of a commander of a fine — what d'ye call 'em? — trireme[1] in the Mediterranean, ordered suddenly to the north; run overland across the Gauls in a hurry; put in charge of one of these craft the legionaries — a wonderful lot of handy men they must have been, too — used to build, apparently by the hundred, in a month or two, if we may believe what we read. Imagine him here — the very end of the world, a sea the colour of lead, a sky the colour of smoke, a kind of ship about as rigid as a concertina — and going up this river with stores, or orders, or what you like. Sand-banks, marshes, forests, savages, — precious little to eat fit for a civilized man, nothing but Thames water to drink.

---

1   trireme] an ancient galley — especially a war-galley — with three sets of rowers.

No Falernian wine[1] here, no going ashore. Here and there a military camp lost in a wilderness, like a needle in a bundle of hay — cold, fog, tempests, disease, exile, and death, — death skulking in the air, in the water, in the bush. They must have been dying like flies here. Oh, yes — he did it. Did it very well, too, no doubt, and without thinking much about it either, except afterwards to brag of what he had gone through in his time, perhaps. They were men enough to face the darkness. And perhaps he was cheered by keeping his eye on a chance of promotion to the fleet at Ravenna[2] by-and-by, if he had good friends in Rome and survived the awful climate. Or think of a decent young citizen in a toga — perhaps too much dice, you know — coming out here in the train of some prefect, or tax-gatherer, or trader even, to mend his fortunes. Land in a swamp, march through the woods, and in some inland post feel the savagery, the utter savagery, had closed round him, — all that mysterious life of the wilderness that stirs in the forest, in the jungles, in the hearts of wild men. There's no initiation either into such mysteries. He has to live in the midst of the incomprehensible, which is also detestable. And it has a fascination, too, that goes to work upon him. The fascination of the abomination — you know, imagine the growing regrets, the longing to escape, the powerless disgust, the surrender, the hate."

He paused.

"Mind," he began again, lifting one arm from the elbow, the palm of the hand outwards, so that, with his legs folded before him, he had the pose of a Buddha preaching in European clothes and without a lotus-flower — "Mind, none of us would feel exactly like this. What saves us is efficiency — the devotion to efficiency. But these chaps were not much account, really. They were no colonists; their administration was merely a squeeze, and nothing more, I suspect. They were conquerors, and for that you want only brute force — nothing to boast of, when you have it, since your strength is just an accident arising from the weakness

---

1 Falernian wine] famous ancient wine from the Falernus Ager district, inland from what is now Naples.

2 Ravenna] once the chief Roman naval base in northern Italy, now an inland city.

of others. They grabbed what they could get for the sake of what was to be got. It was just robbery with violence, aggravated murder on a great scale, and men going at it blind—as is very proper for those who tackle a darkness. The conquest of the earth, which mostly means the taking it away from those who have a different complexion or slightly flatter noses than ourselves, is not a pretty thing when you look into it too much. What redeems it is the idea only. An idea at the back of it; not a sentimental pretence but an idea; and an unselfish belief in the idea—something you can set up, and bow down before, and offer a sacrifice to…."

He broke off. Flames glided in the river, small green flames, red flames, white flames, pursuing, overtaking, joining, crossing each other—then separating slowly or hastily. The traffic of the great city went on in the deepening night upon the sleepless river. We looked on, waiting patiently—there was nothing else to do till the end of the flood; but it was only after a long silence, when he said, in a hesitating voice, "I suppose you fellows remember I did once turn fresh-water sailor for a bit," that we knew we were fated, before the ebb began to run, to hear about one of Marlow's inconclusive experiences.

"I don't want to bother you much with what happened to me personally," he began, showing in this remark the weakness of many tellers of tales who seem so often unaware of what their audience would best like to hear; "yet to understand the effect of it on me you ought to know how I got out there, what I saw, how I went up that river to the place where I first met the poor chap. It was the farthest point of navigation and the culminating point of my experience. It seemed somehow to throw a kind of light on everything about me—and into my thoughts. It was sombre enough, too—and pitiful—not extraordinary in any way—not very clear either. No, not very clear. And yet it seemed to throw a kind of light.

"I had then, as you remember, just returned to London after a lot of Indian Ocean, Pacific, China Seas—a regular dose of the East—six years or so, and I was loafing about, hindering you fellows in your work and invading your homes, just as though I had got a heavenly mission to civilize you. It was very fine for a time, but after a bit I did get tired of resting. Then I began to look for a ship—I should think the hardest work on earth. But the ships wouldn't even look at me. And I got tired of that game, too.

"Now when I was a little chap I had a passion for maps. I would look for hours at South America, or Africa, or Australia, and lose myself in all the glories of exploration. At that time there were many blank spaces on the earth, and when I saw one that looked particularly inviting on a map (but they all look that) I would put my finger on it and say, When I grow up I will go there. The North Pole was one of these places, I remember. Well, I haven't been there yet, and shall not try now. The glamour's off. Other places were scattered about the Equator, and in every sort of latitude all over the two hemispheres. I have been in some of them, and … well, we won't talk about that. But there was one yet—the biggest, the most blank, so to speak—that I had a hankering after.

"True, by this time it was not a blank space any more. It had got filled since my boyhood with rivers and lakes and names. It had ceased to be a blank space of delightful mystery—a white patch for a boy to dream gloriously over. It had become a place of darkness. But there was in it one river especially, a mighty big river, that you could see on the map, resembling an immense snake uncoiled, with its head in the sea, its body at rest curving afar over a vast country, and its tail lost in the depths of the land. And as I looked at the map of it in a shop-window, it fascinated me as a snake would a bird—a silly little bird. Then I remembered there was a big concern, a Company[1] for trade on that river. Dash it all! I thought to myself, they can't trade without using some kind of craft on that lot of fresh water—steamboats! Why shouldn't I try to get charge of one? I went on along Fleet Street, but could not shake off the idea. The snake had charmed me.

"You understand it was a Continental concern, that Trading society; but I have a lot of relations living on the Continent, because it's cheap and not so nasty as it looks, they say.

"I am sorry to own I began to worry them. This was already a fresh departure for me. I was not used to get things that way, you

---

1   Company] the Société Anonyme Belge pour le Commerce du Haut-Congo.

know. I always went my own road and on my own legs where I had a mind to go. I wouldn't have believed it of myself; but, then — you see — I felt somehow I must get there by hook or by crook. So I worried them. The men said 'My dear fellow,' and did nothing. Then — would you believe it? — I tried the women. I, Charlie Marlow, set the women to work — to get a job. Heavens! Well, you see, the notion drove me. I had an aunt, a dear enthusiastic soul. She wrote: 'It will be delightful. I am ready to do anything, anything for you. It is a glorious idea. I know the wife of a very high personage in the Administration, and also a man who has lots of influence with,' etc., etc. She was determined to make no end of fuss to get me appointed skipper of a river steamboat, if such was my fancy.

"I got my appointment — of course; and I got it very quick. It appears the Company had received news that one of their captains had been killed in a scuffle with the natives. This was my chance, and it made me the more anxious to go. It was only months and months afterwards, when I made the attempt to recover what was left of the body, that I heard the original quarrel arose from a misunderstanding about some hens. Yes, two black hens. Fresleven — that was the fellow's name, a Dane — thought himself wronged somehow in the bargain, so he went ashore and started to hammer the chief of the village with a stick. Oh, it didn't surprise me in the least to hear this, and at the same time to be told that Fresleven was the gentlest, quietest creature that ever walked on two legs. No doubt he was; but he had been a couple of years already out there engaged in the noble cause, you know, and he probably felt the need at last of asserting his self-respect in some way. Therefore he whacked the old nigger mercilessly, while a big crowd of his people watched him, thunderstruck, till some man — I was told the chief's son — in desperation at hearing the old chap yell, made a tentative jab with a spear at the white man — and of course it went quite easy between the shoulder blades. Then the whole population cleared into the forest, expecting all kinds of calamities to happen, while, on the other hand, the steamer Fresleven commanded left also in a bad panic, in charge of the engineer, I believe. Afterwards nobody seemed to trouble much about Fresleven's remains, till I got out and stepped into his shoes. I couldn't let it rest, though; but when an opportunity offered at last to meet my predecessor, the grass growing through his ribs was tall enough to hide his bones. They were all there. The supernatural being had not been touched after he fell. And the village was deserted, the huts gaped black, rotting, all askew within the fallen enclosures. A calamity had come to it, sure enough. The people had vanished. Mad terror had scattered them, men, women, and children, through the bush, and they had never returned. What became of the hens I don't know either. I should think the cause of progress got them, anyhow. However, through this glorious affair I got my appointment, before I had fairly begun to hope for it.

"I flew around like mad to get ready, and before forty-eight hours I was crossing the channel to show myself to my employers, and sign the contract. In a very few hours I arrived in a city that always makes me think of a whited sepulchre.[1] Prejudice no doubt. I had no difficulty in finding the Company's offices. It was the biggest thing in the town, and everybody I met was full of it. They were going to run an over-sea empire, and make no end of coin by trade.

"A narrow and deserted street in deep shadow, high houses, innumerable windows with venetian blinds, a dead silence, grass sprouting between the stones, imposing carriage archways right and left, immense double doors standing ponderously ajar. I slipped through one of these cracks, went up a swept and ungarnished staircase, as arid as a desert, and opened the first door I came to. Two women, one fat and the other slim, sat on straw-bottomed chairs, knitting black wool. The slim one got up and walked straight at me—still knitting with down-cast eyes—and only just as I began to think of getting out of her way, as you would for a somnambulist, stood still, and looked up. Her dress was as plain as an umbrella-cover, and she turned round without a word and preceded me into a waiting-room. I gave my name, and looked about. Deal table in the middle, plain chairs all round the

---

1 . whited sepulchre] Cf. Matthew 23: 27-8 "Woe unto you, scribes and Pharisses, hypocrites! for ye are like unto whited sepulchres, which indeed appear beautiful outwardly, but are within full of dead men's bones, and of all uncleaness."

walls, on one end a large shining map, marked with all the colours of a rainbow. There was a vast amount of red—good to see at any time, because one knows that some real work is done in there, a deuce of a lot of blue, a little green, smears of orange, and, on the East Coast, a purple patch, to show where the jolly pioneers of progress drink the jolly lager-beer.[1] However, I wasn't going into any of these. I was going into the yellow. Dead in the centre. And the river was there—fascinating—deadly—like a snake. Ough! A door opened, a white-haired secretarial head, but wearing a compassionate expression, appeared, and a skinny forefinger beckoned me into the sanctuary. Its light was dim, and a heavy writing-desk squatted in the middle. From behind that structure came out an impression of pale plumpness in a frock-coat. The great man himself. He was five feet six, I should judge, and had his grip on the handle-end of ever so many millions. He shook hands, I fancy, murmured vaguely, was satisfied with my French. *Bon voyage.*

"In about forty-five seconds I found myself again in the waiting-room with the compassionate secretary, who, full of desolation and sympathy, made me sign some document. I believe I undertook amongst other things not to disclose any trade secrets. Well, I am not going to.

"I began to feel slightly uneasy. You know I am not used to such ceremonies, and there was something ominous in the atmosphere. It was just as though I had been let into some conspiracy—I don't know—something not quite right; and I was glad to get out. In the outer room the two women knitted black wool feverishly. People were arriving, and the younger one was walking back and forth introducing them. The old one sat on her chair. Her flat cloth slippers were propped up on a foot-warmer, and a cat reposed on her lap. She wore a starched white affair on her head, had a wart on one cheek, and silver-rimmed spectacles hung on the tip of her nose. She glanced at me above the glasses. The swift and indifferent placidity of that look troubled me. Two youths with foolish and cheery countenances were being piloted over, and she threw at them the same quick glance of uncon-

---

1   Red represents British colonies, blue French, orange Portuguese, and purple German.

cerned wisdom. She seemed to know all about them and about me, too. An eerie feeling came over me. She seemed uncanny and fateful. Often far away from there I thought of these two, guarding the door of Darkness, knitting black wool as for a warm pall, one introducing, introducing continuously to the unknown, the other scrutinizing the cheery and foolish faces with unconcerned old eyes. *Ave!*[1] Old knitter of black wool. *Morituri te salutant.*[2] Not many of those she looked at ever saw her again—not half, by a long way.

"There was yet a visit to the doctor. 'A simple formality,' assured me the secretary, with an air of taking an immense part in all my sorrows. Accordingly a young chap wearing his hat over the left eyebrow, some clerk I suppose,—there must have been clerks in the business, though the house was as still as a house in a city of the dead—came from somewhere up-stairs, and led me forth. He was shabby and careless, with ink-stains on the sleeves of his jacket, and his cravat was large and billowy, under a chin shaped like the toe of an old boot. It was a little too early for the doctor, so I proposed a drink, and thereupon he developed a vein of joviality. As we sat over our vermouths he glorified the Company's business, and by-and-by I expressed casually my surprise at him not going out there. He became very cool and collected all at once. 'I am not such a fool as I look,[3] quoth Plato to his disciples,' he said sententiously, emptied his glass with great resolution, and we rose.

"The old doctor felt my pulse, evidently thinking of something else the while. 'Good, good for there,' he mumbled, and then with a certain eagerness asked me whether I would let him measure my head.[4] Rather surprised, I said Yes, when he produced a thing like calipers and got the dimensions back and front and every way, taking notes carefully. He was an unshaven little man in a threadbare coat like a gaberdine, with his feet in slippers, and I thought

---

1   *Ave*] "Hail."

2   *Morituri te salutant*] "Those who are about to die salute you," prefaced by "Hail Caesar," this was the pre-fight salutation of the gladiators in Rome.

3   An attempt at banter rather than a true quotation.

4   In the nineteenth and early twentieth centuries a good deal of spurious science attempted to relate racial characteristics to brain size.

him a harmless fool. 'I always ask leave, in the interests of science, to measure the crania of those going out there,' he said. 'And when they come back, too?' I asked. 'Oh, I never see them,' he remarked; 'and, moreover, the changes take place inside, you know.' He smiled, as if at some quiet joke. 'So you are going out there. Famous.[1] Interesting, too.' He gave me a searching glance, and made another note. 'Ever any madness in your family?' he asked, in a matter-of-fact tone. I felt very annoyed. 'Is that question in the interests of science, too?' 'It would be,' he said, without taking notice of my irritation, 'interesting for science to watch the mental changes of individuals, on the spot, but …' 'Are you an alienist?'[2] I interrupted. 'Every doctor should be—a little,' answered that original, imperturbably. 'I have a little theory which you Messieurs who go out there must help me to prove. This is my share in the advantages my country shall reap from the possession of such a magnificent dependency. The mere wealth I leave to others. Pardon my questions, but you are the first Englishman coming under my observation …' I hastened to assure him I was not in the least typical. 'If I were,' said I, 'I wouldn't be talking like this with you.' 'What you say is rather profound, and probably erroneous,' he said, with a laugh. 'Avoid irritation more than exposure to the sun. Adieu. How do you English say, eh?' 'Good-bye.' 'Ah! Good-bye. Adieu. In the tropics one must before everything keep calm.' … He lifted a warning forefinger…. '*Du calme, du calme. Adieu.*'

"One thing more remained to do—say good-bye to my excellent aunt. I found her triumphant. I had a cup of tea—the last decent cup of tea for many days—and in a room that most soothingly looked just as you would expect a lady's drawing-room to look, we had a long quiet chat by the fireside. In the course of these confidences it became quite plain to me I had been represented to the wife of the high dignitary, and goodness knows to how many more people besides, as an exceptional and gifted creature—a piece of good fortune for the Company—a man you don't get hold of every day. Good heavens! and I was going to

---

1 Famous] Wonderful (slang).
2 alienist] one who treats mental illness.

take charge of a two-penny-half-penny river-steamboat with a penny whistle attached! It appeared, however, I was also one of the Workers, with a capital—you know. Something like an emissary of light, something like a lower sort of apostle. There had been a lot of such rot let loose in print and talk just about that time, and the excellent woman, living right in the rush of all that humbug, got carried off her feet. She talked about 'weaning those ignorant millions from their horrid ways,' till, upon my word, she made me quite uncomfortable. I ventured to hint that the Company was run for profit.

"'You forget, dear Charlie, that the labourer is worthy of his hire,' she said, brightly. It's queer how out of touch with truth women are. They live in a world of their own, and there had never been anything like it, and never can be. It is too beautiful altogether, and if they were to set it up it would go to pieces before the first sunset. Some confounded fact we men have been living contentedly with ever since the day of creation would start up and knock the whole thing over.

"After this I got embraced, told to wear flannel, be sure to write often, and so on—and I left. In the street—I don't know why—a queer feeling came to me that I was an impostor. Odd thing that I, who used to clear out for any part of the world at twenty-four hours' notice, with less thought than most men give to the crossing of a street, had a moment—I won't say of hesitation, but of startled pause, before this commonplace affair. The best way I can explain it to you is by saying that, for a second or two, I felt as though, instead of going to the centre of a continent, I were about to set off for the centre of the earth.

"I left in a French steamer, and she called in every blamed port they have out there,[1] for, as far as I could see, the sole purpose of landing soldiers and custom-house officers. I watched the coast. Watching a coast as it slips by the ship is like thinking about an enigma. There it is before you—smiling, frowning, inviting, grand, mean, insipid, or savage, and always mute with an air of whispering, Come and find out. This one was almost featureless,

---

1 France possessed ports on the west coast of Africa reaching from Algeria to the mouth of the Congo.

as if still in the making, with an aspect of monotonous grimness. The edge of a colossal jungle, so dark-green as to be almost black, fringed with white surf, ran straight, like a ruled line, far, far away along a blue sea whose glitter was blurred by a creeping mist. The sun was fierce, the land seemed to glisten and drip with steam. Here and there grayish-whitish specks showed up clustered inside the white surf, with a flag flying above them perhaps. Settlements some centuries old, and still no bigger than pinheads on the untouched expanse of their background. We pounded along, stopped, landed soldiers; went on, landed custom-house clerks to levy toll in what looked like a God-forsaken wilderness, with a tin shed and a flag-pole lost in it; landed more soldiers — to take care of the custom-house clerks, presumably. Some, I heard, got drowned in the surf; but whether they did or not, nobody seemed particularly to care. They were just flung out there, and on we went. Every day the coast looked the same, as though we had not moved; but we passed various places — trading places — with names like Gran' Bassam, Little Popo; names that seemed to belong to some sordid farce acted in front of a sinister back-cloth. The idleness of a passenger, my isolation amongst all these men with whom I had no point of contact, the oily and languid sea, the uniform sombreness of the coast, seemed to keep me away from the truth of things, within the toil of a mournful and sense-less delusion. The voice of the surf heard now and then was a positive pleasure, like the speech of a brother. It was something natural, that had its reason, that had a meaning. Now and then a boat from the shore gave one a momentary contact with reality. It was paddled by black fellows. You could see from afar the white of their eyeballs glistening. They shouted, sang; their bodies streamed with perspiration; they had faces like grotesque masks — these chaps; but they had bone, muscle, a wild vitality, an intense energy of movement, that was as natural and true as the surf along their coast. They wanted no excuse for being there. They were a great comfort to look at. For a time I would feel I belonged still to a world of straightforward facts; but the feeling would not last long. Something would turn up to scare it away. Once, I remember, we came upon a man-of-war anchored off the coast. There wasn't even a shed there, and she was shelling the bush. It appears the French had one of their wars going on thereabouts. Her ensign dropped limp like a rag; the muzzles of the long six-inch guns stuck out all over the low hull; the greasy, slimy swell swung her up lazily and let her down, swaying her thin masts. In the empty immensity of earth, sky, and water, there she was, incomprehensible, firing into a continent. Pop, would go one of the six-inch guns; a small flame would dart and vanish, a little white smoke would disappear, a tiny projectile would give a feeble screech—and nothing happened. Nothing could happen. There was a touch of insanity in the proceeding, a sense of lugubrious drollery in the sight; and it was not dissipated by somebody on board assuring me earnestly there was a camp of natives—he called them enemies!—hidden out of sight somewhere.

"We gave her her letters (I heard the men in that lonely ship were dying of fever at the rate of three a-day) and went on. We called at some more places with farcical names, where the merry dance of death and trade goes on in a still and earthy atmosphere as of an overheated catacomb; all along the formless coast bordered by dangerous surf, as if Nature herself had tried to ward off intruders; in and out of rivers, streams of death in life, whose banks were rotting into mud, whose waters, thickened into slime, invaded the contorted mangroves, that seemed to writhe at us in the extremity of an impotent despair. Nowhere did we stop long enough to get a particularized impression, but the general sense of vague and oppressive wonder grew upon me. It was like a weary pilgrimage amongst hints for nightmares.

"It was upward of thirty days before I saw the mouth of the big river. We anchored off the seat of the government. But my work would not begin till some two hundred miles farther on. So as soon as I could I made a start for a place thirty miles higher up.

"I had my passage on a little sea-going steamer. Her captain was a Swede, and knowing me for a seaman, invited me on the bridge. He was a young man, lean, fair, and morose, with lanky hair and a shuffling gait. As we left the miserable little wharf, he tossed his head contemptuously at the shore. 'Been living there?' he asked. I said, 'Yes.' 'Fine lot these government chaps—are they not?' he went on, speaking English with great precision and considerable bitterness. 'It is funny what some people will do for a few francs a-month. I wonder what becomes of that kind when it goes up country?' I said to him I expected to see that soon. 'So-o-o!' he exclaimed. He shuffled athwart, keeping one eye ahead vigilantly. 'Don't be too sure,' he continued. 'The other day I took up a man who hanged himself on the road. He was a Swede, too.' 'Hanged himself! Why, in God's name?' I cried. He kept on looking out watchfully. 'Who knows? The sun too much for him, or the country perhaps.'

"At last we opened a reach. A rocky cliff appeared, mounds of turned-up earth by the shore, houses on a hill, others with iron roofs, amongst a waste of excavations, or hanging to the declivity. A continuous noise of the rapids above hovered over this scene of inhabited devastation. A lot of people, mostly black and naked, moved about like ants. A jetty projected into the river. A blinding sunlight drowned all this at times in a sudden recrudescence of flare. 'There's your Company's station,' said the Swede, pointing to three wooden barrack-like structures on the rocky slope. 'I will send your things up. Four boxes did you say? So. Farewell.'

"I came upon a boiler wallowing in the grass, then found a path leading up the hill. It turned aside for the boulders, and also for an undersized railway-truck lying there on its back with its wheels in the air. One was off. The thing looked as dead as the carcass of some animal. I came upon more pieces of decaying machinery, a stack of rusty rails. To the left a clump of trees made a shady spot, where dark things seemed to stir feebly. I blinked, the path was steep. A horn tooted to the right, and I saw the black people run. A heavy and dull detonation shook the ground, a puff of smoke came out of the cliff, and that was all. No change appeared on the face of the rock. They were building a railway. The cliff was not in the way of anything; but this objectless blasting was all the work going on.

"A slight clinking behind me made me turn my head. Six black men advanced in a file, toiling up the path. They walked erect and slow, balancing small baskets full of earth on their heads, and the clink kept time with their footsteps. Black rags were wound round their loins, and the short ends behind waggled to and fro like tails. I could see every rib, the joints of their limbs were like knots in a rope; each had an iron collar on his neck, and all were connected together with a chain whose bights[1] swung between them, rhythmically clinking. Another report from the cliff made me think suddenly of that ship of war I had seen firing into a continent. It was the same kind of ominous voice; but these men could by no stretch of imagination be called enemies. They were called criminals, and the outraged law, like the bursting shells, had come to them, an insoluble mystery from the sea. All their meagre breasts panted together, the violently dilated nostrils quivered, the eyes stared stonily up-hill. They passed me within six inches, without a glance, with that complete, deathlike indifference of unhappy savages. Behind this raw matter one of the reclaimed, the product of the new forces at work, strolled despondently, carrying a rifle by its middle. He had a uniform jacket with one button off, and seeing a white man on the path, hoisted his weapon to his shoulder with alacrity. This was simple prudence, white men being so much alike at a distance that he could not tell who I might be. He was speedily reassured, and with a large, white, rascally grin, and a glance at his charge, seemed to take me into partnership in his exalted trust. After all, I also was a part of the great cause of these high and just proceedings.

"Instead of going up, I turned and descended to the left. My idea was to let that chain-gang get out of sight before I climbed the hill. You know I am not particularly tender; I've had to strike and to fend off. I've had to resist and to attack sometimes — that's only one way of resisting — without counting the exact cost, according to the demands of such sort of life as I had blundered into. I've seen the devil of violence, and the devil of greed, and the devil of hot desire; but, by all the stars! these were strong, lusty, red-eyed devils, that swayed and drove men — men. I tell you. But as I stood on this hillside, I foresaw that in the blinding sunshine of that land I would become acquainted with a flabby, pretending, weak-eyed devil of a rapacious and pitiless folly. How insidious he could be, too, I was only to find out several months later and a thousand miles farther. For a moment I stood appalled, as though

---

1 bights] loops.

by a warning. Finally I descended the hill, obliquely, towards the trees I had seen.

"I avoided a vast artificial hole somebody had been digging on the slope, the purpose of which I found it impossible to divine. It wasn't a quarry or a sandpit, anyhow. It was just a hole. It might have been connected with the philanthropic desire of giving the criminals something to do. I don't know. Then I nearly fell into a very narrow ravine, almost no more than a scar in the hillside. I discovered that a lot of imported drainage-pipes for the settlement had been tumbled in there. There wasn't one that was not broken. It was a wanton smash-up. At last I got under the trees. My purpose was to stroll into the shade for a moment; but no sooner within than it seemed to me I had stepped into the gloomy circle of some Inferno. The rapids were near, and an uninterrupted, uniform, headlong, rushing noise filled the mournful stillness of the grove, where not a breath stirred, not a leaf moved, with a mysterious sound—as though the tearing pace of the launched earth had suddenly become audible.

"Black shapes crouched, lay, sat between the trees leaning against the trunks, clinging to the earth, half coming out, half effaced within the dim light, in all the attitudes of pain, abandonment, and despair. Another mine on the cliff went off, followed by a slight shudder of the soil under my feet. The work was going on. The work! And this was the place where some of the helpers had withdrawn to die.

"They were dying slowly—it was very clear. They were not enemies, they were not criminals, they were nothing earthly now,—nothing but black shadows of disease and starvation, lying confusedly in the greenish gloom. Brought from all the recesses of the coast in all the legality of time contracts, lost in uncongenial surroundings, fed on unfamiliar food, they sickened, became inefficient, and were then allowed to crawl away and rest. These moribund shapes were free as air—and nearly as thin. I began to distinguish the gleam of the eyes under the trees. Then, glancing down, I saw a face near my hand. The black bones reclined at full length with one shoulder against the tree, and slowly the eyelids rose and the sunken eyes looked up at me, enormous and vacant, a kind of blind, white flicker in the depths of the orbs, which died out slowly. The man seemed young—almost a boy—but you know with them it's hard to tell. I found nothing else to do but to offer him one of my good Swede's ship's biscuits I had in my pocket. The fingers closed slowly on it and held—there was no other movement and no other glance. He had tied a bit of white worsted[1] round his neck—Why? Where did he get it? Was it a badge—an ornament—a charm—a propitiatory act? Was there any idea at all connected with it? It looked startling round his black neck, this bit of white thread from beyond the seas.

"Near the same tree two more bundles of acute angles sat with their legs drawn up. One, with his chin propped on his knees, stared at nothing, in an intolerable and appalling manner: his brother phantom rested its forehead, as if overcome with a great weariness; and all about others were scattered in every pose of contorted collapse, as in some picture of a massacre or a pestilence. While I stood horror-struck, one of these creatures rose to his hands and knees, and went off on all-fours towards the river to drink. He lapped out of his hand, then sat up in the sunlight, crossing his shins in front of him, and after a time let his woolly head fall on his breastbone.

"I didn't want any more loitering in the shade, and I made haste towards the station. When near the buildings I met a white man, in such an unexpected elegance of get-up that in the first moment I took him for a sort of vision. I saw a high starched collar, white cuffs, a light alpaca jacket, snowy trousers, a clear necktie, and varnished boots. No hat. Hair parted, brushed, oiled, under a green-lined parasol held in a big white hand. He was amazing, and had a penholder behind his ear.

"I shook hands with this miracle, and I learned he was the Company's chief accountant, and that all the book-keeping was done at this station. He had come out for a moment, he said, 'to get a breath of fresh air.' The expression sounded wonderfully odd, with its suggestion of sedentary desk-life. I wouldn't have mentioned the fellow to you at all, only it was from his lips that I first heard the name of the man who is so indissolubly connected with the memories of that time. Moreover, I respected the fellow.

---

1   worsted] cloth made from a fine smooth yarn spun from wool.

Yes; I respected his collars, his vast cuffs, his brushed hair. His appearance was certainly that of a hairdresser's dummy; but in the great demoralization of the land he kept up his appearance. That's backbone. His starched collars and got-up shirt-fronts were achievements of character. He had been out nearly three years; and, later, I could not help asking him how he managed to sport such linen. He had just the faintest blush, and said modestly, 'I've been teaching one of the native women about the station. It was difficult. She had a distaste for the work.' Thus this man had verily accomplished something. And he was devoted to his books, which were in apple-pie order.

"Everything else in the station was in a muddle,—heads, things, buildings. Strings of dusty niggers with splay feet arrived and departed; a stream of manufactured goods, rubbishy cottons, beads, and brass-wire set into the depths of darkness, and in return came a precious trickle of ivory.

"I had to wait in the station for ten days—an eternity. I lived in a hut in the yard, but to be out of the chaos I would sometimes get into the accountant's office. It was built of horizontal planks, and so badly put together that, as he bent over his high desk, he was barred from neck to heels with narrow strips of sunlight. There was no need to open the big shutter to see. It was hot there, too; big flies buzzed fiendishly, and did not sting, but stabbed. I sat generally on the floor, while, of faultless appearance (and even slightly scented), perching on a high stool, he wrote, he wrote. Sometimes he stood up for exercise. When a truckle-bed with a sick man (some invalid agent from up-country) was put in there, he exhibited a gentle annoyance. 'The groans of this sick person,' he said, 'distract my attention. And without that it is extremely difficult to guard against clerical errors in this climate.'

"One day he remarked, without lifting his head, 'In the interior you will no doubt meet Mr. Kurtz.' On my asking who Mr. Kurtz was, he said he was a first-class agent; and seeing my disappointment at this information, he added slowly, laying down his pen, 'He is a very remarkable person.' Further questions elicited from him that Mr. Kurtz was at present in charge of a trading post, a very important one, in the true ivory-country, at 'the very bottom of there. Sends in as much ivory as all the others put together …' He began to write again. The sick man was too ill to groan. The flies buzzed in a great peace.

"Suddenly there was a growing murmur of voices and a great tramping of feet. A caravan had come in. A violent babble of uncouth sounds burst out on the other side of the planks. All the carriers were speaking together, and in the midst of the uproar the lamentable voice of the chief agent was heard 'giving it up' tearfully for the twentieth time that day…. He rose slowly. 'What a frightful row,' he said. He crossed the room gently to look at the sick man, and returning, said to me, 'He does not hear.' 'What! Dead?' I asked, startled. 'No, not yet,' he answered, with great composure. Then, alluding with a toss of the head to the tumult in the station-yard, 'When one has got to make correct entries, one comes to hate those savages—hate them to the death.' He remained thoughtful for a moment. 'When you see Mr. Kurtz,' he went on, 'tell him from me that everything here'—he glanced at the desk—'is very satisfactory. I don't like to write to him—with those messengers of ours you never know who may get hold of your letter—at that Central Station.' He stared at me for a moment with his mild, bulging eyes. 'Oh, he will go far, very far,' he began again. 'He will be a somebody in the Administration before long. They, above—the Council in Europe, you know—mean him to be.'

"He turned to his work. The noise outside had ceased, and presently in going out I stopped at the door. In the steady buzz of flies the homeward-bound agent was lying flushed and insensible; the other, bent over his books, was making correct entries of perfectly correct transactions; and fifty feet below the doorstep I could see the still tree-tops of the grove of death.

"Next day I left that station at last, with a caravan of sixty men, for a two-hundred-mile tramp.

"No use telling you much about that. Paths, paths, everywhere; a stamped-in network of paths spreading over the empty land, through long grass, through burnt grass, through thickets, down and up chilly ravines, up and down stony hills ablaze with heat; and a solitude, a solitude, nobody, not a hut. The population had cleared out a long time ago. Well, if a lot of mysterious niggers armed with all kinds of fearful weapons suddenly took to travelling on the road between Deal[1] and Gravesend, catching the yokels right and left to carry heavy loads for them, I fancy every farm and cottage thereabouts would get empty very soon. Only here the dwellings were gone, too. Still I passed through several abandoned villages. There's something pathetically childish in the ruins of grass walls. Day after day, with the stamp and shuffle of sixty pair of bare feet behind me, each pair under a 60-lb. load. Camp, cook, sleep, strike camp, march. Now and then a carrier dead in harness, at rest in the long grass near the path, with an empty water-gourd and his long staff lying by his side. A great silence around and above. Perhaps on some quiet night the tremor of far-off drums, sinking, swelling, a tremor vast, faint; a sound weird, appealing, suggestive, and wild—and perhaps with as profound a meaning as the sound of bells in a Christian country. Once a white man in an unbuttoned uniform, camping on the path with an armed escort of lank Zanzibaris,[2] very hospitable and festive—not to say drunk. Was looking after the upkeep of the road, he declared. Can't say I saw any road or any upkeep, unless the body of a middle-aged negro, with a bullet-hole in the forehead, upon which I absolutely stumbled three miles farther on, may be considered as a permanent improvement. I had a white companion, too, not a bad chap, but rather too fleshy and with the exasperating habit of fainting on the hot hillsides, miles away from the least bit of shade and water. Annoying, you know, to hold your own coat like a parasol over a man's head while he is coming-to. I couldn't help asking him once what he meant by coming there at all. 'To make money, of course. What do you think?' he said, scornfully. Then he got fever, and had to be carried in a hammock slung under a pole. As he weighed sixteen stone[3] I had no end of rows with the carriers. They jibbed, ran away, sneaked off with their loads in the night—quite a mutiny. So, one evening, I made a speech in English with gestures, not one of which was lost to the sixty pairs of eyes before me, and the

---

1   Deal] a port on the English Channel in the county of Kent.
2   Zanzibaris] Natives of Zanzibar were often used both as porters and as mercenaries throughout Africa. Stanley's 1887 expedition in relief of Emin Pasha, for example, employed large numbers of Zanzibar natives (see Appendix C).
3   stone] A stone is the equivalent of 14 pounds or 6.3 kilograms.

next morning I started the hammock off in front all right. An hour afterwards I came upon the whole concern wrecked in a bush—man, hammock, groans, blankets, horrors. The heavy pole had skinned his poor nose. He was very anxious for me to kill somebody, but there wasn't the shadow of a carrier near. I remember the old doctor,—'It would be interesting for science to watch the mental changes of individuals, on the spot.' I felt I was becoming scientifically interesting. However, all that is to no purpose. On the fifteenth day I came in sight of the big river again, and hobbled into the Central Station. It was on a back water surrounded by scrub and forest, with a pretty border of smelly mud on one side, and on the three others enclosed by a crazy fence of rushes. A neglected gap was all the gate it had, and the first glance at the place was enough to let you see the flabby devil was running that show. White men with long staves in their hands appeared languidly from amongst the buildings, strolling up to take a look at me, and then retired out of sight somewhere. One of them, a stout, excitable chap with black moustaches, informed me with great volubility and many digressions, as soon as I told him who I was, that my steamer was at the bottom of the river. I was thunderstruck. What, how, why? Oh, it was 'all right.' The 'manager himself' was there. All quite correct. 'Everybody had behaved splendidly! splendidly!'—'you must,' he said in agitation, 'go and see the general manager at once. He is waiting!'

"I did not see the real significance of that wreck at once. I fancy I see it now, but I am not sure—not at all. Certainly the affair was too stupid—when I think of it—to be altogether natural. Still ... But at the moment it presented itself simply as a confounded nuisance. The steamer was sunk. They had started two days before in a sudden hurry up the river with the manager on board, in charge of some volunteer skipper, and before they had been out three hours they tore the bottom out of her on stones, and she sank near the south bank. I asked myself what I was to do there, now my boat was lost. As a matter of fact, I had plenty to do in fishing my command out of the river. I had to set about it the very next day. That, and the repairs when I brought the pieces to the station, took some months.

"My first interview with the manager was curious. He did not ask me to sit down after my twenty-mile walk that morning. He was commonplace in complexion, in feature, in manners, and in voice. He was of middle size and of ordinary build. His eyes, of the usual blue, were perhaps remarkably cold, and he certainly could make his glance fall on one as trenchant and heavy as an axe. But even at these times the rest of his person seemed to disclaim the intention. Otherwise there was only an indefinable, faint expression of his lips, something stealthy—a smile—not a smile—I remember it, but I can't explain. It was unconscious, this smile was, though just after he had said something it got intensified for an instant. It came at the end of his speeches like a seal applied on the words to make the meaning of the commonest phrase appear absolutely inscrutable. He was a common trader, from his youth up employed in these parts—nothing more. He was obeyed, yet he inspired neither love not fear, nor even respect. He inspired uneasiness. That was it! Uneasiness. Not a definite mistrust—just uneasiness—nothing more. You have no idea how effective such a ... a ... faculty can be. He had no genius for organizing, for initiative, or for order even. That was evident in such things as the deplorable state of the station. He had no learning, and no intelligence. His position had come to him—why? Perhaps because he was never ill ... He had served three terms of three years out there ... Because triumphant health in the general rout of constitutions is a kind of power in itself. When he went home on leave he rioted on a large scale—pompously. Jack[1] ashore—with a difference—in externals only. This one could gather from his casual talk. He originated nothing, he could keep the routine going—that's all. But he was great. He was great by this little thing that it was impossible to tell what could control such a man. He never gave that secret away. Perhaps there was nothing within him. Such a suspicion made one pause—for out there there were no external checks. Once when various tropical diseases had laid low almost every 'agent' in the station, he was heard to say, 'Men who come out here should have no entrails.' He sealed the utterance with that smile of his, as though it had been a door opening into a darkness he had in his keeping. You

---

1 Jack] sailor.

fancied you had seen things — but the seal was on. When annoyed at meal-times by the constant quarrels of the white men about precedence, he ordered an immense round table to be made, for which a special house had to be built. This was the station's mess-room. Where he sat was the first place — the rest were nowhere. One felt this to be his unalterable conviction. He was neither civil nor uncivil. He was quiet. He allowed his 'boy' — an overfed young negro from the coast — to treat the white men, under his very eyes, with provoking insolence.

"He began to speak as soon as he saw me. I had been very long on the road. He could not wait. Had to start without me. The up-river stations had to be relieved. There had been so many delays already that he did not know who was dead and who was alive, and how they got on — and so on, and so on. He paid no attention to my explanations, and, playing with a stick of sealing-wax, repeated several times that the situation was 'very grave, very grave.' There were rumours that a very important station was in jeopardy, and its chief, Mr. Kurtz, was ill. Hoped it was not true. Mr. Kurtz was ... I felt weary and irritable. Hang Kurtz, I thought. I interrupted him by saying I had heard of Mr. Kurtz on the coast. 'Ah! so they talk of him down there,' he murmured to himself. Then he began again, assuring me Mr. Kurtz was the best agent he had, an exceptional man, of the greatest importance to the Company; therefore I could understand his anxiety. He was, he said, 'very, very uneasy.' Certainly he fidgeted on his chair a good deal, exclaimed, 'Ah, Mr. Kurtz!' broke the stick of sealing-wax and seemed dumbfounded by the accident. Next thing he wanted to know 'how long it would take to' ... I interrupted him again. Being hungry, you know, and kept on my feet, too, I was getting savage. 'How could I tell?' I said. 'I hadn't even seen the wreck yet — some months, no doubt.' All this talk seemed to me so futile. 'Some months,' he said. 'Well, let us say three months before we can make a start. Yes. That ought to do the affair.' I flung out of his hut (he lived all alone in a clay hut with a sort of verandah) muttering to myself my opinion of him. He was a chattering idiot. Afterwards I took it back when it was borne in upon me startlingly with what extreme nicety he had estimated the time requisite for the 'affair.'

"I went to work the next day, turning, so to speak, my back on that station. In that way only it seemed to me I could keep my hold on the redeeming facts of life. Still, one must look about sometimes; and then I saw this station, these men strolling aimlessly about in the sunshine of the yard. I asked myself sometimes what it all meant. They wandered here and there with their absurd long staves in their hands, like a lot of faithless pilgrims bewitched inside a rotten fence. The word 'ivory' rang in the air, was whispered, was sighed. You would think they were praying to it. A taint of imbecile rapacity blew through it all, like a whiff from some corpse. By Jove! I've never seen anything so unreal in my life. And outside, the silent wilderness surrounding this cleared speck on the earth struck me as something great and invincible, like evil or truth, waiting patiently for the passing away of this fantastic invasion.

"Oh, these months! Well, never mind. Various things happened. One evening a grass shed full of calico, cotton prints, beads, and I don't know what else, burst into a blaze so suddenly that you would have thought the earth had opened to let an avenging fire consume all that trash. I was smoking my pipe quietly by my dismantled steamer, and saw them all cutting capers in the light, with their arms lifted high, when the stout man with moustaches came tearing down to the river, a tin pail in his hand, assured me that everybody was 'behaving splendidly, splendidly,' dipped about a quart of water and tore back again. I noticed there was a hole in the bottom of his pail.

"I strolled up. There was no hurry. You see the thing had gone off like a box of matches. It had been hopeless from the very first. The flame had leaped high, driven everybody back, lighted up everything—and collapsed. The shed was already a heap of embers glowing fiercely. A nigger was being beaten near by. They said he had caused the fire in some way; be that as it may, he was screeching most horribly. I saw him, later, for several days, sitting in a bit of shade looking very sick and trying to recover himself: afterwards he arose and went out—and the wilderness without a sound took him into its bosom again. As I approached the glow from the dark I found myself at the back of two men, talking. I heard the name of Kurtz pronounced, then the words, 'take advantage of this unfortunate accident.' One of the men was the manager. I wished him a good evening. 'Did you ever see anything like it—eh? it is incredible,' he said, and walked off. The other man remained. He was a first-class agent, young, gentlemanly, a bit reserved, with a forked little beard and a hooked nose. He was stand-offish with the other agents, and they on their side said he was the manager's spy upon them. As to me, I had hardly ever spoken to him before. We got into talk, and by-and-by we strolled away from the hissing ruins. Then he asked me to his room, which was in the main building of the station. He struck a match, and I perceived that this young aristocrat had not only a silver-mounted dressing-case but also a whole candle all to himself. Just at that time the manager was the only man supposed to have any right to candles. Native mats covered the clay walls; a collection of spears, assegais,[1] shields, knives was hung up in trophies. The business intrusted to this fellow was the making of bricks—so I had been informed; but there wasn't a fragment of a brick anywhere in the station, and he had been there more than a year—waiting. It seems he could not make bricks without something, I don't know what—straw maybe. Anyways, it could not be found there, and as it was not likely to be sent from Europe, it did not appear clear to me what he was waiting for. An act of special creation perhaps. However, they were all waiting—all the sixteen or twenty pilgrims of them—for something; and upon my word it did not seem an uncongenial occupation, from the way they took it, though the only thing that ever came to them was disease—as far as I could see. They beguiled the time by backbiting and intriguing against each other in a foolish kind of way. There was an air of plotting about that station, but nothing came of it, of course. It was as unreal as everything else—as the philanthropic pretence of the whole concern, as their talk, as their government, as their show of work. The only real feeling was a desire to get appointed to a trading-post where ivory was to be had, so that they could earn percentages. They intrigued and slandered and hated each other only on that account,—but as to effectually lifting a little finger—oh, no. By heavens! there is

---

1   assegais] slender spears designed for throwing.

something after all in the world allowing one man to steal a horse while another must not look at a halter. Steal a horse straight out. Very well. He has done it. Perhaps he can ride. But there is a way of looking at a halter that would provoke the most charitable of saints into a kick.

"I had no idea why he wanted to be sociable, but as we chatted in there it suddenly occurred to me the fellow was trying to get at something—in fact, pumping me. He alluded constantly to Europe, to the people I was supposed to know there—putting leading questions as to my acquaintances in the sepulchral city, and so on. His little eyes glittered like mica discs—with curiosity—though he tried to keep up a bit of superciliousness. At first I was astonished, but very soon I became awfully curious to see what he would find out from me. I couldn't possibly imagine what I had in me to make it worth his while. It was very pretty to see how he baffled himself, for in truth my body was full only of chills, and my head had nothing in it but that wretched steamboat business. It was evident he took me for a perfectly shameless prevaricator. At last he got angry, and, to conceal a movement of furious annoyance, he yawned. I rose. Then I noticed a small sketch in oils, on a panel, representing a woman, draped and blindfolded, carrying a lighted torch. The background was sombre—almost black. The movement of the woman was stately, and the effect of the torch-light on the face was sinister.

"It arrested me, and he stood by civilly, holding an empty half-pint champagne bottle (medical comforts) with the candle stuck in it. To my question he said Mr. Kurtz had painted this—in this very station more than a year ago—while waiting for means to go to his trading-post. 'Tell me, pray,' said I, 'who is this Mr Kurtz?'

"'The chief of the Inner Station,' he answered in a short tone, looking away. 'Much obliged,' I said, laughing. 'And you are the brickmaker of the Central Station. Everyone knows that.' He was silent for a while. 'He is a prodigy,' he said at last. 'He is an emissary of pity, and science, and progress, and devil knows what else. We want,' he began to declaim suddenly, 'for the guidance of the cause intrusted to us by Europe, so to speak, higher intelligence, wide sympathies, a singleness of purpose.' 'Who says that?' I asked.

'Lots of them,' he replied. 'Some even write that; and so *he* comes here, a special being, as you ought to know.' 'Why ought I to know?' I interrupted, really surprised. He paid no attention. 'Yes. To-day he is chief of the best station, next year he will be assistant-manager, two years more and ... but I daresay you know what he will be in two years' time. You are of the new gang—the gang of virtue. The same people who sent him specially also recommended you. Oh, don't say no. I've my own eyes to trust.' Light dawned upon me. My dear aunt's influential acquaintances were producing an unexpected effect upon that young man. I nearly burst into a laugh. 'Do you read the Company's confidential correspondence?' I asked. He hadn't a word to say. It was great fun. 'When Mr. Kurtz,' I continued, severely, 'is General Manager, you won't have the opportunity.'

"He blew the candle out suddenly, and we went outside. The moon had risen. Black figures strolled about listlessly, pouring water on the glow, whence proceeded a sound of hissing; steam ascended in the moonlight, the beaten nigger groaned somewhere. 'What a row the brute makes!' said the indefatigable man with the moustaches, appearing near us. 'Serve him right. Transgression—punishment—bang! Pitiless, pitiless. That's the only way. This will prevent all conflagrations for the future. I was just telling the manager ...' He noticed my companion, and became crestfallen all at once. 'Not in bed yet,' he said, with a kind of servile heartiness; 'it's so natural. Ha! Danger—agitation.' He vanished. I went on to the river-side, and the other followed me. I heard a scathing murmur at my ear, 'Heap of muffs[1]—go to.' The pilgrims could be seen in knots gesticulating, discussing. Several had still their staves in their hands. I verily believe they took these sticks to bed with them. Beyond the fence the forest stood up spectrally in the moonlight, and through the dim stir, through the faint sounds of that lamentable courtyard, the silence of the land went home to one's very heart—its mystery, its greatness, the amazing reality of its concealed life. The hurt nigger moaned feebly somewhere near by, and then fetched a deep sigh that made me mend my pace away from there. I felt a hand

---

1 muffs] bunglers.

introducing itself under my arm. 'My dear sir,' said the fellow, 'I don't want to be misunderstood, and especially by you, who will see Mr. Kurtz long before I can have that pleasure. I wouldn't like him to get a false idea of my disposition....'

"I let him run on, this papier-mâché[1] Mephistopheles,[2] and it seemed to me that if I tried I could poke my forefinger through him, and would find nothing inside but a little loose dirt, maybe. He, don't you see, had been planning to be assistant-manager by-and-by under the present man, and I could see that the coming of that Kurtz had upset them both not a little. He talked precipitately, and I did not try to stop him. I had my shoulders against the wreck of my steamer, hauled up on the slope like a carcass of some big river animal. The smell of mud, of primeval mud, by Jove! was in my nostrils, the high stillness of primeval forest was before my eyes; there were shiny patches on the black creek. The moon had spread over everything a thin layer of silver—over the rank grass, over the mud, upon the wall of matted vegetation standing higher than the wall of a temple, over the great river I could see through a sombre gap glittering, glittering, as it flowed broadly by without a murmur. All this was great, expectant, mute, while the man jabbered about himself. I wondered whether the stillness on the face of the immensity looking at us two were meant as an appeal or as a menace. What were we who had strayed in here? Could we handle that dumb thing, or would it handle us? I felt how big, how confoundedly big, was that thing that couldn't talk, and perhaps was deaf as well. What was in there? I could see a little ivory coming out from there, and I had heard Mr. Kurtz was in there. I had heard enough about it, too— God knows! Yet somehow it didn't bring any image with it—no more than if I had been told an angel or a fiend was in there. I believed it in the same way one of you might believe there are inhabitants in the planet Mars. I knew once a Scotch sailmaker who was certain, dead sure, there were people in Mars. If you asked him for some idea how they looked and behaved, he would

---

1 papier-mâché] a very light material made of mashed paper which is shaped to the desired form and then allowed to harden.
2 Mephistopheles] the chief agent of Lucifer (the devil).

get shy and mutter something about 'walking on all-fours.' If you as much as smiled, he would—though a man of sixty—offer to fight you. I would not have gone so far as to fight for Kurtz, but I went for him near enough to a lie. You know I hate, detest, and can't bear a lie, not because I am straighter than the rest of us, but simply because it appals me. There is a taint of death, a flavour of mortality in lies—which is exactly what I hate and detest in the world—what I want to forget. It makes me miserable and sick, like biting something rotten would do. Temperament, I suppose. Well, I went near enough to it by letting the young fool there believe anything he liked to imagine as to my influence in Europe. I became in an instant as much of a pretence as the rest of the bewitched pilgrims. This simply because I had a notion it somehow would be of help to that Kurtz whom at the time I did not see—you understand. He was just a word for me. I did not see the man in the name any more than you do. Do you see him? Do you see the story? Do you see anything? It seems to me I am trying to tell you a dream—making a vain attempt, because no relation of a dream can convey the dream-sensation, that commingling of absurdity, surprise, and bewilderment in a tremor of struggling revolt, that notion of being captured by the incredible which is of the very essence of dreams...."

He was silent for a while.

"... No, it is impossible; it is impossible to convey the life-sensation of any given epoch of one's existence—that which makes its truth, its meaning—its subtle and penetrating essence. It is impossible. We live, as we dream—alone...."

He paused again as if reflecting, then added—

"Of course in this you fellows see more than I could then. You see me, whom you know...."

It had become so pitch dark that we listeners could hardly see one another. For a long time already he, sitting apart, had been no more to us than a voice. There was not a word from anybody. The others might have been asleep, but I was awake. I listened, I listened on the watch for the sentence, for the word, that would give me the clue to the faint uneasiness inspired by this narrative that seemed to shape itself without human lips in the heavy night-air of the river.

"... Yes — I let him run on," Marlow began again, "and think what he pleased about the powers that were behind me. I did! And there was nothing behind me! There was nothing but that wretched, old, mangled steamboat I was leaning against, while he talked fluently about 'the necessity for every man to get on.' 'And when one comes out here, you conceive, it is not to gaze at the moon.' Mr. Kurtz was a 'universal genius,' but even a genius would find it easier to work with 'adequate tools — intelligent men.' He did not make bricks — why, there was a physical impossibility in the way — as I was well aware; and if he did secretarial work for the manager, it was because 'no sensible man rejects wantonly the confidence of his superiors.' Did I see it? I saw it. What more did I want? What I really wanted was rivets, by heaven! Rivets. To get on with the work — to stop the hole. Rivets I wanted. There were cases of them down at the coast — cases — piled up — burst — split! You kicked a loose rivet at every second step in that station yard on the hillside. Rivets had rolled into the grove of death. You could fill your pockets with rivets for the trouble of stooping down — and there wasn't one rivet to be found where it was wanted. We had plates that would do, but nothing to fasten them with. And every week the messenger, a lone negro, letter-bag on shoulder and staff in hand, left our station for the coast. And several times a week a coast caravan came in with trade goods — ghastly glazed calico that made you shudder only to look at it, glass beads value about a penny a quart, confounded spotted cotton handkerchiefs. And no rivets. Three carriers could have brought all that was wanted to set that steamboat afloat.

"He was becoming confidential now, but I fancy my unresponsive attitude must have exasperated him at last, for he judged it necessary to inform me he feared neither God nor devil, let alone any mere man. I said I could see that very well, but what I wanted was a certain quantity of rivets — and rivets were what really Mr. Kurtz wanted, if he had only known it. Now letters went to the coast every week.... 'My dear sir,' he cried, 'I write from dictation.' I demanded rivets. There was a way — for an intelligent man. He changed his manner; became very cold, and suddenly began to talk about a hippopotamus; wondered whether sleeping on board the steamer (I stuck to my salvage night and day) I wasn't disturbed. There was an old hippo that had the bad habit of getting out on the bank and roaming at night over the station grounds. The pilgrims used to turn out in a body and empty every rifle they could lay hands on at him. Some even had sat up o' nights for him. All this energy was wasted, though. 'That animal has a charmed life,' he said; 'but you can say this only of brutes in this country. No man—you apprehend me?—no man here bears a charmed life.' He stood there for a moment in the moonlight with his delicate hooked nose set a little askew, and his mica eyes glittering without a wink, then, with a curt Good-night, he strode off. I could see he was disturbed and considerably puzzled, which made me feel more hopeful than I had been for days. It was a great comfort to turn from that chap to my influential friend, the battered, twisted, ruined, tin-pot steamboat. I clambered on board. She rang under my feet like an empty Huntley & Palmer biscuit-tin kicked along a gutter; she was nothing so solid in make, and rather less pretty in shape, but I had expended enough hard work on her to make me love her. No influential friend would have served me better. She had given me a chance to come out a bit—to find out what I could do. No, I don't like work. I had rather laze about and think of all the fine things that can be done. I don't like work—no man does—but I like what is in the work,—the chance to find yourself. Your own reality— for yourself, not for others—what no other man can ever know. They can only see the mere show, and never can tell what it really means.

"I was not surprised to see somebody sitting aft, on the deck, with his legs dangling over the mud. You see I rather chummed with the few mechanics there were in that station, whom the other pilgrims naturally despised—on account of their imperfect manners, I suppose. This was the foreman—a boiler-maker by trade—a good worker. He was a lank, bony, yellow-faced man, with big intense eyes. His aspect was worried, and his head was as bald as the palm of my hand; but his hair in falling seemed to have stuck to his chin, and had prospered in the new locality, for his beard hung down to his waist. He was a widower with six young children (he had left them in charge of a sister of his to come out there), and the passion of his life was pigeon-flying. He was an enthusiast and a connoisseur. He would rave about pigeons. After work hours he used sometimes to come over from his hut for a talk about his children and his pigeons; at work, when he had to crawl in the mud under the bottom of the steamboat, he would tie up that beard of his in a kind of white serviette he brought for the purpose. It had loops to go over his ears. In the evening he could be seen squatted on the bank rinsing that wrapper in the creek with great care, then spreading it solemnly on a bush to dry.

"I slapped him on the back and shouted 'We shall have rivets!' He scrambled to his feet exclaiming 'No! Rivets!' as though he couldn't believe his ears. Then in a low voice, 'You ... eh?' I don't know why we behaved like lunatics. I put my finger to the side of my nose and nodded mysteriously. 'Good for you!' he cried, snapped his fingers above his head, lifting one foot. I tried a jig. We capered on the iron deck. A frightful clatter came out of that hulk, and the virgin forest on the other bank of the creek sent it back in a thundering roll upon the sleeping station. It must have made some of the pilgrims sit up in their hovels. A dark figure obscured the lighted doorway of the manager's hut, vanished, then, a second or so after, the doorway itself vanished, too. We stopped, and the silence driven away by the stamping of our feet flowed back again from the recesses of the land. The great wall of vegetation, an exuberant and entangled mass of trunks, branches, leaves, boughs, festoons, motionless in the moonlight, was like a rioting invasion of soundless life, a rolling wave of plants, piled up, crested, ready to topple over the creek, to sweep every little man of us out of his little existence. And it moved not. A deadened burst of mighty splashes and snorts reached us from afar, as though an ichthyosaurus[1] had been taking a bath of glitter in the great river. 'After all,' said the boiler-maker in a reasonable tone, 'why shouldn't we get the rivets?' Why not, indeed! I did not know of any reason why we shouldn't. 'They'll come in three weeks,' I said, confidently.

"But they didn't. Instead of rivets there came an invasion, an infliction, a visitation. It came in sections during the next three

---

1 ichthyosaurus] enormous prehistoric reptile resembling a crocodile.

weeks, each section headed by a donkey carrying a white man in new clothes and tan shoes, bowing from that elevation right and left to the impressed pilgrims. A quarrelsome band of footsore sulky niggers trod on the heels of the donkey; a lot of tents, camp-stools, tin boxes, white cases, brown bales would be shot down in the courtyard, and the air of mystery would deepen a little over the muddle of the station. Five such instalments came, with their absurd air of disorderly flight with the loot of innumerable outfit shops and provision stores, that, one would think, they were lugging, after a raid, into the wilderness for equitable division. It was an inextricable mess of things decent in themselves but that human folly made look like spoils of thieving.

"This devoted band called itself the Eldorado Exploring Expedition, and I believe they were sworn to secrecy. Their talk, however, was the talk of sordid buccaneers: it was reckless without hardihood, greedy without audacity, and cruel without courage; there was not an atom of foresight or of serious intention in the whole batch of them, and they did not seem aware these things are wanted for the work of the world. To tear treasure out of the bowels of the land was their desire, with no more moral purpose at the back of it than there is in burglars breaking into a safe. Who paid the expenses of the noble enterprise I don't know; but the uncle of our manager was leader of that lot.

"In exterior he resembled a butcher in a poor neighbourhood, and his eyes had a look of sleepy cunning. He carried his fat paunch with ostentation on his short legs, and during the time his gang infested the station spoke to no one but his nephew. You could see these two roaming about all day long with their heads close together in an everlasting confab.

"I had given up worrying myself about the rivets. One's capacity for that kind of folly is more limited than you would suppose. I said Hang! — and let things slide. I had plenty of time for meditation, and now and then I would give some thought to Kurtz. I wasn't very interested in him. No. Still, I was curious to see whether this man, who had come out equipped with moral ideas of some sort, would climb to the top after all and how he would set about his work when there."

II

"ONE evening as I was lying flat on the deck of my steamboat, I heard voices approaching—and there were the nephew and the uncle strolling along the bank. I laid my head on my arm again, and had nearly lost myself in a doze, when somebody said in my ear, as it were: 'I am as harmless as a little child, but I don't like to be dictated to. Am I the manager—or am I not? I was ordered to send him there. It's incredible.' ... I became aware that the two were standing on the shore alongside the forepart of the steamboat, just below my head. I did not move; it did not occur to me to move: I was sleepy. 'It *is* unpleasant,' grunted the uncle. 'He has asked the Administration to be sent there,' said the other, 'with the idea of showing what he could do; and I was instructed accordingly. Look at the influence that man must have. Is it not frightful?' They both agreed it was frightful, then made several bizarre remarks: 'Make rain and fine weather—one man—the Council—by the nose'—bits of absurd sentences that got the better of my drowsiness, so that I had pretty near the whole of my wits about me when the uncle said, 'The climate may do away with this difficulty for you. Is he alone there?' 'Yes,' answered the manager; 'he sent his assistant down the river with a note to me in these terms: "Clear this poor devil out of the country, and don't bother sending more of that sort. I had rather be alone than have the kind of men you can dispose of with me." It was more than a year ago. Can you imagine such impudence!' 'Anything since then?' asked the other, hoarsely. 'Ivory,' jerked the nephew; 'lots of it—prime sort—lots—most annoying, from him.' 'And with that?' questioned the heavy rumble. 'Invoice,' was the reply fired out, so to speak. Then silence. They had been talking about Kurtz.

"I was broad awake by this time, but, lying perfectly at ease, remained still, having no inducement to change my position. 'How did that ivory come all this way?' growled the elder man, who seemed very vexed. The other explained that it had come with a fleet of canoes in charge of an English half-caste clerk Kurtz had with him; that Kurtz had apparently intended to return himself, the station being by that time bare of goods and stores, but after coming three hundred miles, had suddenly decided to go back, which he started to do alone in a small dugout with four paddlers, leaving the half-caste to continue down the river with the ivory. The two fellows there seemed astounded at anybody attempting such a thing. They were at a loss for an adequate motive. As to me, I seemed to see Kurtz for the first time. It was a distinct glimpse: the dugout, four paddling savages, and the lone white man turning his back suddenly on the headquarters, on relief, on thoughts of home—perhaps; setting his face towards the depths of the wilderness, towards his empty and desolate station. I did not know the motive. Perhaps he was just simply a fine fellow who stuck to his work for its own sake. His name, you understand, had not been pronounced once. He was 'that man.' The half-caste, who, as far as I could see, had conducted a difficult trip with great prudence and pluck, was invariably alluded to as 'that scoundrel.' The 'scoundrel' had reported that the 'man' had been very ill—had recovered imperfectly.... The two below me moved away then a few paces, and strolled back and forth at some little distance. I heard: 'Military post—doctor—two hundred miles—quite alone now—unavoidable delays—nine months—no news—strange rumours.' They approached again, just as the manager was saying, 'No one, as far as I know, unless a species of wandering trader—a pestilential fellow, snapping ivory from the natives.' Who was it they were talking about now? I gathered in snatches that this was some man supposed to be in Kurtz's district, and of whom the manager did not approve. 'We will not be free from unfair competition till one of these fellows is hanged for an example,' he said. 'Certainly,' grunted the other; 'get him hanged! Why not? Anything—anything can be done in this country. That's what I say; nobody here, you understand, here, can endanger your position. And why? You stand the climate—you outlast them all. The danger is in Europe; but there before I left I took care to——' They moved off and whispered, then their voices rose again. 'The extraordinary series of delays is not my fault. I did my best.' The fat man sighed. 'Very sad.' 'And the pestiferous absurdity of his talk,' continued the other; 'he bothered me enough when he was here. "Each station should be like a beacon on the road towards better things, a centre for trade of course, but also for humanizing, improving, instructing." Conceive you — that ass! And he wants to be manager! No, it's——' Here he got choked by excessive indignation, and I lifted my head the least bit. I was surprised to see how near they were — right under me. I could have spat upon their hats. They were looking on the ground, absorbed in thought. The manager was switching his leg with a slender twig: his sagacious relative lifted his head. 'You have been well since you came out this time?' he asked. The other gave a start. 'Who? I? Oh! Like a charm — like a charm. But the rest — oh, my goodness! All sick. They die so quick, too, that I haven't the time to send them out of the country — it's incredible!' 'H'm. Just so,' grunted the uncle. 'Ah! my boy, trust to this — I say, trust to this.' I saw him extend his short flipper of an arm for a gesture that took in the forest, the creek, the mud, the river, — seemed to beckon with a dishonouring flourish before the sunlit face of the land a treacherous appeal to the lurking death, to the hidden evil, to the profound darkness of its heart. It was so startling that I leaped to my feet and looked back at the edge of the forest, as though I had expected an answer of some sort to that black display of confidence. You know the foolish notions that come to one sometimes. The high stillness confronted these two figures with its ominous patience, waiting for the passing away of a fantastic invasion.

"They swore aloud together — out of sheer fright, I believe — then pretending not to know anything of my existence, turned back to the station. The sun was low; and leaning forward side by side, they seemed to be tugging painfully uphill their two ridiculous shadows of unequal length, that trailed behind them slowly over the tall grass without bending a single blade.

"In a few days the Eldorado Expedition went into the patient wilderness, that closed upon it as the sea closes over a diver. Long afterwards the news came that all the donkeys were dead. I know nothing as to the fate of the less valuable animals. They, no doubt, like the rest of us, found what they deserved. I did not inquire. I was then rather excited at the prospect of meeting Kurtz very soon. When I say very soon I mean it comparatively. It was just two months from the day we left the creek when we came to the bank below Kurtz's station.

"Going up that river was like travelling back to the earliest beginnings of the world, when vegetation rioted on the earth and the big trees were kings. An empty stream, a great silence, an impenetrable forest. The air was warm, thick, heavy, sluggish. There was no joy in the brilliance of sunshine. The long stretches of the waterway ran on, deserted, into the gloom of overshadowed distances. On silvery sandbanks hippos and alligators sunned themselves side by side. The broadening waters flowed through a mob of wooded islands; you lost your way on that river as you would in a desert, and butted all day long against shoals, trying to find the channel, till you thought yourself bewitched and cut off for ever from everything you had known once—somewhere—far away—in another existence perhaps. There were moments when one's past came back to one, as it will sometimes when you have not a moment to spare to yourself; but it came in the shape of an unrestful and noisy dream, remembered with wonder amongst the overwhelming realities of this strange world of plants, and water, and silence. And this stillness of life did not in the least resemble a peace. It was the stillness of an implacable force brooding over an inscrutable intention. It looked at you with a vengeful aspect. I got used to it afterwards; I did not see it any more; I had no time. I had to keep guessing at the channel; I had to discern, mostly by inspiration, the signs of hidden banks; I watched for sunken stones; I was learning to clap my teeth smartly before my heart flew out, when I shaved by a fluke some infernal sly old snag that would have ripped the life out of the tin-pot steamboat and drowned all the pilgrims; I had to keep a look-out for the signs of dead wood we could cut up in the night for next day's steaming. When you have to attend to things of that sort, to the mere incidents of the surface, the reality—the reality, I tell you—fades. The inner truth is hidden—luckily, luckily. But I felt it all the same; I felt often its mysterious stillness watching me at my monkey tricks, just as it watches you fellows performing on your respective tight-ropes for—what is it? half-a-crown a tumble——"

"Try to be civil, Marlow," growled a voice, and I knew there was at least one listener awake besides myself.

"I beg your pardon. I forgot the heartache which makes up the rest of the price. And indeed what does the price matter, if the trick be well done? You do your tricks very well. And I didn't do badly either, since I managed not to sink that steamboat on my first trip. It's a wonder to me yet. Imagine a blindfolded man set to drive a van over a bad road. I sweated and shivered over that business considerably, I can tell you. After all, for a seaman, to scrape the bottom of the thing that's supposed to float all the time under his care is the unpardonable sin. No one may know of it, but you never forget the thump — eh? A blow on the very heart. You remember it, you dream of it, you wake up at night and think of it — years after — and go hot and cold all over. I don't pretend to say that steamboat floated all the time. More than once she had to wade for a bit, with twenty cannibals splashing around and pushing. We had enlisted some of these chaps on the way for a crew. Fine fellows — cannibals — in their place. They were men one could work with, and I am grateful to them. And, after all, they did not eat each other before my face: they had brought along a provision of hippo-meat which went rotten, and made the mystery of the wilderness stink in my nostrils. Phoo! I can sniff it now. I had the manager on board and three or four pilgrims with their staves — all complete. Sometimes we came upon a station close by the bank, clinging to the skirts of the unknown, and the white men rushing out of a tumbledown hovel, with great gestures of joy and surprise and welcome, seemed very strange — had the appearance of being held there captive by a spell. The word ivory would ring in the air for a while — and on we went again into the silence, along empty reaches, round the still bends, between the high walls of our winding way, reverberating in hollow claps the ponderous beat of the stern-wheel. Trees, trees, millions of trees, massive, immense, running up high; and at their foot, hugging the bank against the stream, crept the little begrimed steamboat, like a sluggish beetle crawling on the floor of a lofty portico. It made you feel very small, very lost, and yet it was not altogether depressing, that feeling. After all, if you were small, the grimy beetle crawled on — which was just what you wanted it to do. Where the pilgrims imagined it crawled to I don't know. To some place where they expected to get something, I bet! For me it crawled towards Kurtz — exclusively; but when the steam-pipes started leaking we crawled very slow. The reaches opened before us and closed behind, as if the forest had stepped leisurely across the water to bar the way for our return. We penetrated deeper and deeper into the heart of darkness. It was very quiet there. At night sometimes the roll of drums behind the curtain of trees would run up the river and remain sustained faintly, as if hovering in the air high over our heads, till the first break of day. Whether it meant war, peace, or prayer we could not tell. The dawns were heralded by the descent of a chill stillness; the wood-cutters slept, their fires burned low; the snapping of a twig would make you start. We were wanderers on prehistoric earth, on an earth that wore the aspect of an unknown planet. We could have fancied ourselves the first of men taking possession of an accursed inheritance, to be subdued at the cost of profound anguish and of excessive toil. But suddenly, as we struggled round a bend, there would be a glimpse of rush walls, of peaked grass-roofs, a burst of yells, a whirl of black limbs, a mass of hands clapping, of feet stamping, of bodies swaying, of eyes rolling, under the droop of heavy and motionless foliage. The steamer toiled along slowly on the edge of a black and incomprehensible frenzy. The prehistoric man was cursing us, praying to us, welcoming us—who could tell? We were cut off from the comprehension of our surroundings; we glided past like phantoms, wondering and secretly appalled, as sane men would be before an enthusiastic outbreak in a madhouse. We could not understand because we were too far and could not remember, because we were travelling in the night of first ages, of those ages that are gone, leaving hardly a sign—and no memories.

"The earth seemed unearthly. We are accustomed to look upon the shackled form of a conquered monster, but there—there you could look at a thing monstrous and free. It was unearthly, and the men were—— No, they were not inhuman. Well, you know, that was the worst of it—this suspicion of their not being inhuman. It would come slowly to one. They howled and leaped, and spun, and made horrid faces; but what thrilled you was just the thought of their humanity—like yours—the thought of your remote kinship with this wild and passionate uproar. Ugly. Yes, it was ugly enough; but if you were man enough you would admit to yourself that there was in you just the faintest trace of a response to the terrible frankness of that noise, a dim suspicion of there being a meaning in it which you — you so remote from the night of first ages — could comprehend. And why not? The mind of man is capable of anything — because everything is in it, all the past as well as all the future. What was there after all? Joy, fear, sorrow, devotion, valour, rage — who can tell? — but truth — truth stripped of its cloak of time. Let the fool gape and shudder — the man knows, and can look on without a wink. But he must at least be as much of a man as these on the shore. He must meet that truth with his own true stuff — with his own inborn strength. Principles won't do. Acquisitions, clothes, pretty rags — rags that would fly off at the first good shake. No; you want a deliberate belief. An appeal to me in this fiendish row — is there? Very well; I hear; I admit, but I have a voice, too, and for good or evil mine is the speech that cannot be silenced. Of course, a fool, what with sheer fright and fine sentiments, is always safe. Who's that grunting? You wonder I didn't go ashore for a howl and a dance? Well, no — I didn't. Fine sentiments, you say? Fine sentiments, be hanged! I had no time. I had to mess about with white-lead and strips of woollen blanket helping to put bandages on those leaky steam-pipes — I tell you. I had to watch the steering, and circumvent those snags, and get the tin-pot along by hook or by crook. There was surface-truth enough in these things to save a wiser man. And between whiles I had to look after the savage who was fireman. He was an improved specimen; he could fire up a vertical boiler. He was there below me, and, upon my word, to look at him was as edifying as seeing a dog in a parody of breeches and a feather hat, walking on his hind-legs. A few months of training had done for that really fine chap. He squinted at the steam-gauge and at the water-gauge with an evident effort of intrepidity — and he had filed teeth, too, the poor devil, and the wool of his pate shaved into queer patterns, and three ornamental scars on each of his cheeks. He ought to have been clapping his hands and stamping his feet on the bank, instead of which he was hard at work, a thrall to strange witchcraft, full of improving knowledge. He was useful because he had been instructed; and what he knew was this —

that should the water in that transparent thing disappear, the evil spirit inside the boiler would get angry through the greatness of his thirst, and take a terrible vengeance. So he sweated and fired up and watched the glass fearfully (with an impromptu charm, made of rags, tied to his arm, and a piece of polished bone, as big as a watch, stuck flatways through his lower lip), while the wooded banks slipped past us slowly, the short noise was left behind, the interminable miles of silence—and we crept on, towards Kurtz. But the snags were thick, the water was treacherous and shallow, the boiler seemed indeed to have a sulky devil in it, and thus neither that fireman nor I had any time to peer into our creepy thoughts.

"Some fifty miles below the Inner Station we came upon a hut of reeds, an inclined and melancholy pole, with the unrecognizable tatters of what had been a flag of some sort flying from it, and a neatly stacked wood-pile. This was unexpected. We came to the bank, and on the stack of firewood found a flat piece of board with some faded pencil-writing on it. When deciphered it said: 'Wood for you. Hurry up. Approach cautiously.' There was a signature, but it was illegible—not Kurtz—a much longer word. Hurry up. Where? Up the river? 'Approach cautiously.' We had not done so. But the warning could not have been meant for the place where it could be only found after approach. Something was wrong above. But what—and how much? That was the question. We commented adversely upon the imbecility of that telegraphic style. The bush around said nothing, and would not let us look very far, either. A torn curtain of red twill hung in the doorway of the hut, and flapped sadly in our faces. The dwelling was dismantled; but we could see a white man had lived there not very long ago. There remained a rude table—a plank on two posts; a heap of rubbish reposed in a dark corner, and by the door I picked up a book. It had lost its covers, and the pages had been thumbed into a state of extremely dirty softness; but the back had been lovingly stitched afresh with white cotton thread, which looked clean yet. It was an extraordinary find. Its title was, *An Inquiry into some Points of Seamanship*, by a man Tower, Towson—some such name—Master in his Majesty's Navy. The matter looked dreary reading enough, with illustrative diagrams and repulsive tables of figures, and the copy was sixty years old. I handled this amazing antiquity with the greatest possible tenderness, lest it should dissolve in my hands. Within, Towson or Towser was inquiring earnestly into the breaking strain of ships' chains and tackle, and other such matters. Not a very enthralling book; but at the first glance you could see there a singleness of intention, an honest concern for the right way of going to work, which made these humble pages, thought out so many years ago, luminous with another than a professional light. The simple old sailor, with his talk of chains and purchases,[1] made me forget the jungle and the pilgrims in a delicious sensation of having come upon something unmistakably real. Such a book being there was wonderful enough; but still more astounding were the notes pencilled in the margin, and plainly referring to the text. I couldn't believe my eyes! They were in cipher! Yes, it looked like cipher. Fancy a man lugging with him a book of that description into this nowhere and studying it—and making notes—in cipher at that! It was an extravagant mystery.

"I had been dimly aware for some time of a worrying noise, and when I lifted my eyes I saw the wood-pile was gone, and the manager, aided by all the pilgrims, was shouting at me from the river-side. I slipped the book into my pocket. I assure you to leave off reading was like tearing myself away from the shelter of an old and solid friendship.

"I started the lame engine ahead. 'It must be this miserable trader—this intruder,' exclaimed the manager, looking back malevolently at the place we had left. 'He must be English,' I said. 'It will not save him from getting into trouble if he is not careful,' muttered the manager darkly. I observed with assumed innocence that no man was safe from trouble in this world.

"The current was more rapid now, the steamer seemed at her last gasp, the stern-wheel flopped languidly, and I caught myself listening on tiptoe for the next beat of the boat, for in sober truth I expected the wretched thing to give up every moment. It was like watching the last flickers of a life. But still we crawled. Sometimes I would pick out a tree a little way ahead to measure

---

1 purchases] leverages or tackles.

our progress towards Kurtz by, but I lost it invariably before we got abreast. To keep the eyes so long on one thing was too much for human patience. The manager displayed a beautiful resignation. I fretted and fumed and took to arguing with myself whether or no I would talk openly with Kurtz; but before I could come to any conclusion it occurred to me that my speech or my silence, indeed any action of mine, would be a mere futility. What did it matter what any one knew or ignored? What did it matter who was manager? One gets sometimes such a flash of insight. The essentials of this affair lay deep under the surface, beyond my reach, and beyond my power of meddling.

"Towards the evening of the second day we judged ourselves about eight miles from Kurtz's station. I wanted to push on; but the manager looked grave, and told me the navigation up there was so dangerous that it would be advisable, the sun being very low already, to wait where we were till next morning. Moreover, he pointed out that if the warning to approach cautiously were to be followed, we must approach in daylight—not at dusk, or in the dark. This was sensible enough. Eight miles meant nearly three hours' steaming for us, and I could also see suspicious ripples at the upper end of the reach. Nevertheless, I was annoyed beyond expression at the delay, and most unreasonably, too, since one night more could not matter much after so many months. As we had plenty of wood, and caution was the word, I brought up in the middle of the stream. The reach was narrow, straight, with high sides like a railway cutting. The dusk came gliding into it long before the sun had set. The current ran smooth and swift, but a dumb immobility sat on the banks. The living trees, lashed together by the creepers and every living bush of the undergrowth, might have been changed into stone, even to the slenderest twig, to the lightest leaf. It was not sleep—it seemed unnatural, like a state of trance. Not the faintest sound of any kind could be heard. You looked on amazed, and began to suspect yourself of being deaf—then the night came suddenly, and struck you blind as well. About three in the morning some large fish leaped, and the loud splash made me jump as though a gun had been fired. When the sun rose there was a white fog, very warm and clammy, and more blinding than the night. It did not shift or drive; it was just there, standing all round you like something solid. At eight or nine, perhaps, it lifted as a shutter lifts. We had a glimpse of the towering multitude of trees, of the immense matted jungle, with the blazing little ball of the sun hanging over it—all perfectly still—and then the white shutter came down again, smoothly, as if sliding in greased grooves. I ordered the chain, which we had begun to heave in, to be paid out again. Before it stopped running with a muffled rattle, a cry, a very loud cry, as of infinite desolation, soared slowly in the opaque air. It ceased. A complaining clamour, modulated in savage discords, filled our ears. The sheer unexpectedness of it made my hair stir under my cap. I don't know how it struck the others: to me it seemed as though the mist itself had screamed, so suddenly, and apparently from all sides at once, did this tumultuous and mournful uproar arise. It culminated in a hurried outbreak of almost intolerably excessive shrieking, which stopped short, leaving us stiffened in a variety of silly attitudes, and obstinately listening to the nearly as appalling and excessive silence. 'Good God! What is the meaning——' stammered at my elbow one of the pilgrims,—a little fat man, with sandy hair and red whiskers, who wore side-spring boots, and pink pyjamas tucked into his socks. Two others remained open-mouthed a whole minute, then dashed into the little cabin, to rush out incontinently and stand darting scared glances, with Winchesters at 'ready' in their hands. What we could see was just the steamer we were on, her outlines blurred as though she had been on the point of dissolving, and a misty strip of water, perhaps two feet broad, around her—and that was all. The rest of the world was nowhere, as far as our eyes and ears were concerned. Just nowhere. Gone, disappeared; swept off without leaving a whisper or a shadow behind.

"I went forward, and ordered the chain to be hauled in short, so as to be ready to trip the anchor and move the steamboat at once if necessary. 'Will they attack?' whispered an awed voice. 'We will be all butchered in this fog,' murmured another. The faces twitched with the strain, the hands trembled slightly, the eyes forgot to wink. It was very curious to see the contrast of expressions of the white men and of the black fellows of our crew, who were as much strangers to that part of the river as we, though their homes were only eight hundred miles away. The whites, of course greatly discomposed, had besides a curious look of being painfully shocked by such an outrageous row. The others had an alert, naturally interested expression; but their faces were essentially quiet, even those of the one or two who grinned as they hauled at the chain. Several exchanged short, grunting phrases, which seemed to settle the matter to their satisfaction. Their headman, a young, broad-chested black, severely draped in dark-blue fringed cloths, with fierce nostrils and his hair all done up artfully in oily ringlets, stood near me. 'Aha!' I said, just for good fellowship's sake. 'Catch 'im,' he snapped with a bloodshot widening of his eyes and a flash of sharp teeth—'catch 'im. Give 'im to us.' 'To you, eh?' I asked; 'what would you do with them?' 'Eat 'im!' he said, curtly, and, leaning his elbow on the rail, looked out into the fog in a dignified and profoundly pensive attitude. I would no doubt have been properly horrified, had it not occurred to me that he and his chaps must be very hungry: that they must have been growing increasingly hungry for at least this month past. They had been engaged for six months (I don't think a single one of them had any clear idea of time, as we at the end of countless ages have. They still belonged to the beginnings of time—had no inherited experience to teach them as it were), and of course, as long as there was a piece of paper written over in accordance with some farcical law or other made down the river, it didn't enter anybody's head to trouble how they would live. Certainly they had brought with them some rotten hippo-meat, which couldn't have lasted very long, anyway, even if the pilgrims hadn't, in the midst of a shocking hullabaloo, thrown a considerable quantity of it overboard. It looked like a high-handed proceeding; but it was really a case of legitimate self-defence. You can't breathe dead hippo waking, sleeping, and eating, and at the same time keep your precarious grip on existence. Besides that, they had given them every week three pieces of brass wire, each about nine inches long; and the theory was they were to buy their provisions with that currency in river-side villages. You can see how *that* worked. There were either no villages, or the people were hostile, or the director, who like the rest of us fed out of tins, with an occasional old he-goat thrown in, didn't want to stop the steamer for some more or less recondite reason. So, unless they swallowed the wire itself, or made loops of it to snare the fishes with, I don't see what good their extravagant salary could be to them. I must say it was paid with a regularity worthy of a large and honourable trading company. For the rest, the only thing to eat—though it didn't look eatable in the least—I saw in their possession was a few lumps of some stuff like half-cooked dough, of a dirty lavender colour, they kept wrapped in leaves, and now and then swallowed a piece of, but so small that it seemed done more for the looks of the thing than for any serious purpose of sustenance. Why in the name of all the gnawing devils of hunger they didn't go for us—they were thirty to five—and have a good tuck in for once, amazes me now when I think of it. They were big powerful men, with not much capacity to weigh the conse-quences, with courage, with strength, even yet, though their skins were no longer glossy and their muscles no longer hard. And I saw that something restraining, one of those human secrets that baffle probability, had come into play there. I looked at them with a swift quickening of interest—not because it occurred to me I might be eaten by them before very long, though I own to you that just then I perceived—in a new light, as it were—how unwholesome the pilgrims looked, and I hoped, yes, I positively hoped, that my aspect was not so—what shall I say?—so—unappetizing: a touch of fantastic vanity which fitted well with the dream-sensation that pervaded all my days at that time. Perhaps I had a little fever, too. One can't live with one's finger everlastingly on one's pulse. I had often 'a little fever,' or a little touch of other things—the playful paw-strokes of the wilderness, the preliminary trifling before the more serious onslaught which came in due course. Yes; I looked at them as you would on any human being, with a curiosity of their impulses, motives, capaci-ties, weaknesses, when brought to the test of an inexorable physi-cal necessity. Restraint! What possible restraint? Was it supersti-tion, disgust, patience, fear—or some kind of primitive honour? No fear can stand up to hunger, no patience can wear it out, dis-gust simply does not exist where hunger is; and as to superstition, beliefs, and what you may call principles, they are less than chaff in a breeze. Don't you know the devilry of lingering starvation, its exasperating torment, its black thoughts, its sombre and brooding ferocity? Well, I do. It takes a man all his inborn strength to fight hunger properly. It's really easier to face bereavement, dishonour, and the perdition of one's soul — than this kind of prolonged hunger. Sad, but true. And these chaps, too, had no earthly reason for any kind of scruple. Restraint! I would just as soon have expected restraint from a hyena prowling amongst the corpses of a battlefield. But there was the fact facing me — the fact dazzling, to be seen, like the foam on the depths of the sea, like a ripple on an unfathomable enigma, a mystery greater — when I thought of it — than the curious, inexplicable note of desperate grief in this savage clamour that had swept by us on the river-bank, behind the blind whiteness of the fog.

"Two pilgrims were quarrelling in hurried whispers as to which bank. 'Left.' 'No, no; how can you? Right, right, of course.' 'It is very serious,' said the manager's voice behind me; 'I would be desolated if anything should happen to Mr. Kurtz before we came up.' I looked at him, and had not the slightest doubt he was sincere. He was just the kind of man who would wish to preserve appearances. That was his restraint. But when he muttered something about going on at once, I did not even take the trouble to answer him. I knew, and he knew, that it was impossible. Were we to let go our hold of the bottom, we would be absolutely in the air — in space. We wouldn't be able to tell where we were going to — whether up or down stream, or across — till we fetched against one bank or the other, — and then we wouldn't know at first which it was. Of course I made no move. I had no mind for a smash-up. You couldn't imagine a more deadly place for a shipwreck. Whether drowned at once or not, we were sure to perish speedily in one way or another. 'I authorize you to take all the risks,' he said, after a short silence. 'I refuse to take any,' I said, shortly; which was just the answer he expected, though its tone might have surprised him. 'Well, I must defer to your judgment. You are captain,' he said, with marked civility. I turned my shoulder to him in sign of my appreciation, and looked into the fog. How long would it last? It was the most hopeless look-out. The approach to this Kurtz grubbing for ivory in the wretched bush was beset by as many dangers as though he had been an enchanted princess sleeping in a fabulous castle. 'Will they attack, do you think?' asked the manager, in a confidential tone.

"I did not think they would attack, for several obvious reasons. The thick fog was one. If they left the bank in their canoes they would get lost in it, as we would be if we attempted to move. Still, I had also judged the jungle of both banks quite impenetrable—and yet eyes were in it, eyes that had seen us. The river-side bushes were certainly very thick; but the undergrowth behind was evidently penetrable. However, during the short lift I had seen no canoes anywhere in the reach—certainly not abreast of the steamer. But what made the idea of attack inconceivable to me was the nature of the noise—of the cries we had heard. They had not the fierce character boding of immediate hostile intention. Unexpected, wild, and violent as they had been they had given me an irresistible impression of sorrow. The glimpse of the steamboat had for some reason filled those savages with unrestrained grief. The danger, if any, I expounded, was from our proximity to a great human passion let loose. Even extreme grief may ultimately vent itself in violence—but more generally takes the form of apathy....

"You should have seen the pilgrims stare! They had no heart to grin, or even to revile me: but I believe they thought me gone mad—with fright, maybe. I delivered a regular lecture. My dear boys, it was no good bothering. Keep a look-out? Well, you may guess I watched the fog for the signs of lifting as a cat watches a mouse; but for anything else our eyes were of no more use to us than if we had been buried miles deep in a heap of cotton-wool. It felt like it, too—choking, warm, stifling. Besides, all I said, though it sounded extravagant, was absolutely true to fact. What we afterwards alluded to as an attack was really an attempt at repulse. The action was very far from being aggressive—it was not even defensive, in the usual sense: it was undertaken under the stress of desperation, and in its essence was purely protective.

"It developed itself, I should say, two hours after the fog lifted, and its commencement was at a spot, roughly speaking, about a mile and a half below Kurtz's station. We had just floundered and flopped round a bend, when I saw an islet, a mere grassy hummock of bright green, in the middle of the stream. It was the only thing of the kind; but as we opened the reach more, I perceived it was the head of a long sandbank, or rather of a chain of shallow patches stretching down the middle of the river. They were discoloured, just awash, and the whole lot was seen just under the water, exactly as a man's backbone is seen running down the middle of his back under the skin. Now, as far as I did see, I could go to the right or to the left of this. I didn't know either channel, of course. The banks looked pretty well alike, the depth appeared the same; but as I had been informed the station was on the west side, I naturally headed for the western passage.

"No sooner had we fairly entered it than I became aware it was much narrower than I had supposed. To the left of us there was the long uninterrupted shoal, and to the right a high, steep bank heavily overgrown with bushes. Above the bush the trees stood in serried ranks. The twigs overhung the current thickly, and from distance to distance a large limb of some tree projected rigidly over the stream. It was then well on in the afternoon, the face of the forest was gloomy, and a broad strip of shadow had already fallen on the water. In this shadow we steamed up — very slowly, as you may imagine. I sheered her well inshore — the water being deepest near the bank, as the sounding-pole informed me.

"One of my hungry and forbearing friends was sounding in the bows just below me. This steamboat was exactly like a decked scow. On the deck, there were two little teak-wood houses, with doors and windows. The boiler was in the fore-end, and the machinery right astern. Over the whole there was a light roof, supported on stanchions. The funnel projected through that roof, and in front of the funnel a small cabin built of light planks served for a pilot-house. It contained a couch, two camp-stools, a loaded Martini-Henry[1] leaning in one corner, a tiny table, and the steering-wheel. It had a wide door in front and a broad shutter at each side. All these were always thrown open, of course. I spent my days perched up there on the extreme fore-end of that roof, before the door. At night I slept, or tried to, on the couch. An athletic black belonging to some coast tribe, and educated by my poor predecessor, was the helmsman. He sported a pair of brass

---

1   Martini-Henry] a military rifle.

earrings, wore a blue cloth wrapper from the waist to the ankles, and thought all the world of himself. He was the most unstable kind of fool I had ever seen. He steered with no end of a swagger while you were by; but if he lost sight of you, he became instantly the prey of an abject funk, and would let that cripple of a steamboat get the upper hand of him in a minute.

"I was looking down at the sounding-pole, and feeling much annoyed to see at each try a little more of it stick out of that river, when I saw my poleman give up the business suddenly, and stretch himself flat on the deck, without even taking the trouble to haul his pole in. He kept hold on it though, and it trailed in the water. At the same time the fireman, whom I could also see below me, sat down abruptly before his furnace and ducked his head. I was amazed. Then I had to look at the river mighty quick, because there was a snag in the fairway. Sticks, little sticks, were flying about—thick: they were whizzing before my nose, dropping below me, striking behind me against my pilot-house. All this time the river, the shore, the woods, were very quiet— perfectly quiet. I could only hear the heavy splashing thump of the stern-wheel and the patter of these things. We cleared the snag clumsily. Arrows, by Jove! We were being shot at! I stepped in quickly to close the shutter on the land-side. That fool-helmsman, his hands on the spokes, was lifting his knees high, stamping his feet, champing his mouth, like a reined-in horse. Confound him! And we were staggering within ten feet of the bank. I had to lean right out to swing the heavy shutter, and I saw a face amongst the leaves on the level with my own, looking at me very fierce and steady; and then suddenly, as though a veil had been removed from my eyes, I made out, deep in the tangled gloom, naked breasts, arms, legs, glaring eyes,—the bush was swarming with human limbs in movement, glistening, of bronze colour. The twigs shook, swayed, and rustled, the arrows flew out of them, and then the shutter came to. 'Steer her straight,' I said to the helmsman. He held his head rigid, face forward; but his eyes rolled, he kept on, lifting and setting down his feet gently, his mouth foamed a little. 'Keep quiet!' I said in a fury. I might just as well have ordered a tree not to sway in the wind. I darted out. Below me there was a great scuffle of feet on the iron deck; confused exclamations; a voice screamed, 'Can you turn back?' I caught sight of a V-shaped ripple on the water ahead. What? Another snag! A fusillade burst out under my feet. The pilgrims had opened with their Winchesters, and were simply squirting lead into that bush. A deuce of a lot of smoke came up and drove slowly forward. I swore at it. Now I couldn't see the ripple or the snag either. I stood in the doorway, peering, and the arrows came in swarms. They might have been poisoned, but they looked as though they wouldn't kill a cat. The bush began to howl. Our wood-cutters raised a warlike whoop; the report of a rifle just at my back deafened me. I glanced over my shoulder, and the pilot-house was yet full of noise and smoke when I made a dash at the wheel. The fool-nigger had dropped everything, to throw the shutter open and let off that Martini-Henry. He stood before the wide opening, glaring, and I yelled at him to come back, while I straightened the sudden twist out of that steamboat. There was no room to turn even if I had wanted to, the snag was somewhere very near ahead in that confounded smoke, there was no time to lose, so I just crowded her into the bank—right into the bank, where I knew the water was deep.

"We tore slowly along the overhanging bushes in a whirl of broken twigs and flying leaves. The fusillade below stopped short, as I had foreseen it would when the squirts got empty. I threw my head back to a glinting whizz that traversed the pilot-house, in at one shutter-hole and out at the other. Looking past that mad helmsman, who was shaking the empty rifle and yelling at the shore, I saw vague forms of men running bent double, leaping, gliding, distinct, incomplete, evanescent. Something big appeared in the air before the shutter, the rifle went overboard, and the man stepped back swiftly, looked at me over his shoulder in an extraor-dinary, profound, familiar manner, and fell upon my feet. The side of his head hit the wheel twice, and the end of what appeared a long cane clattered round and knocked over a little camp-stool. It looked as though after wrenching that thing from somebody ashore he had lost his balance in the effort. The thin smoke had blown away, we were clear of the snag, and looking ahead I could see that in another hundred yards or so I would be free to sheer off, away from the bank; but my feet felt so very warm and wet that I had to look down. The man had rolled on his back and stared straight up at me; both his hands clutched that cane. It was the shaft of a spear that, either thrown or lunged through the opening, had caught him in the side just below the ribs; the blade had gone in out of sight, after making a frightful gash; my shoes were full; a pool of blood lay very still, gleaming dark-red under the wheel; his eyes shone with an amazing lustre. The fusillade burst out again. He looked at me anxiously, gripping the spear like something precious, with an air of being afraid I would try to take it away from him. I had to make an effort to free my eyes from his gaze and attend to the steering. With one hand I felt above my head for the line of the steam whistle, and jerked out screech after screech hurriedly. The tumult of angry and warlike yells was checked instantly, and then from the depths of the woods went out such a tremulous and prolonged wail of mournful fear and utter despair as may be imagined to follow the flight of the last hope from the earth. There was a great commotion in the bush; the shower of arrows stopped, a few dropping shots rang out sharply — then silence, in which the languid beat of the stern-wheel came plainly to my ears. I put the helm hard a-starboard at the moment when the pilgrim in pink pyjamas, very hot and agitated, appeared in the doorway. 'The manager sends me——' he began in an official tone, and stopped short. 'Good God!' he said, glaring at the wounded man.

"We two whites stood over him, and his lustrous and inquiring glance enveloped us both. I declare it looked as though he would presently put to us some question in an understandable language; but he died without uttering a sound, without moving a limb, without twitching a muscle. Only in the very last moment, as though in response to some sign we could not see, to some whisper we could not hear, he frowned heavily, and that frown gave to his black death-mask an inconceivably sombre, brooding, and menacing expression. The lustre of inquiring glance faded swiftly into vacant glassiness. 'Can you steer?' I asked the agent eagerly. He looked very dubious; but I made a grab at his arm, and he understood at once I meant him to steer whether or no. To tell you the truth, I was morbidly anxious to change my shoes and socks. 'He is dead,' murmured the fellow, immensely impressed. 'No doubt about it,' said I, tugging like mad at the shoe-laces. 'And by the way, I suppose Mr. Kurtz is dead as well by this time.'

"For the moment that was the dominant thought. There was a sense of extreme disappointment, as though I had found out I had been striving after something altogether without a substance. I couldn't have been more disgusted if I had travelled all this way for the sole purpose of talking with Mr. Kurtz. Talking with.... I flung one shoe overboard, and became aware that that was exactly what I had been looking forward to—a talk with Kurtz. I made the strange discovery that I had never imagined him as doing, you know, but as discoursing. I didn't say to myself, 'Now I will never see him,' or 'Now I will never shake him by the hand,' but, 'now I will never hear him.' The man presented himself as a voice. Not of course that I did not connect him with some sort of action. Hadn't I been told in all the tones of jealousy and admiration that he had collected, bartered, swindled, or stolen more ivory than all the other agents together? That was not the point. The point was in his being a gifted creature, and that of all his gifts the one that stood out preeminently, that carried with it a sense of real presence, was his ability to talk, his words—the gift of expression, the bewildering, the illuminating, the most exalted and the most contemptible, the pulsating stream of light, or the deceitful flow from the heart of an impenetrable darkness.

"The other shoe went flying unto the devil-god of that river. I thought, By Jove! it's all over. We are too late; he has vanished—the gift has vanished, by means of some spear, arrow, or club. I will never hear that chap speak after all,—and my sorrow had a startling extravagance of emotion, even such as I had noticed in the howling sorrow of these savages in the bush. I couldn't have felt more of lonely desolation somehow, had I been robbed of a belief or had missed my destiny in life.... Why do you sigh in this beastly way, somebody? Absurd? Well, absurd. Good Lord! mustn't a man ever——Here give me some tobacco." ...

There was a pause of profound stillness, then a match flared, and Marlow's lean face appeared, worn, hollow, with downward folds and dropped eyelids, with an aspect of concentrated attention; and as he took vigorous draws at his pipe, it seemed to retreat and advance out of the night in the regular flicker of the tiny flame. The match went out.

"Absurd!" he cried. "This is the worst of trying to tell.... Here you all are, each moored with two good addresses, like a hulk with two anchors, a butcher round one corner, a policeman round another, excellent appetites, and temperature normal—you hear—normal from year's end to year's end. And you say, Absurd! Absurd be—exploded! Absurd! My dear boys, what can you expect from a man who out of sheer nervousness had just flung overboard a pair of new shoes! Now I think of it, it is amazing I did not shed tears. I am, upon the whole, proud of my fortitude. I was cut to the quick at the idea of having lost the inestimable privilege of listening to the gifted Kurtz. Of course I was wrong. The privilege was waiting for me. Oh, yes, I heard more than enough. And I was right, too. A voice. He was very little more than a voice. And I heard—him—it—this voice—other voices—all of them were so little more than voices—and the memory of that time itself lingers around me, impalpable, like a dying vibration of one immense jabber, silly, atrocious, sordid, savage, or simply mean, without any kind of sense. Voices, voices—even the girl herself—now——"

He was silent for a long time.

"I laid the ghost of his gifts at last with a lie," he began, suddenly. "Girl! What? Did I mention a girl? Oh, she is out of it—completely. They—the women I mean—are out of it—should be out of it. We must help them to stay in that beautiful world of their own, lest ours gets worse. Oh, she had to be out of it. You should have heard the disinterred body of Mr. Kurtz saying, 'My Intended.' You would have perceived directly then how completely she was out of it. And the lofty frontal bone of Mr. Kurtz! They say the hair goes on growing sometimes, but this—ah—specimen, was impressively bald. The wilderness had patted him on the head, and, behold, it was like a ball—an ivory ball; it had caressed him, and—lo!—he had withered; it had taken him, loved him, embraced him, got into his veins, consumed his flesh, and sealed his soul to its own by the inconceivable ceremonies of some devilish initiation. He was its spoiled and pampered favourite. Ivory? I should think so. Heaps of it, stacks of it. The old mud shanty was bursting with it. You would think there was not a single tusk left either above or below the ground in the whole country. 'Mostly fossil,' the manager had remarked, disparagingly. It was no more fossil than I am; but they call it fossil when it is dug up. It appears these niggers do bury the tusks sometimes—but evidently they couldn't bury this parcel deep enough to save the gifted Mr. Kurtz from his fate. We filled the steamboat with it, and had to pile a lot on the deck. Thus he could see and enjoy as long as he could see, because the appreciation of this favour had remained with him to the last. You should have heard him say, 'My ivory.' Oh yes, I heard him. 'My Intended, my ivory, my station, my river, my——.' Everything belonged to him. It made me hold my breath in expectation of hearing the wilderness burst into a prodigious peal of laughter that would shake the fixed stars in their places. Everything belonged to him—but that was a trifle. The thing was to know what he belonged to, how many powers of darkness claimed him for their own. That was the reflection that made you creepy all over. It was impossible—it was not good for one either—trying to imagine. He had taken a high seat amongst the devils of the land—I mean literally. You can't understand. How could you?—with solid pavement under your feet, surrounded by kind neighbours ready to cheer you or to fall on you, stepping delicately between the butcher and the policeman, in the holy terror of scandal and gallows and lunatic asylums—how can you imagine what particular region of the first ages a man's untrammelled feet may take him into by the way of solitude—utter solitude without a policeman—by the way of silence—utter silence, where no warning voice of a kind neighbour can be heard whispering of public opinion? These little things make all the great difference. When they are gone you must fall back upon your own innate strength, upon your own capacity for faithfulness. Of course you may be too much of a fool to go wrong—too dull even to know you are being assaulted by the powers of darkness. I take it, no fool ever made a bargain for his soul with the devil: the fool is too much of a fool, or the devil too much of a devil—I don't know which. Or you may be such a thunderingly exalted creature as to be altogether deaf and blind to anything but heavenly sights and sounds. Then the earth for you is only a standing place—and whether to be like this is your loss or your gain I won't pretend to say. But most of us are neither one nor the other. The earth for us is a place to live in, where we must put up with sights, with sounds, with smells, too, by Jove!—breathe dead hippo, so to speak, and not be contaminated. And there, don't you see? your strength comes in, the faith in your ability for the digging of unostentatious holes to bury the stuff in—your power of devotion, not to yourself, but to an obscure, back-breaking business. And that's difficult enough. Mind, I am not trying to excuse or even explain—I am trying to account to myself for—for—Mr. Kurtz—for the shade of Mr. Kurtz. This initiated wraith from the back of Nowhere honoured me with its amazing confidence before it vanished altogether. This was because it could speak English to me. The original Kurtz had been educated partly in England, and—as he was good enough to say himself—his sympathies were in the right place. His mother was half-English, his father was half-French. All Europe contributed to the making of Kurtz; and by-and-by I learned that, most appropriately, the International Society for the Suppression of Savage Customs had intrusted him with the making of a report, for its future guidance. And he had written it, too. I've seen it. I've read it. It was eloquent, vibrating with eloquence, but too high-strung, I think. Seventeen pages of close writing he had found time for! But this must have been before his—let us say—nerves, went wrong, and caused him to preside at certain midnight dances ending with unspeakable rites, which—as far as I reluctantly gathered from what I heard at various times—were offered up to him—do you understand?—to Mr. Kurtz himself. But it was a beautiful piece of writing. The opening paragraph, however, in the light of later information, strikes me now as ominous. He began with the argument that we whites, from the point of development we had arrived at, 'must necessarily appear to them [savages] in the nature of supernatural beings—we approach them with the might as of a deity,' and so on, and so on. 'By the simple exercise of our will we can exert a power for good practically unbounded,' etc. etc. From that point he soared and took me with him. The peroration was magnificent, though difficult to remember, you know. It gave me the notion of an exotic Immensity ruled by an august Benevolence. It made me tingle with enthusiasm. This was the unbounded power of eloquence—of words—of burning noble words. There were no practical hints to interrupt the magic current of phrases, unless a kind of note at the foot of the last page, scrawled evidently much later, in an unsteady hand, may be regarded as the exposition of a method. It was very simple, and at the end of that moving appeal to every altruistic sentiment it blazed at you, luminous and terrifying, like a flash of lightning in a serene sky: 'Exterminate all the brutes!' The curious part was that he had apparently forgotten all about that valuable postscriptum, because, later on, when he in a sense came to himself, he repeatedly entreated me to take good care of 'my pamphlet' (he called it), as it was sure to have in the future a good influence upon his career. I had full information about all these things, and, besides, as it turned out, I was to have the care of his memory. I've done enough for it to give me the indisputable right to lay it, if I choose, for an everlasting rest in the dust-bin of progress, amongst all the sweepings and, figuratively speaking, all the dead cats of civilization. But then, you see, I can't choose. He won't be forgotten. Whatever he was, he was not common. He had the power to charm or frighten rudimentary souls into an aggravated witch-dance in his honour; he could also fill the small souls of the pilgrims with bitter misgivings: he had one devoted friend at least, and he had conquered one soul in the world that was neither rudimentary nor tainted with self-seeking. No; I can't forget him, though I am not prepared to affirm the fellow was exactly worth the life we lost in getting to him. I missed my late helmsman awfully,—I missed him even while his body was still lying in the pilot-house. Perhaps you will think it passing strange this regret for a savage who was no more account than a grain of sand in a black Sahara. Well, don't you see, he had done something, he had steered; for months I had him at my back—a help—an instrument. It was a kind of partnership. He steered for me—I had to look after him, I worried about his deficiencies, and thus a subtle bond had been created, of which I only became aware when it was suddenly broken. And the intimate profundity of that look he gave me when he received his hurt remains to this day in my memory—like a claim of distant kinship affirmed in a supreme moment.

"Poor fool! If he had only left that shutter alone. He had no restraint, no restraint—just like Kurtz—a tree swayed by the wind. As soon as I had put on a dry pair of slippers, I dragged him out, after first jerking the spear out of his side, which operation I confess I performed with my eyes shut tight. His heels leaped together over the little door-step; his shoulders were pressed to my breast; I hugged him from behind desperately. Oh! he was heavy; heavy, heavier than any man on earth, I should imagine. Then without more ado I tipped him overboard. The current snatched him as though he had been a wisp of grass, and I saw the body roll over twice before I lost sight of it for ever. All the pilgrims and the manager were then congregated on the awning-deck about the pilot-house, chattering at each other like a flock of excited magpies, and there was a scandalized murmur at my heartless promptitude. What they wanted to keep that body hanging about for I can't guess. Embalm it, maybe. But I had also heard another, and a very ominous, murmur on the deck below. My friends the wood-cutters were likewise scandalized, and with a better show of reason—though I admit that the reason itself was quite inadmissible. Oh, quite! I had made up my mind that if my late helmsman was to be eaten, the fishes alone should have him. He had been a very second-rate helmsman while alive, but now he was dead he might have become a first-class temptation, and possibly cause some startling trouble. Besides, I was anxious to take the wheel, the man in pink pyjamas showing himself a hopeless duffer at the business.

"This I did directly the simple funeral was over. We were going half-speed, keeping right in the middle of the stream, and I listened to the talk about me. They had given up Kurtz, they had given up the station; Kurtz was dead, and the station had been burnt—and so on—and so on. The red-haired pilgrim was beside himself with the thought that at least this poor Kurtz had been properly avenged. 'Say! We must have made a glorious slaughter of them in the bush. Eh? What do you think? Say?' He positively danced, the bloodthirsty little gingery beggar. And he had nearly fainted when he saw the wounded man! I could not help saying, 'You made a glorious lot of smoke, anyhow.' I had seen, from the way the tops of the bushes rustled and flew, that almost all the shots had gone too high. You can't hit anything unless you take aim and fire from the shoulder; but these chaps fired from the hip with their eyes shut. The retreat, I maintained—and I was right—was caused by the screeching of the steam-whistle. Upon this they forgot Kurtz, and began to howl at me with indignant protests.

"The manager stood by the wheel murmuring confidentially about the necessity of getting well away down the river before dark at all events, when I saw in the distance a clearing on the river-side and the outlines of some sort of building. 'What's this?' I asked. He clapped his hands in wonder. 'The station!' he cried. I edged in at once, still going half-speed.

"Through my glasses I saw the slope of a hill interspersed with rare trees and perfectly free from undergrowth. A long decaying building on the summit was half buried in the high grass; the large holes in the peaked roof gaped black from afar; the jungle and the woods made a background. There was no enclosure or fence of any kind; but there had been one apparently, for near the house half-a-dozen slim posts remained in a row, roughly trimmed, and with their upper ends ornamented with round carved balls. The rails, or whatever there had been between, had disappeared. Of course the forest surrounded all that. The river-bank was clear, and on the water-side I saw a white man under a hat like a cart-wheel beckoning persistently with his whole arm. Examining the edge of the forest above and below, I was almost certain I could see movements—human forms gliding here and there. I steamed past prudently, then stopped the engines and let her drift down. The man on the shore began to shout, urging us to land. 'We have been attacked,' screamed the manager. 'I know—I know. It's all right,' yelled back the other, as cheerful as you please. 'Come along. It's all right. I am glad.'

"His aspect reminded me of something I had seen—something funny I had seen somewhere. As I manoeuvred to get alongside, I was asking myself. 'What does this fellow look like?' Suddenly I got it. He looked like a harlequin. His clothes had been made of some stuff that was brown holland probably, but it was covered with patches all over, with bright patches, blue, red, and yellow,—patches on the back, patches on the front, patches on elbows, on knees; coloured binding around his jacket, scarlet edging at the bottom of his trousers; and the sunshine made him look extremely gay and wonderfully neat withal, because you could see how beautifully all this patching had been done. A beardless, boyish face, very fair, no features to speak of, nose peeling, little blue eyes, smiles and frowns chasing each other over that open countenance like sunshine and shadow on a wind-swept plain. 'Look out, captain!' he cried; 'there's a snag lodged in here last night.' What! Another snag? I confess I swore shamefully. I had nearly holed my cripple, to finish off that charming trip. The harlequin on the bank turned his little pug-nose up to me. 'You English?' he asked, all smiles. 'Are you?' I shouted from the wheel. The smiles vanished, and he shook his head as if sorry for my disappointment. Then he brightened up. 'Never mind!' he cried, encouragingly. 'Are we in time?' I asked. 'He is up there,' he replied, with a toss of the head up the hill, and becoming gloomy all of a sudden. His face was like the autumn sky, overcast one moment and bright the next.

"When the manager, escorted by the pilgrims, all of them armed to the teeth, had gone to the house this chap came on board. 'I say, I don't like this. These natives are in the bush.' I said. He assured me earnestly it was all right. 'They are simple people,' he added; 'well I am glad you came. It took me all my time to keep them off.' 'But you said it was all right,' I cried. 'Oh, they meant no harm,' he said; and as I stared he corrected himself, 'Not exactly.' Then vivaciously, 'My faith, your pilot-house wants a clean up!' In the next breath he advised me to keep enough steam on the boiler to blow the whistle in case of any trouble. 'One good screech will do more for you than all your rifles. They are simple people,' he repeated. He rattled away at such a rate he quite overwhelmed me. He seemed to be trying to make up for lots of silence, and actually hinted, laughing, that such was the case. 'Don't you talk with Mr. Kurtz?' I said. 'You don't talk with that man—you listen to him,' he exclaimed with severe exaltation. 'But now——' He waved his arm, and in the twinkling of an eye was in the uttermost depths of despondency. In a moment he came up again with a jump, possessed himself of both my hands, shook them continuously, while he gabbled: 'Brother sailor ... honour ... pleasure ... delight ... introduce myself ... Russian ... son of an arch-priest ... Government of Tambov[1] ... What? Tobacco! English tobacco; the excellent English tobacco! Now, that's brotherly. Smoke? Where's a sailor that does not smoke?'

"The pipe soothed him, and gradually I made out he had run away from school, had gone to sea in a Russian ship; ran away again; served some time in English ships; was now reconciled with the arch-priest. He made a point of that. 'But when one is young one must see things, gather experience, ideas; enlarge the mind.' 'Here!' I interrupted. 'You can never tell! Here I met Mr. Kurtz,' he said, youthfully solemn and reproachful. I held my tongue after that. It appears he had persuaded a Dutch trading-house on the coast to fit him out with stores and goods, and had started for the interior with a light heart, and no more idea of what would happen to him than a baby. He had been wandering about that river for nearly two years alone, cut off from everybody and everything. 'I am not so young as I look. I am twenty-five,' he said. 'At first old Van Shuyten would tell me to go to the devil,' he narrated with keen enjoyment; 'but I stuck to him, and talked and talked, till at last he got afraid I would talk the hind-leg off his favourite dog, so he gave me some cheap things and a few guns, and told me he hoped he would never see my face again. Good old Dutchman, Van Shuyten. I've sent him one small lot of ivory a year ago, so that he can't call me a little thief when I get back. I hope he got it. And for the rest I don't care. I had some wood stacked for you. That was my old house. Did you see?'

"I gave him Towson's book. He made as though he would kiss me, but restrained himself. 'The only book I had left, and I thought I had lost it,' he said, looking at it ecstatically. 'So many accidents happen to a man going about alone, you know. Canoes get upset sometimes—and sometimes you've got to clear out so quick when the people get angry.' He thumbed the pages. 'You made notes in Russian?' I asked. He nodded. 'I thought they were

---

1   Tambov] Russian town, capital of the government of the same name.

written in cipher,' I said. He laughed, then became serious. 'I had lots of trouble to keep these people off,' he said. 'Did they want to kill you?' I asked. 'Oh, no!' he cried, and checked himself. 'Why did they attack us?' I pursued. He hesitated, then said shamefacedly, 'They don't want him to go.' 'Don't they?' I said, curiously. He nodded a nod full of mystery and wisdom. 'I tell you,' he cried, 'this man has enlarged my mind.' He opened his arms wide, staring at me with his little blue eyes that were perfectly round."

III

"I LOOKED at him, lost in astonishment. There he was before me, in motley, as though he had absconded from a troupe of mimes, enthusiastic, fabulous. His very existence was improbable, inexplicable, and altogether bewildering. He was an insoluble problem. It was inconceivable how he had existed, how he had succeeded in getting so far, how he had managed to remain — why he did not instantly disappear. 'I went a little farther,' he said, 'then still a little farther — till I had gone so far that I don't know how I'll ever get back. Never mind. Plenty time. I can manage. You take Kurtz away quick — quick — I tell you.' The glamour of youth enveloped his particoloured rags, his destitution, his loneliness, the essential desolation of his futile wanderings. For months — for years — his life hadn't been worth a day's purchase; and there he was gallantly, thoughtlessly alive, to all appearance indestructible solely by the virtue of his few years and of his unreflecting audacity. I was seduced into something like admiration — like envy. Glamour urged him on, glamour kept him unscathed. He surely wanted nothing from the wilderness but space to breathe in and to push on through. His need was to exist, and to move onwards at the greatest possible risk, and with a maximum of privation. If the absolutely pure, uncalculating, unpractical spirit of adventure had ever ruled a human being, it ruled this be-patched youth. I almost envied him the possession of this modest and clear flame. It seemed to have consumed all thought of self so completely, that even while he was talking to you, you forgot that it was he — the man before your eyes — who had gone through these things. I did not envy him his devotion to Kurtz, though. He had not meditated over it. It came to him, and he accepted it with a sort of eager fatalism. I must say that to me it appeared about the most dangerous thing in every way he had come upon so far.

"They had come together unavoidably, like two ships becalmed near each other, and lay rubbing sides at last. I suppose Kurtz wanted an audience, because on a certain occasion, when encamped in the forest, they had talked all night, or more probably Kurtz had talked. 'We talked of everything,' he said, quite transported at the recollection. 'I forgot there was such a thing as sleep. The night did not seem to last an hour. Everything! Everything! ... Of love, too.' 'Ah, he talked to you of love!' I said, much amused. 'It isn't what you think,' he cried, almost passionately. 'It was in general. He made me see things—things.'

"He threw his arms up. We were on deck at the time, and the headman of my wood-cutters, lounging near by, turned upon him his heavy and glittering eyes. I looked around, and I don't know why, but I assure you that never, never before, did this land, this river, this jungle, the very arch of this blazing sky, appear to me so hopeless and so dark, so impenetrable to human thought, so pitiless to human weakness. 'And, ever since, you have been with him, of course?' I said.

"On the contrary. It appears their intercourse had been very much broken by various causes. He had, as he informed me proudly, managed to nurse Kurtz through two illnesses (he alluded to it as you would to some risky feat), but as a rule Kurtz wandered alone, far in the depths of the forest. 'Very often coming to this station, I had to wait days and days before he would turn up,' he said. 'Ah, it was worth waiting for!—sometimes.' 'What was he doing? exploring or what?' I asked. 'Oh, yes, of course'; he had discovered lots of villages, a lake, too—he did not know exactly in what direction; it was dangerous to inquire too much—but mostly his expeditions had been for ivory. 'But he had no goods to trade with by that time,' I objected. 'There's a good lot of cartridges left even yet,' he answered, looking away. 'To speak plainly, he raided the country,' I said. He nodded. 'Not alone, surely!' He muttered something about the villages round that lake. 'Kurtz got the tribe to follow him, did he?' I suggested. He fidgeted a little.

'They adored him,' he said. The tone of these words was so extra-ordinary that I looked at him searchingly. It was curious to see his mingled eagerness and reluctance to speak of Kurtz. The man filled his life, occupied his thoughts, swayed his emotions. 'What can you expect?' he burst out; 'he came to them with thunder and lightning, you know—and they had never seen anything like it—and very terrible. He could be very terrible. You can't judge Mr. Kurtz as you would an ordinary man. No, no, no! Now—just to give you an idea—I don't mind telling you, he wanted to shoot me, too, one day—but I don't judge him.' 'Shoot you!' I cried. 'What for?' 'Well, I had a small lot of ivory the chief of that village near my house gave me. You see I used to shoot game for them. Well, he wanted it, and wouldn't hear reason. He declared he would shoot me unless I gave him the ivory and then cleared out of the country, because he could do so, and had a fancy for it, and there was nothing on earth to prevent him killing whom he jolly well pleased. And it was true, too. I gave him the ivory. What did I care! But I didn't clear out. No, no. I couldn't leave him. I had to be careful, of course, till we got friendly again for a time. He had his second illness then. Afterwards I had to keep out of the way; but I didn't mind. He was living for the most part in those villages on the lake. When he came down to the river, sometimes he would take to me, and sometimes it was better for me to be careful. This man suffered too much. He hated all this, and somehow he couldn't get away. When I had a chance I begged him to try and leave while there was time; I offered to go back with him. And he would say yes, and then he would remain; go off on another ivory hunt; disappear for weeks; forget himself amongst these people—forget himself—you know.' 'Why! he's mad,' I said. He protested indignantly. Mr. Kurtz couldn't be mad. If I had heard him talk, only two days ago, I wouldn't dare hint at such a thing.... I had taken up my binoculars while we talked, and was looking at the shore, sweeping the limit of the forest at each side and at the back of the house. The consciousness of there being people in that bush, so silent, so quiet—as silent and quiet as the ruined house on the hill—made me uneasy. There was no sign on the face of nature of this amazing tale that was not so much told as suggested to me in desolate exclamations, completed by shrugs, in interrupted phrases, in hints ending in deep sighs. The woods were unmoved, like a mask—heavy, like the closed door of a prison—they looked with their air of hidden knowledge, of patient expectation, of unapproachable silence. The Russian was explaining to me that it was only lately that Mr. Kurtz had come down to the river, bringing along with him all the fighting men of that lake tribe. He had been absent for several months—getting himself adored, I suppose—and had come down unexpectedly, with the intention to all appearance of making a raid either across the river or down stream. Evidently the appetite for more ivory had got the better of the—what shall I say?—less material aspirations. However he had got much worse suddenly. 'I heard he was lying helpless, and so I came up—took my chance,' said the Russian. 'Oh, he is bad, very bad.' I directed my glass to the house. There were no signs of life, but there was the ruined roof, the long mud wall peeping above the grass, with three little square window-holes, no two of the same size; all this brought within reach of my hand, as it were. And then I made a brusque movement, and one of the remaining posts of that vanished fence leaped up in the field of my glass. You remember I told you I had been struck at the distance by certain attempts at ornamentation, rather remarkable in the ruinous aspect of the place. Now I had suddenly a nearer view, and its first result was to make me throw my head back as if before a blow. Then I went carefully from post to post with my glass, and I saw my mistake. These round knobs were not ornamental but symbolic; they were expressive and puzzling, striking and disturbing—food for thought and also for the vultures if there had been any looking down from the sky; but at all events for such ants as were industrious enough to ascend the pole. They would have been even more impressive, those heads on the stakes, if their faces had not been turned to the house. Only one, the first I had made out, was facing my way. I was not so shocked as you may think. The start back I had given was really nothing but a movement of surprise. I had expected to see a knob of wood there, you know. I returned deliberately to the first I had seen—and there it was, black, dried, sunken, with closed eyelids,—a head that seemed to sleep at the top of that pole, and, with the shrunken dry lips showing a narrow white line of the teeth, was smiling, too, smiling continuously at some endless and jocose dream of that eternal slumber.

"I am not disclosing any trade secrets. In fact, the manager said afterwards that Mr. Kurtz's methods had ruined the district. I have no opinion on that point, but I want you clearly to understand that there was nothing exactly profitable in these heads being there. They only showed that Mr. Kurtz lacked restraint in the gratification of his various lusts, that there was something wanting in him—some small matter which, when the pressing need arose, could not be found under his magnificent eloquence. Whether he knew of this deficiency himself I can't say. I think the knowledge came to him at last—only at the very last. But the wilderness had found him out early, and had taken on him a terrible vengeance for the fantastic invasion. I think it had whispered to him things about himself which he did not know, things of which he had no conception till he took counsel with this great solitude—and the whisper had proved irresistibly fascinating. It echoed loudly within him because he was hollow at the core.... I put down the glass, and the head that had appeared near enough to be spoken to seemed at once to have leaped away from me into inaccessible distance.

"The admirer of Mr. Kurtz was a bit crestfallen. In a hurried, indistinct voice he began to assure me he had not dared to take these—say, symbols—down. He was not afraid of the natives; they would not stir till Mr. Kurtz gave the word. His ascendancy was extraordinary. The camps of these people surrounded the place, and the chiefs came every day to see him. They would crawl.... 'I don't want to know anything of the ceremonies used when approaching Mr. Kurtz,' I shouted. Curious, this feeling that came over me that such details would be more intolerable than those heads drying on the stakes under Mr. Kurtz's windows. After all, that was only a savage sight, while I seemed at one bound to have been transported into some lightless region of subtle horrors, where pure, uncomplicated savagery was a positive relief, being something that had a right to exist—obviously—in the sunshine. The young man looked at me with surprise. I suppose it did not occur to him that Mr. Kurtz was no idol of mine. He forgot I hadn't heard any of these splendid monologues on, what was it? on love, justice, conduct of life—or what not. If it had come to crawling before Mr. Kurtz, he crawled as much as the veriest savage of them all. I had no idea of the conditions, he said: these heads were the heads of rebels. I shocked him excessively by laughing. Rebels! What would be the next definition I was to hear? There had been enemies, criminals, workers—and these were rebels. Those rebellious heads looked very subdued to me on their sticks. 'You don't know how such a life tries a man like Kurtz,' cried Kurtz's last disciple. 'Well, and you?' I said. 'I! I! I am a simple man. I have no great thoughts. I want nothing from anybody. How can you compare me to? ...' His feelings were too much for speech, and suddenly he broke down. 'I don't understand,' he groaned. 'I've been doing my best to keep him alive, and that's enough. I had no hand in all this. I have no abilities. There hasn't been a drop of medicine or a mouthful of invalid food for months here. He was shamefully abandoned. A man like this, with such ideas. Shamefully! Shamefully! I—I—haven't slept for the last ten nights...'

"His voice lost itself in the calm of the evening. The long shadows of the forest had slipped down hill while we talked, had gone far beyond the ruined hovel, beyond the symbolic row of stakes. All this was in the gloom, while we down there were yet in the sunshine, and the stretch of the river abreast of the clearing glittered in a still and dazzling splendour, with a murky and over-shadowed bend above and below. Not a living soul was seen on the shore. The bushes did not rustle.

"Suddenly round the corner of the house a group of men appeared, as though they had come up from the ground. They waded waist-deep in the grass, in a compact body, bearing an improvised stretcher in their midst. Instantly, in the emptiness of the landscape, a cry arose whose shrillness pierced the still air like a sharp arrow flying straight to the very heart of the land; and, as if by enchantment, streams of human beings—of naked human beings—with spears in their hands, with bows, with shields, with wild glances and savage movements, were poured into the clearing by the dark-faced and pensive forest. The bushes shook, the grass swayed for a time, and then everything stood still in attentive immobility.

"'Now, if he does not say the right thing to them we are all done for,' said the Russian at my elbow. The knot of men with the stretcher had stopped, too, halfway to the steamer, as if petrified. I saw the man on the stretcher sit up, lank and with an uplifted arm, above the shoulders of the bearers. 'Let us hope that the man who can talk so well of love in general will find some particular reason to spare us this time,' I said. I resented bitterly the absurd danger of our situation, as if to be at the mercy of that atrocious phantom had been a dishonouring necessity. I could not hear a sound, but through my glasses I saw the thin arm extended commandingly, the lower jaw moving, the eyes of that apparition shining darkly far in its bony head that nodded with grotesque jerks. Kurtz — Kurtz — that means short in German — don't it?[1] Well, the name was as true as everything else in his life — and death. He looked at least seven feet long. His covering had fallen off, and his body emerged from it pitiful and appalling as from a winding-sheet. I could see the cage of his ribs all astir, the bones of his arm waving. It was though an animated image of death carved out of old ivory had been shaking its hand with menaces at a motionless crowd of men made of dark and glittering bronze. I saw him open his mouth wide — it gave him a weirdly voracious aspect, as though he had wanted to swallow all the air, all the earth, all the men before him. A deep voice reached me faintly. He must have been shouting. He fell back suddenly. The stretcher shook as the bearers staggered forward again, and almost at the same time I noticed that the crowd of savages was vanishing without any perceptible movement of retreat, as if the forest that had ejected these beings so suddenly had drawn them in again as the breath is drawn in a long aspiration.

"Some of the pilgrims behind the stretcher carried his arms — two shot-guns, a heavy rifle, and a light revolver-carbine — the thunderbolts of that pitiful Jupiter. The manager bent over him murmuring as he walked beside his head. They laid him down in one of the little cabins — just a room for a bedplace and a camp-

---

1   Kurtz] [pronounced "koorts"] is the German word for "short;" "klein" is the German word for "small." (The agent whom Conrad and the *Roi de Belges* party were trying to rescue in 1890 was Georges Klein.)

stool or two, you know. We had brought his belated correspondence, and a lot of torn envelopes and open letters littered his bed. His hand roamed feebly amongst these papers. I was struck by the fire of his eyes and the composed languor of his expression. It was not so much the exhaustion of disease. He did not seem in pain. This shadow looked satiated and calm, as though for the moment it had had its fill of all the emotions.

"He rustled one of the letters, and looking straight in my face said, 'I am glad.' Somebody had been writing to him about me. These special recommendations were turning up again. The volume of tone he emitted without effort, almost without the trouble of moving his lips, amazed me. A voice! a voice! It was grave, profound, vibrating, while the man did not seem capable of a whisper. However, he had enough strength in him—factitious no doubt—to very nearly make an end of us, as you shall hear directly.

"The manager appeared silently in the doorway; I stepped out at once and he drew the curtain after me. The Russian, eyed curiously by the pilgrims, was staring at the shore. I followed the direction of his glance.

"Dark human shapes could be made out in the distance, flitting indistinctly against the gloomy border of the forest, and near the river two bronze figures, leaning on tall spears, stood in the sunlight under fantastic head-dresses of spotted skins, warlike and still in statuesque repose. And from right to left along the lighted shore moved a wild and gorgeous apparition of a woman.

"She walked with measured steps, draped in striped and fringed cloths, treading the earth proudly, with a slight jingle and flash of barbarous ornaments. She carried her head high; her hair was done in the shape of a helmet; she had brass leggings to the knee, brass wire gauntlets to the elbow, a crimson spot on her tawny cheek, innumerable necklaces of glass beads on her neck; bizarre things, charms, gifts of witch-men, that hung about her, glittered and trembled at every step. She must have had the value of several elephant tusks upon her. She was savage and superb, wild-eyed and magnificent; there was something ominous and stately in her deliberate progress. And in the hush that had fallen suddenly upon the whole sorrowful land, the immense wilderness, the colossal body of the fecund and mysterious life seemed to look at her, pensive, as though it had been looking at the image of its own tenebrous and passionate soul.

"She came abreast of the steamer, stood still, and faced us. Her long shadow fell to the water's edge. Her face had a tragic and fierce aspect of wild sorrow and of dumb pain mingled with the fear of some struggling, half-shaped resolve. She stood looking at us without a stir, and like the wilderness itself, with an air of brooding over an inscrutable purpose. A whole minute passed, and then she made a step forward. There was a low jingle, a glint of yellow metal, a sway of fringed draperies, and she stopped as if her heart had failed her. The young fellow by my side growled. The pilgrims murmured at my back. She looked at us all as if her life had depended upon the unswerving steadiness of her glance. Suddenly she opened her bared arms and threw them up rigid above her head, as though in an uncontrollable desire to touch the sky, and at the same time the swift shadows darted out on the earth, swept around on the river, gathering the steamer into a shadowy embrace. A formidable silence hung over the scene.

"She turned away slowly, walked on, following the bank, and passed into the bushes to the left. Once only her eyes gleamed back at us in the dusk of the thickets before she disappeared.

"'If she had offered to come aboard I really think I would have tried to shoot her,' said the man of patches, nervously. 'I had been risking my life every day for the last fortnight to keep her out of the house. She got in one day and kicked up a row about those miserable rags I picked up in the storeroom to mend my clothes with. I wasn't decent. At least it must have been that, for she talked like a fury to Kurtz for an hour, pointing at me now and then. I don't understand the dialect of this tribe. Luckily for me, I fancy Kurtz felt too ill that day to care, or there would have been mischief. I don't understand.... No—it's too much for me. Ah, well, it's all over now.'

"At this moment I heard Kurtz's deep voice behind the curtain: 'Save me!—save the ivory, you mean. Don't tell me. Save *me*! Why, I've had to save you. You are interrupting my plans now. Sick! Sick! Not so sick as you would like to believe. Never mind. I'll carry my ideas out yet—I will return. I'll show you what can be done. You with your little peddling notions — you are inter-fering with me. I will return. I....'

"The manager came out. He did me the honour to take me under the arm and lead me aside. 'He is very low, very low,' he said. He considered it necessary to sigh, but neglected to be con-sistently sorrowful. 'We have done all we could for him — haven't we? But there is no disguising the fact, Mr. Kurtz has done more harm than good to the Company. He did not see the time was not ripe for vigorous action. Cautiously, cautiously — that's my principle. We must be cautious yet. The district is closed to us for a time. Deplorable! Upon the whole, the trade will suffer. I don't deny there is a remarkable quantity of ivory — mostly fossil. We must save it, at all events — but look how precarious the position is — and why? Because the method is unsound.' 'Do you,' said I, looking at the shore, 'call it "unsound method?"' 'Without doubt,' he exclaimed, hotly. 'Don't you?' ... 'No method at all,' I mur-mured after a while. 'Exactly,' he exulted. 'I anticipated this. Shows a complete want of judgment. It is my duty to point it out in the proper quarter.' 'Oh,' said I, 'that fellow — what's his name? — the brickmaker, will make a readable report for you.' He appeared confounded for a moment. It seemed to me I had never breathed an atmosphere so vile, and I turned mentally to Kurtz for relief — positively for relief. 'Nevertheless I think Mr. Kurtz is a remarkable man,' I said with emphasis. He started, dropped on me a cold heavy glance, said very quietly, 'he *was*,' and turned his back on me. My hour of favour was over; I found myself lumped along with Kurtz as a partisan of methods for which the time was not ripe: I was unsound! Ah! but it was something to have at least a choice of nightmares.

"I had turned to the wilderness really, not to Mr. Kurtz, who, I was ready to admit, was as good as buried. And for a moment it seemed to me as if I also were buried in a vast grave full of unspeakable secrets. I felt an intolerable weight oppressing my breast, the smell of the damp earth, the unseen presence of victo-rious corruption, the darkness of an impenetrable night.... The Russian tapped me on the shoulder. I heard him mumbling and stammering something about 'brother seaman — couldn't con-ceal — knowledge of matters that would affect Mr. Kurtz's reputation.' I waited. For him evidently Mr. Kurtz was not in his grave; I suspect that for him Mr. Kurtz was one of the immortals. 'Well!' said I at last, 'speak out. As it happens, I am Mr. Kurtz's friend—in a way.'

"He stated with a good deal of formality that had we not been 'of the same profession,' he would have kept the matter to himself without regard to consequences. 'He suspected there was an active ill will towards him on the part of these white men that——'You are right,' I said, remembering a certain conversation I had overheard. 'The manager thinks you ought to be hanged.' He showed a concern at this intelligence which amused me at first. 'I had better get out of the way quietly,' he said, earnestly. 'I can do no more for Kurtz now, and they would soon find some excuse. What's to stop them? There's a military post three hundred miles from here.' 'Well, upon my word,' said I, 'perhaps you had better go if you have any friends amongst the savages near by.' 'Plenty,' he said. 'They are simple people—and I want nothing, you know.' He stood biting his lip, then: 'I don't want any harm to happen to these whites here, but of course I was thinking of Mr. Kurtz's reputation—but you are a brother seaman and——' 'All right,' said I, after a time. 'Mr. Kurtz's reputation is safe with me.' I did not know how truly I spoke.

"He informed me, lowering his voice, that it was Kurtz who had ordered the attack to be made on the steamer. 'He hated sometimes the idea of being taken away—and then again.... But I don't understand these matters. I am a simple man. He thought it would scare you away—that you would give it up, thinking him dead. I could not stop him. Oh, I had an awful time of it this last month.' 'Very well,' I said. 'He is all right now.' 'Ye-e-es,' he muttered, not very convinced apparently. 'Thanks,' said I; 'I shall keep my eyes open.' 'But quiet—eh?' he urged, anxiously. 'It would be awful for his reputation if anybody here——' I promised a complete discretion with great gravity. 'I have a canoe and three black fellows waiting not very far. I am off. Could you give me a few Martini-Henry cartridges?' I could, and did, with proper secrecy. He helped himself, with a wink at me, to a handful of my tobacco. 'Between sailors—you know—good English tobacco.' At the door of the pilot-house he turned round—'I say, haven't you a pair of shoes you could spare?' He raised one leg. 'Look.' The soles were tied with knotted strings sandal-wise under his bare feet. I rooted out an old pair, at which he looked with admiration before tucking it under his left arm. One of his pockets (bright red) was bulging with cartridges, from the other (dark blue) peeped 'Towson's Inquiry,' etc., etc. He seemed to think himself excellently well equipped for a renewed encounter with the wilderness. 'Ah! I'll never, never meet such a man again. You ought to have heard him recite poetry—his own, too, it was, he told me. Poetry!' He rolled his eyes at the recollection of these delights. 'Oh, he enlarged my mind!' 'Good-bye,' said I. He shook hands and vanished in the night. Sometimes I ask myself whether I had ever really seen him—whether it was possible to meet such a phenomenon! …

"When I woke up shortly after midnight his warning came to my mind with its hint of danger that seemed, in the starred darkness, real enough to make me get up for the purpose of having a look round. On the hill a big fire burned, illuminating fitfully a crooked corner of the station-house. One of the agents with a picket of a few of our blacks, armed for the purpose, was keeping guard over the ivory; but deep within the forest, red gleams that wavered, that seemed to sink and rise from the ground amongst confused columnar shapes of intense blackness, showed the exact position of the camp where Mr. Kurtz's adorers were keeping their uneasy vigil. The monotonous beating of a big drum filled the air with muffled shocks and a lingering vibration. A steady droning sound of many men chanting each to himself some weird incantation came out from the black, flat wall of the woods as the humming of bees comes out of a hive, and had a strange narcotic effect upon my half-awake senses. I believe I dozed off leaning over the rail, till an abrupt burst of yells, an overwhelming outbreak of a pent-up and mysterious frenzy, woke me up in a bewildered wonder. It was cut short all at once, and the low droning went on with an effect of audible and soothing silence. I glanced casually into the little cabin. A light was burning within, but Mr. Kurtz was not there.

"I think I would have raised an outcry if I had believed my eyes. But I didn't believe them at first—the thing seemed so impossible. The fact is I was completely unnerved by a sheer blank fright, pure abstract terror, unconnected with any distinct shape of physical danger. What made this emotion so over-powering was — how shall I define it? — the moral shock I received, as if something altogether monstrous, intolerable to thought and odious to the soul, had been thrust upon me unexpectedly. This lasted of course the merest fraction of a sec-ond, and then the usual sense of commonplace, deadly danger, the possibility of a sudden onslaught and massacre, or something of the kind, which I saw impending, was positively welcome and composing. It pacified me, in fact, so much, that I did not raise an alarm.

"There was an agent buttoned up inside an ulster[1] and sleeping on a chair on deck within three feet of me. The yells had not awakened him; he snored very slightly; I left him to his slumbers and leaped ashore. I did not betray Mr. Kurtz — it was ordered I should never betray him — it was written I should be loyal to the nightmare of my choice. I was anxious to deal with this shadow by myself alone, — and to this day I don't know why I was so jealous of sharing with any one the peculiar blackness of that experience.

"As soon as I got on the bank I saw a trail — a broad trail through the grass. I remember the exultation with which I said to myself, 'He can't walk — he is crawling on all-fours — I've got him.' The grass was wet with dew. I strode rapidly with clenched fists. I fancy I had some vague notion of falling upon him and giving him a drubbing. I don't know. I had some imbecile thoughts. The knitting old woman with the cat obtruded herself upon my memory as a most improper person to be sitting at the other end of such an affair. I saw a row of pilgrims squirting lead in the air out of Winchesters held to the hip. I thought I would never get back to the steamer, and imagined myself living alone and unarmed in the woods to an advanced age. Such silly things — you know. And I remember I confounded the beat of the drum with the beating of my heart, and was pleased at its calm regularity.

---

1   ulster] long loose overcoat, worn by both sexes, originally made in Ulster, Ireland.

"I kept to the track though—then stopped to listen. The night was very clear; a dark blue space, sparkling with dew and starlight, in which black things stood very still. I thought I could see a kind of motion ahead of me. I was strangely cocksure of everything that night. I actually left the track and ran in a wide semicircle (I verily believe chuckling to myself) so as to get in front of that stir, of that motion I had seen—if indeed I had seen anything. I was circumventing Kurtz as though it had been a boyish game.

"I came upon him, and, if he had not heard me coming, I would have fallen over him, too, but he got up in time. He rose, unsteady, long, pale, indistinct, like a vapour exhaled by the earth, and swayed slightly, misty and silent before me; while at my back the fires loomed between the trees, and the murmur of many voices issued from the forest. I had cut him off cleverly; but when actually confronting him I seemed to come to my senses, I saw the danger in its right proportion. It was by no means over yet. Suppose he began to shout? Though he could hardly stand, there was still plenty of vigour in his voice. 'Go away—hide yourself,' he said, in that profound tone. It was very awful. I glanced back. We were within thirty yards from the nearest fire. A black figure stood up, strode on long black legs, waving long black arms, across the glow. It had horns—antelope horns, I think—on its head. Some sorcerer, some witch-man, no doubt: it looked fiend-like enough. 'Do you know what you are doing?' I whispered. 'Perfectly,' he answered, raising his voice for that single word: it sounded to me far off and yet loud, like a hail through a speaking-trumpet. If he makes a row we are lost, I thought to myself. This clearly was not a case for fisticuffs, even apart from the very natural aversion I had to beat that Shadow—this wandering and tormented thing. 'You will be lost,' I said—'utterly lost.' One gets sometimes such a flash of inspiration, you know. I did say the right thing, though indeed he could not have been more irretrievably lost than he was at this very moment, when the foundations of our intimacy were being laid—to endure—to endure—even to the end—even beyond.

"'I had immense plans,' he muttered irresolutely. 'Yes,' said I; 'but if you try to shout I'll smash your head with——' There was

not a stick or a stone near. 'I will throttle you for good,' I corrected myself. 'I was on the threshold of great things,' he pleaded, in a
voice of longing, with a wistfulness of tone that made my blood
run cold. 'And now for this stupid scoundrel——' 'Your success
in Europe is assured in any case,' I affirmed, steadily. I did not
want to have the throttling of him, you understand—and indeed
it would have been very little use for any practical purpose. I tried
to break the spell—the heavy, mute spell of the wilderness—that
seemed to draw him to its pitiless breast by the awakening of forgotten and brutal instincts, by the memory of gratified and monstrous passions. This alone, I was convinced, had driven him out
to the edge of the forest, to the bush, towards the gleam of fires,
the throb of drums, the drone of weird incantations; this alone
had beguiled his unlawful soul beyond the bounds of permitted
aspirations. And, don't you see, the terror of the position was not
in being knocked on the head—though I had a very lively sense
of that danger, too—but in this, that I had to deal with a being to
whom I could not appeal in the name of anything high or low. I
had, even like the niggers, to invoke him—himself—his own
exalted and incredible degradation. There was nothing either
above or below him, and I knew it. He had kicked himself loose
of the earth. Confound the man! he had kicked the very earth to
pieces. He was alone, and I before him did not know whether I
stood on the ground or floated in the air. I've been telling you
what we said—repeating the phrases we pronounced—but
what's the good? They were common everyday words—the
familiar, vague sounds exchanged on every waking day of life. But
what of that? They had behind them, to my mind, the terrific
suggestiveness of words heard in dreams, of phrases spoken in
nightmares. Soul! If anybody had ever struggled with a soul, I am
the man. And I wasn't arguing with a lunatic either. Believe me
or not, his intelligence was perfectly clear—concentrated, it is
true, upon himself with horrible intensity, yet clear; and therein
was my only chance—barring, of course, the killing him there
and then, which wasn't so good, on account of unavoidable noise.
But his soul was mad. Being alone in the wilderness, it had
looked within itself, and, by heavens! I tell you, it had gone mad. I
had—for my sins, I suppose—to go through the ordeal of look-

ing into it myself. No eloquence could have been so withering to one's belief in mankind as his final burst of sincerity. He struggled with himself, too. I saw it,—I heard it. I saw the inconceivable mystery of a soul that knew no restraint, no faith, and no fear, yet struggling blindly with itself. I kept my head pretty well; but when I had him at last stretched on the couch, I wiped my forehead, while my legs shook under me as though I had carried half a ton on my back down that hill. And yet I had only supported him, his bony arm clasped round my neck—and he was not much heavier than a child.

"When next day we left at noon, the crowd, of whose presence behind the curtain of trees I had been acutely conscious all the time, flowed out of the woods again, filled the clearing, covered the slope with a mass of naked, breathing, quivering, bronze bodies. I steamed up a bit, then swung downstream, and two thousand eyes followed the evolutions of the splashing, thumping, fierce river-demon beating the water with its terrible tail and breathing black smoke into the air. In front of the first rank, along the river, three men, plastered with bright red earth from head to foot, strutted to and fro restlessly. When we came abreast again, they faced the river, stamped their feet, nodded their horned heads, swayed their scarlet bodies; they shook towards the fierce river-demon a bunch of black feathers, a mangy skin with a pendent tail—something that looked like a dried gourd; they shouted periodically together strings of amazing words that resembled no sounds of human language; and the deep murmurs of the crowd, interrupted suddenly, were like the responses of some satanic litany.

"We had carried Kurtz into the pilot-house: there was more air there. Lying on the couch, he stared through the open shutter. There was an eddy in the mass of human bodies, and the woman with helmeted head and tawny cheeks rushed out to the very brink of the stream. She put out her hands, shouted something, and all that wild mob took up the shout in a roaring chorus of articulated, rapid, breathless utterance.

"'Do you understand this?' I asked.

"He kept on looking out past me with fiery, longing eyes, with a mingled expression of wistfulness and hate. He made no answer, but I saw a smile, a smile of indefinable meaning, appear on his colourless lips that a moment after twitched convulsively. 'Do I not?' he said slowly, gasping, as if the words had been torn out of him by a supernatural power.

"I pulled the string of the whistle, and I did this because I saw the pilgrims on deck getting out their rifles with an air of anticipating a jolly lark. At the sudden screech there was a movement of abject terror through that wedged mass of bodies. 'Don't! don't you frighten them away,' cried someone on deck disconsolately. I pulled the string time after time. They broke and ran, they leaped, they crouched, they swerved, they dodged the flying terror of the sound. The three red chaps had fallen flat, face down on the shore, as though they had been shot dead. Only the barbarous and superb woman did not so much as flinch, and stretched tragically her bare arms after us over the sombre and glittering river.

"And then that imbecile crowd down on the deck started their little fun, and I could see nothing more for smoke.

"The brown current ran swiftly out of the heart of darkness, bearing us down towards the sea with twice the speed of our upward progress; and Kurtz's life was running swiftly, too, ebbing, ebbing out of his heart into the sea of inexorable time. The manager was very placid, he had no vital anxieties now, he took us both in with a comprehensive and satisfied glance: the 'affair' had come off as well as could be wished. I saw the time approaching when I would be left alone of the party of 'unsound method.' The pilgrims looked upon me with disfavour. I was, so to speak, numbered with the dead. It is strange how I accepted this unforeseen partnership, this choice of nightmares forced upon me in the tenebrous land invaded by these mean and greedy phantoms.

"Kurtz discoursed. A voice! a voice! It rang deep to the very last. It survived his strength to hide in the magnificent folds of eloquence the barren darkness of his heart. Oh, he struggled! he struggled! The wastes of his weary brain were haunted by shadowy images now — images of wealth and fame revolving obsequiously round his unextinguishable gift of noble and lofty expression. My Intended, my station, my career, my ideas — these were the subjects for the occasional utterances of elevated sentiments. The shade of the original Kurtz frequented the bedside of the hollow sham, whose fate it was to be buried presently in the mould of primeval earth. But both the diabolic love and the unearthly hate of the mysteries it had penetrated fought for the possession of that soul satiated with primitive emotions, avid of lying fame, of sham distinction, of all the appearances of success and power.

"Sometimes he was contemptibly childish. He desired to have kings meet him at railway-stations on his return from some ghastly Nowhere, where he intended to accomplish great things. 'You show them you have in you something that is really profitable, and then there will be no limits to the recognition of your ability,' he would say. 'Of course you must take care of the motives—right motives—always.' The long reaches that were like one and the same reach, monotonous bends that were exactly alike, slipped past the steamer with their multitude of secular[1] trees looking patiently after this grimy fragment of another world, the forerunner of change, of conquest, of trade, of massacres, of blessings. I looked ahead—piloting. 'Close the shutter,' said Kurtz suddenly one day; 'I can't bear to look at this.' I did so. There was a silence. 'Oh, but I will wring your heart yet!' he cried at the invisible wilderness.

"We broke down—as I had expected—and had to lie up for repairs at the head of an island. This delay was the first thing that shook Kurtz's confidence. One morning he gave me a packet of papers and a photograph—the lot tied together with a shoestring. 'Keep this for me,' he said. 'This noxious fool' (meaning the manager) 'is capable of prying into my boxes when I am not looking.' In the afternoon I saw him. He was lying on his back with closed eyes, and I withdrew quietly, but I heard him mutter, 'Live rightly, die, die ...' I listened. There was nothing more. Was he rehearsing some speech in his sleep, or was it a fragment of a phrase from some newspaper article? He had been writing for the papers and meant to do so again, 'for the furthering of my ideas. It's a duty.'

"His was an impenetrable darkness. I looked at him as you peer down at a man who is lying at the bottom of a precipice where

---

1 secular] centuries old.

the sun never shines. But I had not much time to give him, because I was helping the engine-driver to take to pieces the leaky cylinders, to straighten a bent connecting-rod, and in other such matters. I lived in an infernal mess of rust, filings, nuts, bolts, spanners, hammers, ratchet-drills—things I abominate, because I don't get on with them. I tended the little forge we fortunately had aboard; I toiled wearily in a wretched scrap-heap—unless I had the shakes too bad to stand.

"One evening coming in with a candle I was startled to hear him say a little tremulously, 'I am lying here in the dark waiting for death.' The light was within a foot of his eyes. I forced myself to murmur, 'Oh, nonsense!' and stood over him as if transfixed.

"Anything approaching the change that came over his features I have never seen before, and hope never to see again. Oh, I wasn't touched. I was fascinated. It was as though a veil had been rent. I saw on that ivory face the expression of sombre pride, of ruthless power, of craven terror—of an intense and hopeless despair. Did he live his life again in every detail of desire, temptation, and surrender during that supreme moment of complete knowledge? He cried in a whisper at some image, at some vision—he cried out twice, a cry that was no more than a breath—

"'The horror! The horror!'

"I blew the candle out and left the cabin. The pilgrims were dining in the mess-room, and I took my place opposite the manager, who lifted his eyes to give me a questioning glance, which I successfully ignored. He leaned back, serene, with that peculiar smile of his sealing the unexpressed depths of his meanness. A continuous shower of small flies streamed upon the lamp, upon the cloth, upon our hands and faces. Suddenly the manager's boy put his insolent black head in the doorway, and said in a tone of scathing contempt—

"'Mistah Kurtz—he dead.'

"All the pilgrims rushed out to see. I remained, and went on with my dinner. I believe I was considered brutally callous. However, I did not eat much. There was a lamp in there—light, don't you know—and outside it was so beastly, beastly dark. I went no more near the remarkable man who had pronounced a judgment upon the adventures of his soul on this earth. The voice was gone. What else had been there? But I am of course aware that next day the pilgrims buried something in a muddy hole.

"And then they very nearly buried me.

"However, as you see, I did not go to join Kurtz there and then. I did not. I remained to dream the nightmare out to the end, and to show my loyalty to Kurtz once more. Destiny. My destiny! Droll thing life is — that mysterious arrangement of merciless logic for a futile purpose. The most you can hope from it is some knowledge of yourself — that comes too late — a crop of unextinguishable regrets. I have wrestled with death. It is the most unexciting contest you can imagine. It takes place in an impalpable grayness, with nothing underfoot, with nothing around, without spectators, without clamour, without glory, without the great desire of victory, without the great fear of defeat, in a sickly atmosphere of tepid scepticism, without much belief in your own right, and still less in that of your adversary. If such is the form of ultimate wisdom, then life is a greater riddle than some of us think it to be. I was within a hair's-breadth of the last opportunity for pronouncement, and I found with humiliation that probably I would have nothing to say. This is the reason why I affirm that Kurtz was a remarkable man. He had something to say. He said it. Since I had peeped over the edge myself, I understand better the meaning of his stare, that could not see the flame of the candle, but was wide enough to embrace the whole universe, piercing enough to penetrate all the hearts that beat in the darkness. He had summed up — he had judged. 'The horror!' He was a remarkable man. After all, this was the expression of some sort of belief; it had candour, it had conviction, it had a vibrating note of revolt in its whisper, it had the appalling face of a glimpsed truth — the strange commingling of desire and hate. And it is not my own extremity I remember best — a vision of grayness without form filled with physical pain, and a careless contempt for the evanescence of all things — even of this pain itself. No! It is his extremity that I seem to have lived through. True, he had made that last stride, he had stepped over the edge, while I had been permitted to draw back my hesitating foot. And perhaps in this is the whole difference; perhaps all the wisdom, and all truth, and all sincerity, are just compressed into that inappreciable moment of time in which we step over the threshold of the invisible. Perhaps! I like to think my summing-up would not have been a word of careless contempt. Better his cry — much better. It was an affirmation, a moral victory paid for by innumerable defeats, by abominable terrors, by abominable satisfactions. But it was a victory! That is why I have remained loyal to Kurtz to the last, and even beyond, when a long time after I heard once more, not his own voice, but the echo of his magnificent eloquence thrown to me from a soul as translucently pure as a cliff of crystal.

"No, they did not bury me, though there is a period of time which I remember mistily, with a shuddering wonder, like a passage through some inconceivable world that had no hope in it and no desire. I found myself back in the sepulchral city resenting the sight of people hurrying through the streets to filch a little money from each other, to devour their infamous cookery, to gulp their unwholesome beer, to dream their insignificant and silly dreams. They trespassed upon my thoughts. They were intruders whose knowledge of life was to me an irritating pretence, because I felt so sure they could not possibly know the things I knew. Their bearing, which was simply the bearing of commonplace individuals going about their business in the assurance of perfect safety, was offensive to me like the outrageous flauntings of folly in the face of a danger it is unable to comprehend. I had no particular desire to enlighten them, but I had some difficulty in restraining myself from laughing in their faces, so full of stupid importance. I daresay I was not very well at that time. I tottered about the streets — there were various affairs to settle — grinning bitterly at perfectly respectable persons. I admit my behaviour was inexcusable, but then my temperature was seldom normal in these days. My dear aunt's endeavours to 'nurse up my strength' seemed altogether beside the mark. It was not my strength that wanted nursing, it was my imagination that wanted soothing. I kept the bundle of papers given me by Kurtz, not knowing exactly what to do with it. His mother had died lately, watched over, as I was told, by his Intended. A clean-shaved man, with an official manner and wearing gold-rimmed spectacles, called on me one day and made inquiries, at first circuitous, afterwards suavely pressing, about what he was pleased to denominate certain 'documents.' I was not surprised, because I had had two rows with the manager on the subject out there. I had refused to give up the smallest scrap out of that package, and I took the same attitude with the spectacled man. He became darkly menacing at last, and with much heat argued that the Company had the right to every bit of information about its 'territories.' And said he, 'Mr. Kurtz's knowledge of unexplored regions must have been necessarily extensive and peculiar—owing to his great abilities and to the deplorable circumstances in which he had been placed: therefore——' I assured him Mr. Kurtz's knowledge, however extensive, did not bear upon the problems of commerce or administration. He invoked then the name of science. 'It would be an incalculable loss if,' etc., etc. I offered him the report on the 'Suppression of Savage Customs,' with the postscriptum torn off. He took it up eagerly, but ended by sniffing at it with an air of contempt. 'This is not what we had a right to expect,' he remarked. 'Expect nothing else,' I said. 'There are only private letters.' He withdrew upon some threat of legal proceedings, and I saw him no more; but another fellow, calling himself Kurtz's cousin, appeared two days later, and was anxious to hear all the details about his dear relative's last moments. Incidentally he gave me to understand that Kurtz had been essentially a great musician. 'There was the making of an immense success,' said the man, who was an organist, I believe, with lank gray hair flowing over a greasy coat-collar. I had no reason to doubt his statement; and to this day I am unable to say what was Kurtz's profession, whether he ever had any—which was the greatest of his talents. I had taken him for a painter who wrote for the papers, or else for a journalist who could paint—but even the cousin (who took snuff during the interview) could not tell me what he had been— exactly. He was a universal genius—on that point I agreed with the old chap, who thereupon blew his nose noisily into a large cotton handkerchief and withdrew in senile agitation, bearing off some family letters and memoranda without importance. Ultimately a journalist anxious to know something of the fate of his 'dear colleague' turned up. This visitor informed me Kurtz's proper sphere ought to have been politics 'on the popular side.' He had furry straight eyebrows, bristly hair cropped short, an eyeglass on a broad ribbon, and, becoming expansive, confessed his opinion that Kurtz really couldn't write a bit—'but heavens! how that man could talk. He electrified large meetings. He had faith—don't you see?—he had the faith. He could get himself to believe anything—anything. He would have been a splendid leader of an extreme party.' 'What party?' I asked. 'Any party,' answered the other. 'He was an—an—extremist.' Did I not think so? I assented. Did I know, he asked, with a sudden flash of curiosity, 'what it was that had induced him to go out there?' 'Yes,' said I, and forthwith handed him the famous Report for publication, if he thought fit. He glanced through it hurriedly, mumbling all the time, judged 'it would do,' and took himself off with this plunder.

"Thus I was left at last with a slim packet of letters and the girl's portrait. She struck me as beautiful—I mean she had a beautiful expression. I know that the sunlight can be made to lie, too, yet one felt that no manipulation of light and pose could have conveyed the delicate shade of truthfulness upon those features. She seemed ready to listen without mental reservation, without suspicion, without a thought for herself. I concluded I would go and give her back her portrait and those letters myself. Curiosity? Yes; and also some other feeling perhaps. All that had been Kurtz's had passed out of my hands: his soul, his body, his station, his plans, his ivory, his career. There remained only his memory and his Intended—and I wanted to give that up, too, to the past, in a way—to surrender personally all that remained of him with me to that oblivion which is the last word of our common fate. I don't defend myself. I had no clear perception of what it was I really wanted. Perhaps it was an impulse of unconscious loyalty, or the fulfilment of one of these ironic necessities that lurk in the facts of human existence. I don't know. I can't tell. But I went.

"I thought his memory was like the other memories of the dead that accumulate in every man's life—a vague impress on the brain of shadows that had fallen on it in their swift and final passage; but before the high and ponderous door, between the tall houses of a street as still and decorous as a well-kept alley in a cemetery, I had a vision of him on the stretcher, opening his mouth voraciously, as if to devour all the earth with all its mankind. He lived then before me; he lived as much as he had ever lived—a shadow insatiable of splendid appearances, of frightful realities; a shadow darker than the shadow of the night, and draped nobly in the folds of a gorgeous eloquence. The vision seemed to enter the house with me—the stretcher, the phantom-bearers, the wild crowd of obedient worshippers, the gloom of the forests, the glitter of the reach between the murky bends, the beat of the drum, regular and muffled like the beating of a heart—the heart of a conquering darkness. It was a moment of triumph for the wilderness, an invading and vengeful rush which, it seemed to me, I would have to keep back alone for the salvation of another soul. And the memory of what I had heard him say afar there, with the horned shapes stirring at my back, in the glow of fires, within the patient woods, those broken phrases came back to me, were heard again in their ominous and terrifying simplicity. I remembered his abject pleading, his abject threats, the colossal scale of his vile desires, the meanness, the torment, the tempestuous anguish of his soul. And later on I seemed to see his collected languid manner, when he said one day, 'This lot of ivory now is really mine. The Company did not pay for it. I collected it myself at a very great personal risk. I am afraid they will try to claim it as theirs though. H'm. It is a difficult case. What do you think I ought to do—resist? Eh? I want no more than justice.'... He wanted no more than justice—no more than justice. I rang the bell before a mahogany door on the first floor, and while I waited he seemed to stare at me out of the glassy panel—stare with that wide and immense stare embracing, condemning, loathing all the universe. I seemed to hear the whispered cry, 'The horror! The horror!'

"The dusk was falling. I had to wait in a lofty drawing-room with three long windows from floor to ceiling that were like three luminous and bedraped columns. The bent gilt legs and backs of the furniture shone in indistinct curves. The tall marble fireplace had a cold and monumental whiteness. A grand piano stood massively in a corner; with dark gleams on the flat surfaces like a sombre and polished sarcophagus. A high door opened—closed. I rose.

"She came forward, all in black, with a pale head, floating towards me in the dusk. She was in mourning. It was more than a year since his death, more than a year since the news came; she seemed as though she would remember and mourn for ever. She took both my hands in hers and murmured, 'I had heard you were coming.' I noticed she was not very young—I mean not girlish. She had a mature capacity for fidelity, for belief, for suffering. The room seemed to have grown darker, as if all the sad light of the cloudy evening had taken refuge on her forehead. This fair hair, this pale visage, this pure brow, seemed surrounded by an ashy halo from which the dark eyes looked out at me. Their glance was guileless, profound, confident, and trustful. She carried her sorrowful head as though she were proud of that sorrow, as though she would say, I—I alone know how to mourn for him as he deserves. But while we were still shaking hands, such a look of awful desolation came upon her face that I perceived she was one of those creatures that are not the playthings of Time. For her he had died only yesterday. And, by Jove! the impression was so powerful that for me, too, he seemed to have died only yesterday—nay, this very minute. I saw her and him in the same instant of time—his death and her sorrow—I saw her sorrow in the very moment of his death. Do you understand? I saw them together—I heard them together. She had said, with a deep catch of the breath, 'I have survived' while my strained ears seemed to hear distinctly, mingled with her tone of despairing regret, the summing up whisper of his eternal condemnation. I asked myself what I was doing there, with a sensation of panic in my heart as though I had blundered into a place of cruel and absurd mysteries not fit for a human being to behold. She motioned me to a chair. We sat down. I laid the packet gently on the little table, and she put her hand over it.... 'You knew him well,' she murmured, after a moment of mourning silence.

"'Intimacy grows quickly out there,' I said, 'I knew him as well as it is possible for one man to know another.'

"'And you admired him,' she said. 'It was impossible to know him and not to admire him. Was it?'

"'He was a remarkable man,' I said, unsteadily. Then before the appealing fixity of her gaze, that seemed to watch for more words on my lips, I went on, 'It was impossible not to——'

"'Love him,' she finished eagerly, silencing me into an appalled dumbness. 'How true! how true! But when you think that no one knew him so well as I! I had all his noble confidence. I knew him best.'

"'You knew him best,' I repeated. And perhaps she did. But with every word spoken the room was growing darker, and only her forehead, smooth and white, remained illumined by the unextinguishable light of belief and love.

"'You were his friend,' she went on. 'His friend,' she repeated, a little louder. 'You must have been, if he had given you this, and sent you to me. I feel I can speak to you—and oh! I must speak. I want you—you who have heard his last words—to know I have been worthy of him.... It is not pride.... Yes! I am proud to know I understood him better than any one on earth—he told me so himself. And since his mother died I have had no one—no one—to—to——'

"I listened. The darkness deepened. I was not even sure whether he had given me the right bundle. I rather suspect he wanted me to take care of another batch of his papers which, after his death, I saw the manager examining under the lamp. And the girl talked, easing her pain in the certitude of my sympathy; she talked as thirsty men drink. I had heard that her engagement with Kurtz had been disapproved by her people. He wasn't rich enough or something. And indeed I don't know whether he had not been a pauper all his life. He had given me some reason to infer that it was his impatience of comparative poverty that drove him out there.

"'... Who was not his friend who had heard him speak once?' she was saying. 'He drew men towards him by what was best in them.' She looked at me with intensity. 'It is the gift of the great,' she went on, and the sound of her low voice seemed to have the accompaniment of all the other sounds, full of mystery, desolation, and sorrow, I had ever heard—the ripple of the river, the soughing of the trees swayed by the wind, the murmurs of the crowds, the faint ring of incomprehensible words cried from afar, the whisper of a voice speaking from beyond the threshold of an eternal darkness. 'But you have heard him! You know!' she cried.

"'Yes, I know,' I said with something like despair in my heart, but bowing my head before the faith that was in her, before that great and saving illusion that shone with an unearthly glow in the darkness, in the triumphant darkness from which I could not have defended her—from which I could not even defend myself.

"'What a loss to me—to us!' she corrected herself with beautiful generosity; then added in a murmur, 'To the world.' By the last gleams of twilight I could see the glitter of her eyes, full of tears—of tears that would not fall.

"'I have been very happy—very fortunate—very proud,' she went on. 'Too fortunate. Too happy for a little while. And now I am unhappy for—for life.'

"She stood up; her fair hair seemed to catch all the remaining light in a glimmer of gold. I rose, too.

"'And of all this,' she went on, mournfully, 'of all his promise, and of all his greatness, of his generous mind, of his noble heart, nothing remains—nothing but a memory. You and I——'

"'We shall always remember him,' I said, hastily.

"'No!' she cried. 'It is impossible that all this should be lost—that such a life should be sacrificed to leave nothing—but sorrow. You know what vast plans he had. I knew of them, too—I could not perhaps understand—but others knew of them. Something must remain. His words, at least, have not died.'

"'His words will remain,' I said.

"'And his example,' she whispered to herself. 'Men looked up to him—his goodness shone in every act. His example——'

"'True,' I said; 'his example, too. Yes, his example. I forgot that.'

"'But I do not. I cannot—I cannot believe—not yet. I cannot believe that I shall never see him again, that nobody will see him again, never, never, never.'

"She put out her arms as if after a retreating figure, stretching them back and with clasped pale hands across the fading and narrow sheen of the window. Never see him! I saw him clearly enough then. I shall see this eloquent phantom as long as I live, and I shall see her, too, a tragic and familiar Shade, resembling in this gesture another one, tragic also, and bedecked with powerless charms, stretching bare brown arms over the glitter of the infernal stream, the stream of darkness. She said suddenly very low, 'He died as he lived.'

"'His end,' said I, with dull anger stirring in me, 'was in every way worthy of his life.'

"'And I was not with him,' she murmured. My anger subsided before a feeling of infinite pity.

"'Everything that could be done——' I mumbled.

"'Ah, but I believed in him more than any one on earth—more than his own mother, more than—himself. He needed me! Me! I would have treasured every sigh, every word, every sign, every glance.'

"I felt like a chill grip on my chest. 'Don't,' I said, in a muffled voice.

"'Forgive me. I—I—have mourned so long in silence—in silence…. You were with him—to the last? I think of his loneliness. Nobody near to understand him as I would have understood. Perhaps no one to hear….'

"'To the very end,' I said, shakily. 'I heard his very last words….' I stopped in a fright.

"'Repeat them,' she murmured in a heart-broken tone. 'I want—I want—something—something—to—to live with.'

"I was on the point of crying at her, 'Don't you hear them?' The dusk was repeating them in a persistent whisper all around us, in a whisper that seemed to swell menacingly like the first whisper of a rising wind. 'The horror! the horror!'

"'His last word—to live with,' she insisted. 'Don't you understand I loved him—I loved him—I loved him!'

"I pulled myself together and spoke slowly.

"'The last word he pronounced was—your name.'

"I heard a light sigh and then my heart stood still, stopped dead short by an exulting and terrible cry, by the cry of inconceivable triumph and of unspeakable pain. 'I knew it—I was sure!'… She knew. She was sure. I heard her weeping; she had hidden her face in her hands. It seemed to me that the house would collapse before I could escape, that the heavens would fall upon my head. But nothing happened. The heavens do not fall for such a trifle. Would they have fallen, I wonder, if I had rendered Kurtz that justice which was his due? Hadn't he said he wanted only justice? But I couldn't. I could not tell her. It would have been too dark—too dark altogether...."

Marlow ceased, and sat apart, indistinct and silent, in the pose of a meditating Buddha. Nobody moved for a time. "We have lost the first of the ebb," said the Director, suddenly. I raised my head. The offing was barred by a black bank of clouds, and the tranquil waterway leading to the uttermost ends of the earth flowed sombre under an overcast sky—seemed to lead into the heart of an immense darkness.

Appendix A: Comments by Conrad

1. Conrad, from 'Geography and Some Explorers'

.... Education is a great thing, but Doctor Barth gets in the way. Neither will the monuments left by all sorts empire builders suppress for me the memory of David Livingstone. The words "Central Africa" bring before my eyes an old man with a rugged, kind face and a clipped, gray moustache, pacing wearily at the head of a few black followers along the reed-fringed lakes towards the dark native hut on the Congo headwaters in which he died, clinging in his very last hour to his heart's unappeased desire for the sources of the Nile.

That passion had changed him in his last days from a great explorer into a restless wanderer refusing to go home any more. From his exalted place among the blessed of militant geography and with his memory enshrined in Westminster Abbey, he can well afford to smile without bitterness at the fatal delusion of his exploring days, a notable European figure and the most venerated perhaps of all the objects of my early geographical enthusiasm.

Once only did that enthusiasm expose me to the derision of my schoolboy chums. One day, putting my finger on a spot in the very middle of the then white heart of Africa, I declared that some day I would go there. My chums' chaffing was perfectly justifiable. I myself was ashamed of having been betrayed into mere vapouring. Nothing was further from my wildest hopes. Yet it is fact that, about eighteen years afterwards, a wretched little stern-wheel steamboat I commanded lay moored to the bank of an African river.

Everything was dark under the stars. Every other white man on board was asleep. I was glad to be alone on deck, smoking the pipe of peace after an anxious day. The subdued thundering mutter of the Stanley Falls hung in the heavy night air of the last navigable reach of the Upper Congo, while no more than ten miles away, in Reshid's camp just above the Falls, the yet unbroken power of the Congo Arabs slumbered uneasily. Their day was over. Away in the middle of the stream, on a little island nestling all black in the foam of the broken water, a solitary little light glimmered feebly, and I said to myself with awe, "This is the very spot of my boyish boast."

A great melancholy descended on me. Yes, this was the very spot. But there was no shadowy friend to stand by my side in the night of the enormous wilderness, no great haunting memory, but only the unholy recollection of a prosaic newspaper "stunt" and the distasteful knowledge of the vilest scramble for loot that ever disfigured the history of human conscience and geographical exploration. What an end to the idealized realities of a boy's daydreams! I wondered what I was doing there, for indeed it was only an unforeseen episode, hard to believe in now, in my seaman's life. Still, the fact remains that I have smoked a pipe of peace at midnight in the very heart of the African continent, and felt very lonely there.

But never so at sea. There I never felt lonely, because there I never lacked company.

[Source: Joseph Conrad, *Tales of Hearsay and Last Essays* (London: J.M. Dent, 1955) 16-7.]

2. From Conrad's Congo Diary

Arrived at Matadi on the 13th of June, 1890.

Mr. Gosse, chief of the station (O.K.) retaining us for some reason of his own.

Made the acquaintance of Mr. Roger Casement, which I should consider as a great pleasure under any circumstances and now it becomes a positive piece of luck. Thinks, speaks well, most intelligent and very sympathetic.

Feel considerably in doubt about the future. Think just now that my life amongst the people (white) around here cannot be very comfortable. Intend avoid acquaintances as much as possible.

Through Mr. R.C. have made the acquain^{ce} of Mr. Underwood, the Manager of the English Factory (Hatton & Cookson) in Kalla Kalla. Av^{ge} com^{al}—hearty and kind. Lunched there on the 21st.

24th. Gosse and R.C. gone with a large lot of ivory down to Boma. On G.['s] return intend to start up the river. Have been myself busy packing ivory in casks. Idiotic employment. Health good up to now.

Wrote to Simpson, to Gov. B., to Purd., to Hope, to Capt. Fround, and to Mar. Prominent characteristic of the social life here; people speaking ill of each other.

Saturday, 28th June. Left Matadi with Mr. Harou and a caravan of 31 men. Parted with Casement in a very friendly manner. Mr. Gosse saw us off as far as the State station.

First halt, M'poso. 2 Danes in Company.

Sund[ay], 29th. Ascent of Pataballa sufficiently fatiguing. Camped at 11 A.M. at Nsoke river. Mosquitos [always spelt thus].

Monday, 30th. to Congo da Lemba after passing black rocks. Long ascent. Harou giving up. Bother. Camp bad. Water far. Dirty. At night Harou better.

Tuesday, 1st July. Left early in a heavy mist, marching towards Lufu river. Part route through forest on the sharp slope of a high mountain. Very long descent. Then market place from where short walk to the bridge (good) and camp. V.G. Bath. Clear river. Feel well. Harou all right. 1st chicken, 2 P.[M.] No sunshine to-day.

Wednesday, 2nd July. Started at 5:30 after a sleepless night. Country more open. Gently undulating hills. Road good, in perfect order. (District of Lukungu.) Great market at 9.30. Bought eggs and chickens. Feel not well to-day. Heavy cold in the head. Arrived at 11 at Banza Manteka. Camped on the market place. Not well enough to call on the missionary. Water scarce and bad. Camp^g place dirty. 2 Danes still in Company.

Thursday, 3rd July. Left at 6 A.M. after a good night's rest. Crossed a low range of hills and entered a broad valley, or rather plain, with a break in the middle. Met an off^{er} of the State inspecting. A few minutes afterwards saw at a camp^g place the dead body of a Backongo. Shot? Horrid smell.

Crossed a range of mountains, running N.W.—S.E. by a low pass. Another broad flat valley with a deep ravine through the centre. Clay and gravel. Another range parallel to the first mentioned, with a chain of low foothills running close to it. Between the two came to camp on the banks of the Luinzono river. Camp^g place clean. River clear. Gov^t Zanzibari with register. Canoe. 2 Danes camp^g on the other bank. Health good.

General tone of landscape gray-yellowish (dry grass) with reddish patches (soil) and clumps of dark green vegetation scattered sparsely about. Mostly in steep gorges between the high mountains or in ravines cutting the plain.

Noticed Palma Christi—Oil Palm. Very straight, tall and thick trees in some Places. Name not known to me. Villages quite invisible. Infer their existence from calbashes [sic] suspended to palm trees for the "Malafu." Good many caravans and travellers. No women, unless on the market place.

Bird notes charming. One especially a flute-like note. Another, kind of "boom" ressembling [sic] the very distant baying of a hound. Saw only pigeons and few green parroquets. Very small and not many. No birds of prey seen by me.

Up to 9 A.M. sky clouded and calm. Afterwards gentle breeze from the Nth generally and sky clearing. Nights damp and cool. White mists on the hills up about half way. Water effects very beautiful this morning. Mists generally raising before sky clears.

Distance 15 miles. general direction N.N.E.—S.S.W.

Friday, 4th July. Left camp at 6 A.M. after a very unpleasant night. Marching across a chain of hills and then in a maze of hills. At 8.15 opened out into an undulating plain. Took bearings of a break in the chain of mountains on the other side. Bearing N.N.E. Road passes through that. Sharp ascents up very steep hills not very high. The higher mountains recede sharply and show a low hilly country. At 9:30 market place. At 10 passed. R. Lukanga and at 10:30 camped on the Mpwe R.

To-day's march. Direction N.N.E. ½. —N. Dist^{ce} 13 miles.

Saw another dead body lying by the path in an attitude of meditative repose.

In the evening three women, of whom one albino, passed our camp; horrid chalky white with pink blotches; red eyes; red hair; features very negroid and ugly. Moisquitos. At night when the moon rose heard shouts and drumming in distant villages. Passed a bad night.

Saturday, 5th July. Left at 6:15. Morning cool, even cold, and very damp. Sky densely overcast. Gentle breeze from N.E. Road through a narrow plain up to R. Kwilu. Swift flowing and deep, 50 yds. wide. Passed in canoes. After^{ds} up and down very steep hills intersected by deep ravines. Main chain of heights running mostly N.W.—S.E. or W. and E. at times. Stopped at Manyamba. Camp^g place bad—in hollow—water very indifferent. Tent set at 10:15. N.N.E. Dist^{ce} 12 m.

To-day fell into a muddy puddle—beastly! The fault of the man that carried me. After camp^g went to a small stream, bathed and washed clothes. Getting jolly well sick of this fun.

To-morrow expect a long march to get to Nsona, 2 days from Manyanga. No sunshine to-day.

Sunday 6th July. Started at 5:40. The route at first hilly, then, after a sharp descent, traversing a broad plain. At the end of it a large market place. At 10 sun came out. After leaving the market passed another plain, then, walking on the crest of a chain of hills, passed 2 villages and at 11 arrived at Nsona. Village invisible.

Direction about N.N.E. Distance 18 miles.

In this camp (Nsona) there is a good camp^g place. Shady, water far and not very good. This night no mosquitos owing to large fires, lit all round our tent. Afternoon very close: night clear and starry.

Monday, 7th July. Left at 6, after a good night's rest, on the road to Inkandu, which is some distance past Lukunga Govt. station. Route very accidented. Succession of round steep hills. At times walking along the crest of a chain of hills. Just before Lukunga our carriers took a wide sweep to the southward till the station bore Nth. Walking through long grass for 1½ hours. Crossed a broad river about 100 feet wide and 4 deep.

After another ½ hour's walk through manioc plantations in good order rejoined our route to the E^d of the Lukunga sta^{on}, walking along an undulating plain towards the Inkandu market on a hill. Hot, thirsty and tired. At 11 arrived on the m^{ket} place. About 200 people. Business brisk. No water; no cam^g place. After remaining for one hour left in search of resting place. Row with carriers. No water. At last about 1½ P.M. camped on an exposed hill side near a muddy creek. No shade. Tent on a slope. Sun heavy. Wretched.

Direction N.E. by N.—Distance 22 miles.

Night miserably cold. No sleep. Mosquitos.

Tuesday, 8th July. Left at 6 A.M. About ten minutes from camp left main Gov^t path for the Manyanga track. Sky overcast. Rode up and down all the time, passing a couple of villages. The country presents a confused wilderness of hills, landslips on their sides showing red. Fine effect of red hill covered in places by dark green vegetation. ½ hour before beginning the descent got a glimpse of the Congo. Sky clouded.

To-day's march—3 h. General direction N. by E. Dist^{ce} 9½ miles.

Arrived at Manyanga at 9 A.M. Received most kindly by Messrs. Heyn and Jaeger. Most comfortable and pleasant halt.

Stayed here till the 25. Both have been sick. Most kindly care taken of us. Leave with sincere regrets.

Friday, the 25th July, 1890. Left Manyanga at 2½ P.M. with plenty of hammock carriers. H. lame and not in very good form. Myself ditto but not lame. Walked as far as Mafiela and camped—2 h.

Saturday, 26th. Left very early. Road ascending all the time. Passed villages. Country seems thickly inhabited. At 11 arrived at large market place. Left at noon and camped at 1 P.M.

General direction E ½ N-W ½ S. Sun visible at 8 A.M. Very hot. Distance 18 miles.

Sunday, 27th. Left at 8 A.M. Sent luggage carriers straight on to Luasi, and went ourselves round by the Mission of Sutili. Hospitable reception by Mrs. Comber. All the missio. absent. The looks of the whole establishment eminently civilized and very refreshing to see after the lots of tumbled down hovels in which the State & Company agents are content to live. Fine buildings. Position on a hill. Rather breezy.

Left at 3 P.M. At the first heavy ascent met Mr. Davis, Miss., returning from a preaching trip. Rev. Bentley away in the south with his wife. This being off the road, no section given.

Distance traversed about 15 miles. gen. direction E.N.E.

At Luasi we get on again on to the Gov^t road.

Camped at 4½ P.M. with Mr. Heche in company. To-day no sunshine. Wind remarkably cold. Gloomy day.

Monday, 28th. Left camp at 6:30 after breakfasting with Heche. Road at first hilly. Then walking along the ridges of hill chains with valleys on both sides. The country more open and there is much more trees growing in large clumps in the ravines.

Passsed Nzungi and camped, 11, on the right bank of the Ngoma, a rapid little river with rocky bed. Village on a hill to the right.

General direction E.N.E.—Distance 14 miles.

· No sunshine. Gloomy cold day. Squalls.

Tuesday, 29th. Left camp at 7, after a good night's rest. Continuous ascent; rather easy at first. Crossed wooded ravines and the river Lunzadi by a very decent bridge. At 9 met Mr. Louette escorting a sick agent of the comp^y back to Matadi. Looking very well. Bad news from up the river. All the steamers disabled—one wrecked. Country wooded. at 10:30 camped at Inkissi.

General direction E.N.E.—Dist^ce 15 miles.

Sun visible at 6:30. Very warm day.

Inkissi River very rapid; is about 100 yards broad. Passage in canoes. Banks wooded very densely, and valley of the river rather deep, but very narrow.

To-day did not set the tent, but put up in Gov^t shimbek. Zanzibari in charge—very obliging. Met ripe pineapple for the first time. On the road to-day passed a skeleton tied up to a post. Also white man's grave—no name—heap of stones in the form of a cross. Health good now.

Wednesday, 30th. Left at 6 A.M. intending to camp at Kinfumu. Two hours sharp walk brought me to Nsona na Nsefe. Market. ½ hour after Harou arrived very ill with billious [*sic*] attack and fever. Laid him down in Gov^t shimbek.

Dose of ipec^a Vomiting bile in enormous quantities. At 11 gave him 1 gramme of quinine and lots of hot tea. Hot fit ending in heavy perspiration. At 2 P.M. put him in hammock and started for Kinfumu. Row with carriers all the way. Harou suffering much through the jerks of the hammock. Camped at a small stream. At 4 Harou better; fever gone.

General direction N.E. by E. ½ E. Distance 13 miles.

Up till noon sky clouded and strong N.W. wind very chilling. From 1 P.M. to 4 P.M. sky clear and very hot day. Expect lots of bother with carriers to-morrow. Had them all called and made a speech, which they did not understand. They promise good behaviour.

Thursday, 31st. Left at 6. Sent Harou ahead, and followed in ½ an hour.

Road presents several sharp ascents, and a few others easier but rather long. Notice in places sandy surface soil instead of hard clay as heretofore; think however that the layer of sand is not very thick and that the clay would be found under it. Great difficulty in carrying Harou. Too heavy—bother! Made two long halts to rest the carriers. Country wooded in valleys and on many of the ridges.

At 2:30 P.M. reached Luila at last, and camped on right bank. Breeze from S.W.

General direction of march about N.E. ½ E. Distance, est^d 16 miles.

Congo very narrow and rapid. Kinzilu rushing in. A short distance up from the mouth, fine waterfall. Sun rose red. From 9 A.M. infernally hot day. Harou very little better. Self rather seedy. Bathed. Luila about 60 feet wide. Shallow.

Friday, 1st of August, 1890. Left at 6:30 A.M. after a very indifferently passed night. Cold, heavy mists. Road in long ascents and sharp dips all the way to Mfumu Mbé. After leaving there, a long and painful climb up a very steep hill; then a long descent in Mfumu Kono, where a long halt was made. Left at 12:30 P.M. towards Nselemba. Many ascents. The aspect of the country entirely changed. Wooded hills with openings. Path almost all the afternoon thro' a forest of light trees with dense undergrowth.

After a halt on a wooded hillside, reached Nselemba at 4.10 P.M. Put up at Gov^t shanty. Row between the carriers and a man, stating himself in Gov^t employ, about a mat. Blows with sticks raining hard. Stopped it.

Chief came with a youth about 13 suffering from gun-shot wound in the head. Bullet entered about an inch above the the right eyebrow and came out a little inside the roots of the hair, fairly in the middle of the brow in a line with the bridge of the nose. Bone not damaged apparently. Gave him a little glycerine to put on the wound made by the bullet coming out.

Harou not very well. Mosquitos—frogs—beastly! Glad to see the end of this stupid tramp. Feel rather seedy. Sun rose red. Very hot day. Wind Sth.

General direction of march N.E. by N. Distance about 17 miles.

[Source: Richard Curle, ed., *Last Essays* (London: J.M. Dent, 1926) 159–71.]

3. Letter to Madame Poradowska

Kinshasa, 26 September 1890

Dearest and best of Aunts!

I received your three letters all at once on my return from Stanley Falls, where I went as supernumerary in the vessel *Roi des Belges* to learn the river. ★★★ My days here are dreary. Make no mistake about that! I am truly sorry to have come here. Indeed, I regret it bitterly. ★★★

Everything is repellent to me here. Men and things, but expecially men. And I am repellent to them, too. From the manager in Africa—who has taken the trouble of telling a good many people that I displease him intensely—down to the lowest mechanic, all have a gift for getting on my nerves; and consequently I am perhaps not as pleasant to them as I might be. The manager is a common ivory-dealer with sordid instincts who considers himself a merchant though he is only a kind of African shopkeeper. His name is Delcommune. He hates the English, and I am of course regarded as an Englishman here. I can hope for neither promotion nor increase of salary while he remains here. Moreover, he has said that he is but little bound here by promises made in Europe, so long as they are not in the contract. Those made me by M. Wauters are not. Likewise I can look forward to nothing, as I have no vessel to command. The new boat will be finished in June of next year, perhaps. In the meanwhile my status here is vague, and I have been having troubles because of this. So there you are!

As a crowning joy, my health is far from good. *Keep the secret for me,* but the truth is that in going up the river I had the fever four times in two months, and then at the Falls (its native country) I had an attack of dysentery lasting five days. I feel rather weak physically and a little bit demoralized, and upon my word I think I am homesick for the sea and long to look again on the plains of that salt-water which has so often cradled me, which has so many times smiled at me under the glittering sunshine of a beautiful day, which many times too has flung the threat of death in my face with a whirl of white foam whipped by the wind under a dark December sky. I regret having to miss all that. But what I regret most of all is having bound myself for three years. True, it is hardly likely I shall serve them out. Either those in authority will pick a German quarrel with me to ship me home (and on my soul I sometimes wish they would), or another attack of dysentery will send me back to Europe, if not into the other world, which last would be a final solution to all my troubles!

For four whole pages I have been talking about myself! I have said nothing of the delight with which I read your descriptions of men and things at home. Truly, while reading your dear letters I forgot Africa, the Congo, the black savages and white slaves (of whom I am one) who inhabit it. I was happy for an hour. Know that it is not a small thing (or an easy thing) to make a human being happy for a *whole* hour. You may well be proud of having done it. And so my heart goes out to you in a burst of gratitude and sincerest, deepest affection. When shall we meet again? Alas, meeting leads to parting, and the more often one meets, the more painful become the separations. Fatality.

While seeking a practical remedy for the disagreeable situation into which I have got myself, I have thought of a little plan—still pretty much up in the air—with which you might perhaps help me. It seems that this Company or another affiliated with it is going to have some ocean-going vessels, and even has one already. Probably that big (or fat?) banker who rules the roost at home will have a sizeable interest in the other Company. If my name could be submitted for the command of one of their ships (whose home-port will be Antwerp), I might on each voyage run off to Brussels for a day or two when you are there. That would be ideal! If they decided to call me home to take a command, I should of course bear the expense of my return passage. This is perhaps not a very practical idea, but if you return to Brussels during the winter you might find out through M. Wauters what is going on, mightn't you, dear little aunt. ★★★

I must close. I leave in an hour by canoe for Bamou, to select wood and have it cut to build the station here. I shall remain encamped in the forest two or three weeks, unless ill. I rather like that. Doubtless I can have a shot or two at buffalo or elephant. ★★★

[Source: Frederick R. Karl & Laurence Davies, eds., *The Collected Letters of Joseph Conrad, Vol. 1, 1861-1897* (Cambridge: CUP, 1983) 61-3.]

4. Conversations with Conrad as recollected by Edward Garnett

I agree with M. Jean-Aubry that Conrad's Congo experiences were the turning-point in his mental life and that its effects on him determined his transformation from a sailor to a writer. According to his emphatic declaration to me, in his early years at sea he had "not a thought in his head." "I was a perfect animal," he reiterated, meaning, of course, that he had reasoned and reflected hardly at all over all the varieties of life he had encountered. The sinister voice of the Congo with its murmuring undertone of human fatuity, baseness and greed had swept away the generous illusions of his youth, and had left him gazing into the heart of an immense darkness.

★ ★ ★

Great quickness of eye was one of Conrad's gifts. I remember while sitting one evening with him in the Café Royal I asked him, after a painted lady had brushed haughtily past our table, what he had specially noticed about her. "The dirt in her nostril," he replied instantly. On this acute sense rested his faculty of selecting the telling detail, an unconscious faculty, so he said. I remarked once of the first draft of *The Rescuer*, that as a seaman he must have noted professionally the details of the rainstorm at sea described in Chapter III. Conrad denied this, and asserted that all such pictures of nature had been stored up unconsciously in his memory, and that they only sprung into life when he took up the pen. That Conrad's memory had extraordinary wealth of observation to draw on I had an illuminating proof in *Heart of Darkness*. Some time before he wrote this story of his Congo experience he narrated it at length one morning while we were walking up and down under a row of Scotch firs that leads down to the Cearne. I listened enthralled while he gave me in detail a very full synopsis of what he intended to write. To my surprise when I saw the printed version I found that about a third of the most striking incidents had been replaced by others of which he had said nothing at all. The effect of the written narrative was no less sombre than the spoken, and the end was more consummate; but I regretted the omission of various scenes, one of which described the hero lying sick to death in a native hut, tended by an old negress who brought him water from day to day, when he had been abandoned by all the Belgians "She saved my life," Conrad said; "the white men never came near me." When on several occasions in those early years I praised his psychological insight he questioned seriously whether he possessed such a power and deplored the lack of opportunities for intimate observation that a sailor's life had offered him. On one occasion on describing to him a terrible family tragedy of which I had been an eye-witness, Conrad became visibly ill-humoured and at last cried out with exasperation: "Nothing of the kind has ever come my way! I have spent half my life knocking about in ships, only getting ashore between voyages. I know nothing, nothing! except from the outside. I have to guess at everything!" This was of course the artist's blind jealousy speaking, coveting the experiences he had not got, and certainly he could have woven a literary masterpiece out of the threads I held, had he known the actors.

[Source: "Introduction" to *Letters from Conrad 1895-1924* (London: The Nonesuch Press, 1928).]

5. Letter to William Blackwood, 31 December 1898.

.... It is a narrative after the manner of *youth* [sic] told by the same man dealing with his experience on a river in Central Africa. The *idea* in it is not as obvious as in *youth*—or at least not so obviously presented. I tell you all this, for tho' I have no doubts as to the *workmanship* I do not know whether the *subject* will commend itself to you for that particular number.

[Blackwood has invited Conrad to contribute to the thousandth number of *Blackwood's Magazine* ('Maga').]

The title I am thinking of is *'The Heart of Darkness'* but the narrative is not gloomy. The criminality of inefficiency and pure selfishness when tackling the civilising work on Africa is a justifiable idea. The subject is of our time distinctly—though not topically treated. It is a story as much as my [*An*] *Outpost of Progress* was but, so to speak, 'takes in' more—is a little wider—is less concentrated upon individuals.

[Source: William Blackburn, ed., *Joseph Conrad: Letters to William Blackwood and David S. Meldrum* (Durham: Duke UP, 1958) 36-7.]

6. Letter to R.B. Cunninghame Graham, 8 February 1899.

I am simply in the seventh heaven, to find you like the *H of D* so far. You bless me indeed. Mind you don't curse me by and by for the very same thing. There are two more instalments in which the idea is so wrapped up in secondary notions that You—even You!—may miss it. And also you must remember that I don't start with an abstract notion. I start with definite images and as their rendering is true some little effect is produced. So far the note struck chimes in with your convictions— mais après? There is an après. But I think that if you look a little into the episodes you will find in them the right intention though I fear nothing that is practically effective....

[Source: C. T. Watts, ed., *Joseph Conrad's Letters to R.B. Cunninghame Graham* (Cambridge: CUP, 1969) 116.]

7. Letter to William Blackwood, 31 May 1902.

I know exactly what I am doing. Mr George Blackwood's incidental remark in his last letter that the story is not fairly begun yet is in a measure correct but, on a large view, beside the point. For, the writing is as good as I can make it (first duty), and in the light of the final incident, the whole story in all its descriptive detail shall fall into its place — acquire its value and its significance. This is my method based on deliberate conviction. I've never departed from it. I call your own kind self to witness and I beg to instance Karain — Lord Jim (where the method is fully developed) — the last pages of Heart of Darkness where the interview of the man and the girl locks in — as it were — the whole 30000 words of narrative description into one suggestive view of a whole phase of life, and makes of that story something quite on another plane than an anecdote of a man who went mad in the Centre of Africa. And *Youth* itself (which I delight to know you like so well) exists only in virtue of my fidelity to the idea and the method.

[Source: William Blackburn, ed., *Joseph Conrad: Letters to William Blackwood and David S. Meldrum*, 154.]

8. Letter to Elsie Hueffer, 3 December 1902.

I ought to have answered your letter before this; but I have been plunged in a torpor so profound that even your attack on my pet Heart of Darkness could do no more than make me roll my eyes ferociously. Then for another day I remained prone revolving thoughts of scathing reply. At last — I arose and ...

Seriously — I don't know that you are wrong. I admit that your strictures are intelligible to me; and every criticism that is intelligible (a quality by no means common) must have some truth in it, if not the whole truth. I mean intelligible to the author of course. As I began by saying — yours is to me; therefore I, in a manner, bear witness to its truth, with (I confess) the greatest reluctance. And, of course, I don't admit the whole of your case. What I distinctly admit is the fault of having made Kurtz too symbolic or rather symbolic at all. But the story being mainly a vehicle for conveying a batch of personal impressions I gave the rein to my mental laziness and took the line of the least resistance. This is then the whole Apologia pro Vita Kurtzii — or rather for the tardiness of his vitality.

[Source: Frederick R. Karl & Laurence Davies eds., *The Collected Letters of Joseph Conrad*, vol.II, 1898-1902 (Cambridge: CUP, 1986) 461.]

9. Letter to Edward Garnett, 22 December 1902.

With my usual brutality I've neglected to express my feelings very much awakened by your review of *Youth*.

How nice they are I renounce to tell. My dearest fellow you quite overcome me. And your brave attempt to grapple with the foggishness of *H. of D*, to explain what I myself have tried to shape blindfold, as it were, has touched me profoundly. You are the Seer of the Figures in the Carpet....

The ruck takes its tone from you. You know how to serve a friend! I notice the reviews as they come in since your article. *Youth* is an epic: that's settled. And the *H. of D*. is this and that and the other thing—they aren't so positive because in this case they aren't intelligent enough to catch on to your indications. But anyhow it's a high water mark. If it hadn't been for you it would have been, dreary bosh—an incoherent bogie tale. Yes. That note too was sounded only you came just in time....

[Source: Edward Garnett, ed., *Letters from Conrad 1895 to 1924* (London: Nonesuch Press, 1928) 187-88.]

Appendix B: Contemporary Reviews

1. Edward Garnett (unsigned)

The publication in volume form of Mr. Conrad's three stories, "Youth," "Heart of Darkness," "The End of the Tether," is one of the events of the literary year. These stories are an achievement in art which will materially advance his growing reputation. Of the stories, "Youth" may be styled a modern English epic of the Sea. "The End of the Tether" is a study of an old sea captain who, at the end of forty years' trade exploration of the Southern seas, finding himself dispossessed by the perfected routine of the British empire overseas he has helped to build, falls on evil times, and faces ruin calmly, fighting to the last. These two will be more popular than the third, "Heart of Darkness," "a study of the white man in Africa" which is most amazing, a consummate piece of artistic *diablerie*. On reading "Heart of Darkness" on its appearance in *Blackwood's Magazine* our first impression was that Mr. Conrad had, here and there, lost his way. Now that the story can be read, not in parts, but from the first page to the last at a sitting, we retract this opinion and hold "Heart of Darkness" to be the high-water mark of the author's talent....

"Heart of Darkness," to present its theme bluntly, is an impression, taken from life, of the conquest by the European whites of a certain portion of Africa, an impression in particular of the civilising methods of a certain great European Trading Company face to face with the "nigger." We say this much because the English reader likes to know where he is going before he takes art seriously, and we add that he will find the human life, black and white, in "Heart of Darkness" an uncommonly and uncannily serious affair. If the ordinary reader, however, insists on taking the subject of a tale very seriously, the artist takes his method of presentation more seriously still, and rightly so. For the art of "Heart of Darkness"—as in every psychological masterpiece—lies in the relation of the things of the spirit to the things of the flesh, of the invisible life to the visible, of the sub-conscious life within us, our obscure motives and instincts, to our conscious actions, feelings and outlook. Just as landscape art implies the artist catching the exact relation of a tree to the earth from which it springs, and of the earth to the sky, so the art of "Heart of Darkness" implies the catching of infinite shades of the white man's uneasy, disconcerted, and fantastic relations with the exploited barbarism of Africa; it implies the acutest analysis of the deterioration of the white man's *morale*, when he is let loose from European restraint, and planted down in the tropics as an "emissary of light" armed to the teeth, to make trade profits out of the "subject races." The weirdness, the brilliance, the psychological truth of this masterly analysis of two Continents in conflict, of the abysmal gulf between the white man's system and the black man's comprehension of its results, is conveyed in a rapidly rushing narrative which calls for close attention on the reader's part. But the attention once surrendered, the pages of the narrative are as enthralling as the pages of Dostoevsky's *Crime and Punishment*. The stillness of the sombre African forests, the glare of sunshine, the feeling of dawn, of noon, of night on the tropical rivers, the isolation of the unnerved, degenerating whites staring all day and every day at the Heart of Darkness which is alike meaningless and threatening to their own creed and conceptions of life, the helpless bewilderment of the unhappy savages in the grasp of their flabby and rapacious conquerors—all this is a page torn from the life of the Dark Continent—a page which has been hitherto carefully blurred and kept away from European eyes. There is no "intention" in the story, no *parti pris*, no prejudice one way or the other; it is simply a piece of art, fascinating and remorseless, and the artist is but intent on presenting his sensations in that sequence and arrangement whereby the meaning or the meaninglessness of the white man in uncivilised Africa can be felt in its really significant aspects....

[Source: "Mr. Conrad's New Book," *Academy and Literature* (6 December 1902) 606-07.]

2. Hugh Clifford, "The Art of Mr. Joseph Conrad"

To a small—a still inexplicably small—circle of readers the publication of a new book written by Mr. Joseph Conrad ranks as a notable event, an event the comparative infrequency of which makes it all the more remarkable in an age when many of our authors have an "output" as regular, and almost as copious, as a Welsh coal-mine. "Almayer's Folly," Mr. Conrad's first novel, appeared early in 1895, and "Youth," the most recent addition to his works, is only the fifth book which has come from his pen during the last eight years. That, as such matters are reckoned to-day, is slow production, and an examination of any one of the volumes which bear this author's name upon their title-pages will serve to convince that these books, at any rate, are *written*—really written—as are but few of the works with which each succeeding publishing season inundates us. It is not merely that by no conceivable effort of fancy can the reader conjure up a picture of Mr. Conrad shouting his "copy" into a phonograph, or dictating it to a breathless stenographer; nor is it only that his work is honourably distinguished by its author's care, sincerity, and conscientious determination to give the public naught save his best, though these things are manifest in every line. Much more is meant, for indeed Mr. Conrad's stories resemble nothing so nearly as some elaborate piece of mosaic. Each of them is made up of an immense number of minute atoms, one and all of which bear witness to the skill and finished workmanship brought to their fashioning, one and all of which, apart from their individual beauty, are essential to the whole whereof they form the parts, so that that whole, lacking any tiniest fragment, would be marred and incomplete. This is why Mr. Conrad's books, to be appreciated at their full worth, must not only be read, but must be read more than once. The mind of their author is so subtle, he has put into them so much thought, so much delicacy of touch, so much that is at once allusive and elusive, that at every reperusal some hitherto undetected nicety is revealed. And in this very fact, perhaps, is to be sought the secret not only of Mr. Conrad's success, but also of his failure. His success, within limits, has been undoubted; for his work cannot fail to make a deep impression upon every lover of literary technique, and to afford keen pleasure to all who are capable of prizing, as its rarity deserves, a creative and imaginative talent which in this case is surely not far removed from genius. On the other hand, however, the very refinements and subtleties inseparable from his habit of thought and literary method have caused his books to make but a faint appeal to the general public. Give a dog a bad name, and hang him; call a book "stiff reading," and let it go by the board! This, seemingly, has been the attitude of the majority of readers towards Mr. Conrad's works in the past. It remains to be seen whether his new book, "Youth, and Two other Stories," just published by Messrs. Blackwood (6s.), will succeed in effecting anything in the nature of a wholesale conversion.

It is to be feared that the chances in favour of any such result are not over great, for "Youth," it must be confessed, furnishes as much "stiff reading" as any of its predecessors. That is to say, the book makes a constant, insistent appeal to the intelligence of the reader: it cannot be taken up idly to while away an hour; it cannot be skimmed or skipped; it must be read word by word, sentence by sentence, paragraph by paragraph, if it is to create the impression which the author has designed to produce. Also, to be quite honest, the admission must be made that Mr. Conrad's style is occasionally difficult. It does not run in any well-worn groove, for its owner is no apostle of the obvious; to the casual reader it may at times appear to be laboured, even self-conscious. A closer study of it, however, should lead to the conviction that this style is individual, instinctive, moulded on no ready-made model; that it is the one and only mode of expression adapted to the purposes of its author, or indeed possible to him; that it is in no sense an affectation; and, moreover, that it is exactly suited to the subjects of which he treats.

Enough, perhaps, has been said concerning Mr. Conrad's manner, for though with him mere manner is of more account than with any writer of our time (Mr. Henry James alone excepted), his matter, after all, is of greater significance and of even higher value. "Description," said Byron at a time when his genius was at its ripest, "description is my forte"; and the same might be said with truth by Mr. Conrad. Description unquestionably is his forte, and the most remarkable of his gifts is the power which his strength in this direction gives him for the absolute creation of atmosphere. He is a realist in that he writes of a real world which he has seen for himself with his own eyes; but he rises superior to the trammels of ordinary realism because he has not only looked long and thoughtfully upon land and sea, so that he can write of them with the truth and certainty born of sure knowledge, but because also he has caught the very spirit of them, and has the art so to breathe it into his pages that his readers become imbued with it too. Those who have struggled round the Cape with Mr. Conrad on board the 'Narcissus' have felt the sting of the salt spray on their cheeks, the winds of all the world buffeting them; those who have wandered with him through the mazes of the Malay Archipelago have gasped and sweated in the stifling heat and the dense forests of tropical Asia, though in body they have never even touched the hem of the East; and those of us who know the lands of which he writes have been carried back to distant scenes with so much vividness that we have awakened with a shock of surprise to find the fogs of London gripping us by the throat and dimming our eyesight. But in no one of his books, in the opinion of the present writer, has Mr. Conrad displayed his peculiar genius with more triumphant success than in that which has just seen the light. It contains three stories—"Youth," "The Heart of Darkness," and "The End of the Tether"—all of which have appeared serially in the pages of *Blackwood's Magazine*, a publication that still maintains its ancient reputation for preferring good literature to names that look well upon the bills.

"The Heart of Darkness," the story which holds the central place in this enthralling book, has of set purpose been left to the last for mention, because to the present writer it makes a stronger appeal than anything which its author has yet written, and appears to him to represent Mr. Conrad at his very best. Space, however, forbids any detailed examination of the story. It is a sombre study of the Congo—the scene is obviously intended for the Congo, though no names are mentioned—in which, while the inefficiency of certain types of European "administrators" is mercilessly gibbeted, the power of the wilderness, of contact with barbarism and elemental men and facts, to effect the demoralisation of the white man is conveyed with marvellous force. The denationalisation of the European, the "going Fantee" of civilised man, has been treated often enough in fiction since Mr. Grant Allen wrote the story of the Rev. John Creedy, and before, but never has the "why of it" been appreciated by any author as Mr. Conrad here appreciates it, and never, beyond all question, has any writer till now succeeded in bringing the reason, and the ghastly unreason, of it all home to sheltered folk as does Mr. Conrad in this wonderful, this magnificent, this terrible study. Mr. Kurtz, the victim of this hideous obsession, the man whom the wilderness had "found out," on whom it had taken a terrible vengeance, to whom it had "whispered things about himself that he did not know, things of which he had no conception till he took counsel with this great solitude," and to whom "the whisper had proved irresistibly fascinating," makes his appearance very late in the story, and then only for a few moments. He is the climax, so to speak, up to which every word of the story has been leading, certainly, inevitably, from the very first; and this is how it comes to pass that when at last he is met with, the reader finds that he is utterly in accord with his surroundings,—in the innermost chamber of the Heart of Darkness.

It has not been possible in the space of a newspaper article to give more than the barest outline of Mr. Conrad's new book, and anything resembling a serious analysis of it is obviously out of the question. But it is hoped that enough may have been said to lead one or two readers, who else might have passed it by, to study the book for themselves. "I do not like work—no man does," says Mr. Conrad, speaking through the mouth of Marlow. "But I like what is in work,—the chance to find yourself. Your own reality—for yourself, not for others—what no other man can know. They can only see the mere show, and never can tell what it really means." That is profoundly true in the sense that a man's work always means far more to him than it can mean to any other living soul; but Mr. Conrad's work, at any rate, means very much to others, even to those who, to his thinking, can perhaps only "see the mere show."

[Source: *The Spectator* (29 November 1902) 827-28.]

3. "Mr. Conrad's New Book" (unsigned)

Mr. Joseph Conrad's latest volume, *Youth*, contains three stories, of which the one that gives the title is the shortest. This and the second one may be regarded as a kind of sequence. The third and longest, 'The End of the Tether,' is admirable, but in comparison with the others the tension is relaxed.... The other two, though not of such scope and design, are of the quality of *Lord Jim*—that is to say, they touch the high-water mark of English fiction and continue a great expression of adventure and romance. Both stories follow Mr. Conrad's particular convention; they are the outpourings of Marlow's experiences. It would be useless to pretend that they can be very widely read. Even to those who are most impressed an excitement so sustained and prolonged, in which we are braced to encounter so much that menaces and appals, must be something of a strain.

"Heart of Darkness" is, again the adventure of youth, an adventure more significant than the mere knockabout of the world. It is youth in the toils, a struggle with phantoms worse than the elements, 'a weary pilgrimage amongst hints for nightmares,' a destructive experience.

[gives an outline of the plot with quotations]

It must not be supposed that Mr. Conrad makes attack upon colonisation, expansion, even upon Imperialism. In no one is the essence of the adventurous spirit more instinctive. But cheap ideals, platitudes of civilisation are shrivelled up in the heat of such experiences. The end of this story brings us back to the familiar, reassuring region of common emotions, to the grief and constancy of the woman who had loved Kurtz and idealises his memory. It shows us how far we have travelled.

Those who can read these two stories in sympathy with Mr. Conrad's temperament will find in them a great expression of the world's mystery and romance. They show the impact upon an undaunted spirit of what is terrible and obscure; they are adventure in terms of experience; they represent the sapping of life that cannot be lived on easy terms. Mr. Conrad's style is his own—concentrated, tenacious, thoughtful, crammed with imaginative detail, breathless, yet missing nothing. Its grim earnestness bends to excursions of irony, to a casual humour, dry, subdued to its surroundings. Phrases strike the mind like lines of verse; we weary under a tension that is never slackened. He is one of the greatest of sea-writers and the most subjective of them. His storms are not the picturesque descriptions of gigantic phenomena, we see them in the "weary, serious faces," in the dreadful concentration of the actors. Mr. Conrad is intensely human and, we may add with some pride of fellowship, intensely modern. By those who seek for the finest expositions of the modern spirit "Youth" and "Heart of Darkness" cannot be neglected.

[Source: *Manchester Guardian* (10 December 1902) 3.]

4. "Youth" (unsigned)

Telling tales, just spinning yarns, has gone out of fashion since the novel has become an epitome of everything a man has to say about anything. The three stories in *Youth* by Joseph Conrad are in this reference a return to an earlier taste. The yarns are of the sea, told with an astonishing zest; and given with vivid accumulation of detail and iterative persistency of emphasis on the quality of character and scenery. The method is exactly the opposite of Mr. Kipling's. It is a little precious; one notes a tasting of the quality of phrases and an occasional indulgence in poetic rhetoric. But the effect is not unlike Mr. Kipling's. In the first story, "Youth," the colour, the atmosphere of the East is brought out as in a picture. The concluding scene of the "Heart of Darkness" is crisp and brief enough for Flaubert, but the effect—a woman's ecstatic belief in a villain's heroism—is reached by an indulgence in the picturesque horror of the villain, his work and his surroundings, which is pitiless in its insistence, and quite extravagant according to the canons of art. But the power, the success in conveying the impression vividly, without loss of energy is undoubted and is refreshing. "The End of the Tether," the last of the three, is the longest and best....

[Source: *The Times Literary Supplement* 48 (12 December 1902) 372.]

5. (Unsigned)

The art of Mr. Conrad is exquisite and very subtle. He uses the tools of his craft with the fine, thoughtful delicacy of a mediaeval clock-maker. With regard to his mastery of the *conte* opinions are divided, and many critics will probably continue to hold that his short stories are not short stories at all, but rather concentrated novels. And the contention is not unreasonable. In more ways than one Mr. Conrad is something of a law unto himself, and creates his own forms, as he certainly has created his own methods. Putting aside all considerations of mere taste, one may say at once that Mr. Conrad's methods command and deserve the highest respect, if only by reason of their scholarly thoroughness. One feels that nothing is too minute, no process too laborious for this author. He considers not material rewards, but the dignity of his work, of all work. He does not count the hours of labour or the weight of weariness involved in the production of a flawless page or an adequately presented conception; but he has the true worker's eye, the true artist's pitilessness, in the detection and elimination of the redundant word, the idle thought, the insincere idiom, or even for the mark of punctuation misplaced. The busy, boastful times we live in are not rich in such sterling literary merits as these; and for that reason we may be the more thankful to an author like Mr. Conrad for the loyalty which prevents his sending a scamped page to press.

A critical writer has said that all fiction may roughly be divided into two classes; that dealing with movement and adventure, and the other dealing with characterization, the analysis of the human mind. In the present, as in every one of his previous books, Mr. Conrad has stepped outside these boundaries, and made his own class of work as he has made his own methods. All his stories have movement and incident, most of them have adventure, and the motive in all has apparently been the careful analysis, the philosophic presentation, of phases of human character. His studious and minute drawing of the action of men's minds, passions, and principles forms fascinating reading. But he has another gift of which he himself may be less conscious, by means of which his other more incisive and purely intellectual message is translated for the proper understanding of simpler minds and plainer men. That gift is the power of conveying atmosphere, and in the exercise of this talent Mr. Conrad has few equals among our living writers of fiction. He presents the atmosphere in which his characters move and act with singular fidelity, by means of watchful and careful building in which the craftsman's methods are never obtrusive, and after turning the last page of one of his books we rise saturated by the very air they breathed. This is a great power, but, more or less, it is possessed by other talented writers of fiction. The rarity of it in Mr. Conrad lies in this, that he can surround both his characters and his readers with the distinctive atmosphere of a particular story within the limits of a few pages. This is an exceptional gift, and the more to be prized in Mr. Conrad for the reason that he shows some signs of growing over-subtle in his analysis of moods, temperaments, and mental idiosyncrasies. It is an extreme into which all artists whose methods are delicate, minute, and searching are apt to be led. We have at least one other analyst of temperament and mood in fiction whose minute subtlety, scrupulous restraint, and allusive economy of words resemble Mr. Conrad's. And, becoming an obsession, these characteristics tend to weary the most appreciative reader. With Mr. Conrad, however, these rather dangerous intellectual refinements are illumined always by a vivid wealth of atmosphere, and translated simply by action, incident, strong light and shade and distinctive colouring.... "The Heart of Darkness" is a big and thoughtful conception, the most important part of the book, as "The End of the Tether" is the most fascinating.

[Source: *Athenaeum* (20 December 1902) 824.]

6. "Some Stories by Joseph Conrad" (unsigned)

The three stories by Joseph Conrad in the volume called "Youth and Other Stories" are all of the sea, of strange lands and of abnormal human beings entrapped under abnormal conditions. The author's exceptional power is manifest in two directions: in his ability to portray extraordinary scenery and in his equal ability to impress a character upon the credulity of his readers. Although the adventures he describes are frequently little short of marvelous and are laid among scenes wholly alien to commonplace life, they are wrought into a tissue of truth so firm and so tough as to resist the keenest scepticism. The personages who move about the ships, thread unbroken forests, establish control over swarms of savages by means of the spoken word, lie and cheat, struggle and work, make money and lose it and talk interminably; these personages are sufficiently interesting in their various activities to lure one through many a patch of wordy underbrush to the welcome clearing where they are plainly to be seen. Their creator treats them with peculiar detachment. He wavers between the objective and the subjective method. Apparently he wishes to move swiftly along his line of adventure toward his termination but his progress frequently is checked by the attacks of analytical modification that overcome him at quite regular intervals. This entanglement of psychological with external phenomena is more or less wearying, as there is no very delicate adjustment between the mental and physical situations and we are conscious sometimes of wishing that we might be allowed to supply our own moralising. For example, the author might have pointed the path to us with a much greater economy of words, in such passages as the following culled at random from "Heart of Darkness"...

> Of course you may be too much of a fool to go wrong—too dull even to know you are being assaulted by the powers of darkness... your power of devotion, not to yourself, but to an obscure, backbreaking business.

These little speeches which occur at — to the reader in quest of happenings — the most inopportune moments when a ship is burning or a man is dying, are undeniably loquacious, although usually opposite enough. They sap one's vitality of mind and cast the shadow of dullness over what otherwise would be stimulating. Nevertheless, Mr. Conrad has been amazingly successful in managing to convey a sense of solidity and veracity. Not even his Kurtz, the man of impenetrable darkness of soul, is either a bloodless or an incredible figure. Like certain caricatures that in their fidelity to the main facts make ordinary portraiture unconvincing, these grotesque figures drive home to the imagination.

[Source: *New York Times Saturday Review of Books and Art* (4 April 1903) 224.]

7. *The Monthly Review* (unsigned)

A most depressing book is *Youth* … full of power, of life, of terrible adventure, of a kind of grim poetry. It seems to be etched rather than written; the relentless cruelty of nature to man, of man to natural man, is bitten in with an acid. The magic is all black magic — a sense of weird unholiness poisons the air. Strength and endurance are put to the torture; they emerge conquering, but with little joy of their conquest. Of the three heroes of these three stories, the first, as if in mockery of the title, is a man of sixty, and the last has seen sixty-five. The spirit of youth is in them yet; there lies the tragedy … There is in the author that sympathy with the very elements of emotion which distinguishes the mind of true, original force....

[Source: *The Monthly Review* (7 April 1903) 21-2.]

Appendix C: Historical Documents

1. Excerpt from Stanley's Diaries: Finding Livingstone

[Stanley's account of his discovery of Livingstone in 1871—a meeting in central Africa which still holds our imagination.]

But, during Susi's absence, the news had been conveyed to the Doctor that it was surely a white man that was coming, whose guns were firing, and whose flag could be seen; and the great Arab magnates of Ujiji— Mohammed bin Sali, Sayd bin Majid, Abid bin Suliman, Mohammed bin Gharib, and others—had gathered together before the Doctor's house, and the Doctor had come out from his veranda to discuss the matter and await my arrival.

In the meantime, the head of the Expedition had halted, and the kirangozi was out of the ranks, holding his flag aloft, and Selim said to me, "I see the Doctor, sir. Oh, what an old man! He has got a white beard." And I——what would I not have given for a bit of friendly wilderness, where, unseen, I might vent my joy in some mad freak, such as idiotically biting my hand, turning a somersault, or slashing at trees, in order to allay those exciting feelings that were well-nigh uncontrollable. My heart beats fast, but I must not let my face betray my emotions, lest it shall detract from the dignity of a white man appearing under such extraordinary circumstances.

So I did that which I thought was most dignified. I pushed back the crowds, and, passing from the rear, walked down a living avenue of people, until I came in front of the semicircle of Arabs, before which stood the "white man with the grey beard."

As I advanced slowly towards him I noticed he was pale, that he looked wearied and wan, that he had grey whiskers and moustache, that he wore a bluish cloth cap with a faded gold band on a red ground round it, and that he had on a red-sleeved waistcoat, and a pair of grey tweed trousers.

I would have run to him, only I was a coward in the presence of such a mob—would have embraced him, but that I did not know how he would receive me; so I did what moral cowardice and false pride suggested was the best thing—walked deliberately to him, took off my hat, and said:

"Dr. Livingstone, I presume?"

"Yes," said he, with a kind, cordial smile, lifting his cap slightly.

I replaced my hat on my head, and he replaced his cap, and we both grasped hands. I then said aloud:

"I thank God, Doctor, I have been permitted to see you."

He answered, " I feel thankful that I am here to welcome you."

[Source: Henry M. Stanley, *How I Found Livingstone: Travels, Adventures and Discoveries in Central Africa: Including Four Months' Residence with Dr. Livingstone; with a Memoir of Dr. Livingstone* (London: Sampson Low, Marston, Low and Searle, 1874 rev. ed.) 330-1.]

2. Excerpt from Stanley's Diaries: The Second Central African Expedition, 1874-1877

["In the undiscovered Africa of the last century, an explorer could still exercise the two functions proper to his craft. He could explore with a view to proving or disproving a theory—in Stanley's case that the Rivers Lualaba and Congo were one; and he could still have the exitement of discoving and the satisfaction of describing places and peoples that had never been seen by European eyes before." From the introduction to Richard Stanley & Alan Neane, eds., *The Exploration Diaries of H.M. Stanley* (London: William Kimber, 1961) vii.]

.... summoned the people to arms, who presently appeared with shields and spears to interrupt our descent.

For two hours we fought with them at the end of which, finding they had retired, we continued our descent as far as the Mikonju River. Mwana-Ntaba ends at the south bank of the Mikonju and the country of the Baswa tribe begins who soon manifested their aversion to strangers by challenging us and coming up from the islands in the Rapids to us. On rounding the point at the north bank of the Mikonju we soon saw the reason of their ferocity in the Rapids, which was an obstacle to delay us and to give them an opportunity to test our prowess and courage. We accepted the challenge after peace was refused, and a few rounds sent them flying. Near the Rapids on the right, bank we constructed a strong camp. Elephants very numerous by recent tracks. Slept undisturbed save by shrill weird cries of the lemur and gorilla.

January 4th:

Baswa Rapids [*re-named the First Cataract of the Stanley Falls*].

While engaged in making several coils of rope out of the lianes or con-
volvuli we were disturbed again by the Baswa who were again repelled,
while each successful shot was responded to with wild cries of surprise,
rage, and sorrow mixed. A small party was sent to survey the right bank
below, but the whole force of the river almost rushed with intense
impetuosity against the right bank which formed a deep bend, barring
all possibility of proceeding by the right branch and numerous wrecks of
canoes strewed along shore testified to the destructive force of the
waters. I then manned 2 double canoes and crossed above the Rapids to
the left bank along which ran a small stream though deep and but little
disturbed, which presently broke into numerous foamy streams among
rocky islands covered with mangrove, others with palms, bananas, and
fields of the fierce Baswa tribe. One small branch still continued its quiet
flow but presently this fell also rapidly over sheets of dark brown rock.

January 7th:

This morning continued our labours, and by noon we were all
embarked in our canoes and afloat once more. Descended cautiously
about 4 miles along the left bank, and landed at Cheandoah Island of the
Baswa tribe who had challenged us to war. Landed a force and captured
the Island after three shots! The suddenness of our arrival had completely upset their calculations and their spirit. We captured about 30 goats
and had an abundance of food, bananas, chickens, eggs with an immense
amount of native African booty consisting of spears, knives, shields, iron
wire, etc. We also captured a woman and child to whom we were
indebted for names of places and other local information, amongst
which we heard of a terrible tribe called the Bakumu Cannibals who
make a clean sweep of tribes such as the Wavinza, Mwana-Ntaba and
Baswa. They are armed with bows and arrows. We are told also that
they have heard of us and mean to see of what stuff we are made.

January 31st:

Voyage continues from Divari Island.

Today I thought I would try to pass one day without fighting, but just as
we left Divari Island we rounded a point where amplest preparations had
been made. They had been up all night with drums, building a palisade,
making charms, etc. Uganza and Irende opposite had also come up with
canoes which they had hidden behind our little island to demonstrate
when opportunity offered to our disadvantage. We therefore floated
quietly down by them, probably without a shot, had not a mischievous

fellow rose up and swayed his spear. He was hushed with one shot, and no more was attempted. We then thought it would be advisable to steer close to the islands and look resolutely away from the natives, but after passing Mawembe some distance, we were followed by six or seven canoes who pulled lustily after us and called out to others hidden behind the small island to advance and eat us. A few harmless shots allayed their rage for our flesh and we came down peacefully to camp on an uninhabited island 17 miles north-west of Mawembe.

The utmost vigilance is necessary each night to prevent theft of canoes and night surprises, for the natives are very capable of it. By day, also, for the islands are numerous and communications of alarm and war combinations rapid enough to excite admiration, by means of their enormous wooden drums which are heard at a great distance.

February 3rd:
.... Livingstone called floating down the Lualaba a foolhardy feat. So it is, and were I to do it again, I would not attempt [*it*] without 200 guns. The natives, besides being savage, ferocious to an extreme degree, are powerful and have means by land and water to exercise to great lengths their ferocity. I pen these lines with half a feeling that they will never be read by any other white person; still as I persist in continuing the journey, I persist in writing, leaving events and their disposal to an All-Wise Providence. If we shall suffer on this journey, we suffer for the injuries done to the tribes above by Mtagamoyo and his confederates, for they have made the name of the Wasambye synonymous with robbers and pirates.

Day and night we are pained with the dreadful drumming which announces our arrival and their fears of our purposes. We have no interpreter, and cannot make ourselves understood.

Either bank is equally powerful, to go from one side to the other is like jumping from the frying pan into the fire. It may be said truly that we are now "Running the gauntlet."

February 7th:
[*Rubunga.*] River called Ikuta Yacongo.
Thank God. An anxious day has terminated with tranquillity to a long disturbed mind. Twenty-six fights on this river have reduced my ammunition so low, and we were still so far from the coast, that I began to fear we should find ourselves hemmed by savage enemies without means of resistance.

We floated down the river from 6.30 a.m. to 11 a.m. among the islands, having previously solemnly addressed the men, told them we had no food; if natives would not sell, we should have to take it by force, or storming. Each gun, spear, and even knife was therefore made ready. At 11 a.m. we sighted the village of Rubunga. Floated steadily towards it. Three canoes came to meet us without the usual savage demonstrations. We welcomed this as a good sign but not understanding what they said, they ran away and shields and spears presently bristled along the banks. Arriving near, dropped anchor, showed copper rings, brass wire, red beads, shells. They were baits, but what suspense, how slow to bite at them. What patience! Men clamoured for food; Prudence whispered Patience. Natives were slow to adopt peace. We showed bananas and drew in our stomachs to illustrate their emptiness. Finally, they made signs for us to go to a small island opposite and they would bring us food. We went and we waited a couple of hours. We saw them packing goats, bananas, food, such things as we looked at with greedy eyes, in their canoes and paddling with them down river. Our men eyed them solemnly and murmured:"You see what fools we are to put trust in a heathen's word. The cunning devils only wanted us to give them time to hide their things. When we do assault the place, as we must do, there will be but little left to satisfy hunger."

"Well, my men," I said, "wait a little and if they do not come to us we will go to them and eat them."

At 1 p.m. we crossed over, savage at heart and desperately hungry, most of the men with the resolve to waste no words but to shoot and take the place and forage at will. The boat led the way as usual, but I saw the natives so clearly, they presented such easy targets that a blind man might have shot a dozen, that I relented, thinking it a pity to shoot people who took no pains to conceal themselves. Besides, their conduct, though somewhat distrustful was not to be compared with the arrogant savages we had run the gauntlet lately.

I told them in a mixture of Kiswahili, Kikusu and Kibaswa, that if they did not bring food, I must take it or we would die. They must sell it for beads, red, blue, or green, copper or brass wire or shells, or.... I drew significant signs across the throat. It was enough, they understood at once, and we hailed it heartily. To confirm their understanding, I threw them ashore a copper bracelet and a string of shells. They clapped hands, laughed, we hurrahed, made blood brotherhood, before we steered from the anchorage before the village and peace was concluded.

These natives outdo all I have seen for tattooing.

[Source: Richard Stanley & Alan Neane, eds., *The Exploration Diaries of H.M. Stanley* (London: William Kimber, 1961) 149-61.]

3. Excerpts from the Diaries of William G. Stairs: The "Emin Pasha" Congo Expedition with Stanley

15th April Up before 5:00 a.m., but the last of the column had not left camp till 6:30. The march today was a five-hour one, but I was rearguard and took six and one-half hours to get all the men in to camp.

Crossed two small and one fairly large river, the latter by means of a long bridge. Saw the Congo glittering in the distance, running between two walls of solid rock. Came upon some natives holding market on the side of the track. Most of them ran away as the Zanzibaris came up. They are very much afraid of our men and well so, for a greater crowd of stealing ruffians it would be hard to find. The natives had bananas, fish, beans, roots, and various things for sale for which they took brass wire and handkerchiefs as payment.

Close to the market impaled on a high pole we saw the dried up remains of a native who had killed one of his tribe in the market place and suffered for it by being impaled as we found him. We also saw a native bird trap set ready for use. This consisted of nooses made of fibres hung down from a vine, stretched between two poles. It was placed on the edge of a small patch of bush and about 30 feet above the ground. It is said to be very effective in catching doves and pigeons, and is very difficult to see against a background of bush.

We reached camp in the rearguard about 12:30 p.m.; the day being very hot we felt the march pretty much. Our camp is in a small village of about twelve huts called Inkissi. Mr. Stanley has one for himself, and four of us, Parke, Nelson, Jameson, and myself have another. On the outside of our hut the natives have all sorts of charms stuck up to keep away sickness and bad luck; there are fowls' heads, chilies [sic], feathers, rags, and all sorts of odds and ends, so we should be well protected. Unfortunately, however, these charms do not serve to keep away earwigs and ants of which there are any quantity.

Jephson is ahead getting the boat ready for crossing the Inkissi River tomorrow. Barttelot is camped with his men about 600 yards in rear of us. The Soudanese "bucked up" a bit today; but they still are very bad.

Old Stanley is getting a bit worked up now. He is a most excitable man, with a violent temper when roused, but it soon subsides. He says and does a great many foolish things when he is in this state for which afterwards he must be sorry. He is not a man who has had any fine feelings cultivated in his youth. I should say, outwardly and to strangers he is most polite and charming, but under this there runs a much different kind of strain. I only hope we shall all pull well together to make a success of this expedition, but he holds such a tremendous leverage over us, that for a single slip any of us might be put down as incompetent and dismissed at once.

16th April Rained heavily during the night and on till nearly seven o'clock. We then made a start by companies for the Inkissi River, about 600 yards from camp, reached the river which was much swollen and started crossing the men over in the steel boat. Jephson had tried bending [sic] cables over, but the current was too strong and the weight of the boat parted the cables so Stanley decided to row the men over, which we did—about twenty-four men or forty loads at a time. We found it took about one hour to get each company over. We also have 150 Congo porters carrying loads for us. These we had to ferry over the river.

The Inkissi River is by far the largest and most rapid river we have yet crossed, taking down twice as much water as the Kwilu or Upozo, I should say. The steel boat is a great success and will be most useful to us as we get on and encounter more rivers to cross. We hear that the steamers at Stanley Pool are all ready to take all of us up-stream but seventy. This is very good news as we had been thinking the difficulty of getting steamers would be very great. I believe there are only four steamers all told on the river above Stanley Pool, viz., *Le Stanley* (stern wheeler) [and subsequently referred to as the *Stanley*], the *En Avant*, the *A.I.A.,* and one steamer belonging to the General Sanford expedition [the *Florida*], which is now far away up some tributary of the Congo and cannot be got at.

I met a very nice chap today on the road, in charge of some of the Sanford expedition porters, carrying machinery and parts of the hull of a steamer up-river for trading purposes on the upper waters of the Congo and its branches. He asked me to breakfast and gave me two eggs as a present, which was a most acceptable gift under such circumstances as we are placed in. All these fellows and the officers of the Congo Free State travel from place to place like lords: they have the very best of tinned goods of all sorts—jams, bacon, oatmeal, tea, coffee, condensed milk, tinned fish, besides fruits, and whatever else the country yields. They generally have three or four native boys as servants, carry swell tents and beds, and generally do themselves up well. In fact, I know one of two officers of the CFS [Congo Free State who] get carried about by porters wherever they go. These Belgian officers are very hospitable to us as we pass by the different stations, but they appear to us to be the wrong sort of men to have as agents of a young state such as this is. They seem to lack energy and push, to be too fond of staying indoors at the stations and as a rule [are] very ignorant of the country above [Stanley] Pool.

The Sanford expedition is a trading company, organized by an American (General Sanford) for the purposes of procuring ivory and Indiarubber from the natives on the upper waters of the Congo and sending in down-country to Banana [Point] and thence to the Liverpool markets. They already, I believe, have one steamer on the river above [Stanley] Pool, and one more is now on its way up-country. I believe the manager is an American naval lieutenant called Taunt.

Jameson gets some very pretty butterflies and beetles now. He must have some hundreds of beauties in his boxes by this time. We should be at Stanley Pool in five days from this, and are already six days behind time. On the whole though, we have not done badly. It must be remembered that our men on starting were very soft, that their loads were heavy — 65 pounds — with blankets, rifle and fifteen days' ration besides, that the rivers have all swollen, giving us much trouble, and that the men have suffered greatly from dysentery and could not be pushed.

We camped for the day after crossing and got all the men over by 4:30 p.m., our camp being on a clear space just above the bush patch lining the Inkissi River.

17 *April* Left the Inkissi camp at six o'clock and started off on a five-hour march. My men going along well, we reached camp in five hours and ten minutes. The road was very good, the only obstacles being two small rivers and a bad hill. We passed through two small villages, one of which our men looted, taking all the manioca roots and driving off the poor frightened natives like so many sheep. I sailed in at last with a big stick and drove them off, but not before they had filled their blankets with *chakula*.

Tippu Tib's people travel and camp with us every day. We have great fun with the women on the march. They are a jolly laughing crew. One passes them every day, as they travel very slowly. We often lift up their loads for them and give them biscuits, and in return they offer us manioca roots — beastly things they are too. Tippu himself is a very good chap and so are most of his followers. There is one fellow, though, called Salim who speaks English, a proper brute. We all dislike him, he is such a sneak. There will be trouble with him some day unless he is nipped a bit by Stanley.

On the march I always keep my headman Rashid and my two boys close at hand to lift up the men's loads onto their heads. This I find to be the best way. The other chiefs I send ahead with the men to encourage them on. Rashid is a splendid fellow, far away the best of the men. He is so quiet and yet when he likes he can use the stick very well. All the men like him and would do anything for him. I am very fortunate in getting such a good man for head chief. My boys are both fairly good little chaps, but they take a lot of teaching and get a fair amount of *fimto* (stick) every day. Our camp is on a hillside in some scrubby bush and close to good water. The distance from last camp is about 10½ miles.

Our grub on this expedition is very bad. In fact much worse than bushmen or surveyors in New Zealand or Canada get. [...]

18th April Up at five o'clock. Had a cup of tea and some biscuits as usual and away on the march by six o'clock. Jephson and the boat came along with us today; the heavy boat loads impede us a great deal at bad places. It would be better if they would march a few hours in rear of us, I fancy. Stanley told me this morning some news which may turn out to be very bad. He had letters saying that the *Stanley* was the only steamer available for taking us up river and that the English mission had declined to lend their steamer to us. Now the *Stanley* can only take 200 men and loads, and towing two lighters she might take about 100 more, for a total of 300 men. He also showed me a letter from the American Baptist mission saying that pending instructions to the contrary, they would lend us their steamer the *Peace*, taking sixty men and loads. It is by no means certain that we will be able to get this steamer, as this mail may bring contrary instructions from America. To tell the truth, the missionaries are frightened to lend their steamer to an armed body of men, ready to fight any opposing natives up the river, as the natives seeing the *Peace*, might fancy it was the missionaries and so the "Gospel" would suffer. [...]

20th April Away from camp early, the morning being a good one for marching. Passed two native villages on the way and about 11:30 drew up in the a third and camped for the day. An old chief called Makoko came to interview Stanley. Makoko has a beard 6 feet long and wears it twisted up into two short spirals of about 3 inches each. He is seventy-five years old and was in power when Stanley came down the river on his first trip. We reached a point 2,770 feet above sea level, the highest altitude between Stanley Pool and the sea. The name of this village is Makoko. There are about fifteen huts and the usual plantations of bananas and manioca roots. This is one of the few villages that the natives have not cleared out from; almost all the others we found devoid of natives. They had been scared by the advance, of our men. [...]

23rd April In camp and hot as the very mischief. Several lengthy interviews between the head of the Free State, Stanley, and some chiefs took place in the morning. Food is absolutely unobtainable here for the men; our rice is finished; we can get no manioca for the men; there is no meat; what are we to do? Can we leave two hundred or three hundred men here to starve and pillage? The missionaries have again and again refused [us] their steamer. Something must be done and we must get out of this as soon as possible to Bolobo where there is food. Today the CFS [Congo Free State] seized for us the steamer *Peace*, or rather requisitioned it, so as to avoid danger to the state and we have go her now for our use up the river. [...]

We have thus secured three steamers, the *Stanley* (200 men), the *Peace* (160 men and loads), and the *Henry Reed*. We also have got from Mr. Swinbourne the hull of the steamer *Florida* of the Sanford expedition, our own steel boat, two lighters, and one of the mission whale boats will be towed behind the steamers. Stanley Pool has not been a station for five or six years, with the very best of rich land on almost every side, yet here today there is a famine. Acres of bananas and manioca could have been planted, but no, everything is ivory from morning to night; all are concerned [with] getting down the greatest quantity of ivory. The [policies of the CFS] will never make anything of a state. The ivory soon will be exhausted, except far up the river and then times will get very bad, much worse than they are now. Things appear to have gone down very much since Stanley's time, from all accounts.

In the evening, Jameson came down-river, having shot two hippopotami, only one of which he managed to get. We had the meat brought up to the camp and distributed as rations to the men. We took some for ourselves and had some steaks, which were very good.

1st May Started loading the *Henry Reed* with Tippu Tib's people and goods. At 8:30 a.m. we sent her off up-river and thus made a start on what will probably be a journey of forty days. We next loaded up the *Florida* with Jameson's and my men in her and made her fast to the *Stanley* and [the] *Peace* and the whale boat *Plymouth* and a state lighter. [...] There were the missionary and his wife, Mr. Greshoff, another German gentleman, Troup, Swinbourne, Casement, Baron Steinworth, and an engineer of the Dutch house. They gave us a vociferous cheer, which we returned. Soon after we left, the *Peace* followed and we lost sight of her after half an hour or so, apparently she returned to Kinshassa. However, a day or so will tell. At last we have started and all are glad, the men especially, as their rations of *matako* rods were not nearly sufficient for the famine prices at Stanley Pool. [...]

We are taking 606 men up-river, those with Parke and Barttelot amount to about 160 more. We should therefore have about 600 men to take up to the [Stanley] Falls and will probably leave 100 of these there in an entrenched camp we are to form.

We are very much crowded on the *Stanley*. The men simply cannot move but stay in one or nearly the same position all day.[...]

Going up the river we dodge about, crossing from side to side of the channel to miss the rocks and sandbanks. Just now we are not more than 10 yards from the bank, here covered with long grass and small bushes infested by crocodiles. The mosquitoes are said to be very bad along the river banks, but we should be safe with netting rigged up. We landed the mails at the Kimpoko misson station and again landed and camped about 300 yards above.

Kimpoko is an American Baptist mission station, self-supporting to a great extent. There are not less than three white men, I believe. These shoot meat, cut their own wood, build their sheds, etc., farm, [and] in fact employ little or no paid labour on the station. We had a visit from some of them: long, tall, bearded Americans, all keen for news about the expedition. Some of them to a great deal of interest in the Maxim gun which we keep mounted, ready for action. We all slept on board and found it very comfortable and free from mosquitoes. The men camped within 200 yards of the steamer and as usual talked all night.

At 6:00 p.m., we started the men off for firewood, having forty-five axemen and others to carry the wood out. By eight o'clock we had about enough wood for the *Stanley*, and we lit large fires and split up our wood and stowed it away in the hold. The *Stanley* burns a tremendous quantity of wood every day. It takes nearly two hundred loads of sixty pounds each for twelve hours steaming. This wood-cutting will get to be very tiresome work, I should say.

In the dark one cannot watch the men as in daytime and so prevent them getting away. The men are hungry and want to cook their manioca. Then, too, wood is difficult to get and wandering about in the dark in bush is not healthy work for the shirt, as most bushmen know.

2nd May Up at five o'clock and started off forty axemen for wood, Jameson going with them. Shortly afterwards Nelson and Jephson took parties off to fetch and cut wood in. The *Henry Reed* is lying about 100 yards above us with Tippu Tib's people camped close by. We have heard nothing of the *Peace* yet. We suppose something must have fouled her screw and so delayed her. How Stanley must be swearing.

At 10:00 a.m., as the *Peace* had not yet turned up, the captain of the *Stanley* and I went downstream in the *Stanley* to look for her. After steaming about 12 miles, we saw her in a small by-channel. Catching up to her, found that yesterday, soon after starting from Kinshassa, she had broken her rudder. We offered them help but they declined, so we came on, loaded up the men, took on some more firewood, and now as I write, all these steamers are on their way up-stream. We should get to Stanley Pool by dark and camp for the night.

Nelson is a little bit seedy today. It looks like the commencement of a fever. After our start we steamed about two-and-a-half hours more up-river and made fast to the left or south bank between the *Henry Reed* and [the] *Stanley*. As soon as the ropes were out, we disembarked the men for the night, cut grass for the goats and donkeys and then had a very comfortable dinner in the saloon, Walker and Bonny coming off to us in the steel boat. We had a heavy thunderstorm during the night, but did not mind it under a good secure roof.

3rd May Up at 5:00 a.m. and started the men on board as soon as it got light enough to see. By 5:45 we had all on board an[d] soon after the *Peace* steamed by with Stanley on board, giving us order to go on to the Black River. Accordingly, we steamed off and soon left the *Peace* astern. The *Henry Reed* had just started after we got about half a mile up the river.

Tippu Tib's people are sadly wanting in discipline, as can be seen every day. They seem quite indifferent to the passage of time. I suppose they have always been used to take things easily [sic] and so now do not see the use of hurrying. Certainly now is the chance to make up time, if we are to do it. Our captain estimates that it will take nearly forty days to get to Stanley Falls loaded up as we are. This is nearly a week over Stanely's [sic] estimate. Stopped on the left bank about 3:30 p.m., and at once started cutting firewood. By dark we had got enough for fifteen hours, so we knocked off work and had our grub. The men camped close to the steamer. While looking for wood I saw plenty of elephant's tracks evidently a week or so old.

5th May Up shortly after 5:00 a.m. and by 5:30 had all aboard. We found that the *Stanley* was fast in the mud and so had to get fifty or sixty men out to push off. We started at once up-river for Mswata about two hours off, having seen nothing of the *Peace* or [the] *Henry Reed* since yesterday afternoon.

Jephson was a bit seedy yesterday, but feels much better now. We all thought it was another fever, but quinine and "Livingstone's" pills made him all right again.

One begins now to feel the dimensions of the Congo. Here the river is about twice as wide as the "Arm" at Halifax, or say slightly over a mile, but deep and swift, closed in on both sides with high bush-covered hills and grassy slopes, and stretching up and down till lost far away among the hazy blue hills. Far up from here at Bangala, the river widens and shallows and is studded with numbers of small islands, but here it flows on in one solid mass, hardly broken in its shape at all. We see plenty of natives all paddle and standing up and not as the Indians do (viz., kneeling down). There are plenty of fish about here. I should say they would rise well to the fly as we seem them jumping at moths and flies.

By 9:30 we reached Mswata, where we met Parke and Barttelot and their men. Stanley came along in the *Peace* about three hours later and the *Henry Reed* about two hours after the *Peace*. We put our wood on board and as soon as [the] *Stanley* came, issued *matakos* to the men and let them go off for grub.

Mswata was formerly a state station, but has now been abandoned, as many others have up the river. The people in this village are Batekes, quiet, harmless duffers they seem. Our men have brought large quantities of maize, bananas, plantains, manioca, and fish and seem very well satisfied with themselves. There are plenty of goats, fowls, and yams besides the above mentioned sorts of food, but the natives will not take *matako* for goats; they must have cloth.

6th May Up early and away by about 5:30 a.m. The *Peace* led the way at the start, but we soon passed her and in three hours were out of sight of both steamers. We passed Kwamouth about 10:30—saw some huts and the site of the mission station. The Kwa is the largest river entering the Congo; one branch, the Mfini drains Lake Leopold II, then the Kassai, which is largest of all, runs from the southeast and is fed by a great many rivers of good size. The *Stanley* has been up the Kassai for over 450 miles to the junction of the Lueob.[…]

At 4:30 in the afternoon we were going along splendidly, congratulating ourselves at the way in which we were leaving the *Peace* and [the] *Henry Reed* behind. We were all on the bridge talking or reading, when smash, bump on firm rocks went the *Stanley*. The water immediately rushed into two compartments and things looked very bad. However, the Zanzibaris kept very quiet, and in about two minutes we had all the men on board the *Florida* and stood ready to cast her off. We soon found there was not much immediate danger as the rock we were on was of a flat table shape, reaching out over the stern and sides of the *Stanley* and having about 3 feet 6 inches of water at the stern.

While we were shifting the cargo aft and moving men to weigh down the stern, a very bad squall came up and blew us clean off the rock and probably proved our salvation.[…]

The men disembarked and the loads were removed. The captain with the engineers started the work of mending the holes in the steamer's bottom. In the morning of 10 May, *Le Stanley* was ready to resume its travel in the direction of Yambuya—the closest settlement to Stanley Falls on the expedition's route. The latter had been taken over by Tippu Tib in August 1884, and eventually he became its governor on behalf on the Congo Free State.

11th May Away by 5:30 a.m. and after some difficult manoeuvring on the part of the captain to keep clear of shoals we landed our men at Bolobo without any trouble. Hibaka the king, is at present away in Lukolela buying ivory, so we could not see him. His son, however, came down to see us and shortly afterwards we drank palm wine with the head men.[…]

The following three days were uneventful, except that the boiler of the Peace *had broken down, which caused some delay in the progress of the expedition.*

15th May Up early and started organizing another company, loaded the *Henry Reed* with men and the *Peace*, and at 10:30 a.m. both steamers got away. After getting the donkeys and goats on board we put the Soudanese on the *Florida*, and shortly afterwards I embarked my men also on the *Florida*. We now have companies of eighty-five men each; every man [is] armed with a rifle and all the sick, bad men and "goe-goes" [sic] picked out and left behind at Bolobo. We are now much better prepared for fighting than we were formerly.[…]

At Bolobo we left about 125 men, with 50 rifles and 2,000 rounds of ammunition. We calculate on their being there for fifty days. [The] *Stanley* will by that time have come down-river to [Stanley] Pool, will pick Troup up, come to Bolobo and take Bonny and Ward on to [Stanley] Falls. It is to be hoped that Ward and Bonny have no trouble with the natives. We had great difficulty in getting any wood and on landing for the night at a small village, the natives ran away after first threatening to fight us. Soon after, our men commenced to loot in the dark and took a tremendous quantity of food and spears.

We had to knock off getting firewood very soon after eight o'clock and will have to get more in the morning. The spears our men took are very fine ones with long straight hardwood hafts and a broad blade, say 4 inches wide at the swell. They are bound with brass bands, lapping over each other for about 9 inches below the head.[…]

Between 16 May and 19 May travel up the river progressed smoothly, except for a minor problem with the boiler, which was soon rectified. Shooting hippos was the favourite entertainment although none of the animals' bodies were recovered. Stairs complained of the lack of sugar, soap, and candles, and the shortage of tea which was now being rationed at one-fifth of an ounce per day, per man. He blamed Stanley for this highly unsatisfactory supply of provisions.

20th May It is just four months today since we left England, and we have now been two months in Africa. Today there was a big row with Stanley, and after many high words he dismissed both Jephson and myself. Of course we are powerless to do anything or [to] retaliate and had to bear a great deal. After his anger had subsided he took us back, but [since] it was before the men and about them that the row took place discipline must suffer and the men think less of us and become incited to mutiny. I am awfully sorry this has happened as it destroys all harmony among us. At the same time, I will never admit being in the wrong, and consider myself fully justified in doing what I did, viz., throwing away food looted from a friendly [Zanzibaris] village. Of course, some innocent souls suffered, but they must blame the guilty ones for this. I threw away the looted food for two reasons. First, to show them that we considered it wrong to loot from friendly natives. Second, to serve as an example to the looters and to show them that if we could help it they would not profit one iota. I have stood more swearing at, heard more degrading things and swallowed more intemperate language from another man today than I have ever before.

We found plenty of food at Lukolela, and bought a lot of fowls at four *matakos* each. The men got five days' rations each, or one *matako* per day. With these they buy *chaquanga*, bananas, plantains, fowls, or fish. Here they get two small *chaquangas* for one *matako*. This bread is not very tempting to a white man but if cut into very thin slices and fried, it's not bad.

21st May Away from Lukolela at 6:30 a.m., the *Peace* and [the] *Henry Reed* getting half an hour's start [ahead] of us owing to our engineer not having steam up for us. Our wood supply being short, at one o'clock we landed and started cutting wood and soon after decided to stay for the night. We were cutting from 2:00 to 9:00 p.m. before we could get enough wood. I had to knock off as I felt a touch of fever coming on. It was petty [sic] bad for several hours, but the effects of the quinine soon showed themselves. After piling on all the coats and blankets I could get, the perspiration at last came out and I began to feel relieved.

22nd May Away from camp at 6:00 a.m. My fever has gone down a great deal, but still today my head aches horribly. Nelson and Jameson are now much better. The *Peace* and [the] *Henry Reed* camped nearly opposite to us last night, for what reason we cannot understand. Probably they imagined our boiler had gone wrong again. Stopped at 5:15 on the left bank, the *Henry Reed* lying close to us and the *Peace* opposite on the other side of the channel. Could not get any wood as it was pitch dark and the bush was almost impassable. Passed Ngombe about noon.

24th May Today is the queen's birthday. This time we are under the flag of the Congo Free State. Our camp last night was on the left bank in a very good place.[…]

We reached the equator station in the evening, much to the astonishment of the Europeans here who had not heard from down-river for six months and of course did not know what to make of us. They at first thought we were a force coming to retake Stanley Falls from the Arabs. Equator is now abandoned by the state as a station and its buildings have been handed over to the Sanford trading expedition. There is also an Anglo-American Baptist mission station here, with two missionaries and a very nice earth house.

Though the state has abandoned this place, still an officer has been staying here for some time, looking out for Stanley Falls. Unluckily for him, he does not know as much about the state of affairs as we do as we brought news from Zanzibar that had crossed Africa about which he knew nothing. His name is Van Eile, a lieutenant in the Belgian service. There is a chap here called Glove, a young Englishman who formerly was in the service of the Congo Free State but now is in the Sanford company buying ivory from the natives here. He seems a very decent sort of chap. Quite a different cut from the usual milk-watery Belgian officer one meets on the Congo.

The names of the two missionaries I do not know. I suppose they do some work, but the natives are not of the right sort to take to Christianity easily. This is a bad place, taken all round for food. All that is used is obtained from villages some distance off. Some day there will probably be famine here, owing to the same reasons that caused one at [Stanley] Pool viz., that no one plants roots or fruit here, or seems to provide in the slightest for the future.

25th May Barttelot, Jephson, Nelson, and Jameson went out with the axemen first thing in the morning to get our supply of wood, the missionaries kindly giving us permission to cut on their ground behind the houses. I issued rations of *matako* to the men and did some minor jobs, while Parke attended his sick. By noon we had finished getting our wood on board and we noticed that the *Peace* and [the] *Henry Reed* had almost finished with theirs.

Chickens are very dear here. One pays six *matakos* (brass rods) or their equivalent in shells for one small bird and the natives even ask as many as ten for a good fowl. *Chaquanga* is proportionately dear, of course, owing to the great demand and the short supply. We are once more in the northern hemisphere having crossed the line yesterday afternoon. This place [is] about 8° north latitude. It will be noticed that the Congo goes north a little more then bends back again to the south and crosses the line near Stanley Falls and then works away to the SSE and SE. The natives here are very much the same as those we saw at Bolobo, but seem to be bigger men than those down-river.

As we go up-river one notices that the spears, knives, canoes, and shields are getting superior to those down-river. All the full-grown men here carry a bunch of throwing spears and a shield made of webbed fibres. The spears are made very slight, with beautifully worked hafts, as straight as a die. One can get a good one for, say, eight *matakos* and a shield for about fifteen. The shields are small and light, just sufficient to turn a spear, but a slug or bullet would go through at least two of them. They are the most beautifully worked things we have seen in the Congo. If I had some *matakos* and had a chance, I would send some home.

The shield is about 5 feet long and 10 inches wide at the broadest part, made of basket work of several different colours and strengthened by two long ribs of black basket work surrounding canes.

We all went to dinner with Glove and Van Gele in a very comfortable mud and bamboo house of one story. We had hippo meat, butter, palm wine, cabbage, bread, coffee, and tinned peaches, a regal repast after goat, rice and weavilly [sic], stale biscuits, and insipid tea. Van Gele has ascended the Mobangi River for some distance, but was stopped by the rapids. He also went up the Lulanga, a river just above the village of Uranga. This time he was in the *Henry Reed*. They came across a lot of very wild natives who would not allow them to land. After some persuasion and gifts of cloth, I believe he managed to land higher up and opened trade. These natives had never seen a white man before. The proper name of the river emptying into the Congo just here is the Rouki and not Mahinchu as Stanely [sic] has it in his maps.

Van Gele has also been up this river and also the Ikelemba [River] some distance.[...]

In the subsequent five days, Stairs admired the scenery and found it far superior to the famous Thousand Islands of the St. Lawrence River. He noticed that on Friday, 27 May none of the Muslim members of the expedition observed the fast of Ramadan. After a long reflection on the merits of the alternative routes which the expedition could have followed, Stairs appeared to have second thoughts about the wisdom of the choice of the Congo route, particularly in view of the four-hundred-mile stretch of an entirely unknown country which the caravan had to cross.

On Monday, 30 May the expedition arrived at the Bangala State station, where it was greeted with a salute from a Krupp gun.

31st May Up early, getting Barttelot and the *Henry Reed* off. Barttelot took forty of his Soudanese and all Tippu Tib's men and has rations for eighteen days. They go on straight to Stanley Falls, leave Tippu Tib there, try to quiet the country, and then Barttelot and his men come back to the mouth of the Aruwimi where we ought to pick them up. It will be an interesting piece of work, as the Arabs will of course imagine it to be an expedition of the Congo Free State for the retaking of Stanley Falls station and will probably attack, if they do not recognize Tippu Tib.

At noon, the *Peace* left amid cheers and at 1:30 we (in the *Stanley*) followed, having some trouble in getting all our men together.

Bangala is one of the biggest (collection of) villages on the Congo. The station at present is the highest one on the river, we, therefore, have said goodbye to everything that appertains to civilization, and in all probability none of us will see a white man again till we meet Emin Pasha.

We have now seen the whole of the working of the Congo Independent State. We have seen how it treats the different trading houses under its jurisdiction. We have also seen a fair portion of the country it governs and the natives under its charge. Our unanimous opinion is that the state, as [it is] now constructed, is one huge mistake. It was originally intended to be a *free state*, open to all, welcoming all honest trade, countenancing all open dealings with the natives and doing its best to establish postal and other communication between its different stations. Instead of this, what does really exist? A Congo *independent state*, open as regards its officials to all Belgians, is continually at variance with all the trading houses — English, Dutch, French, and Portuguese alike — hindering instead of aiding trade, and absolutely ignoring the importance of even a rough track with bush bridges on such a thoroughfare as that between Mataddi and Stanley Pool.

Certainly the Congo Independent State is a huge unweildy mistake (as managed at present), worked purely in the interests of the king of the

Belgians, who takes the best of care that outside influence is excluded and apparently imagines that some day this place will form a safe deposit for Belgian capital and manufactures. The officers at Bangala were all very good to us and invited us to breakfast and dinner, but underneath everything one could easily see there ran a vein of jealousy which required pretty strong effort on their part to conceal. They imagine, I suppose, that an expedition coming up *their* river [the Congo] in *their* steamers should be composed of Belgians, instead of Englishmen, as it is. This is only what one expects, as everywhere on the Congo the English are cried down and excluded from billets owing to the unpleasant fact that some day the English will control almost all the import trade to this [Congo] River, and also that the Belgians cannot help seeing that those English officers they have had out here have been far ahead of those of any other nationality in the way of managing the state and dealing with the natives.

1st June Away from our moorings by 5:30 a.m. and soon caught up with the *Peace* and kept close behind her all the morning. Yesterday Stanley observed and I worked out the longitude of Bangala. It is in longitude 19°32' E, latitude 1°28' N.

What a subject of conversation that dinner at Bangala has been. How we have talked it over and laughed among ourselves and imagined again and again we were eating butter, meat, and vegetables and drinking Portuguese wine and champagne, but alas, it is farewell to these little comforts for some time. I'm afraid the Belgian officers must think us all frightful gluttons, for certainly none of us spared the grub. We played havoc with their cigars and champagne at dinner and just before they were opening a fine bottle of brandy as a liquer, Stanley rose and we had to adjourn. This was our farewell dinner with white men and Stanley, rising to the occasion, made a long speech exposing the dangers and adventures before us. Referring in "glowing terms" (that's correct!) to the king of the Belgians, [he] stated that it was owning to His Majesty that we were comfortably "roomed and dined" 800 miles up from the sea, and hoped that His Majesty would be spared many years of useful existence and remain the protector of the Free State (I hope the young man will).

The doctor recommends that we should get butter at least three times a day and advises the use of champagne in small quantities. His recommendations, however, do not carry much weight, as of butter there is none and the nearest fiz is at Bangala.

Camped to the left side of a small swampy island at 5:00 p.m. and managed by moonlight to get four or five hours [worth of] wood.

Travel up the Congo River continued. The routine of everyday life consisted mainly of navigational problems such as avoiding the sandbanks and other obstacles and of cutting the wood for fuel during the stops. On 6 June Upoto was reached, where Stairs and the local chief concluded blood-brotherhood.

In this part of the Congo, cowrie shells were used, instead of matakos, *as a medium of exchange. The expedition lost two of its members: a Somali boy and a Sudanese soldier. Both of them died from what appeared to have been "debility and exhaustion."*

12 June Away at 5:15 a.m. Stuck three times on sandbanks. Passed the village of Yalumbo about noon, a very large village with great numbers of canoes. Late in the afternoon we [...] came to the junction of the Congo and Aruwimi, and turned up into the latter river. Stanley took the *Peace* into the bank at Basoko, a large village, and held a palaver with the natives, using his boy Baruti as an interpreter. The result was that we went across to the opposite side of the river and the natives promised to bring us food there in their canoes. They were distinctly averse to our landing and no wonder. Basoko had been twice burned, once by the state and then again by Tippu Tib's Arabs. Baruti, Stanley's boy who had been in England for some time, is the son of the chief of this village. Baruti's friends were there, but his brother failed to recognize him till Baruti had told him the names of his father, mother, and sisters; even then the natives were sceptical, but Baruti said, "Here is the mark of a crocodile's teeth that I got when a boy here," and showing his brother the mark Baruti was welcomed by all, but not allowed to land.[...]

13th June Started at 5:20 a.m. Picked up the *Peace* and found that we were to stop till noon and thus get food from the natives. This, however, did not come off as the Basokos were too much frightened to venture [near] us. Some two small canoes, however, did come and were sent back to induce their friends to cut bananas and send them over to us. We waited till nearly eleven o'clock; Stanley's patience being then exhausted we got up steam and went up the river. Five minutes after leaving our landing place some twenty or thirty natives collected on the spot. This was done so quickly that there can be no doubt that they were in the bush all round the camp, watching our every movement.

The Aruwimi [River] at our camp is just about 900 yards wide and has three bad banks near its centre. The longitude of Karoko is 24°12' E, its latitude is about 1°15' N. It is a great change getting out of the Congo. One can now see both banks at the same time and one's eye takes in everything, whereas on the mighty Congo, distances are too great to allow one to see the river at one sweep. There are a few small islands in this part of the river and the usual number of sandbanks. We follow close to the *Peace* though [the] *Stanley* has been up-river about 96 miles when in the Congo Free State.[…]

Stanley, in his *Through the Dark Continent*, said that the Aruwimi is the same river as Schweinfurther Welle. He now thinks the Aruwimi runs from the direction of Muta Nzige. We steamed till five o'clock and camped on the left bank at a small village, all the natives running away as soon as we came near the bank. We found no food of any sort as the banana trees had just been planted and the natives apparently had only just come there. All day long we pased village after village with scores of people. Sometimes we went within 10 yards of the banks. The natives all appeared vaillant at first, but ran like deer as we approached their village and then came back again when we had passed.

A great many of the natives were painted with white and red clays. They all have distended ears caused by wearing small bits of wood stuck through the flaps. Most of them have their hair done up in different shapes, the prevailing one being much the same as the Bayanzi.

14th June Left camp at 5:10 a.m. and steamed across the river, then worked our way slowly among the sandbanks in a thickish mist. Towards the afternoon we came upon a very large village, probably one of the largest we have yet seen. Here we begin to notice a change in the shape of the huts and for the first time saw the conical palm hut of which there are so many on the upper part of this river. For miles we passed this village, seeing hundreds of natives in hideous head dresses and gaudy with red ochre and white clay. They have most perfect paddles with handles of polished ivory. Some of their paddles also are made of bright red wood, which glitters in the sunlight, the effect being very pretty.[…]

22nd June Wet and miserable. All still at firewood. I came into breakfast at 11:00 a.m., after a long talk with Stanley about the non-arrival of the *Henry Reed*. At last he decided to send me off tomorrow morning with the *Peace* and thirty Zanzibaris, ten days' provisions, and firewood and start down the Aruwimi and up the Congo to search for the *Henry Reed*. His suspicions as to the cause of delay were the following: (1) Tippu Tib might have seized the steamer at Stanley Falls and made the whites prisoners; (2) the Soudanese might not or could not cut enough firewood to keep the steamer going; (3) the Soudanese might have mutinied and shot Barttelot; (4) the steamer might have got on banks, rocks or been delayed owing to fights with natives.

I was to have gone as far as Stanley Falls if necessary. However, at 5:30 p.m. the *Henry Reed* rounded the bend below camp and came on and in half an hour was made fast and we learnt everything. They had trouble with natives, also with getting wood and were delayed half a day at [Stanley] Falls. Tippu Tib landed and was at first fired on. Soon, however, his friends recognized him and there were great rejoicings.

The Arabs have been burning and pillaging a great number of villages up-river, taking all the men and women as slaves to exchange for ivory which they take to Zanzibar. The *Henry Reed* brought down a cow, a present to Ngalyema, the chief at Stanley Falls. Our men were attacked once when cutting firewood and one boy was wounded. I believe Tippu Tib's men killed six or seven and the village was burned and manioc destroyed, so the natives learnt a lesson, I have no doubt. Slight fever today — temperature 103°.

23rd June All hands but the major and Jameson out after firewood. This is the last day's cutting for which all are most thankful.

24th June Both steamers (*Peace* and *Henry Reed*) got away between six and seven o'clock this morning. Thus we have seen the last white men till we reach Emin Pasha.[...]

[Source: Janina M. Konzacki, ed., *Victorian Explorer: The African Diaries of William G. Stairs 1887-1892* (Halifax: Nimbus, 1991). Reprinted with permission.]

4. Stanley on the Congo

.... on my invitation about seventy re-enlisted, and voyaging by the Mediterranean we entered the Congo river once more, in 1879. For nearly six years we laboured at the building of a State out of the immense heart of Africa, where we had endured so much, and in February last year the European Powers recognized our work, and it was agreed to call that region, over a million square miles in extent, the Free and Independent State of the Congo. It has now a regular Government, it has an Endowment Fund which furnishes a quarter of a million of dollars annually for the expenses of its administration. A flotilla of eight steamers navigates the waters of the Upper Congo regularly. There are about three hundred Europeans in Congo State at last accounts. A telegraphic cable lies across the mouth of the great river, and Europe is within twenty-four hours' communication of the State. The romance of the wild land is all gone, but instead we have something approaching to order and system and peaceful intercourse. Every day will now add to its prosperity. Success has amply crowned my efforts; I have been nobly assisted, sustained by many friends, and encouraged by abundant sympathy. Thanks and praise be to God! May He watch over the infant State, and nourish it to mature fullness, to be a shining example to the rest of that Continent, which remained so long Dark and Mysterious.

[From Henry M. Stanley, *Incidents of the Journey through the Dark Continent* (London: Wm Clowes & Sons, 1886) 59-60.]

5. Stanley on his Career

... in England, and the publications of the C.M. Society prove that, for some years afterwards, no great hope of success was entertained, and, as if to add to the public disbelief in the efficacy of missionary effort among negro pagans, there came, almost simultaneously with my return from Africa early in the following year, the sad news that two out of the three missionaries had been massacred. Thus, at the beginning of that year, 1878, the surviving missionary in Uganda was the sole white man in all the regions bordering the African equator.

The publication of this book in the following June excited unusual, indeed, I may truly say extraordinary, interest throughout Europe. It was translated into many languages, and the aggregate sales were prodigious. In this country, in France, Germany, Belgium, and Italy, it was discussed from every point of view. It led to much controversy, personal and general, but the British public did not take kindly to the suggestions for immediate action in Africa contained in it. England lost the opportunity of selecting unquestioned her field for enterprise, and so long was she indifferent to the Continent, and the splendid possibilities that awaited her, that Equatorial Africa was well-nigh closed to her altogether.

It happened that there was one person on the Continent who manifested much more than an abstract interest in Africa, and had, indeed, solicited my services for the development of the Dark Continent — within a few minutes of my return to Europe — but had generously admitted that the people in whose interest I had made my explorations should have the first claim on them. This person was King Leopold II, whose wonderful character and extraordinary ability were then unknown to the world. No Englishman living, not even the geographical expert, paid such close attention to my letters in the *Daily Telegraph*, my book and speeches on African subjects, as did the King, and no man shared my zeal and hopes for Africa as did His Majesty. I waited from January to November, 1878, to see if on this side of the Channel any serious notice was likely to be taken of my suggestions; but finding public feeling impossible to be aroused here, I then crossed the Channel, and accepted the post of chief agent to the *Comité des Etudes du Haut Congo*, of which King Leopold was President....

Resuming my proper subject, I became chief agent on the Congo. Every now and then during the six years that I occupied that position, directing the advance into the Congo basin, reports of our doings frequently reached England in one form or another, and still the trend of events seemed unperceived there, though there was considerable stir in Germany, France, Portugal,and Belgium.

Neither, apparently, were the actions of the Germans on the borders of Cape Colony in 1883-84 of a character to excite alarm, suspicion, or even intelligent alertness in the British mind. Lord Derby was not in the least disturbed by the curious inquisitive tone of Bismarck's despatches relating to South Africa, and Lord Granville failed to comprehend the drift of Bismarck's anxiety about the German settlement at Angra Pequena, or that the presence of a German warship in South African waters signified anything.

When it was too late, however, to prevent the seizure of a large territory neighbouring Cape Colony, the British rubbed their eyes, and found that a European Power, which might make itself unpleasant some day to our South African colonists, had wilfully planted itself in close proximity to the Boer states, with which we had already more than once grave misunderstandings. It was then inferred that a similar move, a little further inland, by either the Boers or Germans, would perpetually confine British South Africa to within the narrow limits of Cape Colony, and a suspicious manoeuvre of a German ship of war in Eastern South Africa confirmed the British Government that longer delay would be disastrous to British interests, and the Warren Expedition, which secured to us Bechuanaland, and an open way to the Zambesi, was the result. But before the Berlin Conference of 1884-85 was held, Germany had become the owner of important possessions at various places in Occidental Africa, and was projecting other surprises of a similar kind....

On the Continent, however, the diplomatic discussions had a most stimulating effect. The people of every state now studied their African maps with a different purpose from the acquisition of mere geographical knowledge. Societies, miscalled "commercial, geographical, or scientific," sprang into existence like mushrooms throughout France, Germany, Italy, Belgium, and Sweden, and in a short time numerous expeditions, disguised by innocent titles, were prepared for Africa.

[Source: Henry M. Stanley, *Through the Dark Continent* (London: George Newnes, 1899) xii–xv.]

6. Advertising Announcement

GEORGE NEWNES, LIMITED, beg to announce that by an arrangement with Messrs. SAMPSON LOW, MARSTON AND COMPANY, Limited, they are now offering to the public in a cheap and attractive form one of the greatest and most popular books of Travel ever published.

MR. H.M. STANLEY AND HIS WORK

AFRICA has always engaged a full share of the interest of the civilised world, and especially during the first half of the century now verging on its close; it was then regarded as a dark and mysterious continent, by far the largest portion of its interior being quite blank on the map of the world.

Now there is not much left of it that has not yielded up its secrets to enterprising explorers. The great valley of the Congo and its Tributaries, the Zambesi Valley, and the great Central Lakes, then equally unknown, are now as familiarly spoken of as Cape Town and Zanzibar.

Among the band of noble adventurers who opened up this great continent, it cannot be questioned that the names of **LIVINGSTONE** and **STANLEY** stand out most prominently. Time, like an ever-rolling stream, passes so quickly that the younger portion of the present generation already look upon the deeds of these men as belonging to ancient history, and yet it is not fifty years since the works of LIVINGSTONE first began to attract the attention of the whole world; and it is not yet thirty years since H.M. STANLEY began his wonderful explorations; it is not too much to say that during the twenty years occupied by him in opening up "THE DARK CONTINENT" he did more by his wonderful tact and indomitable energy than all the great explorers who had gone before him.

The publishers are of opinion that the time has arrived when a new, cheap, and beautifully printed edition of his great work, "THROUGH THE DARK CONTINENT," must certainly prove acceptable to a very large number of readers.

It may not be uninteresting to mention, in proof of Mr. Stanley's immense popularity, that of his four great and expensive works, viz.: **"HOW I FOUND LIVINGSTONE"; "THROUGH THE DARK CONTINENT"; "THE CONGO, and the Founding of a Free State"; "IN DARKEST AFRICA,"** an aggregate of OVER A HUNDRED THOUSAND COPIES have been sold in this country alone, and probably a much larger number in America. They have also been translated into the languages of nearly every civilised country in the world, and it may be safe to assume that the combined issue in Foreign tongues has been at least equal to that in the English language. The subject of which these works treat is as fresh and interesting to-day as it ever was.

7. Henry Morton Stanley, speech on being given the freedom of the city of Swansea

To illustrate the slow growth of ideas among nations, I will quote you a portion of a speech delivered by the great Pitt a hundred years ago. Lord Granville, Bishop Wilberforce, and Sir Bartle Frere in 1873 and Lord Salisbury in 1890 have made some effective speeches about the obnoxious slave traffic and our duties in regard to it, but they bear no comparison... with that delivered by William Pitt in April, 1792. Said he, 'Grieved am I to think that there should be a single person in this country, much more that there should be a single member of the British Parliament, who can look on the present dark, uncultivated, and uncivilized state of Africa as a ground for continuing the slave trade, as a ground for not only refusing to attempt the improvement of that continent, but even for hindering and interrupting every ray of light which might otherwise break in upon it—as a ground for refusing to it the common chance and the common means with which other nations have been blessed of emerging from their barbarism. It has been alleged that Africa labours under a natural incapacity for civilization, that it is enthusiasm or fanaticism to think that she can ever enjoy the knowledge and morals of Europe, that Providence never intended her to rise above barbarism, that Providence has irrevocably doomed her to be only a nursery for slaves. Allow of this principle as applied to Africa, and I should be glad to know why it might not also have been applied to ancient and uncivilized Britain. Why might not some Roman Senator have predicted with equal boldness — "There is a people destined never to be free, a people depressed by the hand of nature below the level of the human species, and created to form a supply of slaves for the rest of the world"? Sir, we were once as obscure among the nations of the earth, as debased in our morals, as savage in our manners, as degraded in our understandings as these unhappy Africans are at present. But in the lapse of a long series of years, by a progression slow and, for a time, almost imperceptible, we have become rich in a variety of acquirements, favoured above measure with the gifts of Providence, unrivalled in commerce, pre-eminent in arts, foremost in the pursuits of philosophy and science, and established in all the blessings of civil society. But had other nations applied to Great Britain the reasoning which some gentlemen now apply to Africa, ages might have passed without our emerging from barbarism, and we might even at this hour have been little superior in morals, in knowledge, or in refinement to the rude inhabitants of Guinea. If we shudder to think of the misery which would still have overwhelmed us had Great Britain continued to the present time as she once was, God forbid that we should any longer subject Africa to the same dreadful scourge and preclude the light of knowledge which has reached every other quarter of the globe from having access into her coasts.

[Source: *The Times* (4 October 1892).]

8. Stanley, speech at a dinner given in his honour by the Lotos Club in New York on 27 November 1886

....[1878] The very day I landed in Europe the King of Italy gave me an express train to convey me to France, and the very moment I descended from it at Marseilles there were three ambassadors from the King of the Belgians who asked me to go back to Africa....

After I had written my book, "Through the Dark Continent," I began to lecture, using these words: "I have passed through a land watered by the largest river of the African continent, and that land knows no owner. A word to the wise is sufficient. You have cloths and hardware and glassware and gunpowder and these millions of natives have ivory and gums and rubber and dyestuffs, and in barter there is good profit." [Applause.]

The King of the Belgians commissioned me to go to that country. My expedition when we started from the coast numbered 300 colored people and fourteen Europeans. We returned with 3,000 trained black men and 300 Europeans. The first sum allowed me was $50,000 a year, but it has ended at something like $700,000 a year. Thus, you see, the progress of civilization. We found the Congo, having only canoes. Today there are eight steamers. It was said at first that King Leopold was a dreamer. He dreamed he could unite the barbarians of Africa into a confederacy and call it the Free State, but on February 25, 1885, the Powers of Europe and America also ratified an act, recognizing the territories acquired by us to be the free and independent State of the Congo. Perhaps when the members of the Lotos Club have reflected a little more upon the value of what Livingstone and Leopold have been doing, they will also agree that these men have done their duty in this world and in the age that they lived, and that their labor has not been in vain on account of the great sacrifices they have made to the benighted millions of dark Africa. [Loud and enthusiastic applause.]

[Source: H.M. Stanley, "Through the Dark Continent," Lewis Copeland, ed., *The World's Great Speeches* (New York: Dover Publications, 1958) 667-68.]

9. Cecil Rhodes, from speech on 18 July 1899 at Cape Town

"And, sir, my people have changed. I speak of the English people, with their marvellous common sense, coupled with their powers of imagination—all thoughts of a Little England are over. They are tumbling over each other, Liberals and Conservatives, to show which side are the greatest and most enthusiastic Imperialists. The people have changed, and so do all the parties, just like the Punch and Judy show at a country fair. The people have found out that England is small, and her trade is large, and they have also found out that other people are taking their share of the world, and enforcing hostile tariffs. The people of England are finding out that "trade follows the flag," and they have all become Imperialists. They are not going to part with any territory. And the bygone ideas of nebulous republics are over. The English people intend to retain every inch of land they have got, and perhaps, sir, they intend to secure a few more inches. And so the thought of my country has changed. When I began this business of annexation, both sides were most timid. They would ask one to stop at Kimberley, then they asked one to stop at Khama's country. I remember Lord Salisbury's Chief Secretary imploring me to stop at the Zambesi. Mr. Mayor, excuse me for using the word "I," but unfortunately I have been alone in these efforts. Now, sir, they won't stop anywhere; they have found out that the world is not quite big enough for British trade and the British flag; and that the operation of even conquering the planets is only something which has yet to be known. I have little doubt about the Colonial people, and in saying so, I cover in the Colonial people the Dutch as well as the English. Notwithstanding my past little temporary difficulty, if we were all to accept equal rights, I feel convinced that we should all be united on the proposition that Africa is not, after all, big enough for us."

[Source: "Vindex" ed., *Cecil Rhodes: His Political Life and Speeches* (London: Chapman & Hall, 1900) 642-43.]

10. Joseph Chamberlain: Speech 11 November 1895

[The Right Hon. Joseph Chamberlain was Secretary of State for the Colonies.]

.... I will venture to claim two qualifications for the great office which I hold, and which, to my mind, without making invidious distinctions, is one of the most important that can be held by any Englishman. These qualifications are that, in the first place, I believe in the British Empire— (cheers)—and, in the second place, I believe in the British race. (Renewed cheering.) I believe that the British race is the greatest of governing races that the world has ever seen. (More cheering.) I say that not merely as an empty boast, but as proved and evidenced by the success which we have had in administering the vast dominions which are connected with these small islands. (Cheers.) I think a man who holds my office is bound to be sanguine, is bound to be confident, and I have both those qualifications. (Laughter, and cheers.)...

[Source: "A Young Nation," *Foreign and Colonial Speeches* (London: George Routledge & Sons, 1897) 89.]

11. W.M. Thackeray on the Race Question

To Mrs. Carmichael-Smyth, 26 January 1853

.... I don't believe Blacky *is* my man and my brother, though God forbid I should own him or flog him, or part him from his wife and children. But the question is a much longer [one than] is set forth in Mrs Stowe's philosophy: and I shan't speak about it, till I know it, or till it's my business, or I think I can do good.

To Mrs. Carmichael-Smyth, 13 February 1853

.... They are not my men and brethren, these strange people with retreating foreheads, with great obtruding lips and jaws: with capacities for thought, pleasure, endurance quite different to mine. They are not suffering as you are impassioning yourself for their wrongs as you read Mrs Stowe, they are grinning and joking in the sun; roaring with laughter as they stand about the streets in squads; very civil, kind and gentle, even winning in their manner when you accost them at gentlemen's houses, where they do all the service. But they don't seem to me to be the same as white men, any more than asses are the same animals as horses; I don't mean this disrespectfully, but simply that there is such a difference of colour, habits, conformation of brains, that we must acknowledge it, and can't by any rhetorical phrase get it over; Sambo is not my man and my brother; the very aspect of his face is grotesque and inferior.... As soon as the cheap substitute is found, depend on it the Planter, who stoutly pleads humanity now as the one of the reasons why he can't liberate his people, will get rid of them quickly enough; & the price of the slave-goods will fall so that owners won't care to hold such an unprofitable & costly stock.

[Source: Gordon N. Ray, ed., *The Letters and Private Papers of William Makepeace Thackeray, Vol. III, 1852-1856* (London: 1946) 187, 198.]

12. D. Crawford, F.R.G.S. (Konga Vantu)

How little you knew of the African puzzle is seen when it leaks out that the very name ("Africa!") is utterly unknown to the negro. Africa? He never heard such a hideous word. It is a mere tag, a mere ticket stuck on the back of this poor Continent by outsiders. A perfect parable all this of Africa, the land, and the African, the man. A straw indicates the current, and if we know not the name, then we know less of the nature of black place and black person, of black man and *blacker manners*. [Editor's italics]

Even before sighting the African coast, and while still far out at sea, we saw the whole coming problem in another panoramic parable. This time it is a romantic river reading us a lesson, and by way of warning that the confluence of the Congo might soon be expected, here is our blue Atlantic painted a muddy brown eight miles out into the ocean. Parable, surely, of the ugly fact we are soon to prove that evil African communications corrupt good European manners.

There, in that monster mouth of the Congo, yawning seven miles wide, and vomiting its dirty contents into the blue Atlantic — there, I say, you see the sad and symbolic story of decadence on the West Coast of Africa. For the fearful fact must be faced that all things European degenerate in Central Africa — European provisions go bad, European fruits, European dogs degenerate. So, too, European men and women.

★ ★ ★ ★

This advancing into Africa seems to have a strange reciprocal effect on a newcomer. Day by day, what in fact is happening is that Africa invades you a metaphoric mile, the Dark Continent flooding your insular English being at every pore.

[Source: D. Crawford, *Thinking Black: Twenty-two Years without a Break in the Long Grass of Central Africa* (London: 1912) xiii–xv, 94.]

13. From Benjamin Kidd

In the first place, the attempt to acclimatize the white man in the tropics must be recognized to be a blunder of the first magnitude. All experiments based upon the idea are mere idle and empty enterprises foredoomed to failure. Excepting only the deportation of the African races under the institution of slavery, probably no other idea which has held the mind of our civilization during the last three hundred years has led to so much physical and moral suffering and degradation, or has strewn the world with the wrecks of so many gigantic enterprises.... If the white man cannot be permanently acclimatized in the tropics, even where for the time being he has become relatively numerous, under the effects of evil conditions of the past, the government of all such regions must, if the ideas and standards which have prevailed in the past be allowed to continue, tend ultimately in one direction. It must tend to become the government of a large native population by a permanently resident European caste cut off from the moral, ethical, political, and physical conditions, which have produced the European. This is the real problem in many States in the tropical parts of central and northern South America. We cannot look for good government under such conditions; we have no right to expect it. In climatic conditions which are a burden to him; in the midst of races in a different and lower stage of development; divorced from the influences which have produced him, from the moral and political environment from which he sprang, the white man does not in the end, in such circumstances, tend so much to raise the level of the races amongst whom he has made his unnatural home, as he tends himself to sink slowly to the level around him.

We come, therefore, to a clearly defined position. If we have to meet the fact that by force of circumstances the tropics *must* be developed, and if the evidence is equally emphatic that such a development can only take place under the influences of the white man, we are confronted with a larger issue than any mere question of commercial policy or of national selfishness. The tropics in such circumstances can only be governed as a trust for civilization, and with a full sense of the responsibility which such a trust involves.

In any forecast of the future of our civilization, one of the most important of the questions presenting themselves for consideration is that of the future relationship of the European peoples to what are called the lower races....

The relationships of the Western peoples to the inferior races, with which they have come into contact in the course of the expansion they have undergone, is one of the most interesting subjects in history.

... No one can doubt that it is within the power of the leading European peoples of today — should they so desire — to parcel out the entire equatorial regions of the earth into a series of satrapies, and to administer their resources, not as in the past by a permanently resident population, but from the temperate regions, and under the direction of a relatively small European official population. And this without any fear of effective resistance from the inhabitants. *Always, however, assuming that there existed a clear call of duty or necessity to provide the moral force necessary for such action.*

.... We have evidence of a general feeling, which recognizes the immense future importance of the tropical regions of the earth to the energetic races, in that partition of Africa amongst the European powers which forms one of the most remarkable signs of the times at he end of the nineteenth century....

Lastly, it will materially help towards the solution of this and other difficult problems, if we are in a position, as it appears we shall be, to say with greater clearness in the future, than we have been able to do in the past, what it is constitutes superiority and inferiority of race. We shall probably have to set aside many of our old ideas on the subject. Neither in respect alone of colour, nor of descent, nor even of the possession of high intellectual capacity, can science give us any warrant for speaking of one race as superior to another. The evolution which man is undergoing is, over and above everything else, a social evolution. There is, therefore, but one absolute test of superiority. It is only the race possessing in the highest degree the qualities contributing to social efficiency that can be recognized as having any claim to superiority.

But these qualities are not as a rule of the brilliant order, nor such as strike the imagination. Occupying a high place amongst them are such characteristics as strength and energy of character, humanity, probity and integrity, and simple-minded devotion to conceptions of duty in such circumstances as may arise.

[Source: Benjamin Kidd, *The Control of the Tropics* (New York & London: 1898) 48-98.]

14. From Roger Casement's Congo Report

[Roger Casement (1864-1916) began his consular services on the West coast of Africa in 1898. In 1903 he was requested by the British Government to report on the alleged atrocities in the Belgian Congo. His Report caused a sensation and was an important factor in the movement which led to the extinction of the Congo Free State in 1908. Conrad's first meeting with Casement is described in the opening entry (13 June 1890) of *The Congo Diary*: "Made the acquaintance of Mr. Roger Casement, which I should consider as a great pleasure under any circumstances and now it becomes a positive piece of luck. Thinks, speaks well, most intelligent and very sympathetic."]

Mr. Casement to the Marquess of Lansdowne
London, December 11, 1903
.... Perhaps the most striking change observed during my journey into the interior was the great reduction observable everywhere in native life. Communities I have formerly known as large and flourishing centres of population are today entirely gone, or now exist in such diminished numbers as to be no longer recognisable.

.... Bolobo used to be one of the most important native settlements along the South bank of the Upper Congo, and the population in the early days of civilised rule numbered fully 40,000 people, chiefly of the Bobangi tribe. Today the population is believed to be not more than 7,000·to 8,000 souls.

When I visited the Government station at P★★★, the chief of that post showed me ten sacks of gum which he said had been just brought in by a very small village in the neighbourhood. For this quarter of a ton of gum-copal he said he had paid the village one piece of blue drill—a rough cotton cloth which is valued locally after adding the cost of transport, at 11½ fr. apiece. By the Congo Government "Bulletin Official" of this year (No. 4, April 1903) I found that 339½ tons of gum-copal were exported in 1902, all from the Upper Congo, and that this was valued at 473,490 fr. The value per ton would, therefore, work out at about 561. The fortnightly yield of each village would therefore seem to be worth a maximum of 141 (probably less), for which a maximum payment of 11½ fr. is made. At one village I visited I found the majority of the inhabitants getting ready the gum-copal and the supply of fish which they had to take to P★ on the morrow. They were putting it into canoes to paddle across the lake—some 20 miles—and they left with their loads in the night from along side my steamer. These people told me that they frequently received, instead of cloth, 150 brass rods (7½ fr.) for the quarter of a ton of gum-copal they took fortnightly.

M.P. called on us to get out of the rain, and in conversation with M.Q. in presence of myself and R., said: 'The only way to get rubber is to fight for it. The natives are paid 35 centimes per kilog., it is claimed, but that includes a large profit on the cloth; the amount of rubber is controlled by the number of guns, and not the number of bales of cloth. The S.A.B. on the Bussira, with 150 guns, get only 10 tons (rubber) a month: we, the State, at Mombovo, with 130 guns, get 13 tons per month.' 'So you count by guns?' I asked him.'Partout,' M.P. said. 'Each time the corporal goes out to get rubber cartridges are given to him. He must bring back all not used; and for every one used, he must bring back a right hand.' M.P. told me that sometimes they shot a cartridge at an animal in hunting; they then cut off a hand from a living man. As to the extent to which this is carried on, he informed me that in six months they, the State, on the Momboyo River, had used 6,000 cartridges, which means that 6,000 people are killed or mutilated. It means more than 6,000 for the people have told me repeatedly that the soldiers kill children with the butt of their guns.

The region drained by the Lulongo being of great fertility has, in the past, maintained a large population. In the days prior to the establishment of civilized rule in the interior of Africa, this river offered a constant source of supply to the slave markets of the Upper Congo. The towns around the lower Lulongo River raided the interior tribes, whose prolific humanity provided not only servitors, but human meat for those stronger than themselves. Cannibalism had gone hand in hand with slave raiding, and it was no uncommon spectacle to see gangs of human beings being conveyed for exposure and sale in the local markets. I had in the past, when travelling on the Lulongo River, more than once viewed such a scene. On one occasion a woman was killed in the village I was passing through, and her head and other portions of her were brought and offered for sale to some of the crew of the steamer I was on. Sights of this description are to-day impossible in any part of the country I traversed, and the full credit for their suppression must be given to the authorities of the Congo Government. It is, perhaps, to be regretted that in its efforts to suppress such barbarous practices the Congo Government should have had to rely upon, often, very savage agencies wherewith to combat savagery. The troops employed in punitive measures were—and often are—themselves savages only removed by outward garb from those they are sent to punish.

... that the Congo Government itself did not hesitate some years ago to purchase slaves (required as soldiers or workmen), who could be obtained for sale by the most deplorable means: —

> Le chef Ngulu de Wangata est envoyé dans la Maringa, pour m'y acheter des esclaves. Prière à M.M. les agents de l'A.B.I.R. de bien vouloir me signaler les méfaits que celui-ci pourrait commettre en route.
>
> Le Capitiaine-Commamdant
(Signé) Sarrazzyn
Colquilhatville, le 1er Mai, 1896

This document was shown to me during the course of my journey. The officer who issued this direction was, I was informed, for a considerable period chief executive authority of the district: and I heard him frequently spoken of by the natives who referred to him by the sobriquet he had earned in the district, "Widjima," or "Darkness."...

★ ★ ★ ★

The Concession Companies, I believe, account for the armed men in their service on the ground that their factories and agents must be protected against the possible violence of the rude forest dwellers with whom they deal; but this legitimate need for safeguarding European establishments does not suffice to account for the presence, far from those establishments, of large numbers of armed men quartered throughout the native villages, and who exercise upon their surroundings an influence far from protective. The explanation offered me of this state of things was that, as the "impositions" laid upon the natives were regulated by law, and were calculated on the scale of public labour the Government had a right to require of the people, the collection of these "impositions" had to be strictly enforced. *When I pointed out that the profit of this system was not reaped by the Government but by a Commercial Company, and figured in the public returns of that Company's affairs as well as in the official Government statistics as the outcome of commercial dealings with the natives, I was informed that the "impositions" were in reality trade, " for, as you observe, we pay the natives for the produce they bring in." "But," I observed, "you told me just now that these products did not belong to the natives, but to you, the Concessionaire, who owned the soil; how, then, do you buy from them*

what is already yours?" "We do not buy the india-rubber. What we pay to the
native is a remuneration for his labour in collecting our produce on our land, and
bringing it to us." [Editor's italics]

Since it was thus to the labour of the native alone that the profits of
the Company were attributed, I inquired whether he was not protected
by contract with his employer; but I was here referred back to the statement that the natives performed these services as a public duty required
of him by his Government. He was acquitting himself of an "imposition"
laid upon him by the Government, "of which we are but the collectors
by right of our Concession." "Your Concession, then, implies," I said,
"that you have been conceded not only a certain area of land, but also
the people dwelling on the land?" This however, was not accepted either,
and I was assured that the people were absolutely free, and owed no service to any one but to the Government of the country. But there was no
explanation offered to me that was not at once contradicted by the next.
One said it was a tax, an obligatory burden laid upon the people, such as
all Governments have the undoubted right of imposing; but this failed to
explain how, if a tax, it came to be collected by the agents of a trading
firm, and figured as the outcome of the trade dealings with the people,
still less, how, if it were a tax, it could be justly imposed every week or
fortnight in the year, instead of once, or at most, twice a year.

Another asserted that it was clearly legitimate commerce with the
natives because these were well paid and very happy. He could not then
explain the presence of so many armed men in their midst, or the reason
for tying the men, women and children, and of maintaining in each
trading establishment a local prison termed a "maison des otages,"
wherein recalcitrant native traders endured long periods of confinement.

. A third admitted that there was no law on the Congo Statute Book
constituting his trading establishment a Government taxing station, and
that since the product of his dealings with the natives figured in his
Company's balance-sheets as trade, and he paid customs duty to the
Government on export, and a dividend to the shareholders, and as he
himself drew a commission of 2 per cent on his turnover, it must be
trade; but this exponent could not explain how if these operations were
purely commercial, they rested on a privilege denied to others, for since,
as he asserted, the products of his district could neither be worked nor
bought by any one but himself, it was clear they were not merchandise,
which, to be merchandise, must be marketable. The summing up of the
situation by the majority of those with whom I sought to discuss it was
that, in fact, it was forced labour conceived in the true interest of the
native who, if not controlled in this way, would spend his days in idleness, unprofitable to himself and the general community.

As Z★ lies upon the main stream of the Lulongo River, and is often touched at by passing steamers, I chose for the next inspection a town lying somewhat off this beaten track, where my coming would be quite unexpected. Steaming up a small tributary of the Lulongo, I arrived, unpreceded by any rumour of my coming, at the village of A★. In an open shed I found two sentries of the La Lulanga Company guarding fifteen native women, five of whom had infants at the breast, and three of whom were about to become mothers. The chief of these sentries, a man called S— who was bearing a double-barreled shot-gun, for which he had a belt of cartridges — at once volunteered an explanation of the reason for these women's detention. Four of them, he said, were hostages who were being held to insure the peaceful settlement of a dispute between two neighboring towns, which had already cost the life of a man. His employer, the agent of the La Lulanga Company at B— near by, he said, had ordered these women to be seized and kept until the Chief of the offending town to which they belonged should come in to talk over the palaver. The sentry pointed out that this was evidently a much better way to settle such troubles between native towns than to leave them to be fought out among the people themselves.

The remaining eleven women, whom he indicated, he said he had caught and was detaining as prisoners to compel their husbands to bring in the right amount of india-rubber required of them on next market day. When I asked if it was a woman's work to collect india-rubber, he said, "No; that, of course, it was man's work." "Then why do you catch the women and not the men?" I asked. "Don't you see," was the answer, "if I caught and kept the men, who would work the rubber? But if I catch their wives, the husbands are anxious to have them home again, and so the rubber is brought in quickly and quite up to the mark." When I asked what would become of these women if their husbands failed to bring in the right quantity of rubber on the next market day, he said at once that then they would be kept there until their husbands had redeemed them. Their food, he explained, he made the Chief of A★★ provide, and he himself saw it given to them daily. They came from more than one village of the neighborhood, he said, mostly from the Ngombi or inland country, where he often had to catch women to insure the rubber being brought in in sufficient quantity. It was an institution, he explained, that served well and saved much trouble. When his master came each fortnight to A★★ to take away the rubber so collected, if it was found to be sufficient, the women were released and allowed to return with their husbands, but if not sufficient they would undergo continued detention. The sentry's statements were clear and explicit, as were equally those of several of the villagers with whom I spoke. The sentry further explained, in answer to my inquiry, that he caught women in this way by direction of his employers. That it was a custom generally adopted and found to work well; that the people were very lazy, and that this was much the simplest way of making them do what was required of them. When asked if he had any use for his shot-gun, he answered that it had been given by the white man "to frighten people and make them bring in rubber," but that he had never otherwise used it. I found that the two sentries at A★ were complete masters of the town.

The praiseworthy official would be he whose district yielded the best and biggest supply of that commodity; and, succeeding in this, the means whereby he brought about the enhanced value of that yield would not, it may be believed, be too closely scrutinized.

A State without resources is inconceivable. On what legitimate grounds could the exemption of natives from all taxes be based, seeing that they are the first to benefit by the material and moral advantages introduced into Africa? As they have no money, a contribution in the shape of labour is required from them. It has been said that, if Africa is ever to be redeemed from barbarism, it must be by getting the negro to understand the meaning of work by the obligation of paying taxes: —

> It is a question (of native labour) which has engaged my most careful attention in connection with West Africa and other Colonies. To listen to the right honourable gentleman, you would almost think that it would be a good thing for the native to be idle. I think it is a good thing for him to be industrious; and by every means in our power we must teach him to work. ... No people ever have lived in the world's history who would not work. In the interests of the natives all over Africa, we have to teach them to work.

Such was the language used by Mr. Chamberlain in the House of Commons on the 6th August, 1901;....

[Source: Peter Singleton-Gates, ed., *The Black Diaries: An Account of Roger Casement's Life and Times, with a Collection of his Diaries and Public Writings* (Paris: Olympia Press, 1957).]

15. E.D. Morel on Belgian Colonialism in the Congo

["The expropriation has been unique. The massacres have been unique. But there is another element which adds a last grotesque touch to this horror. It is the words of piety and philanthropy, the odious sustained hypocrisy which have cloaked these dreadful deeds." From the introduction by Arthur Conan Doyle to E.D. Morel's *Great Britain and the Congo* (London: 1909) xvi.]

★ ★ ★ ★

To argue, as some have done, that it is not our business, is an absurdity. We made it our business in 1884 and 1885, when we recognised the flag of King Leopold's enterprise as the symbol of "a humane and benevolent" enterprise, sent the Lord Mayor and Sheriffs of London in state to Brussels to present a congratulatory address, and subsequently played a leading part in the deliberations of the Berlin Conference, which, but for our concurrence, would never have been held. (119-20)

.... the [Belgian] Premier, M. de Smet de Naeyer, who pronounced the classic phrase in this story of the Congo: "The native is entitled to nothing. What is given to him is a pure gratuity."

"Of that phrase," said M. Lorand, three years later, recalling it to the [Belgian] Chamber, "a man has been found to make a system." (166)

Extract from King Leopold's speech at Antwerp on June 12, 1909: — ".... If these vast Congo territories, many of which as yet unoccupied and unproductive, were exploited would they not furnish us with the resources required for many things? The Colonial Law provides that the product of customs receipts and taxes shall be exclusively devoted to the needs of the colony. But apart from these budgetary resources, is the nation not free to give to its sons the right of obtaining from the lands as yet unappropriated and from the mines as yet untapped, the resources which will increase the openings available to their activity? Thus without calling upon the tax-payer, revenues can be secured from the Congo's virgin soil. Why should not lands and mines in the Congo be attributed to the promoters of Banks in the Far East, of founders of Belgian Steamship Companies? Revenues drawn from the Congo would thus relieve the Chambers in facing the necessities of national expenditure. Is it not legitimate that the unworked lands of the Congo should contribute to ensure our general prosperity? If we desire that our colony shall enrich the Belgian working man we must leave none of its riches untapped.

"Gentlemen, if the people of Antwerp will take up this task, I am convinced that the results will be brilliant. The greatest satisfaction of my life has been to give the Congo to Belgium. The Congo is richer than you think. The duty of a Sovereign is to enrich the nation. *Vive* the prosperity of Antwerp!" (290)

[Source: E.D. Morel, *Great Britain and the Congo* (London: 1909).]

16. Mark Twain on King Leopold

"To appreciate to the full this scathing satire upon the Sovereign of the Congo State, there are two points which should be noted.

The first is that King Leopold himself, personally, has been the real and sole Governor of the Congo territory since 1885.

The second point is that King Leopold has ever posed as a philanthropist, a benefactor to the Church, a pillar of the Christian faith, a generous donor to Arts and Sciences." From E.D. Morel's Preface to the 1907 edition of M. Twain's *King Leopold's Soliloquy*.]

★ ★ ★ ★

.... They tell it all: how I am wiping a nation of friendless creatures out of existence by every form of murder, for my private pocket's sake, and how every shilling I get costs a rape, a mutilation or a life. But they never say, although they know it, that I have labored in the cause of religion at the same time and all the time, and have sent missionaries there (of a "convenient stripe," as they phrase it), to teach them the error of their ways and bring them to Him who is all mercy and love, and who is the sleepless guardian and friend of all who suffer. They tell only what is against me, they will not tell what is in my favour.

They tell how England required of me a Commission of Inquiry into Congo atrocities, and how, to quiet that meddling country, with its disagreeable Congo Reform Association, made up of earls and bishops and John Morleys and university grandees and other dudes, more interested in other people's business than in their own. I appointed it. Did it stop their mouths? No, they merely pointed out that it was a commission composed wholly of my "Congo butchers," "the very men whose acts were to be inquired into." They said it was equivalent to appointing a commission of wolves to inquire into depredations committed upon a sheepfold. *Nothing* can satisfy a cursed Englishman!....

[*Meditative pause*] Well ... no matter, I *did* beat the Yankees, anyway! there's comfort in that. [*Reads with mocking smile, the President's Order of Recognition of April 22, 1884*]

... the government of the United States announces its sympathy with and approval of the humane and benevolent purposes of (my Congo scheme), and will order the officers of the United States, both on land and sea, to recognize its flag as the flag of a friendly government.

Possibly the Yankees would like to take that back, now, but they will find that my agents are not over there in America for nothing. But there is no danger; neither nations nor governments can afford to confess a blunder. [*With a contented smile, begins to read from "Report by Rev. W.M. Morrison, American missionary in the Congo Free State"*]

I furnish herewith some of the many atrocious incidents which have come under my own personal observation; they reveal the *organized system* of plunder and outrage which has been perpetrated and is now being carried on in that unfortunate country by King Leopold of Belgium. I say King Leopold, because he and he *alone* is now responsible, since he is the *absolute sovereign. He styles himself such.* When our government in 1884 laid the foundation of the Congo Free State, by recognizing its flag, little did it know that this concern, parading under the guise of philanthropy, was really King Leopold of Belgium, one of the shrewdest, most heartless and most conscienceless rulers that ever sat on a throne. This is apart from his known corrupt morals, which have made his name and his family a byword in two continents. Our government would most certainly not have recognized that flag had it known that it was really King Leopold individually who was asking for recognition; had it known that it was setting up in the heart of Africa an *absolute monarchy*; had it known that, having put down African slavery in our own country at great cost of blood and money, it was *establishing a worse form of slavery right in Africa.*

[*With evil joy*] Yes, I certainly was a shade too clever for the Yankees. It hurts; it gravels them. They can't get over it! Puts a shame upon them in another way, too, and a graver way; for they never can rid their records of the reproachful fact that their vain Republic, self-appointed Champion and Promoter of the Liberties of the World, is the only democracy in history that has lent its power and influence to the establishing of an *absolute monarchy!*

[*Contemplating, with an unfriendly eye, a stately pile of pamphlets*] Blister the meddlesome missionaries! They write tons of these things. They seem to be always around, always spying, always eye-witnessing the happenings; and everything they see they commit to paper. They are always prowling from place to place; the natives consider them their only friends; they go to them with their sorrows; they show them their scars and their wounds, inflicted by my soldier police; they hold up the stumps of their arms and lament because their hands have been chopped off, as punishment for not bringing in enough rubber, and as proof to be laid before my officers that the required punishment was well and truly carried out. One of these missionaries saw eighty-one of these hands drying over a fire for transmission to my officials—and of course he must go and set it down.... And that British consul, Mr. Casement, is just like them. He gets hold of a *diary which had been kept by one of my government officers*, and, although it is a private diary and intended for no eye but its owner's, Mr. Casement is so lacking in delicacy and refinement as to print passages from it.

Now as to the mutilations. You can't head off a Congo critic and make him stay headed-off; he dodges, and straightway comes back at you from another direction. They are full of slippery arts. When the mutilations (severing hands, unsexing men, etc.) began to stir Europe, we hit upon the idea of excusing them with a retort which we judged would knock them dizzy on that subject for good and all, and leave them nothing more to say; to wit, we boldly laid the custom on the natives, and said we did not invent it, but only followed it. Did it knock them dizzy? did it shut their mouths? Not for an hour. They dodged, and came straight back at us with the remark that "if a Christian king can perceive a saving moral difference between inventing bloody barbarities, and *imitating them from savages*, for charity's sake let him get what comfort he can out of his confession!"

It is most amazing, the way that that consul acts—that spy, that busy-body. [*Takes up pamphlet "Treatment of Women and Children in the Congo State; what Mr. Casement Saw in 1903"*] Hardly two years ago! Intruding that date upon the public was a piece of cold malice. It was intended to weaken the force of my press syndicate's assurances to the public that my severities in the Congo *ceased*, and ceased utterly, *years and years ago*. This man is fond of trifles—revels in them, gloats over them, pets them, fondles them, sets them all down. One doesn't need to drowse through his monotonous report to see that; the mere sub-headings of its chapters prove it. [*Reads*]

Two hundred and forty persons, *men, women and children*, compelled to supply government with *one ton* of carefully prepared foodstuffs *per week*, receiving in remuneration, all told, the princely sum of 15s. 10d!

Very well, it was liberal. It was not much short of a penny a week for each nigger. It suits this consul to belittle it, yet he knows very well that I could have had both the food and the labor for nothing. I can prove it by a thousand instances. [*Reads*]

Expedition against a village behindhand in its (compulsory) supplies; result, slaughter of sixteen persons; among them three women and a boy of five years. Ten carried off, to be prisoners till ransomed; among them a child, who died during the march.

But he is careful not to explain that we are *obliged* to resort to ransom to collect debts, where the people have nothing to pay with. Families that escape to the woods sell some of their members into slavery and thus provide the ransom. He knows that I would stop this if I could find a less objectionable way to collect their debts....

It is all the same old thing—tedious repetitions and duplications of shop-worn episodes; mutilations, murders, massacres, and so on, and so on, till one gets drowsy over it. Mr. Morel intrudes at this point, and contributes a comment which he could just as well have kept to himself—and throws in some italics, of course; these people can never get along without italics:

It is one heartrending story of human misery from beginning to end, and *it is all recent.*

Meaning 1904 and 1905. I do not see how a person can act so. This Morel is a king's subject, and reverence for monarchy should have restrained him from reflecting upon me with that exposure. This Morel is a reformer; a Congo reformer. That sizes *him* up. He publishes a sheet in Liverpool called " The West African Mail," which is supported by the voluntary contributions of the sap-headed and the soft-hearted; and every week it steams and reeks and festers with up-to-date "Congo atrocities" of the sort detailed in this pile of pamphlets here. I will suppress it. I suppressed a Congo atrocity book there, after it was actually in print; it should not be difficult for me to suppress a newspaper.

[*Studies some photographs of mutilated negroes—throws them down. Sighs*] The kodak has been a sore calamity to us. The most powerful enemy that has confronted us, indeed. In the early years we had no trouble in getting the press to "expose" the tales of the mutilations as slanders, lies, inventions of busy-body American missionaries and exasperated foreigners who had found the "open door" of the Berlin-Congo charter closed against them when they innocently went out there to trade; and by the press's help we got the Christian nations everywhere to turn an irritated and unbelieving ear to those tales and say hard things about the tellers of them. Yes, all things went harmoniously and pleasantly in those good days, and I was looked up to as the benefactor of a down-trodden and friendless people. Then all of a sudden came the crash! That is to say, the incorruptible *kodak*— and all the harmony went to hell! The only witness I have encountered in my long experience that I couldn't bribe. Every Yankee missionary and every interrupted trader sent home and got one; and now—oh, well, the pictures get sneaked around everywhere, in spite of all we can do to ferret them out and suppress them. Ten thousand pulpits and ten thousand presses are saying the good word for me all the time and placidly and convincingly denying the mutilations. Then that trivial little kodak, that a child can carry in its pocket, gets up, uttering never a word, and knocks them dumb!...

[Source: Mark Twain, *King Leopold's Soliloquy: A Defense of his Congo Rule* (Boston, MA: P. R. Warren Co., 1905) 9-40.]

17. Letter from George Gissing to his brother Algernon, 23 January 1885.

Very hateful the account of all this throat-cutting in Africa. The way in which it is written about, shows the completest barbarism still existing under the surface; in fact the whole affair is amazing if one dwells upon it. Any day we may be brought into contact with the same slaughtering, evidently. The masses of men are still in a state of partially varnished savagery; the more wonder that anyone is able to rise above it.

[Source: Algernon & Ellen Gissing, eds., *Letters of George Gissing: To Members of his Family* (London: Constable, 1927) 152.]

18. Olaudah Equiano (c 1745-97): Benin in Pre-Colonial Times

[Olaudah Equiano's autobiography was published in 1789; the following excerpts deal with Equiano's early life.]

THAT part of Africa known by the name of Guinea to which the trade for slaves is carried on extends along the coast above 3,400 miles, from the Senegal to Angola, and includes a variety of kingdoms. Of these the most considerable is the kingdom of Benin, both as to extent and wealth, the richness and cultivation of the soil, the power of its king, and the number and warlike disposition of the inhabitants. It is situated nearly under the line and extends along the coast about 170 miles, but runs back into the interior part of Africa to a distance hitherto I believe unexplored by any traveller, and seems only terminated at length by the empire of Abyssinia, near 1,500 miles from its beginning. This kingdom is divided into many provinces or districts, in one of the most remote and fertile of which, called Eboe, I was born in the year 1745, situated in a charming fruitful vale, named Essaka. The distance of this province from the capital of Benin and the sea coast must be considerable, for I had never heard of white men or Europeans, nor of the sea, and our subjection to the king of Benin was little more than nominal; for every transaction of the government, as far as my slender observation extended, was conducted by the chiefs or elders of the place. The manners and government of a people who have little commerce with other countries are generally very simple, and the history of what passes in one family or village may serve as a specimen of a nation. My father was one of those elders or chiefs I have spoken of and was styled Embrenché, a term as I remember importing the highest distinction, and signifying in our language a *mark* of grandeur. This mark is conferred on the person entitled to it by cutting the skin across at the top of the forehead and drawing it down to the eyebrows, and while it is in this situation applying a warm hand and rubbing it until it shrinks up into a thick *weal* across the lower part of the forehead. Most of the judges and senators were thus marked; my father had long borne it. I had seen it conferred on one of my brothers, and I was also *destined* to receive it by my parents. Those Embrenché or chief men decided disputes and punished crimes, for which purpose they always assembled together. The proceedings were generally short, and in most cases the law of retaliation prevailed. I remember a man was brought before my father and the other judges for kidnapping a boy, and although he was the son of a chief or senator, he was condemned to make recompense by a man or woman slave. Adultery, however, was sometimes punished with slavery or death, a punishment which I believe is inflicted on it throughout the most of the nations of Africa, so sacred among them is the honour of the marriage bed and so jealous are they of the fidelity of their wives. Of this I recollect an instance—a woman was convicted before the judges of adultery, and delivered over, as the custom was, to her husband, to be punished. Accordingly he determined to put her to death: but it being found just before her execution that she had an infant at her breast, and no woman being prevailed on to perform the part of a nurse, she was spared on account of the child. The men however do not preserve the same constancy to their wives which they expect from them, for they indulge in a plurality, though seldom in more than two. Their mode of marriage is thus: both parties are usually betrothed when young by their parents, (though I have known the males to betroth themselves). On this occasion a feast is prepared, and the bride and bridegroom stand up in the midst of all their friends who are assembled for the purpose, while he declares she is thenceforth to be looked upon as his wife, and that no other person is to pay any addresses to her. This is also immediately proclaimed in the vicinity, on which the bride retires from the assembly. Some time after she is brought home to her husband, and then another feast is made to which the relations of both parties are invited: her parents then deliver her to the bridegroom accompanied with a number of blessings, and at the same time they tie round her waist a cotton string of the thickness of a goose-quill, which not but married women are permitted to wear: she is now considered as completely his wife, and at this time the dowry is given to the new married pair, which generally consists of portions of land, slaves, and cattle, household goods, and implements of husbandry. These are offered by the friends of both parties, besides which the parents of the bridegroom present gifts to those of the bride, whose property she is looked upon before marriage; but after it she is esteemed the sole property of her husband. The ceremony being now ended, the festival begins, which is celebrated with bonfires and loud acclamations of joy accompanied with music and dancing.

We are almost a nation of dancers, musicians, and poets. Thus every great event such as a triumphant return from battle or other cause of public rejoicing is celebrated in public dances, which are accompanied with songs and music suited to the occasion. The assembly is separated into four divisions, which dance either apart or in succession, and each with a character peculiar to itself. The first division contains the married men, who in their dances frequently exhibit feats of arms and the representation of a battle. To these succeed the married women, who dance in the second division. The young men occupy the third and the maidens the fourth. Each represents some interesting scene of real life, such as a great achievement, domestic employment, a pathetic story, or some rural sport, and as the subject is generally founded on some recent event it is therefore ever new. This gives our dances a spirit and variety which I have scarcely seen elsewhere. We have many musical instruments, particularly drums of different kinds, a piece of music which resembles a guitar, and another much like a stickado. These last are chiefly used by betrothed virgins who play on them on all grand festivals.

As our manners are simple, our luxuries are few. The dress of both sexes is nearly the same. It generally consists of a long piece of calico or muslin, wrapped loosely round the body somewhat in the form of a highland plaid. This is usually dyed blue, which is our favourite colour.

It is extracted from a berry and is brighter and richer than any I have seen in Europe. Besides this our women of distinction wear golden ornaments, which they dispose with some profusion on their arms and legs. When are women are not employed with the men in tillage, their usual occupation is spinning and weaving cotton, which they afterwards dye and make into garments. They also manufacture earthen vessels, of which we have many kinds. Among the rest tobacco pipes, made after the same fashion and used in the same manner, as those in Turkey.

Our manner of living is entirely plain, for as yet the natives are unacquainted with those refinements in cookery which debauch the taste: bullocks, goats, and poultry, supply the greatest part of their food. These constitute likewise the principal wealth of the country and the chief articles of its commerce. The flesh is usually stewed in a pan; to make it savoury we sometimes use also pepper and other spices, and we have salt made of wood ashes. Our vegetables are mostly plantains, eadas, yams, beans, and Indian corn. The head of the family usually eats alone; his wives and slaves have also their separate tables. Before we taste food we always wash our hands: indeed our cleanliness on all occasions is extreme, but on this it is an indispensable ceremony. After washing, libation is made by pouring out a small portion of the drink on the floor, and tossing a small quantity of the food in a certain place for the spirits of departed relations, which the natives suppose to preside over their conduct and guard them from evil. They are totally unacquainted with strong or spirituous liquors, and their principal beverage is palm wine. This is got from a tree of that name by tapping it at the top and fastening a large gourd to it, and sometimes one tree will yield three or four gallons in a night. When just drawn it is of a most delicious sweetness, but in a few days it acquires a tartish and more spirituous flavour, though I never saw anyone intoxicated by it. The same tree also produces nuts and oils. Our principal luxury is in perfumes; one sort of these is an odoriferous wood of delicious fragrance, the other a kind of earth, a small portion of which thrown into the fire diffuses a more powerful odour. We beat this wood into powder and mix it with palm oil, with which both men and women perfume themselves.

In our buildings we study convenience rather than ornament. Each master of a family has a large square piece of ground, surrounded with a moat or fence or enclosed with a wall made of red earth tempered, which when dry is as hard a brick. Within this are his houses to accommodate his family and slaves which if numerous frequently present the appearance of a village. In the middle stands the principal building, appropriated to the sole use of the master and consisting of two apartments, in one of which he sits in the day with his family. The other is left apart for the reception of his friends. He has besides these a distinct apartment in which he sleeps, together with his male children. On each side are the apartments of his wives, who have also their separate day and night houses. The habitations of the slaves and their families are distributed throughout the rest of the enclosure. These houses never exceed one storey in height: they are always built of wood or stakes driven into the ground, crossed with wattles, and neatly plastered within and without. The roof is thatched with reeds. Our day-houses are left open at the sides, but those in which we sleep are always covered, and plastered in the inside with a composition mixed with cow-dung to keep off the different insects which annoy us during the night. The walls and floors also of these are generally covered with mats. Our beds consist of a platform raised three or four feet from the ground, on which are laid skins and different parts of a spungy tree called plantain. Our covering is calico or muslin, the same as our dress. The usual seats are a few logs of wood, but we have benches, which are generally perfumed to accommodate strangers: these compose the greater part of our household furniture. Houses so constructed and furnished require but little skill to erect them. Every man is a sufficient architect for the purpose. The whole neighbourhood afford their unanimous assistance in building them and in return receive and expect no other recompense than a feast.

As we live in a country where nature is prodigal of her favours, our wants are few and easily supplied; of course we have few manufactures. They consist for the most part of calicoes, earthenware, ornaments, and instruments of war and husbandry. But these make no part of our commerce, the principal articles of which, as I have observed, are provisions. In such a state money is of little use; however we have some small pieces of coin, if I may call them such. They are made of something like an anchor, but I do not remember either their value or denomination. We have also markets, at which I have been frequently with my mother. These are sometimes visited by stout mahogany-coloured men from the south-west of us: we call them *Oye-Eboe*, which term signifies red men living at a distance. They generally bring us fire-arms, gunpowder, hats, beads, and dried fish. The last we esteemed a great rarity as our waters were only brooks and springs. These articles they barter with us for odoriferous woods and earth, and our salt of wood ashes. They always carry slaves through our land, but the strictest account is exacted of their manner of procuring them before they are suffered to pass. Sometimes indeed we sold slaves to them, but they were only prisoners of war, or such among us as had been convicted of kidnapping, or adultery, and some other crimes which we esteemed heinous. This practice of kidnapping induces me to think that, notwithstanding all our strictness, their principal business among us was to trepan our people. I remember too they carried great sacks along with them, which not long after I had an opportunity of fatally seeing applied to that infamous purpose....

All our industry is exerted to improve those blessings of nature. Agriculture is our chief employment, and everyone, even the children and women, are engaged in it. Thus we are all habituated to labour from our earliest years. Everyone contributes something to the common stock, and as we are unacquainted with idleness we have no beggars. The benefits of such a mode of living are obvious. The West India planters prefer the slaves of Benin or Eboe to those of any other part of Guinea for their hardiness, intelligence, integrity, and zeal. Those benefits are felt by us in the general healthiness of the people, and in their vigour and activity; I might have added too in their comeliness. Deformity is indeed unknown amongst us, I mean that of shape. Numbers of the natives of Eboe now in London might be brought in support of this assertion, for in regards to complexion, ideas of beauty are wholly relative. I remember while in Africa to have seen three negro children who were tawny, and another quite white, who were universally regarded by myself and the natives in general, as far as related to their complexions, as deformed. Our women too were in my eyes at least uncommonly graceful, alert, and modest to a degree of bashfulness; nor do I remember to have ever heard of an instance of incontinence amongst them before marriage. They are also remarkably cheerful. Indeed cheerfulness and affability are two of the leading characteristics of our nation.

Our tillage is exercised in a large plain or common, some hours walk from our dwellings, and all the neighbours resort thither in a body. They use no beasts of husbandry, and their only instruments are hoes, axes, shovels, and beaks, or pointed iron to dig with. Sometimes we are visited by locusts, which come in large clouds so as to darken the air and destroy our harvest. This however happens rarely, but when it does a famine is produced by it. I remember an instance or two wherein this happened. This common is often the theatre of war, and therefore when our people go out to till their land they not only go in a body but generally take their arms with them for fear of a surprise, and when they apprehend an invasion they guard the avenues to their dwellings by driving sticks into the ground, which are so sharp at one end as to pierce the foot and are generally dipped in poison. From what I can recollect of these battles, they appear to have been irruptions of one little state or district on the other to obtain prisoners or booty. Perhaps they were incited to this by those traders who brought the European goods I mentioned amongst us. Such a mode of obtaining slaves in Africa is common, and I believe more are procured this way and by kidnapping than any other. When a trader wants slaves he applies to a chief for them and tempts him with his wares. It is not extraordinary if on this occasion he yields to the temptation with as little firmness, and accepts the price of his fellow creatures' liberty with as little reluctance as the enlightened merchant. Accordingly he falls on his neighbours and a desperate battle ensues. If he prevails and take prisoners, he gratifies his avarice by selling them; but if his party be vanquished and he falls into the hands of the enemy, he is put to death: for as he has been known to foment their quarrels it is thought dangerous to let him survive, and no ransom can save him, though all other prisoners may be redeemed....

As to religion, the natives believe that there is one Creator of all things and that he lives in the sun and is girded round with a belt that he may never eat or drink; but according to some he smokes a pipe, which is our own favourite luxury. They believe he governs events, especially our deaths or captivity, but as for the doctrine of eternity, I do not remember to have ever heard of it: some however believe in the transmigration of souls in a certain degree. Those spirits which are not transmigrated, such as their dear friends or relations, they believe always attend them and guard them from the bad spirits of their foes. For this reason they always before eating, as I have observed, put some small portion of the meat and pour some of their drink, on the ground for them, and they often make oblations of the blood of beasts or fowls at their graves. I was very fond of my mother and almost constantly with her. When she went to make these oblations at her mother's tomb, which was a kind of small solitary thatched house, I sometimes attended her. There she made her libations and spent most of the night in cries and lamentations. I have been often extremely terrified on these occasions. The loneliness of the place, the darkness of the night, and the ceremony of libation, naturally awful and gloomy, were heightened by my mother's lamentations; and these, concurring with the doleful cries of birds by which these places were frequented, gave an inexpressible terror to the scene.

We compute the year from the day on which the sun crosses the line, and on its setting that evening there is a general shout throughout the land; at least I can speak from my own knowledge throughout our vicinity. The people at the same time make a great noise with rattles, not unlike the basket rattles used by children here, though much larger, and hold up their hands to heaven for a blessing. It is then the greatest offerings are made, and those children whom our wise men foretell will be fortunate are then presented to different people....

We practised circumcision like the Jews and made offerings and feasts on that occasion in the same manner as they did. Like them also, our children were named from some event, some circumstance, or fancied foreboding at the time of their birth. I was named *Olaudah*, which in our language signifies vicissitude or fortunate; also, one favoured, and having a loud voice and well spoken. I remember we never polluted the name of the object of our adoration; on the contrary it was always mentioned with the greatest reverence, and we were totally unacquainted with swearing and all those terms of abuse and reproach which find their way so readily and copiously into the languages of more civilized people. The only expressions of that kind I remember were 'May you rot', or 'may you swell', or 'may a beast take you'.

I have before remarked that the natives of this part of Africa are extremely cleanly. This necessary habit of decency was with us a part of religion, and therefore we had many purifications and washings; indeed almost as many and used on the same occasions, if my recollection does not fail me, as the Jews. Those that touched the dead at any time were obliged to wash and purify themselves before they could enter a dwelling-house. Every woman too, at certain times, was forbidden to come into a dwelling-house or touch any person or anything we ate. I was so fond of my mother I could not keep from her or avoid touching her at some of those periods, in consequence of which I was obliged to be kept out with her in a little house made for that purpose till offering was made, and then we were purified.

Though we had no places of public worship, we had priests and magicians or wise men. I do not remember whether they had different offices or whether they were united in the same persons, but they were held in great reverence by the people. They calculated our time and foretold events, as their name imported, for we called them Ah-affoe-way-cah, which signifies calculators or yearly men, our year being called Ah-affoe. They wore their beards, and when they died they were succeeded by their sons. Most of their implements and things of value were interred along with them. Pipes and tobacco were also put into the grave with the corpse, which was always perfumed and ornamented, and animals were offered in sacrifice to them. None accompanied their funerals but those of the same profession or tribe. These buried them after sunset and always returned from the grave by a different way from that which they went.

These magicians were also our doctors or physicians. They practised bleeding by cupping, and were very successful in healing wounds and expelling poisons. They had likewise some extraordinary method of discovering jealousy, theft, and poisoning, the success of which no doubt they derived from their unbounded influence over the credulity and superstition of the people. I do not remember what those methods were, except that as to poisoning …

The natives are extremely cautious about poison. When they buy any eatable the seller kisses it all round before the buyer to show him it is not poisoned, and the same is done when any meat or drink is presented, particularly to a stranger …

My father, besides many slaves, had a numerous family of which seven lived to grow up, including myself and a sister who was the only daughter. As I was the youngest of the sons, I became, of course, the greatest favourite with my mother and was always with her; and she used to take particular pains to form my mind. I was trained from my earliest years in the art of war, my daily exercise was shooting and throwing javelins, and my mother adorned me with emblems after the manner of our greatest warriors. In this way I grew up till I was turned the age of 11, when an end was put to my happiness in the following manner. Generally when the grown people in the neighbourhood were gone far in the fields to labour, the children assembled together in some of the neighbours' premises to play, and commonly some of us used to get up a tree to look out for any assailant or kidnapper that might come upon us, for they sometimes took these opportunities of our parents' absence to attack and carry off as many as they could seize. One day, as I was watching at the top of a tree in our yard, I saw one of those people come into the yard of our next neighbour but one to kidnap, there being many stout young people in it. Immediately on this I gave the alarm of the rogue and he was surrounded by the stoutest of them, who entangled him with cords so that he could not escape till some of the grown people came and secured him. But alas! ere long it was my fate to be thus attacked and to be carried off when none of the grown people were nigh. One day, when all our people were gone out to their works as usual and only I and my dear sister were left to mind the house, two men and a woman got over our walls, and in a moment seized us both, and without giving us time to cry out or make resistance they stopped our mouths and ran off with us into the nearest wood. Here they tied our hands and continued to carry us as far as they could till night came on, when we reached a small house where the robbers halted for refreshment and spent the night. We were then unbound but were unable to take any food, and being quite overpowered by fatigue and grief, our only relief was some sleep, which allayed our misfortune for a short time. The next morning we left the house and continued travelling all the day …

From the time I left my own nation I always found somebody that understood me till I came to the sea coast. The languages of different nations did not totally differ, nor were they so copious as those of the Europeans, particularly the English. They were therefore easily learned, and while I was journeying thus through Africa I acquired two or three different tongues ...

I was again sold and carried through a number of places till, after travelling a considerable time, I came to a town called Tinmah in the most beautiful country I had yet seen in Africa. It was extremely rich, and there were many rivulets which flowed through it and supplied a large pond in the centre of the town, where the people washed. Here I first saw and tasted coconuts, which I thought superior to any nuts I had ever tasted before; and the trees, which were loaded, were also interspersed amongst the houses, which had commodious shades adjoining and were in the same manner as ours, the insides being neatly plastered and whitewashed. Here I also saw and tasted for the first time sugarcane. Their money consisted of little white shells the size of the fingernail. I was sold here for 172 of them by a merchant who lived and brought me there....

All the nations and people I had hitherto passed through resembled our own in their manner, customs, and language: but I came at length to a country the inhabitants of which differed from us in all those particulars. I was very much struck with this difference, especially when I came among a people who did not circumcise and ate without washing their hands. They cooked also in iron pots and had European cutlasses and crossbows, which were unknown to us, and fought with their fists among themselves. Their women were not so modest as ours, for they ate and drank and slept with their men. But above all, I was amazed to see no sacrifices or offerings among them. In some of those places the people ornamented themselves with scars, and likewise filed their teeth very sharp. They wanted sometimes to ornament me in the same manner, but I would not suffer them, hoping that I might some time be among a people who did not thus disfigure themselves, as I thought they did. At last I came to the banks of a large river, which was covered with canoes in which the people appeared to live with their household utensils and provisions of all kinds. I was beyond measure astonished at this, as I had never before seen any water larger than a pond or a rivulet: and my surprise was mingled with no small fear when I was put into one of these canoes and we began to paddle and move along the river. We continued going on thus till night, and when we came to land and made fires on the banks, each family by themselves, some dragged their canoes on shore, others stayed and cooked in theirs and laid in them all night.

Those on the land had mats of which they made tents, some in the shape of little houses: in these we slept, and after the morning meal we embarked again and proceeded as before. I was often very much astonished to see some of the women, as well as the men, jump into the water, dive to the bottom, come up again, and swim about. Thus I continued to travel, sometimes by land, sometimes by water, through different countries and various nations, till at the end of six or seven months after I had been kidnapped I arrived at the sea coast.

[Source: Paul Edwards, ed., *The Interesting Narrative —Equiano's Travels: His Autobiography* (New York: Praegar, 1967) 1-24.]

19. Commander R.H. Bacon, Intelligence Officer to the Benin Expedition

TRULY has Benin been called The City of Blood. Its history is one long record of savagery of the most debased kind. In the earlier part of this century, when it was the centre of the slave trade, human suffering must here have reached its most acute form, but it is doubtful if even then the wanton sacrifice of life could have exceeded that of more recent times. Nothing that can be called religion exists within its limits, only paganism of the most unenlightened description, with certain rites and observances, which, from their ferocious cruelty, have caused Benin to be the capital of superstitious idolatry and barbarity for more than a hundred miles inland. The Benin Juju is the Juju bowed to by tribes even beyond the Kukuruku country, and even holds the more civilised Jakri or water tribes, now for some years under English protection, in a half doubtful belief.

Juju is a term of wide meaning, and embraces every form of superstitious offering to, or imaginary decree of, a god, from the gin-bottle hung on a branch to a human sacrifice, the culmination of their magic and atrocities. The King to a large extent has had the right of placing the ban of Juju on anything in his kingdom by the exercise of his mystical powers, and this he has often done with articles of commerce, such as rubber and ivory; and so by his arbitrary decrees, and the servile superstition of his subjects, prevented the trade in these articles passing through his dominions. One of the Jujus of the Beni is never to cross water; hence they never enter canoes, and all the river trade is done by Jakris or Ijos; therefore each large waterside Benin town has its Jakri village or settlement, inhabited by the agents of the chiefs and their men during trading operations.

This complete isolation from the water, and therefore to a great extent from contact with white men, must have done much to prevent the smallest seeds of civilisation finding their way to the capital. The King himself is supposed to have his limiting Jujus, one of which is that he must never enter the town until he is made king, nor ever after leave it. To what extent this Juju is binding, and how it may work to his ultimate death, or capture, from his betrayal by his subjects, now that he has fled from the city, will be interesting to see...

The history of the painful massacre is too well known to recapitulate. But there are one or two points it is well to dwell on.

Firstly, The King sent a message to say that he was "making his father," and did not wish to receive the mission.

Secondly, Mr. Phillips sent a message to the King to tell him that the mission was of importance and could not be delayed, to which an answer was sent that the King would receive the mission.

Now, "making one's father" is an African native custom, which takes place once a year, and is an excuse for general holiday making, eating, drinking and dancing; and, in the case of the more debased natives, sacrifices, human and otherwise. That King Duboar would not have cared to have Englishmen present at Benin during his fiendish orgies one can well imagine; but, at the same time, would not a gallant man like Phillips probably think that the presence of his mission might restrain the blood-lust of the King and Juju priests, and perhaps save some poor creatures from an untimely death?.. We have heard the Little England wail of interfering with the prerogatives of native royalty. There are, however, some prerogatives of native royalty that make interference necessary.

The massacre took place on January 4, 1897 ... it was not till the 15th that orders were received from the Admiralty to organise an expedition against Benin....

An average nigger of low type lies without compunction if there is the slightest thing to be gained by it, and often, when nothing can be gained one way or the other, out of absolute indifference to telling a lie or the truth.... The brain of the black man is also very slow; when once fairly on a subject it works well, and he has a good memory, but change from one point to another and apparently his brain cannot do so quickly, and it will take some few minutes of waiting and patient interrogation before he thoroughly gets in touch with the new subject. They are not, therefore, easy people to manipulate from an intelligence point of view.

Nearing Ologbo the Maxim was played on the bush to dislodge any enemy that might have been in ambush. No firing was returned, and at 8.10 the force disembarked by wading ashore.

In most of the Juju compounds was a well for the reception of the bodies.

The one lasting remembrance of Benin in my mind is its smells. Crucifixions, human sacrifices, and every horror the eye could get accustomed to, to a large extent, but the smells no white man's internal economy could stand. Four times in one day I was practically sick from them, and many more times on the point of being so. Every person who was able, I should say, indulged in a human sacrifice, and those who could not, sacrificed some animal and left the remains in front of his house. After a day or so the whole town seemed one huge pest-house.

And these pits! who could describe them; out of one a Jakri boy was pulled with drag-ropes from under several corpses; he said he had been in five days. But it is incredible that he could have lived that time in such a place; *one day, or two at the outside, must have killed even a black man.* [Editor's italics]

Blood was everywhere; smeared over bronzes, ivory, and even the walls, and spoke the history of that awful city in a clearer way than writing ever could. And this had been going on for centuries! Not the lust of one king, not the climax of a bloody reign, but the religion (save the word!) of the race. The Juju held sway for a hundred miles all round, and that in the older and more flourishing times of the city must have been practised with, if possible, greater intensity than at the present day.

Human sacrifice undoubtedly differs in criminal degree, as do the various grades of every other barbaric custom.

It should be remembered that no one blames Abraham for his attempted sacrifice of Isaac, doing it with sorrow from absolutely conscientious motives, and cases where the blame to the individual must be comparatively small still remain. For instance, a not uncommon form in some parts is for a chief at times to kill a slave to take a message to his father, or some reverenced person, in the land of shades. On these occasions a slave is sent for and given the message, and told when he gets to the next world to give it to the chief's father. The slave repeats the message, absolutely believes that when he dies he will find the old chief, give him the message, and then enter his service in the far-off world. He is then killed quite willingly and peaceably, for the confidence of the black slave in his chief is unbounded. Again, the killing of wives and slaves to accompany the dead man to the next world is not without its redeeming side. But the atrocities of Benin, originating in blood lust and desire to terrorise the neighbouring states, the brutal love of mutilation and torture, and the wholesale manner in which the caprices of the King and Juju were satisfied, could only have been the result of centuries of stagnant brutality.

... But buried in the dirt of ages, in one house, were several hundred unique bronze plaques, suggestive of almost Egyptian design, but of really superb casting. Castings of wonderful delicacy of detail, and some magnificently carved tusks were collected... Of other ivory work, some bracelets suggestive of Chinese work and two magnificent leopards were the chief articles of note; bronze groups of idols, and two large and beautifully-worked stools were also found, and must have been of very old manufacture.

Leaving the compound and facing north there was immediately in front a clear space, forming, so to speak, the delta of the road leading to the water at Ikpoba. On the right was a crucifixion tree with a double crucifixion on it, the two poor wretches stretched out facing the west, with their arms bound together in the middle. The construction of this tree was peculiar, being absolutely built for the purpose of crucifixion. At the base were skulls and bones, literally strewn about; the débris of former sacrifices. The other crucifixion tree was used for single crucifixion only, and here a woman was crucified, and again the green shrubs at the base of the tree were full of bones and skulls.

... It is useless to continue describing the horrors of the place, everywhere death, barbarity, and blood, and smells that it hardly seemed right for human beings to smell and yet live.

And yet the town was not without its beauty of a sort. Plenty of trees and green all round, the houses built in no set fashion, but each compound surrounded by its own bushes and shady avenues. It seemed a place suggestive of peace and plenty; *let us now hope it may one day become so.* [Editor's italics]

... Glad we were to leave Benin, but sorry enough to say good-bye to the friends we had so recently made, and whose friendship the expedition had so speedily cemented;—good luck go with them, and may England always have such men to hold her rights for her in any part of the world where sudden trouble may arise! Their work for the next few months will not exactly be a bed of roses up in Benin, holding the place till the Beni come in and settle down. Treacherous though they are, it is unlikely they will try and recapture the place after the lessons received from the Maxims and breech-loaders of our troops. Their Juju is broken, their fetich places burned; the King's House is the Palace of the White Chief, and their own Palava House the assembly place where they will be dictated to as to terms of surrender and their future behaviour. The crucifixion trees have disappeared, and they cannot fail to see that peace and the good rule of the white man mean happiness, contentment, and security...

Time will show the effect of our possession of Benin. On the trade of the Benin River it cannot fail to be beneficial. The removal of trade Jujus, and increased security to travellers of all sorts, must not only bring the products of the country itself to European markets, but also increase the passage of trade from the interior. Moreover, the capture of the ancient city, at nearly the same time as the destruction of the power of Beda, farther inland, will greatly increase the prestige of the white man, and make him safer and more respected in his travels through the neighbouring countries.

[Source: *Benin: The City of Blood* (London & New York: Edward Arnold, 1897) 13-129.]

20. Captain Alan Boisragon, One of the Two Survivors, Commandant of the Niger Coast Protectorate Force

Juju here is everything, religion, superstition, custom, anything. And with it go such gentle customs as human sacrifices, cannibalism, twin-killing, and others. Of course all these customs are being abolished as fast as possible, and every year sees law and order brought into fresh big tracts of country where before all these brutalities used to take place. As far as human sacrifices are concerned, life in these parts, anyway the life of a slave, is not valued at much, and the gentle savage cannot understand why we should object to a few men being killed for a big man's funeral, or for some similar purpose, when such has been the custom of the country ever since there were people in it. Then the big man who is about to die also objects strongly, for he says that no one in the other world will believe that he has been a big man in this, unless he brings a certain amount of slaves with him to show what he can do in that line. He also thinks it is very hard lines that, after having spent so much money in celebrating his relative's funeral and in purchasing slaves for his own, he cannot do what he likes with his own goods and chattels. It is the anniversary of the death of the chief's grandmother's aunt, up go a few slaves; a new market is to be opened, up goes a wretched slave; nothing seemed to be celebrated properly in this Juju land unless it was accompanied by the death of some unfortunates. Of course I am talking about Benin City and such-like places, where the rule of the

Protectorate had not yet reached, for if we could get at them there was always punishment for any town or village committing human sacrifices after having been warned not to.

Cannibalism was also one of the sweet things of the past all over the Protectorate. Even the Brass natives, who were a fairly civilised people, most of whom could talk English, and in whose town, Nimbe, there was a mission-station, with a sweet little church, were not beyond it. And after their successful raid on Akassa, mentioned above, most of them killed and ate the Kroo boy prisoners they had taken there. There was one brilliant exception, Chief Warri, now the head chief of that part of the world, who kept his prisoners, treated them exceedingly well, and sent them all down to the Vice-Consulate afterwards. Amongst the cannibals was the son of a chief just returned from England, where he had been for some years being educated in a missionary college. There happened to be a French father from the Roman Catholic Mission at Onicha on the Niger, in Nimbe, the capital of the Brassmen, at the time, who of course wasn't allowed to go away, but was otherwise well treated. This educated, civilised chief's son, waltzing about the town with a Kroo boy's leg over his shoulder, came across the father, and said "Father, have a bit." Civilisation had not gone very deep.

The killing of twins is another wretched, insane custom that seems to have been in force for centuries, but which is also being stopped all over the Protectorate. The usual thing was when a wretched woman gave birth to twins for the babies to be killed or thrown into the bush to die, and the unfortunate mother to be driven away, never allowed to come near any town or village, and most probably to die of starvation in the bush. The house in which the twins were born, and everything in it, was destroyed, and the father had to pay sacrifices of sheep and fowls by way of purifying the village again. After that he could take another wife, but could never have his former wife back, or even see her again. Now villages, called twin villages, have been made in several places, where the unfortunate mothers can go and live, while the babies are saved and brought up by someone else.

In conclusion, I should like to quote an extract from a letter of a comrade of the late Mr. Phillips: — "... The loss which the British nation has sustained during the last sixty years, through the deaths of so many brave soldiers, bluejackets, and civilians in the glorious work of rescuing the native races in West Africa from the horrors of human sacrifice, cannibalism, and the tortures of fetish worship, must ever be a matter of deep regret and sadness to all; but it cannot fail to make us proud of our countrymen who have nobly and courageously done their duty with the greatest enthusiasm, undergoing hardship and privation inseparable from the trying climate of the West African Coast, and exhibiting in their conduct an entire disregard of personal danger."

[Source: *The Benin Massacre* (London: Methuen, 1897) 29-33, 189-90.]

Appendix D: Major Textual Changes

[Following are the major changes from the manuscript (as in *Joseph Conrad: Heart of Darkness*, ed. Robert Kimborough [New York: Norton, 1983]) and magazine versions of the text (*Blackwood's Edinburgh Magazine*, February-April, 1899).]

I, 65   *Ms:* got. That's all. The best of them is they didn't get up pretty fictions about it. Was there, I wonder, an association on a philanthropic basis to develop Britain, with some third rate king for a president and solemn old senators discoursing about it approvingly and philosophers with uncombed beards praising it, and men in market places crying it up. Not much! And that's what I like! No! No! It was just, *etc.*

I, 66   *Ms:* river. A big steamer came down all a long blaze of lights like a town viewed from the sea bound to the utter-most ends of the earth and timed to the day, to the very hour with nothing unknown in her path [,] no mystery on her way, nothing but a few coaling stations. She went fullspeed, noisily, an angry commotion of the waters followed her spreading from bank to bank — passed, vanished all at once — timed from port to port, to the very hour. And the early suddenly seemed shrunk to the size of a pea spinning in the heart of an immense darkness full of sparks born, scattered, glowing, going out beyond the ken of men. We looked on, *etc.*

I, 75   *Ms:* river where my work was waiting for me. We went up some twenty miles and anchored off the seat of the government. I had heard enough in Europe about its advanced state of civilization: the papers, nay the very paper vendors in the sepulchral city were boasting about the steam tramway and the hotel — especially the hotel. I beheld that wonder. It was like a symbol at the gate. It stood alone, a grey high cube of iron with two tiers of galleries outside towering above one of those ruinous-looking foreshores you come upon at home in out-of-the-way places where refuse is thrown out. To make the resemblance complete it wanted only a drooping post bearing a board with the legend: rubbish shot here, and the symbol would have had the clearness of the naked truth. Not that a man could not be found even there, just as a precious stone is sometimes found in a dust-bin.

I had one dinner in the hotel and found out the tramway ran only twice a day, at mealtimes. It brought I believe the whole government with the exception of the governor general down from the hill to be fed by contract. They filled the dining room, uniforms and civil clothes [,] sallow faces, purposeless expressions. I was astonished at their number. An air of weary bewilderment at finding themselves where they were sat upon all the faces, and in their demeanour they pretended to take themselves seriously just as the greasy and dingy place that was like one of those infamous eating shops you find near the slums of cities, where everything is suspicious, the linen, the crockery, the food [,] the owner [,] the patrons, pretended to be a sign of progress; as the enormous baobab on the barren top of the hill amongst the government buildings [,] soldier's huts, wooden shanties, corrugated iron hovels, soared, spread out a maze of denuded boughs as though it had been a shade giving tree, as ghastly as a skeleton that posturing in showy attitudes would pretend to be, a man.

I was glad to think my work only began two hundred miles away from there. I could not be too far away from that comedy of light at the door of darkness. As soon as I could I left for a place thirty miles higher up. From there I would have to walk on the caravan road some hundred and seventy miles more to the starting point of inland navigation.

I had my passage, *etc.*

I, 75   *Ms*: perhaps. The little steamer had no speed to speak of and I was rather impatient to see the first establishment, the shore station of my company. We had left the coast belt of forest and barren, stony hills came to view right and left of the stream, bordering flat strips of reedy coarse grass. [*Canceled:* As we rounded a point I heard far ahead a powerful and muffled detonation as of a big gun. After a time there was another. It reminded me of the ship shelling the continent. "What's that?" I asked. "Railway station," answered the Swede curtly, preparing to make a crossing to the south bank.]

At last we opened a reach, *etc.*

I, 80   *Ms canceled*: Klein (and the next three times; thereafter, Kurtz).

I, 83   *Ms*: explain. It could be seen from a distance as he walked
         about the station grounds, a silent perambulating, glancing
         figure—with the air of being very much alone. It was
         unconscious, *etc.*

II, 97   *Ms*: confidence. But there was nothing, there could be noth-
         ing. The thick voice was swallowed up, the confident gesture
         was lost in the high stillness that fronted these two mean and
         atrocious figures with its ominous air [of] patient waiting, *etc.*

II, 100 *Ms:* surroundings. It could only be obtained by conquest—
         or by surrender, but we passed on indifferent, surprising, less
         than phantoms, wondering and secretly *etc.*

II, 100 *Ms:* faces. You know how it is when we hear the band of the
         regiment. A martial noise—and you pacific father, mild
         guardian of a domestic heartstone [*sic*] suddenly find yourself
         thinking of carnage. The joy of killing—hey? Or did you
         never, when listening to another kind of music, did you never
         dream yourself capable of becoming a saint—if—if. Aha!
         Another noise, another appeal, another response. All true. All
         there—in you. Not for you tho' the joy of killing—or the
         felicity of being a saint. Too many things in the way, business,
         houses, omnibuses, police[,] the man next door. You don't
         know my respectable friends how much you owe to the man
         next door. He is a great fact. There[']s very few places on
         earth where you haven't a man next door to you or some-
         thing of him, the merest trace, his footprint—that's enough.
         You heard the yells and saw the dance and there was the man
         next door to call you names if you felt an impulse to yell and
         dance yourself. Another kindly appeal too, and, by Jove, if you
         did not watch yourself, if you had no weak spot in you where
         you could take refuge, you would perceive a responsive stir.
         Why not! Especially if you had a brain. There's all the past as
         well as all the future in a man's mind. And no kind neighbor
         to hang you promptly. The discretion of the wilderness, the
         night, the darkness of the land that would hide everything.
         Principles? Principles—acquisitions, clothes, rags, rags that
         fall off if you gave yourself a good shake. There was the naked
         truth—dancing, howling, praying, cursing. Rage. Fear. Joy.
         Who can tell. It was an appeal. Who's that grunting? You
         don't think I went ashore to dance too. Not I. I had to mess

about with white lead and strips of blanket bandaging those leaky steam pipes—I tell you. And I had to watch the steering, and I had to look after the savage who was fireman. He was being improved—he was improved. He could fire up a vertical boiler, *etc.*

II, 114   *Ms:* worse. That's a monster-truth with many maws to whom we've got to throw every year—or every day—no matter— no sacrifice is too great—a ransom of pretty, shining lies— not very new perhaps—but spotless, aureoled, tender. Oh, she, *etc.*

II, 116   *Ms canceled after* contaminated: To say there's no dead hippo won't do. And there, *etc.*

II, 117   *Ms canceled:* brutes. Kill every single brute of them.

II, 117   *Ms:* upon 'my career.' His Intended, his ivory, his future, his career.

III, 125   *Ms and Blackwood's:* symbolic of some cruel and forbidden knowledge. They were, *etc.*

III, 125   *Ms and Blackwood's:* invasion. It had tempted him with all the sinister suggestions of its loneliness. I think, *etc.*

III, 126   *Ms:* all. And his was a sturdy allegiance, soaring bravely above the facts which it could see with a bewilderment and a sorrow akin to despair. I had, *etc.*

III, 129   *Ms and Blackwood's:* and she stopped. Had her heart failed her, or had her eyes veiled with that mournfulness that lies over all the wild things of the earth seen the hopelessness of longing that will find out sometimes even a savage soul in the loneliness [*Blackwood's:* lonely darkness] of its being? Who can tell. Perhaps she did not know herself. The young fellow, *etc.*

III, 129   *Ms:* embrace. Her sudden gesture was as startling as a cry but not a sound was heard. The formidable silence of the scene completed the memorable impression. *Blackwood's:* embrace. Her sudden gesture seemed to demand a cry, but the unbroken silence that hung over the scene was more formidable than any sound could be. *1902*: embrace. A formidable silence hung over the scene.

III, 134   *Ms and Blackwood's*: thing that seemed released from one grave only to sink forever into another. 'You will, *etc.*

III, 136   *Ms*: to one's belief in mankind, *added 1902.*

III, 137–8 *Ms*: My Intended, my ivory, my station, my career, my ideas.

III, 138   *Ms*: 'Oh, but I will make you serve my ends.'

III, 138   *Ms*: die nobly

III, 139   *Ms and Blackwood's*: rent. I saw on that ivory visage the expression of strange pride, of mental power, of avarice, of blood-thirstiness, of cunning, of excessive terror, of intense and hopeless despair. Did he live his life through in every detail of desire[,] temptation[,] and surrender during that short and supreme moment? [*Ms only continues:*] He cried at some image, at some vision, he cried with a cry that was no more than a breath —
    "Oh! the horror!"
    I blew the candle out and left the cabin. Never before in his life had he been such a master of his magnificent gift as in his last on earth.
    The pilgrims, *etc.*

III, 143   *Ms and Blackwood's*: yet that face on paper seemed to be a reflection of truth itself. One felt, *etc.*

III, 143   *Ms and Blackwood's*: features. She looked out trustfully. She seemed ready, *etc.*

III, 143   *Ms and Blackwood's*: well-kept sepulchre.

III, 144   *Ms and Blackwood's*: simplicity: 'I have lived—supremely! [*Blackwood's only*: What do you want here?] I have been dead—and damned.' 'Let me go—I want more of it.' More of what? More blood, more heads on stakes, more adoration, rapine, and murder. I remembered, *etc.*

III, 144   *Ms:* cry, 'Oh! the horror!'

III, 146   *Ms and Blackwood's:* lamp. But in the box I brought to his bed-
            side there were several packages [*Blackwood's only:* pretty well
            alike, all] tied with shoe-strings and probably he had made a
            mistake. And the girl, *etc.*

III, 147   *Ms:* the infernal stream that flows from the heart of darkness.

[Reprinted with permission of the Beinecke Rare Book and Manuscript
Library, Yale University.]

'Arthur Eugene Constant Hodister' [Congo Illustre, 1891]

'Roi des Belges' [from Alexandre Delcommune, *Vingt Années de Vie Africaine* (Brussels: 1920)]

"King Leopold," cartoon *c.* 1905 [Anti-Slavery International, London]

'Stanley and the Chief of Wangata, *c.* 1876' ['Musée Royal de l'Afrique Centrale,' reproduced in Ruth Slade, *King Leopold's Congo* (1962)]

'East African Ivory Traders, 1880s'
[Royal Commonwealth Society, reproduced in "International Cultural Corporation of Australia," *Commonwealth in Focus* (1982)]

'The sternwheeler "Hornbill" and trading canoes on the Eyong River at Okopedi, Southern Nigeria, 1909.' This photo points to similarities between the British and Belgian colonial enterprises. [Royal Commonwealth Society, reproduced in "International Cultural
Corporation of Australia," *Commonwealth in Focus* (1982)]

'Kinshassa Station' [H.M. Stanley, *The Congo: Founding of its Free State* (London: 1885)]

Appendix F: The Photographs of Alice Harris

Alice Harris was the wife of the Reverend John Harris, a missionary in the Congo Free State for several years, until August 1905. Alice Harris documented the atrocities to which the native rubber workers and their families were subjected.

When they returned to England the Reverend Harris gave evidence to the Commission of Enquiry on the Congo and also spoke at public meetings in London and elsewhere; Alice Harris's photographs, in the form of lantern slides, were presented as illustrations during the lectures. In 1906 both became organizing secretaries of the Congo Reform Association. In 1909 the Reverend Harris became "the organizing secretary of the Anti-Slavery and Aborigines Protection Society (the two societies were amalgamated in 1909), a position he held until his death in 1941."[1]

The photographs remained in the collection of the organization now known as Anti-Slavery International in London, and are reproduced here with the permission of Anti-Slavery International.

[This appendix has been prepared by Rachel Bennett of the University of Alberta, with the assistance of Jeff Howarth and Caroline Moorhead of Anti-Slavery International.]

---

1   Roger Louis and Jean Stengers, *E.D. Morel's "History of the Congo Reform Movement"* (Oxford: Clarendon Press, 1960) 204.

'Ivory collecting,' Congo, *c.* 1900–1904

'Three Anglo-Belgian Rubber and Exploration Company Militiamen (ABIR [Anglo-Belgian India Rubber]) and prisoner,' *c.* 1900–1904

'Boy rubber collecting,' Congo, *c.* 1900–1904

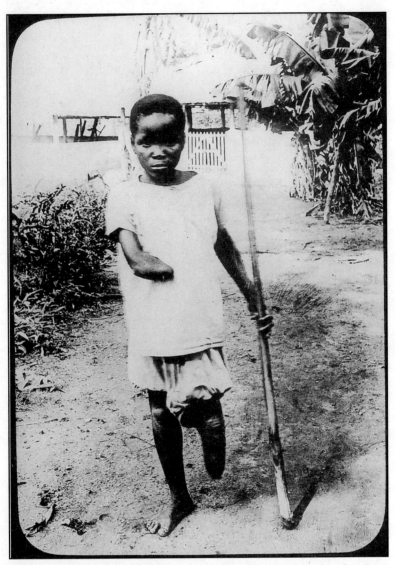

'Child, Congo, *c.* 1900-1904.' The Casement Report and photographs such as these "produced concrete evidence to show that in many districts the inhabitants were living under a system of forced labour, exacted from them by methods which sometimes involved murder and mutilation" (Ruth Slade, *King Leopold's Congo* [Oxford: Oxford University Press, 1962] 185).

'Nsala, of the district of Wala, looking at the severed hand and foot of his five-year-old daughter, Boali, a victim of the Anglo–Belgian India Rubber (ABIR) militia.'

'British Missionaries, with men holding hands severed from victims, named Bolenge and Lingomo, by ABIR militiamen,' 1904.

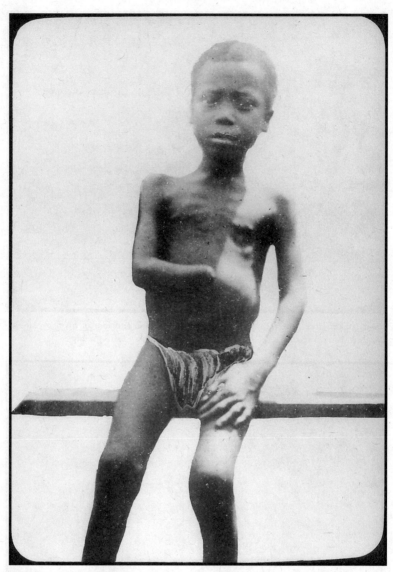

'Child, Congo,' c. 1900–1904

'Two youths of the Equator district. The hands of Mola, seated, have been destroyed by gangrene after being tied up tightly by soldiers. The right hand of Yoka, standing, was cut off by soldiers wanting to claim him as killed.' c. 1900–1904

'Young man with mutilated hand,' Congo, *c.* 1900–1904.

Appendix G: Map of the Congo